· P

The Seadragon's Daughter

"This fast-paced adventure does not disappoint; Troop's Dela-Sangre series continues to impress and delight, raising the bar for inventive fantasy."　　　　　—*Booklist*

"A dark and edgy novel. . . . The main characters are well developed and consistent, if sometimes unsettling. . . . Troop's mythology is inventive."　　　　　—*Romantic Times*

Dragon Moon

"This is, like the first volume, an entertaining, action-oriented story deepened by a dollop of thoughtful ambiguity."—*Locus*

"Troop has powerful command of his fanciful scenario. . . . The author also has a gift, sharper than ever, for suspense and action, and his dragon mythology is every bit as inventive, beguiling—and sexy—as anything Anne Rice has written about vampires."　　　　　—*South Florida Sun-Sentinel*

"Surpasses its predecessor in imagination and humor, and leaves the reader wanting more People of the Blood tales."　　　　　—*Starlog*

"I am amazed at the ingenuity of this story. . . . Filled with adventure, this contemporary fantasy skewers our vision of the world."　　　　　—*SF Site*

"A rousing adventure tale worthy of its predecessor."　　　　　—*Booklist*

continued . . .

The Dragon DelaSangre

Named by *Booklist* as One of the Top Ten Horror Novels
of Recent Years

"Comparisons with *Interview with the Vampire* are almost
inevitable. . . . However, *DelaSangre* ultimately carves out
its own territory. . . . Unabashed fun, with just enough moral
ambiguity to raise it above the level of a pure popcorn book.
A promising debut." —*Locus*

"Any book that has us cheering for a human-eating dragon
is definitely well written." —*Chicago Sun-Times*

"As . . . fascinating as the man who wrote it."
—*The Miami Herald*

"The most original fantasy I've read in years, its strength
coming in no small part from Alan Troop's remarkable ability to deliver a sympathetic but distinctly non-human pro-
tagonist. . . . I loved this book!"
—Tanya Huff, author of *Summon the Keeper*

THE DRAGON DELASANGRE SERIES

The Dragon DelaSangre
Dragon Moon
The Seadragon's Daughter

A
Host of
Dragons

Alan F. Troop

A ROC BOOK

ROC

Published by New American Library, a division of
Penguin Group (USA) Inc., 375 Hudson Street,
New York, New York 10014, USA
Penguin Group (Canada), 90 Eglinton Avenue East, Suite 700, Toronto,
Ontario M4P 2Y3, Canada (a division of Pearson Penguin Canada Inc.)
Penguin Books Ltd., 80 Strand, London WC2R 0RL, England
Penguin Ireland, 25 St. Stephen's Green, Dublin 2,
Ireland (a division of Penguin Books Ltd.)
Penguin Group (Australia), 250 Camberwell Road, Camberwell, Victoria 3124,
Australia (a division of Pearson Australia Group Pty. Ltd.)
Penguin Books India Pvt. Ltd., 11 Community Centre, Panchsheel Park,
New Delhi - 110 017, India
Penguin Group (NZ), cnr Airborne and Rosedale Roads, Albany,
Auckland 1310, New Zealand (a division of Pearson New Zealand Ltd.)
Penguin Books (South Africa) (Pty.) Ltd., 24 Sturdee Avenue,
Rosebank, Johannesburg 2196, South Africa

Penguin Books Ltd., Registered Offices:
80 Strand, London WC2R 0RL, England

First published by Roc, an imprint of New American Library,
a division of Penguin Group (USA) Inc.

First Printing, January 2006
10 9 8 7 6 5 4 3 2 1

For all my mentors—Gene Troop, Stan Peal,
Seymour Spelton and Harold Shapiro.
None of them taught me anything about writing,
but they all taught me a hell of a lot about life.

Acknowledgments

To Susan, my wife, my favorite reader and my life partner and true love for the past eighteen years. To Rocky Marcus, who's been aboard for this ride from the very beginning, chapter by chapter, and whose enthusiasm and advice have always helped to keep me writing. And to Jason and Allison, David and Susana, Leah and Jay, Mike and Wendy and Leon and Laura—who all bless our lives. To Katie in England—hi. And to Delaney—sorry you're still too young to read this.

1

I notice the stranger as soon as I finish pulling our Grady White into our slip at Monty's. Slouched against the white concrete wall of the dockmaster's office, he stares in our direction, his eyes shielded against the bright Miami sun by dark sunglasses, his muscular arms crossed over a broad chest. I think little of it. People at marinas watch boats come and go all the time.

But the man continues to watch as Chloe and I and our son and daughter get off of our boat. When he still stares as we make our way down the dock, I glare back at him. He surprises me by not looking away. Instead, he smiles as if he were watching a buddy approach.

Chloe notices him too and says, "Who is that?"

"I have no idea," I say, wondering what the man has in mind, whether he's a salesman waiting to pitch a product or a con man hoping to score off a mark. Dressed as he is, in a tan silk shirt, brown linen pants and pointed leather loafers, he might belong up at Monty's Restaurant but he certainly isn't waiting to go boating for the day.

I sigh. Months have passed since the last time Chloe wanted to go anywhere on a family outing. Last night, after all that time, after all the days that she spent silent and withdrawn from me, she suggested we go to *Calle Ocho*—all of us. I smiled and agreed, even though I had little desire to spend a day surrounded by thousands of people.

This morning when Chloe woke and grinned at me, I knew my choice was the right one. She joked and laughed with the children and me as we were all getting ready, even hugging me twice. I want nothing to happen today that might dim her mood.

Though the stranger has given no offense and made no threatening move, something about him makes me tense my muscles. I know the man probably can't pose any threat that either I or Chloe or even our nine-year-old son or four-year-old daughter can't overcome. Still, when we near him, I move slightly in front of my family, my pulse quickening, my senses alert. *"Always trust your instincts,"* my father, Don Henri DelaSangre, taught me. *"It's better to be wrong than sorry."*

I stop in front of the man. "Is there something you wanted from me?" I say, looking at him.

He uncrosses his arms and stands straight, the change in posture emphasizing his height advantage—a few inches over my own six feet, two inches. His long, dark, slicked-back hair barely moves as he shakes his head. *"Nein,"* he says, "I was just admiring your family. They're very handsome, especially the little girl. She's *liebenswert* . . . how you say . . . adorable?"

The man speaks with a fairly thick but understandable German accent. I look back at my daughter and nod. "Yes, she is, thank you," I say, and we walk on to the parking lot.

I take no great pride from the man's compliment. People often stop to admire the children. Just as I often catch men staring at my wife and women glancing at me. We are no ordinary family. For creatures like us, beauty and youth are simple things to achieve. After all, we can change anything about our appearances that we wish, whenever we wish—except for our emerald green eyes.

When I was younger, I modeled my own features, including my white skin, blond hair and cleft chin after popular movie stars. My wife, Chloe, who grew up in inland Jamaica without exposure to either movies or television, chose to look like an islander, her chocolate brown skin offering a striking contrast to her eyes.

The children have made divergent choices. Henri has so far copied my looks, while Lizzie has taken what she prefers from both of our features, giving herself Chloe's more rounded face, but with my cleft chin, and adopting my blond hair, but making it wiry like her mother's. Even her mocha skin color is a blend, darker than mine and many shades lighter than Chloe's.

We stop by our two cars, Chloe's new red Porsche Boxster and my new dark green Porsche Cayenne SUV. I smile just looking at the two cars, remembering the good time we had shopping for a new car for her. By the time Chloe and I finished test-driving every model the dealer had, we were laughing and hugging like we did in the old days.

So when she couldn't make her mind up between the Boxster and the Cayenne I couldn't resist saying, "We're rich. We can afford it. Let's get both." I'm not sure who was more delighted, the salesman or Chloe, but I know, for an evening, it was like I had my old wife back. She didn't turn distant again until the next morning.

I hope today will be at least as good for us. We haven't had many good days since I returned from Andros Island almost two years ago.

"Pops, he's still looking," my son Henri says.

I resist the urge to tell him to call me Papa—like he used to. The boy has only a few months to go before his tenth birthday. As much as I'd like him to not act older, I know it's inevitable. Turning, I glance back at the marina. The German has a cell phone to his ear but, just as Henri said, he has his eyes on us.

"There's no law against staring," I say, shrugging and opening the door to the Cayenne. "Come on, get in, we're going to a street festival. Your mom says it's going to be fun."

We leave the car at the Coconut Grove station and ride Metrorail uptown to Brickell. The smells and sounds of *Calle Ocho* reach us as soon as we walk north two blocks from the station and turn onto Southwest Eighth Street. Even though we're still three blocks from the beginning of the festival, too many people already crowd the sidewalks and spill over onto the street.

I wrinkle my nose at the odors filling the air—the scents of countless humans intermixed with the aromas of grilled meat, chicken, pork, sausage, onions and all types of Latin delicacies—and wish my kind had never been blessed with such an acute sense of smell.

Lizzie, seated on my shoulders, her hands on my head for balance, says, "It smells funny here."

"Supposed to. We're around a bunch of humans," Henri, walking to my right, says, with all the authority of an older brother.

I take in another breath, frown at the smell and the growing crowd, and turn to Chloe on my left. "Are you sure we want to do this?"

She looks at me, studies my expression and laughs. "It's *Carnaval*, Peter. Of course I'm sure. They say this is the largest Hispanic festival in the country . . ."

"They also say more than a million people are going to cram themselves into just twenty-three blocks," I say and glance up at the clear, blue March sky. "It's beautiful today. We could go to Fairchild Gardens or Metrozoo."

Chloe's smile fades and her voice turns brittle. "I want to go to *Calle Ocho*. I think it will be fun for the kids."

I ignore the harsh tone she uses and resist the urge to bark back. We've argued too much, for too long.

The crowd on the sidewalk picks up speed as we walk under I-95 and cross into Little Havana. People begin to stream onto the street. It's as if we've left Miami and traveled to another country. Most buildings look as if they were built in the fifties or before. None are over two stories. Storefronts display signs in Spanish.

Loudspeakers blare Latin music everywhere, filling the air with the pulsing rhythms of salsa, meringue, samba, rumba and mambo. Cubans, Puerto Ricans, South and Central Americans chatter in Spanish, laughing and dancing as they push their way through the crowd.

A large Latino woman lurches toward me and I sidestep just before she dances into me. "*Excusa*," she says and dances on. Lizzie laughs, points to a magician on a nearby stage and says, "Over there, Papa, please!"

I look at Chloe. "Don't you think she should have something to eat before she does anything else? I know she's good at controlling herself but she's never been in the middle of so much temptation."

"Lizzie, honey, are you hungry?" Chloe says.

Lizzie shakes her head and points at the stage. "I want to get down and go watch," she says.

Chloe smiles at her and turns to me. "Why don't I take the kids to the stage and you go get burgers for everybody?"

I nod and lift Lizzie off my shoulders. I marvel at how well she behaves. At this age, Henri had just begun to be able to control his hunger. It takes only a moment for the crowd to swallow my wife and children and I walk off to find a food concession where I can get four very rare hamburgers.

Food booths line both sides of the street and after only a few minutes of pushing through the crowd I find one cooking hamburgers. Ordinarily just being in the middle of a crowd of them, enduring their jostles and bumps, would make me want to lash out. But all their smiles and laughter soon have me smiling with them.

Though it's not even noon yet, the line at the hamburger concession already juts a quarter of the way into the street. I get at its end and wait my turn, smiling and swaying to the beat of a salsa tune.

A young woman, not more than twenty and at the point that her body's begun to thicken but not yet turn to fat, pauses near me, undulating her hips to the rhythm. I study her as she dances, examine the lines and shape of her body, and she flashes me a grin and thrusts her hips harder.

I smile back and look away before I grow too hungry. The woman misunderstands my interest. True, at another time in my life I might have been willing to take her as a bedmate, but she stirs another hunger in me today.

My stomach growls and I smile even wider. How shocked she'd be if she knew my only interest was how tasty she would be. How horrified she'd be if I showed her my true form.

A drunken man dances into me and I stop smiling. He begins to dance with the young woman, loses his balance and slams into me again. I stifle a growl and shove him away, suddenly tired of all of them, of their music and food, and their dancing and their laughter. At best, my family and I can come and watch them, but we can never truly be part of them.

If only these humans prancing around me, feeding so happily on meat from cows and pigs and sheep, could know that they are not the lords of the planet they think themselves to be, that another species sits atop the food chain. I wish I could tell them that there are others who feed on them, others who can speak with thoughts alone and change shapes at will—that dragons do exist.

"Peter!" Chloe mindspeaks to me. *"I don't know where Lizzie is!"*

2

"Did Henri see where she went?" I mindspeak, glad that our kind has the ability to communicate by thought alone. Had Chloe needed to shout, the crowd's laughter and chatter and the loud, omnipresent music would certainly have drowned out her words.

But Chloe ignores my question. *"Lizzie, where are you?"* she mindspeaks.

I stare in the direction of the magic show's stage but too many people crowd the street for me to see any sign of Chloe, let alone either of my children. I wait for my daughter to respond, clenching and unclenching my fists at the thought that any harm could come to her.

A quarter of a minute and then a half passes with no answer. I let out an almost inaudible growl and turn to leave the hamburger line. A large Cuban man has the misfortune to stand in my way. I shove him, hard, and rush by him. He shouts, *"Cabron!"* but I pay no attention as I push through the crowd. I have no time to waste on creatures like him. My daughter may be missing and may God help whoever might be responsible for it.

"Henri," I mindspeak. *"Do you have any idea where your sister is?"*

"I wasn't supposed to be watching her. I was watching the show . . ."

"No one thinks it's your fault, Henri," Chloe mindspeaks. *"Elizabeth DelaSangre, where are you? You answer me right now!"*

Another quarter of a minute passes and I let out a sigh when my daughter finally responds, *"Yes, Mama."*

"Where are you?"

"A man lost his puppy."

"And where did this happen?"

"The man told me he lost his puppy and he asked me to help find it and he said then he'd bring me back."

A groan escapes my lips. Neither Chloe nor I have ever cautioned our children about strangers. We live by ourselves on our own small island, far from the mainland. Between the solitude of our homestead and the children's natural defenses, we had never thought such warnings necessary.

"Lizzie can you describe where you are?" Chloe mindspeaks as I near the magic show's stage. I study the sea of faces without seeing either Chloe or Henri.

"I'm walking with the man," Lizzie mindspeaks. *"He's nice."*

Henri mindspeaks. *"Let me try. Lizzie! Are you on a street?"*

"No. Not now. Now we're on a sidewalk."

"Can you see a street sign, like on Sesame Street*? Can you name the numbers on it?"*

"You know I know how to do that."

Chloe spots me first and waves. I wave back and look around. The Southwest Fifth Avenue intersection lies only a dozen yards away. I point toward the intersection and motion for us to meet there. Chloe nods and begins to work her way through the crowd with Henri right behind her.

I arrive at the intersection just before Lizzie mindspeaks, *"I see one! I see a street sign!"*

Chloe and Henri join me, my son beaming as he answers his sister. *"Tell me what numbers you see."*

"A number six . . . and a number nine."

"Great," I say out loud. "She could be at Sixth Street and Ninth Avenue or Ninth Street and Sixth Avenue. We need to ask her where the letters are on the signs."

"Why waste any more time?" Chloe says. She points to the south. "You take Ninth Street. I'll take Southwest Sixth." Before I can even nod, she turns and runs north toward Sixth.

I look at my son and say, *"Henri, you stay here and keep asking your sister questions. You're doing great."* Henri flashes me a wide smile and I race south.

The crowd diminishes as soon as I leave Southwest Eighth Street. By Ninth, except for a few couples and families making their way to *Calle Ocho*, the street is empty. Henri continues to question his sister, and I shake my head and wonder at his patience when she names random letters from the street sign, giving us no clue as to which number is a street or an avenue.

I turn right on Southwest Ninth Street. Small one-story concrete homes, most painted white, some with flat roofs, others with asphalt shingles or barrel tiles, crowd each side of the street. Security bars on most of the windows testify to the area's resistance to all attempts at gentrification.

Ordinarily I'd expect to find people out and about. But today no one sits on any of the porches. No children play in any of the yards. I shrug. I can't imagine many residents choosing to sit at home with the most important Latin festival in the country going on only a block away. I look up the sidewalk on the street's north side and see no sign of a man walking with a little girl.

Cutting across the street, I look west. A block away, a group of four adults and six children approaches Sixth Avenue on the south side's sidewalk.

"Lizzie, is he holding you?" Henri mindspeaks.

"No."

"I want you to walk slower."

"What about the puppy?"

"Forget the puppy! Slow down!"

My eyes fixed in front of me, I get on the south side's sidewalk and run west toward Sixth Avenue.

"Now he's angry with me. He grabbed my shoulders very hard. He's pushing me. It's your fault!" Lizzie mindspeaks.

"Run away!"

"He's too strong. I can't!"

The group reaches Sixth Avenue and crosses the street, on their way, I suppose, to *Calle Ocho*. With them out of the way, I finally see a man in faded jeans and a green T-shirt a quarter block west of them, walking toward Seventh Avenue.

Henri mindspeaks. *"Then fall down!"*

The man stumbles over something and comes to a halt. I continue toward him as he leans over, lifts something, readjusts for its weight and walks on.

"I did what you said but he picked me up. Now he's holding me too tight. I don't like him anymore," Lizzie mindspeaks and I catch a glimpse of her wiry blond hair showing over the man's shoulder.

"*I see them!*" I mindspeak, racing forward. "*They're on their way toward Seventh Avenue.*"

Chloe mindspeaks, "*I'm at Southwest Sixth Street and Seventh Avenue now. I'll cut south and head them off.*"

"*Mama! Papa!*" Lizzie mindspeaks.

"*Don't worry, Lizzie, we're all coming,*" Henri mindspeaks.

A half a block still remains between the man and me when someone in a black Mercedes sedan, parked in the driveway of a plywood-shuttered house near the end of the block, swings open the car's rear door. Except for a quick glimpse of a hand, the car's dark-tinted windows prevent me from seeing anything else of the car's inhabitants.

As soon as the car door opens, Lizzie's abductor begins to speed up, breaking into more of a trot than a full run. I groan. Running as fast as I can, I have little chance of stopping the man before he reaches the Mercedes. "*Lizzie!*" I mindspeak. "*I want you to make a claw and cut the man with it, very deep.*"

"*I'm not allowed. Not in front of people. You told me that.*"

"*You're allowed this time. Shape shift your finger into a claw and hurt him. You have to do it now. He's going to hurt you.*"

"*Do what your father says!*" Chloe mindspeaks.

"*Yes, Mama,*" Lizzie mindspeaks. A few moments later the man's back stiffens. He stops and drops Lizzie.

"*Run, Lizzie!*" I mindspeak.

But the man sweeps her up again, pins her arms against her sides and dashes toward the sedan. A tall, muscular man emerges from the car's open door and waves him on. He wears linen pants and dark sunglasses, and I gasp before I notice his short-cropped, blond, almost white hair and beefy face and realize he can't be the German man we encountered at Monty's dock.

Chloe rounds the corner from Seventh Avenue, sees the man holding Lizzie and shouts, "That's my daughter! Leave her alone!"

I yell, "Put her down—now!"

The blond man darts back into the car and slams the door shut. The car's motor starts and the Mercedes shoots out of the driveway just as Chloe reaches it. She grabs at a door but the Mercedes accelerates out of her reach.

The car speeds west. I stare at it. I can make out the model number—C500—but I want to remember its license number too. I see only a bare rear bumper. "Shit!" I say. "No tag."

With the car gone, Lizzie's abductor drops her and runs between the two nearest houses. Lizzie shouts, "Mama!" and as Chloe rushes to her, I speed after the man.

He's shorter than I am and thinner, with a frame like a runner's and I expect a difficult chase. To my surprise I close on him by the time he reaches the houses' backyards. I lunge for the back of his T-shirt, grab it and yank him to a stop.

"Okay," he says, raising his arms, his chest heaving. "Okay, okay. You got me."

When he turns, I see the reason for his slow pace and lack of resistance. Blood flows from three gouges ripped in his T-shirt, soaking the whole front of his shirt red and dripping down his jeans. Its rich aroma fills the air around him. Just the first whiff of it makes saliva flood my mouth.

The man gasps for air, grimacing with each breath. "That kid fucked me up, man. Look at me. It hurts just to breathe.

Who the fuck lets a little girl have a knife?" he says. "Listen, call the cops already. I need an ambulance!"

I glare at the man. It takes all my control to resist ripping the pathetic creature to pieces. I want to shout at him, to beat him, to make him understand that no one should ever take any child from their family. Instead I just shake my head. "It wasn't a knife," I say. "And no one's calling the police."

His eyes widen. "What the fuck does that mean?" he says and takes a step back, away from me. "I'm hurt here, man. Bad. I need medical attention. You have to . . ."

I lunge forward, grab his throat and choke off his words. "You can tell me what I have to do after I get you out of sight," I growl, and drag him toward the back of the shuttered house. The man gurgles an incomprehensible reply and suddenly tries to break free. I only tighten my grip, and he grabs at my fingers with both hands and tries to pry my fingers from his throat, contorting and twisting his body at the same time—digging his heels into the grass to slow our progress.

He may as well have saved his energy. I have him at the back of the house in only a few moments. He continues to struggle, but even uninjured, he would be no match for me or any of my kind. I maintain my grip on his throat with one hand, rip the plywood off the house's rear jalousie door with the other and then punch my free fist through the door's glass slats. Reaching through for the door lock and opening the door, I mindspeak, "*Chloe, did anyone see any of this?*"

"*I don't think so. The street's empty.*"

"*Good. Is Henri here yet?*"

"*Right next to me,*" she mindspeaks.

"*Come to the back of the shuttered house. The door's open.*"

I drag the man into the house and throw him against the far wall. He falls to the floor, gasping for air. "Your name?" I say.

The man hacks out a few weak coughs and pushes himself off the floor, grimacing as he sits up and leans his back against the wall. "What are you going to do to me?" he groans. "Can't you see I'm already bleeding? I could die here. Is that what you want?" He looks around the empty room, illuminated only by the open door, and sneers at the dusty floor and water-stained walls. "Ya want me to die, sitting in this shithole?" he says.

"Don't worry. If you cooperate, this won't take too long," I say. "Listen carefully. That was my daughter you grabbed. You saw what she did to you. Imagine what I could do if I wanted . . ."

He shakes his head. "Oh, man, please, don't. I'm hurt bad enough as it is. I didn't harm your daughter. Just call the police. Let them take care of this. With my record, they'll put me away forever. You can count on it."

"I told you, no police. This is between you and me and my family."

"I'm bleeding, man! I'm in pain. Please, I need help."

I shrug. "You won't die . . . yet." I hold my right index finger in front of his face and will it to change form. As familiar as the sensation is, I still smile at the small thrill of pleasure and pain that runs through me as my finger's skin ripples and then turns scaly.

The man's eyes grow wide and then wider still when my finger grows longer, its nail thickening and curving into a long, sharp claw. I run the tip of it down his face and trace a thin red line from his right cheekbone to his jaw as I say, "What's your name?"

The man touches his cheek, feels the blood beginning to well up and moans. "Shit, man. What the hell are you? Please, no more. You don't have to hurt me, okay? Name's Maldonado, Enrique Maldonado. They call me Ricky."

Chloe comes into the house, carrying Lizzie, the girl's arms wrapped around her neck and her legs around her midriff. Henri walks in beside them. All three glare at Ricky.

He barely glances at them. "It was a business deal. That's all," Ricky says, his eyes focused on my claw. "No one wanted her hurt. Hell, I'm not into little girls, man. I don't think they were, either. I wouldn't have taken the job if I thought they were." He raises his right hand, palm out. "I swear. They told me it was a custody thing. They said they didn't want her hurt in any way. I was just supposed to de-liver her to them."

"Who are they?" Chloe says.

Ricky jerks his head in her direction. "You think people arranging things like this hand out their business cards? No one ever gave me any names. You saw the blond guy in the car. He was one of them. There were two others, big guys too, like him. But the blond one was the only one who talked to me."

I say, "Don't you have a number or any way of contact-ing them?"

The man shifts position and groans. "This hurts, man. Real bad." He studies his blood-soaked T-shirt. "I'm still bleeding. I need to get some bandages or something."

"You need to answer my questions," I say, pressing the sharp tip of my claw under his chin.

Ricky sucks in a breath. "They contacted me—or at least the blond guy did. I hang out a lot at the bar at the Quarter-deck. You know, the one in the Grove on Bird Avenue."

I nod. While I've never gone in, I've driven by the restaurant dozens of times. In the evenings, pickups, cars and motorcycles, some new and a large number old and shabby, pack the parking lot.

"I just got out of County a few weeks ago and I was at the bar complaining how hard it was to find work if you had a record and the blond guy came over to me and said he might have something for me."

"And you have no idea who these men are or how I can find them?"

"Not really." Ricky shakes his head. "The blond guy took my number. He called me just a little while ago and told me they'd pick me up. They brought me to *Calle Ocho* in that Mercedes you saw. The blond guy handed me two grand and pointed out your daughter to me. He told me where to meet them and that there would be another three when I delivered. And that's all I know."

He looks up at me. "Can we call the cops now? Please, man. I've told you everything."

"Surely there's something else," Chloe says. "You must have noticed something more about those men."

The man thinks for a moment and then says, "The blond guy had an accent."

I cock an eyebrow. "German?" I say.

"Nah." He shakes his head. "Sounded more Russian or something like that."

"Chloe, it's time to close the door," I mindspeak.

"Are you sure we should?"

"You said no one saw us outside. No one's come rushing to see what's happened. You know we can't let him live."

Chloe nods.

"What about the puppy?" Lizzie says.

The man shrugs. "There never was any puppy. I made it up."

"It's not nice to lie to little kids," Lizzie says. She looks at the blood soaking through the man's T-shirt. "I'm glad I hurt you." Then she turns to Chloe. "It's all making me hungry, Mama."

Chloe nods. "Me too, honey. Just a few minutes more." She walks back to the door. The light in the room, already dim, dims even more when she closes and locks it.

The loss of light means nothing to me and my family. Our kind prefer to hunt at night, when the dark overtakes the land. As long as we have the slightest glimmer of light, we can see as well as in daylight. Ricky can't. He looks around, trying to stare through the shadows that have overtaken the room, his eyes wide.

"What is with you people?" he says. "I've cooperated. Why don't you call the cops already?"

Henri scowls at the man. "*He could have hurt Lizzie. Let me take care of him, Pops,*" he mindspeaks.

I look at my son. I had my first kill shortly after I turned eight. The boy's almost ten, larger and more mature than I was at that age. Still, I'd rather he wait. It's one thing to take down your prey at the end of a heated hunt and quite another to merely kill a creature. I shake my head. "*Not this time. When you're a little older.*"

"*But I'm almost ten. You know I can do it.*"

"*Another time, Henri.*"

"*No fair.*"

"*Enough, Henri,*" I mindspeak. I turn my attention back to the human. "Ricky, you grabbed the wrong family's child," I say, pressing my claw against his neck. "Think now. Is there anything else you can tell us?"

"Please, man. I told you everything," he says. I run my claw across his neck, deep enough to sever both arteries. Blood spurts from his new wound and he only manages to gurgle, "Hey!" before he collapses.

I step back, away from the blood, and Chloe says, "Now what are we going to do?"

The heavy odor of fresh blood floods the air around us. My stomach growls and I hold my claw to my nose and sniff at the blood on it. No telltale rankness of drugs or disease fouls its aroma. I smile. "I think his meat should be clean," I say. "And since no one has shown up here yet, we should have time enough to feed before we do anything else. Isn't everyone hungry?"

Henri and Lizzie both nod. Chloe says, "Okay, Peter, and then what? People tried to kidnap our daughter."

I stare at Enrique Maldonado's lifeless body. "And the kidnapper's dead," I say as I pull off my shirt and unbutton the top of my shorts. "Right now I'm hungry and so are the children. After we eat, I'll call the office and tell Claudia to send a limo to pick us up a few blocks from here and to arrange for a crew to come clean this mess up. Then I'll have her get Arturo on the phone and tell them both what happened here. Once they hear it, they'll be as upset about all this as we are. I'm sure they'll put every one of their operatives out on the street looking for those men in the Mercedes before the day is over."

Chloe nods. She's well aware of the wealth and power of LaMar Associates, the company my father founded so long ago. And she knows full well that besides their regular employees, Arturo Gomez and Ian Tindall—who comanage the company for me—employ dozens of operatives who are willing to perform any task asked of them, legal or not.

By the time I have my shorts off, Lizzie has already stripped everything off and has begun her change, her small, naked body's skin convulsing and contracting as it forms into scales, her back swelling behind her shoulder blades as her wings begin to unfold. Henri finishes undressing and kicks his clothes aside as he begins to shift shape too.

I do the same, and sigh at the familiar sensations that the stretching and changing of bone and skin and teeth and claws bring. Halfway through my change I glance at Chloe and find her almost naked, her brown skin already turning green, showing the first outlines of her scales.

"*I'm hungry too,*" she mindspeaks.

Even though the children and I complete our changes first, we wait for Chloe to finish shifting her form too. We continue to wait while she makes sure all of our clothing lies far away from even the slightest splatter of blood and then approaches Ricky Maldonado's still form. She pauses by his body. "*I like it better when we hunt for them,*" she mindspeaks. "*There's no excitement in this. Only food.*"

I nod. "*I feel the same way. But this one almost harmed our daughter. He deserved killing. Just because his death was different, should we let his meat go to waste?*"

"*No.*" Chloe cuts a small strip of meat from the man's carcass, as tradition dictates the lead female should. I wait for her to offer the first morsel to me, as tradition also dictates, but she holds it out to Lizzie instead, and looks at me. "*She deserves a special treat today, okay?*"

I nod. My daughter takes it and gulps it down, and then we all rip and bite at the carcass, swallowing chunk after chunk of sweet, fresh meat until only bones and entrails remain.

Afterward sleep tugs at me, as it always does after a large

meal. I lie down on the dusty floor and curl my tail around me. Lizzie lies down next to me, her head nestled on my tail. Henri follows suit. I motion for Chloe to join us but she shakes her head.

"*We should go soon,*" Chloe mindspeaks. "*I don't like that something's going on that I don't understand. I'll feel better when we get the kids back to the island.*"

I sigh. "*Just let us rest for a few minutes. Then I'll call Claudia.*"

Chloe shakes her head. "*No. I'd rather you call her now. I want to take the children home.*"

I stifle a second sigh and sit up, the children sitting too. "*Okay,*" I mindspeak. "*But I don't think any of us are in any danger right now.*"

"*You don't know whether we are or not. We need some sort of plan.*"

"*Let's wait and see what Arturo and Claudia's operatives find out.*" I stand and begin to shift into my human form. "*Then we can decide what type of plan we need, if any.*"

3

Chloe barely speaks to me on the way to Monty's. At the dock, rather than sit in her customary place beside me on the helm seat of our Grady White for the boat ride back to our island, she takes Lizzie and sits on the stern bench with her. Not that her seat stays open for long. Henri eyes it and says, "Can I take the wheel, Pops?"

I smile and move over. The boy has been on the water almost since birth and, at nearly ten, handles boats as well as most adults. I watch as he backs us out of the slip and takes us out Monty's channel. Unlike the many hotdoggers who rocket out of the marina as soon as they clear the dock, Henri watches his speed until we clear the No Wake zone. Even then he accelerates slowly, mindful of the other boats in the channel.

At the last channel marker he looks at me. Knowing what he wants, I nod. Henri beams and slams the throttles forward. Both Yamaha outboards roar to full power and the twenty-seven-foot boat surges forward like it was a smaller speedboat.

Without a glance at the compass, Henri turns the wheel fifteen degrees. The boat curves toward the open bay. Only blue water shows in front of us, but I know, as does Henri, that our home lies in that direction. I stare to the front and watch the water race by. The day's events have left me on edge and ready for combat—with no clear enemy to engage.

I sigh. I've already told Claudia and Arturo what happened. Nothing more can be done until they report back to me. I breathe in the clean salt air, will my muscles to relax and wait for the first sign of our island to rise over the horizon.

Within minutes a small dark smudge appears, the first indication of the trees on Soldier Key, the northernmost of the small barrier islands that reach up from the Florida Keys. Henri readjusts our course a slight bit to the south. Our interest lies two islands south of Soldier Key, on Caya DelaSangre, the island our family has owned for over four hundred years.

A few more minutes pass and another black speck appears on the horizon, Wayward Key, the island just north of ours. Henri readjusts course slightly once again, and I nod and wait for the next dark smudge on the horizon to appear.

Only a few moments later, the black speck rises into sight and I nod and grin. As much as I love the bright sun overhead, the smell of salt spray, and the bump and crash of speeding over the waves, nothing on the bay brings a smile to my lips faster than the sight of my island slowly coming into view.

"Look over there, Pops," Henri says, and points across our bow to the south of us.

It's a Sunday and, like on most nice weekend days, pleasure boaters crowd the bay. At least a dozen motorboats and four sailboats cruise the water in the direction he indicates. I turn toward my son, wrinkle my forehead and he points again, further south. "That one. The big blue sailboat."

I look again, more to our side, and see a large three-masted sailboat, its hull painted bright blue with a thick yellow stripe at its waterline, about a mile south of us, just past the tiny, tree-covered spits of land known as the Ragged Keys. The boat has its sails furled and doesn't seem to be moving.

"Wouldn't you love to sail that one? It has to be over a hundred feet long," Henri says. "Think it ran aground?"

"I doubt it," I say. "It's deep enough where he is. Though if they get any closer to Boca Chita Key, they will get in trouble. It's a beautiful day. They probably just decided to anchor there for the afternoon."

"Can we take a look?"

"Sure," I say and Henri cuts the wheel over so we head straight for the sailboat. "Hey!" Chloe says. "I thought we were going home."

I turn and find her glaring at me, a protective arm around Lizzie. The girl is slumped against her, eyes closed, obviously lost in a deep sleep. I sigh. I know the look on my wife's face as surely as I know what a storm looks like brewing out on the ocean.

When I was little, before my mother died, she used to get the same look on her face—on those few occasions when she was furious with my father. I remember asking my father one time, just after he taught me how to mindspeak masked, so others of our kind couldn't hear our thoughts, if it meant she was going to leave us. {*No, Peter. Our kind mates for life,*} he mindspoke, masked. Then he shook his head and half smiled. {*Of course, no one says we get to be happy for all of that time.*}

Rather than have the children listen to us bicker now, I mask my thoughts to Chloe. {*We're just taking a quick de-*

tour. Henri wanted to take a closer look at that big sail-boat.}

She shakes her head. {*Henri wasn't kidnapped today. Our daughter was. And you wonder why I get angry with you. Sometimes you just don't think. You just go off and do whatever you want without any consideration for the rest of us . . .*}

{*Damn it, Chloe. What difference will it make to Lizzie? The girl's asleep . . .*}

{*You didn't know that when you let Henri turn the boat,*} Chloe mindspeaks.

{*And I doubt Lizzie would mind going to see the boat if she were awake.*}

{*How do you know what she would mind? You thought I wouldn't mind your going back to Andros to see that woman's child.*}

I take a breath and try to keep calm. For the past two years, every fight we've had has turned into a fight over my unfortunate stay on Andros Island. {*I didn't think you wouldn't mind. I thought you shouldn't mind. Dela's not just that woman's child, he's my son too. I couldn't not go see him. Please, Chloe, why do we have to keep doing this? I never chose to go with Lorrel. I never wanted to be involved with her. I don't love her. I love you. I want us to be happy again.*}

{*How can I be happy when you keep going back there?*}

{*I've only gone back once—and only to see my son.*}

{*But you're going to go back again.*}

{*You know as well as I do, I had no choice in what happened. But I will not turn my back on a child of mine.*}

"Wow. We're near the boat. Look at it, Pops. It's huge," Henri says.

I turn away from Chloe and gawk at the size of the sailboat. "It has to be over a hundred and fifty feet," I say.

{*So much for our conversation,*} Chloe mindspeaks.

{*Henri needs my attention too. This is an old argument,
Chloe. Don't you get tired of it? We need to find a way to
stop this. I wish we could go to a marriage counselor, the
way humans do,*} I mindspeak.

"Can I go closer, Pops?" Henri asks.

Chloe sighs loudly enough to be heard from the stern.
{*Go ahead. We can talk later.*}

I nod and Henri steers the Grady White toward the blue
sailboat's sharp bow. As I thought, the boat's anchored, the
anchor chain taut, coming out of the water on a tight angle,
holding the sailboat's bow pointed into the wind, facing toward the ocean. We motor to the outside of the chain, Henri
pointing out the four furled jibs on the bowsprit, the sailboat's three tall, white masts.

"Look how raked they are," he says. "This thing has to
scream when its sails are up."

"I'm sure it's fast," I say.

Henri turns the wheel and guides the Grady White to pass
parallel to the long, blue hull. I study the boat and admire its
high masts and narrow hull. My father would frown at such
modern rigging. "*Sailing is meant to be a marriage between
a boat and the wind and the water,*" he would say. "*If you
want to go fast, buy a motorboat.*"

"Where do you think it's from?" Henri asks.

I look up and realize we've seen no one on the deck or at
any of the portholes. Ordinarily someone waves or at least
shows themselves and answers any shouted questions. I'm
tempted to shout or sound our horn just to see if anyone's

onboard. "I don't know," I say. "Once we get to the stern, we should be able to tell from their flag."

But even with the flag streaming in the wind, proudly showing two white stars on a field of blue with a yellow stripe separating its lower quarter from the rest, neither Henri or I have any idea which country it represents. The home port painted on the stern just under the boat's name leaves us just as clueless.

ANOCHI YAGDO
KORSOU

"What does it mean?" Henri says.

I shrug and look back at Chloe.

"I have no idea," she says. "Let's go home. That boat gives me the creeps."

After we've gone about a tenth of a mile from the sailboat, I turn and look back. Two men, both dressed in white shorts and white T-shirts, now stand on deck amidship. One has binoculars focused in our direction. The other points toward us and seems to be saying something.

Just to see how they will react, I wave in their direction. The man continues to observe us with his binoculars but after a moment he says something to his companion, who stops pointing and makes a short, choppy motion in my direction that could be interpreted as a return wave.

I turn away and watch our island grow larger. I smile when the three-story house my father built from coral stone so long ago starts to show itself, followed by the tallest of our trees. I was born and raised on the island and know every inch of it.

But I have to fight the impulse to turn around and look at the blue sailboat. I feel as if the men's eyes are still on us. I don't shake that feeling until after we've motored into our island's small harbor.

4

In the morning, Chloe goes to help Lizzie get up and I go to wake Henri, as we always do. I grin when I open his large oak door. The boy has taken to sleeping in his natural form, on a bed of hay. In that shape he's now larger than my human form and, judging by his leg and tail hanging off the hay onto the floor, obviously outgrowing his current bedding.

Fortunately Father built all of our home's rooms more than large enough to accommodate whatever form we might choose. "We're going to have to get you more hay," I whisper, and sit beside my son.

He is either too deeply asleep to hear or has chosen to ignore me, and I run my hand over the scaly ridge above his closed eyes and down the side of his long, green neck. "Time to get up," I say. "You promised Chloe you wouldn't be late for breakfast anymore."

The boy lets out a small whimper, stretches his body a little and readjusts his position. I slap him lightly on his rump. "Come on," I say. "It's time to get up."

Henri's eyes open. Yawning, showing off his rows of sharp, pointed teeth, he swishes his tail from side to side, stretches out his legs and extends and retracts his claws.

"Enough, Pops. I'm getting up. You don't have to stay here," he mindspeaks.

I shake my head. I've left too many times before—only to find later that he's gone back to sleep. I get up and sit on his regular bed. "I'll wait here until you shift shape and get dressed," I say.

"Whatever," Henri mindspeaks. He stands, stretches again and snaps his wings open. *"I don't get why you and Mom don't stay in your natural forms more."*

"It's just a matter of what you're more comfortable with," I say. "When I was your age, I went to school like you. I really wanted to be human—like my classmates. So I stayed in that shape as much as I could. I guess I got used to it."

Henri flaps his wings a few times, hard enough to fan bursts of air across the room, and then folds them. He hunches his shoulders and his wings begin to shrink into his back as his color fades from green to a normal, tan, human tone and his scales smooth to skin. *"I don't wish I was human. Then I couldn't fly or hunt. I like my natural form,"* he mindspeaks. *"At Grandpa's I sometimes stayed in it for days."*

I think of Chloe's parents' home, Morgan's Hole, a secluded valley in Jamaica's rugged, almost impassable Cockpit Country. "There's little possibility any humans would discover you there. Here there's no chance to go outside during the day in your natural form. You could be spotted by a passing boater."

Henri shrugs, his naked body now already human—tall for his age and more muscular and wide-shouldered than most, but indistinguishable from any other human boy. "I still like it," he says.

"My father preferred his natural form too. So did your mother."

"My real mom?"

I nod and think of Elizabeth, my first wife, Chloe's sister, dead since Henri's birth and buried beneath the grass overlooking our island's small harbor. "She used to like to sleep like you do, in her natural form on a bed of hay."

Henri pulls on underwear and a beige Coral Bluff school T-shirt. "I like that we're dragons . . ."

"Dragons is what humans call us. We call ourselves People of the Blood," I say.

"I like that too. I just wish we could live the way we wanted without worrying about what humans might think," he says, stepping into a pair of shorts.

"Me too," I say. "Our kind once could. But there are a lot more of them now than there are of us, and they have dangerous weapons. I don't think they'd be very happy if they knew predators like us existed. You can't blame them. No one likes to be eaten." I tousle his hair with my hand.

He grimaces and pushes my hand away. "Pops, you're messing me up!" he says, and rushes to his nightstand for a hairbrush.

We both smell the aroma of warm, raw meat before we reach the top of the wooden staircase that spirals up the center of our house. Henri looks at me. "We aren't late, are we?"

I shake my head. "No. Your mom and Lizzie are just ahead of us."

Lizzie says "Papa!" and runs to me as soon as we enter the great room on the third floor. Max, the massive black dog Henri took as a puppy from our island's pack of watchdogs, barks out a loud woof and pads over to my son, wagging his tail and waiting to be petted.

My daughter wraps herself around me as soon as I sweep her up, and I hug her and carry her with me to the long oak dining table in the center of the room. "Henri," Chloe says from the kitchen as she puts another frozen steak in the microwave, "you're on time. Good. Come here and give me a kiss and then go set the table." She smiles at him. He beams and does what she says.

If Chloe smiled at me that way again, I would beam too. She's barely spoken to me since the ride back yesterday. Last night, in bed, I tried to bring up our conversation but she snapped, "You already asked me why I kept doing this. We don't have to do this anymore," and turned her back to me.

Still, once we're all seated at the table, Chloe looks at me and says, "I talked to Claudia last night."

I nod. Claudia may be my employee but she and my wife have been close friends ever since I first brought Chloe from Jamaica. "And?" I say.

"She said they don't have much to work with. There have to be hundreds of black Mercedes 500C sedans in South Florida, and God knows how many blond Russians—if the guy is really a Russian and if he hasn't already left town. She promised to put all of their people on it but she said we should keep our eyes out and especially watch out for Henri and Lizzie."

"It doesn't surprise me." I cut and eat a piece of my blood-rare steak, closing my eyes for a moment as I savor the meat's rich flavor. "We'll probably have to wait for them to show themselves again before we can figure out what's going on," I say.

"I don't see any reason why we have to wait."

I put down my knife and fork and look at Chloe.

"We could just go to our place in Jamaica for a while," she says. "If it were just you and me, I would have no problem staying here. But I hate that someone grabbed Lizzie. It's been almost a year since we were at Bartlet House anyway. You know the kids like it there. I'm sure they'd be thrilled to ride their horses again. It wouldn't be so terrible if we visited my parents and brother too. Maybe they've heard something from Derek."

I stifle a groan. I like Chloe's younger brother, Philip. Charles and Samantha Blood, her parents, and Derek are another matter entirely. While all remains calm between us now, it's hard to forget that your in-laws once tried to kill you.

"If you want to hear from your older brother just ask me," I say. "From his credit card bills, I'd say Derek's been making his way across Europe. I think he was either in Greece or Turkey a few weeks ago. I'm sure if I tell Arturo to cut off his LaMar Associates credit cards, he'll contact us pretty damned quick."

Chloe makes a face. "That's your deal. You're the one who offered to support him while he went to search for a mate."

I nod. "You're right. And it's been worth every penny to have him out of the way. You know perfectly well that we can't always trust what he'll do."

"He can be a jerk sometimes," Chloe says. "But the question is whether we go to Jamaica or not."

"I can't go," Henri says. "I'm still in school."

Chloe turns to the boy. "We've taken you out of school before."

"But I'm on the sailing team this year. We have a match scheduled with Royce Academy next month. If I don't make it, all the guys will be mad at me."

"I'd rather we didn't go now, too," I say. "We're in the middle of some big deals at the office. They should be done in a couple of months. By then Henri will be out of school too."

"The problem is now." Chloe shakes her head, slow, from side to side to side. "Since when is business so important to you?"

I stare at her. "You know I've been going to the office every day after I drop Henri off at school. What do you think I've been doing there?"

{*Avoiding me,*} Chloe mindspeaks.

Her words silence me for a moment. When I started going to work Chloe said nothing. I took it as a silent assent, just one more thing we wouldn't discuss in our relationship, like how infrequently we have sex anymore.

I study her face now and see no anger, only sadness, and I reach for her hand. She lets me hold it but doesn't respond to my grasp.

{*You know it hasn't been pleasant between us,*} I mindspeak. {*When Henri's in school I'm pretty much alone here. You spend most of your time with Lizzie. You hardly talk to me. It's been easier for me to go to the office during the week. I assumed you were just as glad to have me gone.*}

Chloe pulls her hand away. {*Assume whatever you want. It may be easier for you. It's not easier for me.*}

"You guys are doing it again," Henri says.

Henri has never made a secret about his dislike for our masking our conversations around him. Chloe grins. "It's just grown-up talk," she says.

"And you tell me not to mindspeak with Lizzie masked so you can't hear," Henri says.

I grin too. Ever since the boy learned that he could modulate his mindthoughts, a process much like changing a radio's frequency, he has made a habit of communicating in secret with his sister—an act most often betrayed by Lizzie's inability to keep a straight face.

"And you don't listen," I say. I check my watch. "Finish your breakfast. We have to get you to school." I cut another piece from my steak and say to Chloe, "I have a meeting I really have to go to this morning. I can come home after that. We can talk more then."

She shrugs. "It doesn't matter. I was going to take Lizzie shopping down at the Dadeland Mall anyway."

"If you wait I could go with you," I say. Chloe looks away and I continue to eat while I wait for her to turn back and answer.

"Finished," Henri says. He gets up from his chair, walks over to the windows facing the Wayward Channel to our north, studies the sky and the water and then does the same to the windows facing the ocean and then the windows facing the Ragged Keys to our south. He's been lobbying for a boat of his own and it's part of a daily routine he's instituted to show what a responsible mariner he is.

He ends it, as usual, by staring out the windows overlooking Biscayne Bay and the mainland miles to the east. "Clear skies," he reports. "But there's definitely some wind blowing. We'll have major chop out there today."

I nod.

Henri stays at the window. "Wow. Would you believe that blue sailboat's still out there?"

"Really?" I say. I gulp down my few remaining pieces of steak and join him at the window.

The wind's shifted during the night and the blue sailboat's bow now points toward the mainland, straining on its anchor line as it rises and falls with each successive swell. Other than a large blue inflatable motorboat tied up to its side, everything else looks the same as the day before.

Chloe comes over and stares out of the window too. "What do you think?" she says.

"He's probably just a cruiser," I say. "Other boats have anchored out there for a week or two before. It's not like he's near us. The boat's almost a mile away."

"So you're okay with it being there?"

I stare at the sailboat and shrug. "I don't know. After yesterday everything feels strange. I guess it wouldn't hurt to have Arturo and Claudia check it out. Do you remember the boat's name?"

Chloe shakes her head. "I just remember it was something foreign."

"No problem," I say. "Henri and I can shoot by it and write the name and home port down when we leave. Do you want me to come back after my meeting?"

"No," she says. "It's nice of you to offer . . . but you go do what you need to today and I'll do as I planned."

I nod and go over and kiss Lizzie good-bye. When Henri and I reach the door, Chloe says, "Maybe you'll stay home another day. That could be nice."

"It could," I say, and flash her a smile.

She smiles back and, for a moment, it feels like how we once were.

5

If anything, Henri had underestimated the wind and the chop. After a cold, rough ride across Biscayne Bay that makes me regret my choice of only a T-shirt and shorts to wear, I drop him off at the dock at Coral Bluff, the county's most exclusive private school.

The school points to its reputation for excellence as justification for its exorbitant tuition. As a former student, I'm just as impressed with its convenient bayfront location; only a quarter mile south of downtown Coconut Grove, minutes from Dinner Key Marina and our slip at Monty's.

I motor north to the channel just past Dinner Key's and cut back on the throttles as soon as the boat reaches the protection of the harbor. The Grady White glides toward our dock, the murmured throb of its motors the loudest sound in the marina. Finally shielded from the cold morning wind, I feel the sun's rays and smile as they begin to warm me.

As usual for early on a weekday, I see only a few people on the docks. Except for a middle-aged couple sipping coffee on the bridge of their trawler, all the rest are service people busy painting, hosing down decks and scrubbing hulls.

A bikini-clad blond woman carrying a duffel bag walks out onto the dock while I maneuver the Grady White into its slip. She stops by the sailboat in the slip to the right of mine and puts down the duffel bag. "Need help tying up?" she asks.

I kill the motors and shake my head. "Thanks, but I have it under control."

She nods, opens her duffel bag and begins to take out scuba equipment and flippers. I look at her after I finish securing the boat's lines. She has short blond hair and a long, lean body, shapely in an athletic sort of way. I guess her to be in her midtwenties, about five foot seven—definitely the type I would have pursued when I was single.

I feel a familiar stirring in my loins and sigh. It has been far too long since Chloe and I have had sex.

The blonde looks up and notices my attention. She smiles at me and I grin back. A cold burst of wind hits us. It raises goose bumps on her bare skin and she shivers—just for a moment. "It's chilly this morning," I say. "I sort of wish I'd worn more myself."

"It's an occupational hazard for me," she says and pulls a wet suit out of her duffel bag. "I'll be fine once I get this on." She rummages a little more in the bag and takes out a business card.

I step off the boat. As I take the card from her, our fingers touch and the wind calms enough for me to smell her clean scent and just the slightest moist whiff of her excitement. "Abby Stiles," she says. "I clean hulls. I'm doing Mr. Mack's sailboat next to you."

"Peter DelaSangre," I say. I study the card. Even though I've lived much longer, I know I don't look much older than thirty. It would be so simple, I'm sure; just a glance or two, a few words, a little banter and then a discussion about when and where. But I shake my head. "I do mine myself," I say and offer the card back to her.

She shrugs. "Most of my clients are down south, anyway. I do a lot of the big boats down in Gables Estates."

I let out an appreciative whistle. Almost everyone familiar with the South Miami waterfront knows how exclusive and expensive the area is. "I'm surprised you bother with this."

"Mr. Mack's brother is a client of mine. I do this one as a favor for him. But I can always use more money. Adding yours would have been no big deal. I have to come here anyway to get my boat. It's at the next dock. It beats driving and having to contend with security gates." She grins and looks directly at my eyes. "I'm not the type of girl who likes waiting to be let in."

"I'm sure that's true," I say, returning her stare.

"Keep the card," she says. "The number's my home number too. Call me if you want to."

"Thanks." I put her card in my pocket and turn.

"Love your eyes," she calls out as I walk away. I grin. Even though I know the woman's just reacting to looks that I created, I still like it when women find me attractive, especially after all the days I've spent coping with my wife's indifference, though I hope the woman's never around when Chloe and I are at the dock together. We have little need for anything else to trigger her jealous outbursts.

Because I have to take Henri to school so early and because LaMar Associates occupies the top floors of the Monroe Building, just across Bayshore Drive from Monty's, I arrive at the office far before any of my executives. Sarah, our receptionist, a girlish-looking thirty-year-old who maintains a constant battle with her weight, stands up from her desk as soon as I step off LaMar's private elevator.

"Mr. DelaSangre. Good morning, sir," she says.

"Morning," I say. "Any messages for me?"

Since I have no title and function mostly as an observer, there rarely are any messages. Still, she rummages through the papers on her desk. "No, sir. I don't believe so, sir," she says. Her hands flutter as she stacks and restacks her piles of paper.

I resist shaking my head. I dislike my effect on the woman. I'd hoped once I started to come to work on a regular basis that she'd grow used to my presence. But Sarah's just as nervous today as she was the first time she met me.

My father had warned me about people like that. "*Humans have a wonderful talent for forgetting their animal instincts,*" he said. "*There are a few of them though that can sense our difference. They don't understand it but we make them uneasy. Be careful of them. They can be unpredictable.*"

Sarah hardly impresses me as presenting any danger. I leave before she begins to give off an acrid scent of fear. I have no desire to make her any more uncomfortable than she is.

Once in my office, I look out my window at the whitecaps on the bay, and call Chloe. "The bay's rougher than Henri said. You might want me to come home and take you in the Grady White. It'll handle the waves better than your Donzi."

"It's not that bad out there, Peter. Anyway, it's not like I have the sixteen-footer anymore. You know my 22ZX can outrun you and almost anyone else, in any water."

I'm long used to Chloe's love for speed. When we shopped for a new boat, after the fire that destroyed our harbor, two years ago, she wouldn't look at any craft that couldn't top sixty miles per hour. Compared to my boat, Chloe's new one is a rocket. I have no doubt it can leave mine far behind. "It'll just pound your kidneys more," I say.

"Sounds like fun to me," Chloe says. "Lizzie will love it."

Ian Tindall, LaMar's vice president and legal counsel, has scheduled our meeting for nine thirty. With plenty of time before that, I unroll the plans we'll be discussing and spread them out on my desk. I whistle when I look at them and wonder what my father would think.

When I was a boy, Don Henri took me down to the treasure room beneath our house. My eyes grew wide at the stacks of gold and silver bars and the chests full of coins and jewels that took up two-thirds of the room. "*This is all worth millions,*" he said. "*I'm not even sure just how many. But what good is it? You can't eat it. It's hard to spend. And do you know what's worse?*"

I wanted to find the answer but, honestly, it looked pretty good to me. Finally I shrugged.

"*It doesn't change, boy,*" he said. "*It doesn't do anything for us. If we come back to this room next year it will be the same as it is today. This may look like an unlimited fortune to you, but remember our kind lives for hundreds of years.*

"*I'm over four hundred years old now, Peter. When I was young, if I needed treasure, I took it. Most of what you see here came from my pirate fleet.*" He shook his head. "*Those days are long gone. Once there was enough treasure here to fill this room and the other one next to it. But our real wealth is on the mainland now.*"

I looked at him.

"*I used only a small part of my treasure when I founded*

LaMar Associates. That small investment has grown to a huge fortune. It gives us power and it gives us the money to pay people like the Gomez family and the Tindalls to serve us.

"One day LaMar will be yours and there will be a Gomez and a Tindall who will do as you wish. Be careful with your choices. It will be your responsibility to make sure the business continues to prosper so one day you can pass it on to your children."

I put my finger on the plans and trace it along the outlines of the upscale condominium buildings and walkways. If the city awards us the bid we'll be able to redevelop the railway yards in downtown Miami with no land cost whatsoever. Encompassing more than two full city blocks, Flagler Station will be LaMar's largest project.

I'd originally shaken my head when Ian first proposed it. "It's going to cost hundreds of millions," I said. "We're going to have to turn to more banks." But he assured me the city was desperate to bring upscale housing to the area. And he promised we could buy up the surrounding area for next to nothing before the news got out.

Father certainly never approved of going into debt for any project. With four projects already under way and two other major projects under consideration, I wonder whether we're going to be overextended. Between the acquisition costs for the surrounding area and the planning and the necessary payoffs, LaMar has already borrowed and spent over twenty million dollars.

Someone knocks on my open doorway and I look up and see it's Claudia Gomez, Arturo's daughter and assistant. I smile and motion to her to come in. She gives me a wide grin, and walks over to my desk and stares at the plans. "I don't know about this one, Boss," she says.

Except for the green business suit she's chosen to wear today, its skirt too short and a little too form-fitting, I would take her for an athlete or a boater. Tan and wide-shouldered, square-jawed like her father but far more attractive, she's muscular enough to leave no doubt that she works out on a regular basis. Her dark black hair smells of herbal shampoo and I think a silent thanks that she hasn't inherited her father's propensity for strong cologne.

"I don't know about it either," I say. "But if Ian's right we stand to make a bundle." I look at her and then at my watch. "You're early."

"Don't tell Pops," she says, and we both laugh. Her habitual tardiness is a constant irritation to him, as are her choices of wearing either too short or too tight clothing. "I woke up early. What happened to Lizzie yesterday really bugged me. Toba Mathias was out of town over the weekend. I wanted to get hold of her first thing this morning and put her in charge of looking into it."

I nod. Toba may be one of the smaller operatives LaMar employs, but she's certainly one of the best. "So you didn't find out anything yesterday," I say.

"You know it doesn't work that fast. They have to go through records, check visas, do interviews. I did spend a good bit of the evening last night at the Quarterdeck's bar."

"Get anything there?"

"A couple of propositions." She flashes a smile. "But no blond Russians."

"I have another thing for you." I tell her about the blue sailboat and hand her the piece of paper on which I've written its name and home port. "It's probably nothing but I'd like you to check it out."

Claudia stares at the paper. "The home port's easy," she says. "On my last vacation, I took a cruise that went there."

I cock an eyebrow.

"Korsou is just the native way of writing Curaçao." She continues to look at the paper and shakes her head. "But I have no idea what Anochi Yagdo means. You think it could be someone's name?"

"I don't care about that so much. I want to know whose boat it is. Why they're anchored out near my island."

Ian Tindall storms into my office without knocking. Ordinarily ghost pale, his sunken cheeks glow with a red flush. "Les Tobin just called to cancel our meeting. We've been fucked," he says.

"What are you talking about?" I ask.

Tall and skeletally thin, wearing his customary funereal black Brooks Brothers suit, Ian walks to my desk and starts rolling up my copy of the Flagler Station plans. "Forget about this. It isn't going to happen. The city commission just voted to drop the project."

"Our commissioners voted against us?" Claudia says.

Ian nods, finishes rolling up the plans and dumps them in my wastebasket. "They're all whores. They don't have the class to stay bought."

"What happened?" I say.

"Les said Julio Morales, the city manager, requested a special meeting with the commission, early this morning. First he informed the commission that Central Bank and Heartland Trust had just been taken over by Wallenstein, Bearce Investments in New York."

"But those two banks do most of our financing," Claudia says.

Ian flashes a grim smile and nods. "That's just what

Morales told the commission. He also let them know that neither bank will be allowed to take on any new loans until Wallenstein, Bearce's people perform a full audit. Even then, anything over a million will have to be approved by New York."

"Which leaves us where?" I say.

"Looking for some new bankers," Ian says. "Not that we'll need any for Flagler Station. Morales presented an offer he received from a foreign corporation for a ninety-nine-year lease on the railway property at twenty-five percent above what we offered. He said the corporation making the offer guaranteed they would develop it as a center for biochemical research. They promised they would bring the city at least three thousand high-paying jobs."

Ian shakes his head. "Les said the deal was too good. He swore if he voted against it, he'd never get reelected again."

I think about all the surrounding properties we've just bought and frown. "That leaves us holding a lot of useless property."

"Not totally useless. True, in the short term we'll have a loss, but it's a good one. We'll at least have a substantial tax writeoff for this year." Ian smiles. "If we can content ourselves with being slumlords for a while, and if that company does build what they say, we'll eventually turn the land for a strong return."

"My father taught me that no loss is a good loss," I growl.

"Look, Peter, I'm as upset as you are. We probably won't see any bonuses this year."

I catch a strong whiff of Aramis cologne as Arturo Gomez walks into the office. Claudia stops him at the doorway and whispers just loud enough that I know she's filling him in on what has happened. I watch the two of them a moment, Arturo wearing a beige silk Armani suit today, gray-haired, thicker and a head taller than his daughter but just as square-jawed and fit, and then turn back to Ian. "How much are we going to lose?"

"I'll have to run the figures."

"And there's no way we can turn this around? No extra pressure?"

Ian's face goes blank. While he prefers to leave that part of the business to Arturo and Claudia, he knows perfectly well what I mean by extra pressure. He shakes his head. "There's too much money involved. You can bet if Morales called for a special meeting there was more to the offer than Les said."

"Who are these people?" Arturo says.

His voice is harsh enough for all three of us to turn and look at him. I look at his grim expression and hard eyes and am thankful he works for me and not the other way around.

"Ouder Raad Investering," Ian says. He spells out the name and Claudia writes it down.

"I'll check it out," she says.

Ian nods. "Les said they pronounce it Owder Rad. They're a Netherland Antilles holding corporation, privately held. Morales showed the commission a financial report on them. Their pockets are as deep as or deeper than ours."

Arturo scowls. "Screw their pockets. This is costing us too much money. Do we have the names of any of their principals? I'd like to send them some visitors."

"I don't have any names yet," Ian says. "As soon as I learn more I'll let you know. But I don't think at this point it would be wise to force a change." He holds up both hands. "If you do decide to try something, I don't want to know anything about it. Anyway, it's not the worst thing for us. If we can line up some new banks, it leaves us in better position to join with the Zabros brothers on the Young Circle condo project in Hollywood, and for us to make an offer on Matherby Farm in Homestead." Ian smiles at me. "I know you want that one, Peter."

I nod. Matherby Farm is the last large tract of undeveloped land in the county, big enough to develop a whole community within it. I've already made it clear, if the deal comes to fruition, I want to work with the architects on its design.

But even better than that, the Matherby home and the forty-five-acre hardwood hammock it occupies on the edge of the Everglades, comes with the deal, stables and all. Separated from the rest of the tract by water and swamp, and connected by only a quarter-mile-long, one-lane dirt causeway, it could make for an ideal inland getaway for me and my family.

"See what you can do on both," I say to Ian.

Rather than reply or nod, Ian looks down for a moment as if he's collecting his thoughts. "Of course," he says. "I'll be glad to . . . but, I've been thinking of all the projects we've been adding and, frankly, I could use some more help in my department."

I raise an eyebrow. "Since when do you ask if you can hire someone?"

"I wouldn't if it was a clerk or a junior legal." Ian glances over at Claudia and Arturo. "This is a bit more important. I'd like to bring in an assistant."

Arturo grins. "Since when do you want an assistant?" he says.

Ian frowns at him. "You have Claudia. Why shouldn't I have someone?" He turns back to me. "Actually, I've been thinking about recruiting one ever since you and Arturo put that Santiago woman in my office. I think it will work better for all of us this time if I choose one before you choose one for me again."

I nod. Ian had hated having her in his office and, in the end, she had proved to be a major disappointment for me.

Ian flashes a thin-lipped grin. "And we have a great opportunity right now, my aunt's son just graduated from U of F law school. I don't have any children yet. And you really need someone to back me up the same way Claudia does Arturo. Thad made law review at Florida and his specialty is real estate law. And even if he doesn't look it, he's a Tindall. He understands the special relationship our family has with the DelaSangres. He understands both the risks and rewards of working here."

I look at Arturo.

"I have no problem with it," he says.

"It's fine with me," I say.

Ian nods. "Good. I'll have him get to work on the Matherby deal as soon as he starts. Let him show us how good he is."

My phone rings. I pick it up and Chloe says, "I just thought you'd like to know that the blue sailboat has pulled up anchor. It's turning to motor across the bay, toward Dinner Key." She pauses for a moment. "Funny thing, though. Remember that blue inflatable that was tied up alongside it? It's heading south."

6

With the deal called off, I putter around my office for a few hours before I grow bored reading reports. In truth, the day-to-day minutiae of running a business leaves me cold. Fortunately, LaMar Associates has no need for my services. It runs perfectly well under Arturo, Ian and Claudia's guidance.

I do enjoy sitting in on planning and negotiations. I especially love meeting with architects and contractors, and brainstorming the best way to build something. My father designed and built our home from the first stone up. I've always wished I could have such an opportunity.

The Matherby folder sits in the middle of the pile of papers on the right side of my desk. I pull it out, open it and stare at the picture of Buddy Matherby's wood frame home and sigh. Every local old-timer knows the story of how Buddy's great-grandmother built the house by hand while her husband, Ralph, was out in the Everglades tending the family still.

Once it had been a fine example of pioneer architecture. Now the roof sags on one side of the house and the chimney, mortared stone by stone by Jane Matherby's own hands, has collapsed into a gaping hole. Only a metal, windmill-operated water pump towering over the rear of the house looks substantial. I glance at the report. It recommends demolition of the house. I nod. If the Matherby deal comes to fruition, it will come down—and I'll finally get to build a house the way I want.

I call Chloe on her cell phone. "I'm coming home early," I say.

"Oh, I told you not to," Chloe says. "It's sweet of you, but Lizzie and I are already on the way to Dadeland. . . . We only need to go shoe shopping for her. I could hurry home after that."

"No, it's okay," I say, though I'd rather she did hurry home. "Don't rush. There are some chores I need to get to and anyway, later I have to go back to pick up Henri from school."

"I can do that on the way home." She laughs. "It'll just mean I have to spend a little more time shopping than I planned."

While I can't imagine at this point what else remains for my wife to buy, I say, "Sure," and hang up the phone.

Claudia catches me in the hallway on my way out. "Got something I thought you'd like to hear, Boss."

I turn to her and raise an eyebrow. "The Mercedes?" I say.

She shakes her head. "I don't want to make like it's all that much, but I've received some feedback on your blue sailboat."

"Tell me."

Claudia has a Palm Pilot in her hand. She taps it with a stylus. "We have a connection with a guy at Customs. The *Anochi Yagdo*, your blue sailboat, processed in at Miami

Customs in the middle of February. There aren't that many slips for boats their size so they originally berthed at the Miami Seaport. But the slip was only available until its regular tenant came out of dry dock. They had to leave a couple of days ago."

"Where'd they go?"

She shrugs. "Don't know yet."

"What did they say about who's on board?"

"I told you—I don't have all that much." Claudia stares at her Palm Pilot. "Thirteen crewmen passed through immigration; eleven of them islanders from either Curaçao or Bonaire, and two, the captain and first mate, from Holland."

"And no passengers?"

Claudia shakes her head. "Our guy at Customs said they put on their paperwork that the ship's owner and some of his associates were to fly in and join up with the ship. But they weren't required to list who and from where."

I frown and say, "It would be nice just once to get a full report."

"You know it doesn't work like that Boss. If you want me to wait until I get everything . . ."

"You know I don't," I say. "What about the owner?"

"VastenZeilen out of Bonaire. Which is—would you believe?—another Netherland Antilles holding company."

I groan. "First Udderrad . . ."

"Ouder Raad," Claudia says, "I'm still trying to find out who they are."

"Ouder Raad." I nod. "Two Netherland Antilles holding foreign companies in the same day? And now we're up to our necks in islanders."

"Not necessarily. A lot of people find Curaçao and Bonaire convenient places to set up their corporations. They have strict privacy laws down there. Back in the eighties almost every other big building project around here was financed by Netherland Antilles holding corporations. Later it came out most were controlled by Columbians and Panamanians who needed to launder their drug money."

"Do you think that's what's going on here?"

Claudia shrugs. "I can't say, but probably not. A whole bunch of people were prosecuted so that's pretty much over with now. It could be anyone, from any country. It could even be people from Curaçao. We don't know yet. Remember, there's nothing to say that any of this is anything but a coincidence."

"You know what my father said about coincidences?"

"No. What?"

"He said he didn't believe in them," I say, and start to turn. "If you find out anything else, give me a call."

Claudia reaches out and touches my arm. "Wait, one other thing."

I turn back.

"Pops thought you'd like to know. He just saw the new credit card bills. He says your brother-in-law's in India now."

On the way through Monty's parking lot, I pass by my SUV and Chloe's empty parking space next to it. For a moment I wonder if I should drive down to Dadeland and find my wife and daughter. I shake my head. I've certainly offered to be with her enough today.

I go to the dock and stop by the slip to the left of mine to look at Chloe's Donzi. She'd insisted on a red one with white upholstery, just like the sixteen-footer she'd had before. I check her white dock lines and nod. Chloe only had to be shown once. Each is tied neatly to the appropriate cleat, with the excess wrapped in a tight, flat coil on the dock.

The house band at Monty's outdoor patio breaks into a loud and poor rendition of a Bob Marley song, and I turn my attention to the patio. Couples and groups take up a third of the tables under the restaurant's palm-thatched, open-sided structures.

I smile. On weekdays the restaurant attracts mostly tourists. I wonder if any of them realize that the palm-thatched roofs that shade them have been built to resemble the Seminole Indians' traditional wall-less chickee hut. I wonder if any of them would care.

The band ends its song and, with them silent, the murmur of conversation interspersed with occasional laughter reaches me. I check my watch. With no one waiting for me at home, I have more than enough time to go up to the patio, order a lunch of rare hamburger and sit in the midst of all the activity.

But I could just as well go back to my office where I know all the people. Neither Arturo nor Claudia nor even Ian would ever suggest I leave their presence. I shake my head. Human company will do little to combat the loneliness that has begun to gnaw at me. I need the company of my own kind, my wife and children. I untie my boat's dock lines and get on the Grady White.

I don't notice the *Anochi Yagdo*'s blue hull and three raked masts until I reach the middle of the harbor, where I can see past Grove Harbor Marina to Grove Key. The blue sailboat takes up most of the length of the concrete seawall near Miami's waterfront city hall, one of the few places in Coconut Grove large enough to accommodate it.

It lies only a few minutes out of my way and I consider motoring over to it. But and then what? I take out my cell phone and call Claudia's direct line.

As soon as she answers, I say, "I know where the *Anochi Yagdo* went."

"Where?"

"Look out your window and check out Grove Key Marina, near city hall."

"Son of a bitch," she says. "Couldn't be more under our noses."

"I'd say they're not concerned about hiding from us."

"They might not even know who we are."

I say, "Still . . ."

"I know. I'll have a team watching them within the hour," Claudia says.

If anything the bay is rougher than when we crossed in the morning. I welcome it and throw the throttles forward. The Grady White leaps ahead and smashes through a wave, and I work the wheel to keep the boat on course as it slams its way across the bay, my work momentarily forgotten, my problems with Chloe temporarily out of my mind. The boat responds to my slightest touch, dancing from wave to wave, breaking through some and skimming over others. It collides with a particularly large wave and races past it, leaving a cloud of salt spray behind, and I laugh.

By the time I reach the unmarked channel into our harbor, salt spray coats me from head to toe. I could care less. I maintain the same speed as I steer the boat through the channel, from turn to turn. This is my home. I know each rock that lurks under the water's surface and how close I can come before their hard, sharp edges tear through my boat's fiberglass hull.

When I reach the harbor, I back off the throttles at the last possible moment and coast toward the dock, the Yamahas' yowl dropping to a throaty purr. The pack of dogs that guard the island start to growl and bay—but from a distance. Not one shows itself, not even Max.

I wrinkle my forehead, throw the motors in reverse—to stop the boat's motion—and study the harbor. The stand of red mangrove trees at the far end of the harbor has grown back to about half of the height it had reached before the fire that devastated the harbor two years ago. Nothing there looks unusual or out of place, and I throw the throttles forward again and coast up to the dock.

Again, all looks as it should. The new dock, built exactly as the old one had been, lacks only the crowd of boats we used to keep tied up to it. Except for the two Mistral windsurfers lying at the far end of the dock, Chloe and I have chosen not to replace most of them.

Nothing about my house appears different either. The black singe marks that reach up to the second story of the house's coral wall near the dock only serve as another reminder of the fire and the battle that had raged here.

I shake my head. I can find nothing awry. Still, at least some of the dogs should have come to the dock to see who's arrived. I tie up the Grady White and walk to the wide coral stone steps that lead up to the oak veranda that encircles the house.

Again, except for the absence of any dogs, all looks as it should. I glance down at Chloe's herb garden, examine the patch of grass under the gumbo-limbo tree that serves as my first wife's resting place, look over the bushes and trees toward the Wayward Channel and across the sea oat–covered sand dunes to the ocean. No tracks show on the beach. Nothing looks disturbed.

Putting two fingers to my mouth, I blow out a shrill whistle. Dogs bark back at me from under bushes and behind the dunes. I shake my head when none come. These dogs know my whistle. They understand who is master on this island.

I go to one of the cannon ports Father placed in the coral parapet that circles the veranda and whistle again. Two dogs slink out from under a nearby Barbados Cherry bush, and then another shows itself farther off and then another. I whistle one more time and wait for all the dogs to gather below me.

Chloe and I had counted the pack not too many months before to make sure they hadn't grown too numerous. I look at them now, the dogs bred by my father to be large, with oversize heads and jaws so they more resembled hyenas than any breed of domestic dog, and count them all, adults and puppies.

The total should have come to twenty-seven, including Max, but I count only twenty-four. I whistle again and wait five minutes before I take another count. Still, Max and two other dogs remain uncounted.

One more examination of the grounds reveals nothing new and I turn and walk to the massive oak door that leads into my and Chloe's bedroom. The door has no lock, only a latch, the same as all the other bedroom doors that ring the exterior of the house. Father always boasted, *"We have no need for locks and keys. Our isolation and our dogs are security enough."*

I glance at the massive oak arms room door only a dozen

yards away and grin at the narrow crack in the stone beside it. When it came to the ancient pistols, rifles, cannons and ammunition stored in the four arms rooms located in each quarter of the house, Father opted for the extra security of a latch hidden within the stone itself—just as he secured our treasure room doors with chains and padlocks.

The latch to my room snaps clear, and I throw my door open and click on the light. Nothing looks out of place. No strange scents seem to have invaded the room's air. I breathe in hard to make sure and still smell only the clean, leathery scent of my kind. Yet I have a sense of something not quite right.

A dog bays somewhere in the house, its barks muffled or partially blocked. I rush from my room through the door to the interior landing that circles the second floor. Eleven closed oak doors lead to eleven other bedrooms. I walk from one to the next, starting with Henri's room and then Lizzie's until, by the sixth door, the barks grow louder.

As soon as I open the door, Max jumps out at me and almost knocks me down in his excitement. His tail whips from side to side and he barks and leaps and circles me, obviously thrilled to be rescued from his confinement. "It's okay, boy," I say as I pet him. "It's okay, calm down."

Once I get him to remain in one place, I run my hands over his body and check his fur for any sign of blood or injury. Except for his old scars, I find nothing. I turn and Max follows me down to the bottom level, and pads alongside me as I check out our storerooms and Father's old holding cells and again find nothing out of place.

I enter the last cell, the smallest one, and stand at the foot of the cubicle's narrow cot. While nothing has disturbed the cot's bedding and no foreign scent floats in the air to offend my nostrils, I'm concerned about my family's treasure rooms lying in a chamber directly below. I yank up on the foot of the cot.

It resists for only a second and then begins to rise, the stone floor under the cot cantilevering up with it as a series of counterweights and pulleys go into action. I nod, wait for the bed to rise out of the way and then enter the dark, steep stairwell beneath it, the dog close behind me.

At the stair's bottom I flick on a wall switch and examine the chamber and the two massive treasure room doors. Thick chains and heavy padlocks still secure both, apparently undisturbed.

After a quick inspection of the passageway that leads from the chamber to a hidden door that opens into the bushes by the dock, I backtrack and return to the cell, and lower the cot back into place.

Max stays close by my side the whole way, and continues to follow me as I walk up the spiral staircase to the great room on the third floor. Outside the room, the dog raises his hackles and lets out a low growl. I pause and sniff the air, but I smell nothing strange here, either.

I walk into the room and circle it. Again everything looks as it should. I shrug and sit down at the table but, rather than settle to the floor beside me, Max snorts and turns away. He lets out a long, low growl and walks stiff-legged toward the wooden chest that holds my father's ancient maps and log books.

"What is it?" I say, and get up and join him. Close up, I examine the chest and let out a breath. The clasp securing the top has been left open. I prize my father's old documents. Anytime I take anything out, I always take extra care to close the clasp after I return it.

I lift the top up, examine the chest's contents and shake my head. Nothing has been removed and nothing is out of place. I stare at Max and wish he had a way to tell me what he knows.

"*Chloe,*" I mindspeak.

"*Hi, Peter. I'm just pulling into Monty's parking lot. Did you get to finish those chores you wanted to do?*"

"*No. Something strange has been going on out here. Two dogs are missing,*" I mindspeak. I tell her about the dog pack's odd behavior, Max's confinement and his focus on my father's chest. "*And whatever it may be or may not be, somehow someone left the clasp off the chest. You know I never do that.*"

"*I know what your father taught you about relying on your instincts, but you might be working yourself up. You know that our dogs would have torn apart any human who was foolish enough to step on our island. Besides, did you smell anyone's scent in the house?*"

"*No.*"

"*As far as the clasp—it could have been either Lizzie or Henri. They're always going into that old chest. And about Max. You know how Lizzie's been about opening and closing doors recently.*"

I nod and mindspeak, "*Sure.*" For some reason only known to herself, the child has decided that slamming doors shut is the apex of self-entertainment. Not a day passes that either Chloe or I or both of us don't scold her for slamming doors.

"*So she could easily have accidentally locked Max in that bedroom. I wouldn't have noticed unless he made a commotion.*"

"*And what about the two missing dogs?*" I mindspeak.

"You thought Max was missing too. Maybe they aren't gone. Maybe they just didn't come when you called."

"That's not how they're trained."

"Why don't you go outside and check again? I have to go and pick up Henri."

Outside, I call the dog pack again and take another count. Thanks to Max's presence the number now totals twenty-five. I sigh. Two dogs remain missing. I search from bush to bush, walk across the sand dunes to the beach and walk along the island's coast without finding any sign of them.

"Peter!" Chloe mindspeaks.

"What?"

"You may be right about strange things going on. We just now were coming out of the channel at Henri's school when I looked to my right and saw that blue inflatable—the one that belongs to that sailboat—heading straight toward us at full speed. I jammed my Donzi's throttles as far ahead as I could. If they were after us, they had no chance to catch us. But they may know where our island is. I don't see them anymore. Still, they could be on their way out here."

Just the thought that anyone would dare threaten Chloe and our children makes me clench my fists. Though part of me hopes the inflatable is on the way to my island, after Lizzie's abduction, the business's reversals and now the two missing dogs, it would be a relief to be able to rip into something solid. *"Claudia keeps binoculars in her office,"* I mindspeak. *"Let me call her and find out what she can see."*

Claudia picks up her phone on the second ring. I say, "Get your binoculars and see if you can spot a large, blue inflatable."

"Sure," she says.

Only a few seconds pass before she says, "Okay, I spotted it, but I really don't need any binoculars."

"Where is it?"

"It's coming in Monty's channel. Didn't you say it belonged to the blue sailboat?"

"Yes."

"Well, that's where it's probably heading. Why do you care?"

I explain about Chloe and her concern about being chased.

"Any boat approaching Dinner Key from the south is going to shoot past Coral Bluff's channel," Claudia says. "I understand how upset you guys are about what happened to Lizzie, but you're acting paranoid. The only thing that blue sailboat's done to you is to anchor within a mile of your island. Really, Boss, chill. Let my dad and me do the worrying."

As soon as I hang up, I mindspeak Chloe and explain what Claudia said. "*I feel so foolish,*" she mindspeaks. "*Claudia's right. We're getting ourselves too worked up. It's probably a good idea to try to get back on a normal keel.*"

"*That would be nice,*" I mindspeak. "*Now tell me why I can't find two of our dogs.*"

7

Ordinarily I sleep well, but the image of the man carrying Lizzie down the block and varied visions of the missing dogs keep invading my dreams. I wake at one in the morning, and twenty after two, and three forty-five, to find Chloe only half asleep, tossing beside me. When I wake once again at five thirty, I feel her turn. I ignore her movements and lie still with my eyes closed, hoping I can fall back asleep one more time.

"Are you up?" Chloe says.

I groan. "I guess I am now," I say. I turn to find her on her side, her eyes wide open, focused on me.

As usual, she's chosen to sleep in one of my T-shirts. Its material rides up as she arches her back and stretches, her bare legs extended and her dark body exposed from the midriff down. "I had a terrible night," she says.

"Me too." I sit up in bed and look toward the window and the gloom outside. "But I think the night's not really over yet."

"The sun will be up soon enough," Chloe says. She sits up too, draws up her knees and hugs them. "I couldn't stop thinking about those missing dogs. I think we should look for them one more time as soon as it's light."

"I've already looked. They're not out there."

"We should get up," Chloe says. She clicks her bedside light on, stands and pulls off the T-shirt. I blink at the sudden light, but can't help but study the curves of her naked body, the dark brown of her nipples, the patch of tightly curled black hair between her legs.

"You could get back in bed," I say. "I can think of other things we can do until it's light outside."

Chloe smiles and shakes her head. "I can't say the thought hasn't crossed my mind. It's been a long time for me too, Peter. But I'm not ready just yet. Somehow we need to work something out."

I open my mouth to say something and she puts a slender finger on my lips. "Bear with me," she says. "If I knew what would fix how I feel, I would tell you in an instant. For now, I need to go look for those dogs."

Our small island consists of only a little more than six acres of dry land, but such an area suddenly feels huge when one must search under each bush and tree. Because both the harbor area and the shore facing the Wayward Island channel lack much in the way of natural cover, they are easy for us to search in the predawn dimness. By the time Chloe and I finish with both, the sun has started to rise above the horizon. We leave the center of the island for last and go to the ocean shore next.

As soon as we reach the crest of the sand dune nearest the beach, I look from the north end of the sand to the south. "See," I say. "Nothing. Not a footprint, not a track of a boat being pulled up on shore. Not a bloodstain in sight."

Chloe nods. She walks down the dune and across the beach to the wet sand at the surf line. A roller breaks a few yards off the shore and its white foam rushes up the sand and wets Chloe's legs to the calves. She laughs. "Good thing I wore shorts today," she says, and looks to the north and then to the south.

Her forehead wrinkles and she points a finger to the place where a jumble of large, jagged coral stones mark the end of the beach. A wave smashes into the stones and then recedes, seaweed and sticks and other flotsam left behind it. "What's that?" she says.

I shrug. "You know junk always gets washed up over there."

She starts to walk toward it. "Look at the black thing between the first two rocks. I think it's more than just junk."

We find the dog's body wedged between two large, jagged rocks. I kneel next to it and pick seaweed off of its wet, matted black fur. "I don't think they threw it here," I say. "I think a wave brought it ashore last night."

Chloe nods. She sits on a rock near the beast's massive head. A new wave rushes up to us and wets us as it engulfs the rocks and floods over the dog's carcass. The animal's head moves with the water, first toward the inland and then back toward the sea.

"Poor thing," Chloe says. She reaches for the head with both hands and moves it from side to side. "No resistance at all. Someone broke its neck."

"Someone very strong, very fearless and very unconcerned that we might find the dog's body," I say.

"Either that or they didn't understand how the currents work around here. They could have thrown the dog in the water from any side of the island or even out on the bay." Chloe gets up and clambers over the rocks, her eyes on each space between them.

Finally she stops, turns back and shrugs. "God knows

where the other dog's body is," she says. "At least let's bury this one."

As soon as we return to the house, I call Claudia on her cell phone. "Have you found out anything yet?" I say.

"Not yet, Boss. You know these things take time."

"What about the people you assigned to watch the sailboat?"

"I won't even receive their first report until I get to the office."

"Look. I know you think I'm being paranoid," I say and explain about our missing dogs and how we found one of them just this morning, dead, its neck broken.

"And you think the people on the sailboat are responsible?" Claudia says.

"I don't know. But I would bet anything that the other missing dog is dead too," I say. " I don't like this. Someone has been on our island and has probably been in our house. Someone who's not afraid of our dogs . . . You know those animals. Would you ever set foot on our island without one of us to control them?"

"Not a chance. They'd tear me to pieces."

"Exactly," I say. "All this has made Chloe and me very uneasy about leaving the island unattended. Tell your dad and Ian that I won't be coming to the office for a while. The Flagler Station deal's dead anyway and you don't need me to sit in at this stage of the Zabros brothers' and Matherby Farm projects negotiations."

"Sure. They'll call you if they need to ask you any questions."

"I'm sure they will," I say. "I'm more interested in you calling me with some answers. Soon."

8

Chloe no longer shows any interest in leaving the island. I understand her unease. Even though our island has been attacked before, no one has ever been in our house without our invitation. Both of us have thought of it as our sanctuary in a dangerous world. With that breached, we have no place else to turn to that could be any more secure.

Except for taking Henri back and forth to school, I spend my time at home with Chloe and Lizzie. My daughter takes my new, extended presence at home as proof of my preference for her. "Papa's coming back to spend the day with *me*," she says to Henri each morning when we leave.

She takes to following me around the island as I perform maintenance on the boats and generators and pumps, and she insists on helping when I replace rotted old wood with fresh new timber. "Do you mind that Lizzie's with me so much these days?" I say to Chloe.

She shrugs. "I have her to myself enough. The girl has two parents. I think she's lucky to be able to spend so much time with both."

I have to admit, I enjoy the time Lizzie and I spend together. I'd had Henri to myself for over four years. But, with Lizzie, Chloe has done much of the parenting. I find myself smiling as Lizzie babbles on, telling me about nothing consequential in serious tones. I nod and answer her questions and mostly resist the impulse to grab her up and kiss and hug her until she objects.

Still, after a few weeks, I start looking across the bay toward the mainland and, in the evening, I find myself drawn outside to stare at the dark sky, and the stars and the moon that break up its gloom. I know the feeling well. It's been too long since my last hunt.

A storm front rushes up from the Carribbean and stalls over Miami. Rain and wind take over the last few days of March, churning up the bay and the ocean and darkening the sky. The last of the storm finally leaves early in the evening on the second day of April.

We're in the great room, just finishing dinner when Claudia calls. "Okay, Boss," she says. "I finally have some more stuff."

"Tell me," I say.

"Which do you want first, the sailboat or Ouder Raad?"

"The sailboat."

"Why am I not surprised?" Claudia says. She rustles through some papers near the phone. "We've had three two-man teams doing surveillance around the clock on them. They've reported visitors coming and going by car and by the inflatable . . ."

"And who are they?"

"We're not sure yet. It looks like, besides the captain and crew, there are twelve of them. They don't all come or leave at once, so it's taken us a while to make sure we're not undercounting or overcounting anyone."

I listen as she rustles through more paper. "I think

they're all foreign. At least my guys say that no one on board seems to speak to each other in English. They report hearing a lot of German—though it could be Dutch—and other languages that they can't identify."

"But you don't have any names."

"Not a one. We do have a few pictures of some of them though. But they're really not very good. Our best guy for that is Ernie Roland. We have him covering the city manager right now—just to see if we can find something to convince him to be more supportive. If you want, I can reassign him to the boat detail."

"I want."

"Okay . . . and now about Ouder Raad Investering."

"Yeah?"

"First of all, they're being represented by Holden Grey."

I whistle. "Of Bennett, Teasdale, Grey and Levine?"

"That very law firm, south Florida's finest," Claudia says. "This Ouder Raad has to be loaded. Bennett, Teasdale's hourly rate is so high that it can cost a client five hundred dollars just saying 'Good morning' to one of the partners.

"Anyway, Holden Grey's been one busy lawyer. Ouder Raad seems determined to be a major player in real estate and development—like we are. In the past month he's arranged for them to buy six downtown buildings, including the Seybold Building and the Wyler Complex."

"Weren't we bidding on them?"

"We were. Not anymore."

"Arturo must be pissed off."

"That's an understatement," Claudia says. "Ian's even madder. Pop's pretty sure that Ian invested some of his own money on land next to the Wyler Complex—to convert it to parking. We were going to turn the area into an entertainment center. But now, if Ouder Raad just uses it as an office complex, there won't be any market for his parking."

I smile. It would be just like Ian, or any Tindall, to make such a separate investment. My father always warned me about their potential for dishonesty. *"The Gomez family has served ours since the day I left Spain,"* Don Henri often said. *"None has ever betrayed us. They understand that their fortune is entwined with ours. But the Tindalls, who have served us for hundreds of years too, have never learned that. They must always be watched."*

"Serves him right," I say.

"I agree," Claudia says. "But that's not all on Ouder Raad. They also bought the Hoffsinger Castle in Gables Estates."

I shake my head. I never could understand how Miami's most exclusive waterfront neighborhood ever let anyone build a four-story castle—complete with twenty bedrooms, twenty-five bathrooms, three towers and ten ancient cannons—within its boundaries. Even for someone as rich as Dwayne Hoffsinger, the owner of the country's largest chain of dry cleaners. "Hoffsinger finally unloaded that monstrosity?" I say.

"Word is, he needed the money for a new business venture and quickly. Ouder Raad already has possession. I haven't been able to put the house under surveillance yet. You know how crazy about security Gables Estates is. If you want me to get men in, it will take a while to get them hired as gardeners and groundskeepers."

"Don't bother yet," I say. "I'm more concerned about those twelve men on the sailboat. For now I'd rather you concentrate on them. You already have people researching Ouder Raad, right?"

"Sure."

"Then once we find out more, we can see if we need to put the house under surveillance."

"Okay, Boss," Claudia says. "That's all I have for now. Nothing on the Mercedes yet, or your blond Russian. Oh, Pops said you should come in to the office this Friday. Manny Padron called. He's representing Buddy Matherby. He said Buddy would like to drop by and meet you."

"Meet me? Why?"

"Apparently Matherby's old-fashioned. Manny told Pops Buddy said, 'Only way one old he-coon's going to get on with another is if they both get to sniff each other all over first.' Do you understand that?"

"Sure." I grin. When I was young, folksy sayings like that, spoken in a light Southern drawl, were the mark of a true, native south Floridian. Unfortunately, now, with Miami's growth into an international city, a Southern accent most often identifies the speaker as a visitor. "It's just old-fashioned Florida Cracker speak," I say. "Tell me when he wants the meeting and I'll be there."

Chloe looks at me when I put the phone down. "Well?" she says.

"Still not much," I say, and repeat everything Claudia said to me about the blue sailboat and Ouder Raad.

"So we still don't have any answers." Chloe frowns.

"No, we don't." I walk over to one of the windows overlooking Biscayne Bay. With the sky finally clear, the glow of Miami's lights fills the horizon. I open the window, sniff the air and smile at its freshness.

"Rain's gone," I say.

"So?"

"I think it's time I went out. A little later, of course. I wouldn't mind taking a look at that castle Ouder Raad just bought; maybe go down to Homestead and check out this property, Matherby Farms, we're thinking about developing. There's a part of it, set off by itself, that would make a great inland retreat for us. A place where the kids could go horseback riding and freshwater fishing, like in Jamaica."

"Sounds like that could be nice," Chloe says. She grins at me. "And just maybe you're thinking of doing a little hunting while you're at it, too?"

"It's been a long time," I say. "Want to come?"

"Yes," Chloe says. "But I don't think we should both leave the kids."

"Can I go?" Henri says.

Chloe and I both say, "No," at the same time.

Henri scowls. "When I was in Jamaica, Grampa said I was old enough then, and that was almost two years ago. He said you're not really of the Blood until you've taken your first kill. You keep saying 'Later' to me. You know I can do it."

"You know what happened to those dogs. Things are strange out there right now," I say. "There will be plenty of more times for you to go with me. I'll bring back fresh prey for all of you. I promise."

After Henri and Lizzie have fallen asleep, I go out on the veranda. A light gust of wind blows in from the ocean. It envelopes me with its fresh salt smell, and I smile and look skyward. Only a sliver of the moon shows itself. But with the sky almost clear of clouds, the stars shine their brilliance in every direction.

Most humans would find the night too dark. All the better. I nod and begin to remove my shirt and then my pants. My kind needs only the slightest illumination to see. The dark lets us go where we want, unseen and unnoticed.

Before I begin my change, I glance back at the house and wonder whether I should invite Chloe to come with me again. I shrug. She has already refused my invitation once and, honestly, I like the thought of going aloft alone.

I let out a low growl as soon as my skin begins to tighten. As much as I enjoy living in my human form, as comfortable as I find it, it never thrills me to change into it. But just having my skin tighten and harden and form scales reminds me of the power building inside me.

Pain and pleasure run through my body as my cells shift and my bones and claws and teeth lengthen. I welcome both sensations and flex my shoulders to help my growing wings break through the skin on my back. I growl again as my skin rips open, and hold my arms out and extend my claws, and wait for my tail to finish its growth and my scales to harden into armor and my wings to reach their full thirty-two-foot span.

As soon as the change has finished, I flex my wings and spread them and run into the wind. It takes only a few strong wing-beats for me to go airborne, and I shoot out over the veranda on the ocean side of the island, my underbelly just inches above the tips of the sea oats growing on top of the dunes. I skim past them and across the beach before I begin to spiral and build altitude.

I circle above Caya DelaSangre, gaining altitude on each circuit, noting the dozens of boat lights out on the ocean and the few boats cruising the bay, near to our shore. Below me, lights warm the windows in the great room and the master bedroom of my coral stone house. I smile, knowing that Chloe will leave them on, as would I if she were out. They will serve as a beacon to welcome me when I finally return home.

Ordinarily, I would head out over the ocean to find my human prey on boats far out at sea or on distant islands. Father taught me long ago that caution dictated hunting far from home. *"Humans may be weak creatures, but when threatened they find strength in their numbers and their weapons,"* he lectured. *"Only a fool would hunt where he could be discovered."*

My stomach growls. As usual, changing shape has left me famished. Still, I have things I want to do before I hunt. I bank away from the island and head toward the mainland.

Gables Estates lies to the south, across the bay from my island. I fly over it first, circle around and study the huge homes that crowd each lot. Wide roads run by the front of each house and wide canals provide convenient dockage at their rear. Of course, at least one or two oversize boats sit behind every house.

The largest and most expensive homes sit on the bay, and the dearest of those sit at either end of Gables Estates, where they can look out over the bay from one side of the house and keep their boats in the water on the wide canal behind them. Hoffsinger's castle takes up six lots and dwarfs all of its neighbors on the north end.

I curve out over the bay and descend until my wings almost touch the water. My approach takes me to the north side of the castle and I glide south, just high enough to take in the size of the grounds and to shake my head at the pointed tops of its three towers. After I pass, I fly to the channel that runs into the neighborhood and follow it in from the bay.

Once inside, I follow a wide canal to the north and fly past the castle's rear. Ten black cannons jut out from a false stone wall and point out over the water toward the homes on the other side of the canal. I shake my head and grin, and wonder at the horrified expressions the cannons' arrival must have caused.

Lights show in a few windows in the castle. I turn again and pass a little slower and a little closer. Five men stand and talk near a large picture window by the center of the house. One turns in my direction as I fly by and I speed forward, a black shadow passing by in the dark.

I gain altitude, circle above Gables Estates and frown into the dark. What a poor spy I make. All I've learned is that five men have gathered in the house. From the short glimpse I had of them, I can barely describe their heights, let alone their features.

Better to leave things like that to Arturo and Claudia— though I hate the thought of waiting for Claudia to find a way to insert her people into the area's work force. I look down at all the huge homes, at their expensive cars and boats and shake my head. How many service people must earn their livings here?

And then I remember the blond woman at the dock at Monty's—Abby something. She said she cleaned hulls for some of these people. I smile. The woman seemed ambitious. I'm sure Claudia can find a way to convince her to take on a willing worker like Toba Mathais.

My poor stomach rumbles and aches, and I turn south

and fly toward Homestead. I haven't hunted over the Everglades in years. But I've little doubt I'll find some solitary camper, or a hunter huddled by a fire somewhere out there. Fortunately, Buddy Matherby's farm is right on the way.

9

Clouds crowd the sky and make the night darker the farther west I fly over Homestead. It matters little to me. I still see well enough to make out the streets and the shapes of homes and warehouses. But only the dim glint of moonlight on a windmill's metal tower prevents me from missing Matherby Farm.

A campfire burns at the rear of the house and I spiral down, circling over dark sawgrass-covered swampland and cultivated fields and the treed hammock that holds the Matherby's home. I fly close enough to see a pickup truck parked near the campfire and a Seminole chickee hut just beyond it.

No other lights show for miles in any direction and I nod. Chloe and the kids will like it here. I suddenly find myself looking forward to the meeting on Friday with Buddy Matherby.

Lightning slashes through the air far out over the Everglades, its brief flash revealing gray clouds bunched together all over the sky. I fly past Matherby Farm toward the dark terrain of the Everglades. My stomach aches too much now for me to linger.

I find little difference between flying over the Everglades and soaring over the ocean at night. Except for the areas where the water reflects the brilliance of the stars and moon, both are endless stretches of blackness. I glide over that gloom and search for the light of a campfire or a flashlight, or the red glow of a lit cigarette.

When minutes turn into a quarter of an hour, I gain altitude to see if any lights show farther out. I let out a breath when I see three lights scattered out in the darkness; two to the east toward Florida Bay and one a campfire far away, deep into the Everglades. I head toward the solitary blaze.

Something disturbs the air near me, just slightly, just enough for me to sense that some creature shares the sky near me, to my rear. I whirl around in midair only to find nothing, smell nothing. "*Chloe?*" I mindspeak.

A half minute passes before she answers, "*What, Peter? I was sleeping.*"

"*Sorry,*" I mindspeak. "*I thought I felt you near me.*"

"*That's nice, I guess, but I've been in bed since you left. Maybe it was an owl or another nightbird.*"

"*You're probably right. Go back to sleep.*"

Chloe mindspeaks, "*That's exactly my plan.*"

I look from side to side, and strain to see what bird, if any, flew by me. But nothing shows itself.

While most of the Everglades consists of watery swamp, it's also dotted with hammocks—spots of high ground crowded with trees and brush, each carved into a teardrop-shaped island by the relentless flow of millions of gallons of water making its slow way south, year after year after year. I find the campfire in a large clearing on one of them.

It's burned down to a pile of red embers by the time I arrive over it. A mud-splattered swampbuggy sits on its oversized tires near it, two sleeping bags laid out on the ground by its side. But I spot no sign of anyone nearby.

I circle overhead and try to ignore my growling stomach. Certainly whatever humans ventured so far out here couldn't have wandered too far away from their campsite. Even for the knowledgeable, the Everglades can be a treacherous place.

Saw grass grows everywhere, taller than any human, each high, wide, ragged-edged blade capable of ripping the flesh of any unsuspecting visitor ignorant enough to try to push through it. Water moccasins, alligators and even a few crocodiles cruise the waterways, while rattlers, coral snakes, wild boar and, on rare occasions, panthers and black bears hide in the palmetto scrub thickets on the high ground.

A careless misstep can plunge the unwary into deep water clogged with underwater vines that wrap around kicking feet and hold onto a body even after it's grown still. Worse still are the muddy bogs and quicksand pits that can be found scattered almost anywhere.

Still, no one shows themselves and I circle again and again without finding any more signs of any hunters. Finally, the bark of a rifle shatters the night's calm and I turn toward the sound. A match flares for a moment then extinguishes, only the red, newly lit tip of a cigarette showing in the gloom. I speed in its direction and soon find myself above a man clad in hunter's camouflage.

Knee-deep in water, his rifle laid down on the dry ground of a clearing near him, he grunts as he cuts through the thick hide of a dead alligator with a large hunting knife. "Son of a bitch, Marty!" he shouts, his cigarette dangling in his mouth. "Wouldn't of shot this one if I thought I was going to go through this much trouble without you."

I spiral up a little—to look for Marty—and something

large whirs past me, just out of my sight. I spin in the air and find nothing again.

Below me, the man shouts,"What the fuck was that?" He scrambles out of the water, grabs his rifle and a flashlight, and points both skyward. The flashlight's beam slices through the moist dark air and illuminates my cream-colored underbody.

"God damn!" the hunter bellows and three bullets slam into me before I hear the first crack of his rifle. I yowl, as much from the shock of being hit as from the pain, and dive toward the man.

In my experience, most humans who have seen me rush toward them either freeze or turn and run. This man doesn't even spit his cigarette out of his mouth. He stands in place, his legs spread, his rifle following my movement and fires every remaining bullet in his rifle's magazine.

One buries itself in my chest and another strikes my right wing. The last shot strikes my throat, just below my jaw. I roar into the dark and extend my claws as I continue to plunge.

The man calmly ejects his empty magazine and pulls another from his pouch. I level off a dozen yards in front of him and shoot toward him just as he clicks it into place. He cocks the receiver and tries to take aim at me again just as I reach him. I rip my claws through his flesh and tear a great gaping wound in his midsection in the few moments it takes for me to speed past him.

I bank and turn in time to see the rifle fall from his hands and his legs crumple beneath him. He moans when I land next to him. "Marty, you asshole. Where the fuck are you?" he groans.

While I'd like to know the same thing, the thick aroma of

freshly spilt blood fills my nostrils and makes it impossible for me to ignore my hunger any longer. The man moans again. I look at him and shake my head. My wounds ache too, but I feel no anger toward him. I'll heal soon enough. If he knew how little real damage his bullets did to my armored scales he'd be horrified. His bravery accomplished nothing. I crouch over his body and bite through his neck, and he goes still.

A blood frenzy overtakes me. I rip into the man's carcass and gulp huge chunks of tender flesh, bite after bite, barely chewing, my eyes closed, my mind intent on healing my wounds, pushing out the lead slugs buried in my flesh.

"Jesus!" a voice mutters.

I look up. A heavyset man stands at the edge of the clearing, a large revolver in his right hand. His pants are pulled up but still unzipped, and I guess that a call of nature had kept him from his friend's side. "Jesus," he mutters again and aims at me, his hand shaking, the gun barrel wavering.

Raising up on my hind legs so I tower over the man, my jaws red with the hunter's blood, I bellow out a roar. Marty gasps, fires a shot that whizzes past me, drops his gun and plunges into the nearby thicket. I listen to him scramble through the underbrush and debate whether to follow him now or to feed a little more on my new kill.

But, while I doubt any cellular towers have been built near enough for a signal to get out from this deep in the Everglades, my father taught me all too well that caution must rule my decisions. I take a last bite of tender, sweet flesh and leap into the air.

Slash pine, mahogany and oak trees crowd most of the hammock and prevent my landing anywhere in its interior. I circle overhead and listen as Marty crashes through bush after bush. When the sounds stop, I roar and the man begins to run again. I can only imagine the punishment his body takes from the sharp leaves of each scrub palmetto, from the slaps of low-hanging branches and the stings of countless insects.

Finally he breaks through a thick growth of saw grass and runs into a long, crescent-shaped lagoon. Only knee-deep, the water splashes around him as he heads toward the dry land on the other side. I circle one last time, preparatory to swooping down and seizing the man with my talons before he reaches the cover of the trees just past the water.

After only five or six steps Marty slows. He lifts his feet high for a few more steps and finally stops altogether. Rather than attack, I continue to circle and watch as he struggles to jerk his legs loose, his body sinking with each new, frantic motion.

I wonder why an outdoorsman like him doesn't know that the best way to contend with quicksand is to just lie back and let his body float. But it's obvious that panic has overtaken him.

I shoot down before he sinks much deeper and grunt as I yank him free. The man has to weigh half again as much as his friend. Marty shows no appreciation for my rescue. Not that he should. With me his end is no less certain, just quicker. He screams and kicks and tries to twist away from my claws digging into him. I silence him with a single swipe across his neck.

The smell of his blood envelops me and my stomach rumbles. I shake my head. My wife and children lie in their beds at home, waiting for me to return with fresh meat. I fly back to the clearing to finish feeding on my first kill.

*   *   *

The carcass no longer lies where I left it. I land, lay down my second kill and search the clearing. A panther or bear could possibly have dragged the hunter's body into the bushes just as an alligator or crocodile could have pulled it into the water, but no drag marks, no trail of blood show anywhere on the ground.

I take to the air, careful to keep the clearing and Marty's body in my sight, and search for any sign as to where the first body might have been taken. Nothing looks different. I find no more blood, no other scent of a fresh kill. Finally I shrug and fly back to the clearing to recover the body of my second kill.

Even though it's never been totally out of my sight, I let out a breath when I find it exactly as I left it.

"*Chloe,*" I mindspeak as I fly back toward Homestead. "*Wake up. I'm on the way back.*"

A few moments pass before she mindspeaks, "*Did you have a good hunt?*"

"*A strange one,*" I mindspeak.

"*How so?*"

I sigh into the dark night air and look from side to side. Once again I see nothing. Still, I can't shake the feeling that something, some creature or creatures, lurk in the dark just beyond my vision, their eyes watching my every move. "*I'll tell you all about it when I get back.*"

"*You were successful, weren't you? The children will be disappointed if you return without fresh meat.*"

My stomach growls at the mention of fresh meat. I wonder again what happened to the first hunter's body. I wish I'd had more time to feed and heal away the last remnants of the aches and pains of my wounds.

It takes all of my willpower not to rip a chunk from the large body dangling from my claws. But I'd rather return with my kill whole—even though it weighs so much that it slows my flight and threatens to tear loose from my grip. I can only imagine how wide-eyed my children will be at its bulk.

I sigh again and tighten my hold on Marty's body. *"Don't worry. The children won't be disappointed. Neither will you. I have more than enough for all of us."*

10

As usual these days, Henri takes the helm of the Grady White when we leave to take him to school. I barely watch as he maneuvers the boat out of our harbor and down our channel. The boy has long ago proven his seamanship. I look across the flat bay and study the calm morning water instead.

Henri nudges the throttles forward, faster than I would have chosen, and the boat's bow rises for a moment, then settles as the craft shoots ahead. I ignore the increased yowl of the engines and the boy's desire for too much speed. Not a single boat shows anywhere in sight. Not a single wave exists this morning to disturb our journey.

Besides, only the brisk breeze created by our movement saves me from the sun burning overhead, its heat unhindered by a cloudless blue sky. I look down at the long pants and polo shirt I've chosen to wear for my meeting at ten this morning with Buddy Matherby and frown. The man prides himself on being a good old boy. I probably could just as well have worn my customary cutoffs and T-shirt.

A dolphin's gray fin breaks the water to the north of us, not far from the channel leading to Bear Cut and the Crandon Marina on the west end of Key Biscayne. Two more appear and then another three, the dolphins humping their backs, then diving, then reappearing. "Look," I say, and point in their direction.

Henri glances at them and grins. "Can we go over to them, Pops?"

I check my watch and shake my head. "We need to get you to school. Anyway, this early in the morning they're probably looking for fish, not playmates. We'd just get in their way."

Henri nods and continues toward school. We've come upon hunting pods of dolphins before only to have them either ignore our existence or swim away. "I wish you could teach me how to change into their shape one of these days," he says.

"It's not that easy," I say. I watch the dolphins appear and dive. Ever since Andros, I can't pass any dolphins without thinking of my days on that island. As happy and relieved as I am to have escaped from the Pelk's safehold, I can't help but wonder about my other son and wish he could be with me.

"But you can do it."

I sigh. Why did I ever choose to show him that I had that ability? It only annoyed Chloe and made Henri want to imitate me. "I can," I say. "But I have no idea how to teach you. You know a Pelk had to get into my thoughts to teach me."

"Sure. Lorrel," he says. "You told me all about it. But the Pelk are just dragons too."

"Of the Blood," I say. "And a different castryl."

Henri shrugs and says, "Of the Blood." He adjusts the wheel a few degrees. "But if the Pelk are of the Blood too, why can't we do what they do?"

"Because each castryl has different abilities. We've taught you all that, haven't we?"

"Sure." Henri drones out his words as if he were reciting a lesson in class. "The Zal were the largest and the fire-breathers. The Thryll were the smallest and lived mostly in the trees and air. The Pelk lived in the water and the Undrae lived on the land."

"And which castryl won the Great War?"

"The Undrae."

"Right. And what are we?"

"We're Undrae, Papa."

I nod. "And our kind killed most of the others. No one has seen a Zal in a millennium. The few remaining Thryll and Pelk live hidden away."

"I still wish I could change into a dolphin like the Pelk. I bet Dela will be able to."

Neither Chloe nor I have made any secret of my abduction by the Pelk or my unwilling relationship with Lorrel, the Pelk female who was forced upon me, or the child that our union produced. "Of course he will," I say, glad Chloe can't hear us discuss his half brother. "He's half Pelk. But would you like to live under the water or in caves, and eat only fish and dolphin like he will?"

Henri thinks for a minute, then nods. "Sure, it could be fun . . . some of the time."

Sarah looks up when I step off the elevator and say good morning. "Good morning, Mr. DelaSangre," she says. "Ms. Gomez is in already."

I glance at my watch. "So early?" I say.

A glimmer of a grin appears on Sarah's face and disappears as soon as she notices I'm looking at her. She nods and her hand trembles a little as she points down the hall. "She asked if you'd come by her office as soon as you arrived."

"Of course." I turn and start to walk away.

With a sound that sounds halfway between an "Oh" and a gulp, Sarah says, "Uh, Mr. DelaSangre, one more thing, please. It's something I think I should tell you. I hope it doesn't sound too silly."

"I'm sure it won't," I say, turning back to her.

"Well, I don't know if you've noticed . . . I mean, I try not to show it but, and I don't know why, believe me, but you always make me very nervous—more than anyone else here, more even than Mr. Tindall, who makes everyone nervous, and more than Mr. Gomez. Look at this." She holds out a trembling hand. "No one ever made me feel this way except you. God knows you've always been nothing but nice to me.

"Anyway, that's not exactly what I wanted to say but I had to tell you that first. Anyway, last night, some of my girlfriends and I decided to go to the Quarterdeck—the one over on Bird Road—for happy hour."

Sarah's face flushes a pale pink and she shrugs. "Sometimes it's a fun thing to do, especially on Thursdays. That's the night the Quarterdeck gives two-for-one drinks to women. So it was pretty crowded like it usually is, but my friend Max—that's short for Maxine—she pushed her way to the bar and found us some stools.

"As soon as I sat down, I started to feel the same sort of nerves like I get when I'm near you. I looked around and almost fell off my stool. I thought I saw you sitting a few seats from me. Then I realized he wasn't you. He was wearing sunglasses inside. You never do that. And even though he was built like you and was every bit as tall as you, his blond hair was lighter, almost platinum, and his face was rounder and puffier.

"He was talking to this other man, a pretty rough-looking

guy. I don't know why they let people in that look that way when they want women to come. The two of them talked for a few minutes and then both left." Sarah's face contorts into a nervous smile. "And I felt better as soon as they were gone."

My heart races ahead a few beats as I think about the blond Russian Lizzie's abductor claimed to have met at the Quarterdeck. "And did the blond man have an accent?" I say.

Sarah shakes her head. "It was way too crowded and too loud for me to hear anything they said."

"If we showed you a picture, do you think you could identify him?"

"I don't know. Maybe. But I'm sure I could tell who he was by the way he makes me feel—if he was close to me."

"And you go there every week?"

Sarah shakes her head. "Just once in a while. I don't want you to think like I'm this barfly or I'm at bars all the time looking for guys."

I smile at her and try to look as reassuring as possible. "I don't think that. But the man you describe sounds like someone I've been looking for. If I asked you, would you go back every few nights and watch for that man for me? You won't have to do anything. Just call Claudia if you see him. Do you think you could do that? I'm sure Mr. Gomez will arrange something fair to pay for your time. Bring a friend if you want. We'll cover all of the costs."

"I don't know." Sarah flutters her hands as she speaks. "Not about going. If you want me to, I will. But I don't know that you need to pay me any more money for that. Mr. Gomez has always been most generous . . ."

"Let us worry about the money," I say. "I'll tell Ms. Gomez to work things out with you."

*   *   *

A half-full cup of black coffee, a large purse and an open file sit on Claudia's desk; otherwise no sign shows of her presence. As I walk toward the desk, I hear the hard splatter of her private bathroom's shower. I glance toward the closed bathroom door and nod. If I were to guess, her early arrival has more to do with her last night's activities than any desire to come in early.

I sit at her desk, push the coffee cup and the purse out of the way, and look at the tab on the file. It reads *Anochi Yagdo*. I spread out the file's contents. A log lists the arrivals and departures of the blue sailboat's inflatable as well as whatever cars or taxis come to drop off or pick up either the boat's passengers or crew.

None are identified by name. Of the crew, only the captain and first mate are singled out. The rest of the crew is listed as crew one, crew two and so on. But each of the twelve passengers has a nickname. I go down the list. Blondie catches my attention first. Of all the people listed, he comes and goes the most.

I continue studying the list. Red, Stretch and Samson seem to appear on the list almost as much as Blondie. Goliath merits only three entries while Mr. Muscles, Fat Sam, Longface, Slowpoke, Skinny and Handsome count two apiece. Someone tagged "Old Guy" has only one mention.

The shower stops, its sound replaced moments later by the whine of a hairblower. I go over the list of cars and stop when I see "Black Mercedes." The same description shows over and over the farther down the list I read, but none of Claudia's people have listed which model.

I study the list a second time and don't even realize that the hairblower has stopped until the bathroom door swings open. "Hey, Boss," Claudia says, buttoning the next-to-top button of her silk blouse and smoothing her short skirt as she walks into the office. "See you found the file."

"Yeah," I say, and glance down at her tan, bare feet.

Her face flushes. "Sorry about that. Not very professional of me." She goes to her purse, extracts a pair of high-heeled shoes and flashes me a wide smile. "Not that I ever claimed to be all that professional," she says, and leans on the desk as she slips each shoe on.

Claudia sits in a chair facing me, rummages in the pocketbook and takes out a small, red cloth, zippered makeup bag. She unzips the bag, empties the contents in front of her and picks up a gold compact. After she opens it, she glances up at me. "Now you know my secret—plenty of makeup." She flashes another smile and begins to apply her mascara. "You might want to look under the reports while I'm doing this," she says.

Under the papers I find a small stack of eight-by-ten glossy pictures. The first few show the sailboat and the inflatable from different angles. Each crew member has multiple pictures and I leaf through them quickly, anxious to see what passengers' faces match the nicknames I've read.

I pass by the picture of a redheaded man walking down the ship's gangplank and looking away from the camera almost as rapidly, but stop at the next photo. "I know this one," I say, staring at the man's long, dark, slicked-back hair.

Busy applying lipstick, her lips pursed, Claudia manages to say, "Name's on the back."

Flipping it over I nod at the nickname, SAMSON. "Appropriate," I say. "Now what's his real name?"

Claudia finishes her lips and closes her lipstick. "We have no idea yet, Boss," she says. She gathers up her makeup and begins to put it back in the bag. "We have barely any decent pictures of most of them. The one they call Old Guy has only been seen once."

She puts the makeup bag away and leans over the desk. "Here." She leafs through the pictures until only one remains. "This is what I wanted you to see. Recognize it?"

I stare at the picture of a black Mercedes 500C sedan pulled up in front of the blue sailboat. The long-haired man they identify as Samson stands by a rear window and appears to be deep in conversation with someone inside the car. "It's the same model car as they used when they tried to snatch Lizzie," I say. "And I've talked to that man before— on the dock. He has a German accent."

Claudia nods. "Maybe," she says. "But would you know if it was Dutch or Norwegian instead?"

I shake my head. "Not really."

"Me neither." She gathers up the pictures and looks through them herself. "Just like we can't be sure whether that Mercedes was the one at *Calle Ocho*."

"So what do you suggest we do now?"

"We just got the Mercedes picture last evening. I'm having someone track the license number but, judging from the number, it's a rental or a lease. I don't think we're going to get a sure answer there. As far as the people go, we can work on arranging for some friendly police to try and get a glance at their passports, or we can take a more direct route."

"And?" I say, arching one eyebrow.

"We can grab one of them and see what he wants to tell us."

"And then what do we do with him?"

"You know the answer to that. If he isn't a bad guy it will be a shame." Claudia leafs through the pictures again. "Though I'd be surprised if he didn't tell us some very interesting things. In any case, it's up to you. We'll do it any way you want."

Without the picture of the Mercedes I would never agree to subjecting one of them to a fatal interrogation. But for me, the car makes one coincidence too many. "Do it," I say. "But make it Samson. I have a feeling about him. Some of the others might be innocent."

Claudia leafs through the pictures again and shakes her head. "Don't know about that, Boss." She hands the pictures back to me. "Notice anything strange?"

I go through them one by one and then repeat the action and shrug.

"Look." Claudia takes the pictures back and holds up the one of Samson. "Except for the sunglasses, we have a decent shot of this one's face," she says, and holds up the next and then the next, some taken in daylight and others shot in the dark. "But we only have partials of everyone else. They're all either holding something that blocks their faces or are looking in a bad direction for the camera—as if they knew it was pointed at them."

11

Arturo Gomez walks into the office just as I take Abby Stiles's business card from my pocket. I nod in his direction and hold the card out to Claudia. "You were talking the other day about how difficult it will be to put surveillance in place to watch Ouder Raad's house," I say. "I met this woman a little while ago. She cleans hulls. Most of her clients are in Gables Estates."

Claudia examines the card. Arturo sits down next to her, holds out his manicured hand and she passes it to him. "And you think she'd be interested in working with us?" Claudia says.

"I think she's interested in money. She's in there, on her boat, all the time. If we asked to place one of our operatives with her, someone like Toba, as an assistant, and we made it worth her while, I think she'd cooperate."

"It would help us put someone in there right away." Claudia looks at her father.

He nods and hands the card back to her. "I think Peter's right. Toba would be a good choice. Who's going to suspect a pretty little blonde in a bikini?"

"I'll put it together." Claudia gets up and looks at me. "If you could let me take my seat, I'll make some notes."

After we've switched seats, I tell Claudia and Arturo

about my conversation with Sarah. "It could have been the blond Russian from Lizzie's abduction," I say.

"Certainly won't hurt to send Sarah to the Quarterdeck." Arturo smiles. "Hey, even if we don't catch the Russian, she might get lucky."

Shortly before ten we move to the conference room. A window looking out over Bayshore Drive, Dinner Key Marina and then Biscayne Bay runs the length of the room, and a gleaming, well-polished twenty-two-seat mahogany conference table runs parallel to it. I sit at one end of the table, with Arturo and Claudia to my right.

Ian Tindall joins us only moments later. His new assistant, Thad Campbell, follows close behind him, struggling to carry both a stack of manila folders and three thick rolls of plans. Even though the man is a cousin, I would never take him for a Tindall. Where Ian is tall and skeletal and pale, Thad is short and chubby and well tanned.

I wonder if the man understood what it would be like to work for his cousin. He makes no move to sit when Ian takes the seat to my left. Rather, he deposits one folder and the rolls of plans in front of Ian, another by the seat next to him and then goes around the room, placing folders at the far end of the table for Manny Padron and his client, putting each of the others in front of Arturo, Claudia and me.

When he finally goes to sit, Ian looks up and says, "Where's the coffee and iced water?" Thad scurries out of the room.

Ian opens the folder in front of him and smiles down at the papers. "This is a good one," he says. "Even if we pay the price per acre that Matherby's asking . . . it's still a bargain." Ian looks at me. "Even if you keep the prime acreage you say you want, we'll make out like bandits. Everywhere else around here is already built out. We get this one and we'll be able to build the last great development in the county—and pretty much charge anything we want."

I reach for one of the sets of plans and unroll it in front of me. I study the map of the entire tract. "It *is* huge," I say.

Ian grins. "Larger than Coral Springs up in Broward. We'll be making money off of it for years. Your children will be grown before it's done."

"What about financing?" Arturo says.

"Well forget Central and Heartland. They don't even want to meet to discuss it. I had to go to Pan American on Brickell. They'll play for one over prime."

"But we've never paid over prime," I say.

"What can I tell you?" Ian shrugs. "We never had Central and Heartland turn their backs on us before. Even with one over prime, we'll still make a fortune."

Thad returns with a tray bearing pitchers of ice water and glasses. One of the secretaries follows him with pitchers of coffee and coffee cups. Once all are laid out, Thad again approaches his seat.

He glances at Ian before he sits. Ian looks at his watch and says, "Damn it, they're already fifteen minutes late. Bet it's his goddamned Cuban lawyer. Those people are always late." He scowls at Thad. "Go to the elevator and escort them right in when they arrive."

"But," Thad says, looks at Ian's scowl, thinks better of it, and turns and scurries out again.

When he returns fifteen minutes later, only one person enters the room with him—a dark, short, elderly Cuban wearing a white silk guayabera shirt. Ian makes a show of studying his watch while Thad directs Manny Padron to a seat at the far end of the table and pours a cup of coffee for him. Manny takes the cup, pushes the manila folder out of his way and smiles toward us.

Grim-faced, Thad finally sits next to Ian. He leans over and whispers something to him.

Ian nods. He turns to Manny and scowls. "You're late."

The Cuban shrugs. "You're in Miami. It's a new culture. Get used to it." He picks up his coffee cup, smells the aroma for a few moments and then takes a sip. He nods. "You have better coffee than you do manners," he says.

"And where's your client?" Ian says. "Thad tells me you came up alone. Is he planning on coming even later?"

Manny takes a long sip from his cup and then looks at me. "I wasn't going to come at all, Mr. DelaSangre, but Buddy insisted that he wanted me to apologize to you in person for his absence. He said he'd like to meet up with you one of these days but, without any business reason for it, he was damned if he was going to drive all the way up to the Grove."

"No business reason? We're talking a huge deal here," Ian says.

The Cuban's eyes go hard and he snarls, "Listen, *cabron*, I'm talking to your boss here. Be a good little attorney and let us have a pleasant conversation without any more of your interruptions."

Ian's face flushes red. Before he can blurt another word, I say, "Please go on, Mr. Padron."

"Manners. It's so easy when everyone has good manners." Manny smiles at me and takes another sip from his cup. "Someone else has tendered an offer on Matherby

Farm—a very substantial offer. Buddy is considering it very seriously."

"But we're prepared to pay his asking price," Arturo says.

Manny nods. "I know. Unfortunately that no longer is good enough. Please bear with me. My client has given me very specific instructions. He wants me to let you know he doesn't like changing any deal. He was prepared to accept your offer. But no one shook on it and nothing has been signed. And the new bidders have offered more than fifteen percent over his asking price."

"That's insane!" Ian says.

The Cuban ignores him. "Buddy is uncomfortable with the other offer only because the bidder is from out of town. He'd rather his family's property stayed in local hands like yours."

"I think we could find a way to meet their offer," Arturo says.

"That's not what Buddy wants. He has asked me to solicit a firm final bid from the other party. Once we learn whatever that is—if you still want to bid—he requests that Mr. DelaSangre will please drive to Matherby Farm to deliver the offer himself. If the bid's sufficient, they'll shake hands on it. If not . . ." Manny shrugs. "He hopes at least you'll share dinner with him."

"We'll bid," I say.

"Good. Buddy will like that." The Cuban drinks the rest of his coffee. "Then I'll be on my way. I have things I must tend to."

"May I ask who the other bidder is?" Claudia says.

"You can ask but I'm not at liberty to tell."

"Is it Ouder Raad?" Ian says.

The elderly Cuban stands to his full, although truncated,

height. "Mr. Tindall, you have an unpleasant reputation. I'm afraid it's wholly justified. If we have any future dealings, please let your young associate represent your interests. I find his company far more bearable than yours."

After Padron leaves, Thad struggles to conceal the triumphant grin that keeps trying to break out across his face. Ian makes no such attempt to suppress the frown on his. "You're not planning to offer more than fifteen percent of his asking price, are you?" he says.

"You just told us how valuable the property is. Did it suddenly become worth less?" I turn to Arturo. "Do you think our accountants can work out what we should offer?"

He nods. "I'll have a cost benefit analysis run right away."

Claudia says, "What about Ouder Raad? It has to be them behind this."

"Probably," Ian says. "But there's no law against buying and selling property."

Arturo studies the plans for a few long moments before he says, "Since when did we ever let the law get in the way of what we want?"

12

Claudia calls a little more than a week later, in the morning, just after I return to the island from dropping Henri off at school. "Boss, I think you should come to the office right now," she says. "Pop and I have some things we need to discuss with you."

"So tell me now," I say.

"I'd rather not talk about it on the phone."

"Wait a minute. Don't we pay a fortune to make sure all our cell phone conversations can't be intercepted?"

"It doesn't mean that they aren't. Nothing's foolproof. You'll understand more once you come to the office."

A thin blonde seated at the receptionist's desk looks up at me and smiles when I step off the elevator. "Good morning, Mr. DelaSangre," she says. "I'm Marcia Voss from accounting. Ms. Gomez asked me to fill in for Sarah today."

I nod and she points down the hall, toward Arturo's office. "She and Mr. Gomez are waiting for you in his office."

Only Arturo and Claudia are in the office. Neither smiles when I enter. Arturo motions for me to take one of the leather seats in front of his desk, next to Claudia. As I sit, I say, "Where's Ian?"

"At South Miami Hospital," Claudia says.

I look from her to her father. "Has something happened to him? That's why I had to rush in here?"

Arturo shakes his head. "No. Except for being irritated that I asked him to get involved down there, he's fine. Ordinarily Claudia or I would handle a situation like that. But we have too much else going on right now."

"A situation like what?" I say.

The Cuban frowns and looks at his daughter. "You didn't tell him?"

"You said the cell phones might not be secure," she says.

He sighs and turns back to me. "Sarah's in intensive care right now. A Waste Management crew found her this morning when they went to empty a Dumpster in the back of the Coconut Grove Quarterdeck's parking lot. She was lying on the ground behind it, half-naked and unconscious and very badly bruised."

"She's still out of it," Claudia says. "Whoever beat her did one major job. The doctors were surprised she didn't die. Not one of them will promise she'll recover. They think she may have been raped too, but they couldn't find any DNA."

"And they found her by the Quarterdeck?" I say.

Claudia nods. "I know what you're thinking. She did call me last night. From the bar. She saw the blond guy she told you about but he left right after she arrived. Sarah said she was going to have a few drinks with her friend, Maxine, and then go home. And yes, I already assigned some of our people to track Maxine down and find out what else went on with Sarah last night."

I frown. "I hate that I asked her to go there. It's not like she was an operative. She was just a receptionist."

"You don't know that your request caused this. How do

you know she didn't just leave the bar with the wrong person?" Claudia says.

"And how do you know it wasn't the blond Russian?" I ask.

Claudia shrugs.

"There's more," Arturo says.

I look at him and he tilts his head toward his daughter.

She sucks in a breath when I look at her. "Okay, the night before last, I sent a crew—three of our best guys; Ken Kuntz, Tim Cleaver and Sammy Morris—to pick up your German friend, the one we call Samson. They were supposed to grab him and take him to our warehouse in Hialeah Gardens."

"You remember Lionel Morales, don't you?" she says.

"Sure," I say. "He worked for Castro before he defected to Miami."

"They say he was one of Castro's best interrogators. I had him and an assistant waiting for my crew to arrive at the warehouse. My crew called me at nine fifty that night to confirm that the snatch went well. Morales called at ten forty-five and said that they'd arrived and that the German seemed pliable."

Claudia pauses for a moment and shifts her position in her chair as if she were suddenly uncomfortable. "That's the last I heard from any of them."

"Yesterday afternoon, after no one had called and no one had answered their cell phones, I sent some other men to the warehouse," Arturo says. "They found enough blood on the floor to know that something happened there. But, except for the van Claudia's crew used and Morales's car parked out front, there was no sign of the German or of any of our people."

"And?" I say.

Claudia picks up some papers from Arturo's desk. "According to the surveillance log, a black Mercedes came to the *Anochi Yagdo* at five after ten. That's shortly after the German was taken by our people. It picked up four men and left.

"The same car returned at one forty-six in the morning." Claudia looks up from the paper and gives me a grim smile. "This time it dropped off five people. Guess who the fifth man was?"

I sigh and say, "Samson?"

"Bingo."

"Anyway, I don't like the timing," Arturo growls.

I look at him. "I don't like any of it."

He nods. "Of course not. But why did the Mercedes pick up the German's associates so quickly after our guys snatched him? Our phones are supposed to be secure, but what if they're not?"

"I don't know," I say. I get up, walk over to Arturo's window and stare out at the water and the nearby marinas. It takes only a moment for me to locate the *Anochi Yagdo*. I glare at the blue sailboat. "What do you propose?"

"I'm arranging to replace all of our phones with ones with newer and better technology. We're going to sweep the offices, and Claudia's, Ian's and my homes for bugs too."

"None of that's going to help us one damned bit to find out why these people are here or what they intend to do." I point to the sailboat. "I want to know who they are and where they come from and I want to know it soon."

"So do we, Boss," Claudia says. "We're down five good people. Six, if we count Sarah. We don't intend to let this pass unnoticed. I can have a new crew ready to go by this afternoon."

I stare at the boat and shake my head. "My father taught me—if one approach fails then try another. I don't want any more direct action right now. There's too much happening all at once," I say. "We need to know more. Haven't you been able to find anything else about the boat's owners or passengers?"

"Not yet. Not any more than we already know," Claudia says. "We've tried our friends in the police and at Customs. Ian's working with the officers at Pan American, our new bank, to see if they can get any detailed financial reports on either VastenZeilen or Ouder Raad."

I stifle a growl. "Since when do we sit around waiting for reports? Why don't we send someone down to Curaçao and Bonaire to check out the companies in person?"

Claudia nods. "We can do that."

"And what about the DEA?" I ask. "Didn't you say that people in the drug business used to use Netherland Antilles holding companies to launder money? Wouldn't the DEA have a way of looking into them?"

"That's not a bad idea, Boss. But it's not like we can just call up someone at the Drug Enforcement Agency and ask them to check something out for us," Claudia says. "It's not like we have federal agents on our payroll."

Arturo begins to grin, his smile widening as Claudia's mouth drops open. "Do we?" she says.

"Not on *our* payroll," he says. He opens his desk drawer and rummages through it for a few moments, and takes out a leather-bound journal. He opens it, turns a few pages and nods. "Ian trades favors occasionally with some South American businessmen named Ramirez."

Claudia shakes her head. "If it's the same Ramirez brothers that were in the paper last year, I don't know how you got Ian to deal with them directly. He hates having to associate with people like that."

"He's started to have Thad handle most of our contacts with them these days. But if we didn't have to occasionally move things in and out of the country without bothering with Customs, I doubt either of them would deal with them at all," Arturo says. "But the Ramirezes have a better relationship with Customs than we do—and, according to Ian, they have the Miami DEA section chief in their pocket too."

"Will they help us with him?" I say.

Arturo nods. "Probably. But it will cost us."

I shrug. "So have Ian arrange it."

"No need to wait for Ian," Arturo says. He turns to Claudia. "After this meeting, get with Thad and tell him to make a call and see if the Ramirezes will help us."

Arturo waits for Claudia to nod and then says, "One more thing, Peter."

"There's more?" I say.

"Just your brother-in-law."

"Derek?"

"Derek." Arturo nods. He picks up a memo pad and looks at it. "He called late yesterday. He's in Australia now, staying at the Stamford Plaza in Brisbane." The Latino looks up and flashes a quick grin. "I'd say he lives very well off your money.

"Anyway, he wanted me to give you the hotel's number and his room number." Arturo imitates Derek's upper-class British accent, so different from Chloe's native Jamaican lilt, as he says, "He said he'd appreciate it very much if you'd ring him up as soon as you can."

* * *

After I leave Arturo's office I stand in the hallway and debate whether to call Derek or to return home immediately. Too many strange things have occurred recently. As capable as Chloe may be as a defender of our home and children, especially with the extra lethal help our growing son can now provide, I still feel most secure when I'm with them.

But two years have passed since my brother-in-law left to find a mate of his own. Though Arturo has kept me aware of the bills he's run up in his constant travels from one European country to the next—and recently through the Middle East and Far East—neither Derek nor I have made any attempt to contact each other.

Has he finally found a mate? I know from my own experience how difficult it can be to find a female of our own kind. There's such a small window of opportunity when one of them comes to maturity. Even finding one just as she gives off the wondrous scent of cinnamon and musk that announces her first heat guarantees nothing. Often other suitors appear and must be dealt with.

Certainly Derek's ongoing charges and now his phone call make it perfectly clear that, at least, no opponent has killed him—yet. But they indicate nothing else. And even if I can ignore my own curiosity, Chloe will definitely frown if I mention her brother's call and provide no other information.

I go to my office. As soon as I sit at my desk, I pick up my phone and dial the Stamford Plaza. A sleepy hotel clerk answers on the fifth ring and I give him Derek's room number. I drum my fingers on my desk as the phone rings, over and over, at least a dozen times before someone finally picks up the receiver. A woman says, in a voice made husky by sleep, "*Szervusz?*"

I pause for a moment, and glance at the numbers Arturo gave me—to make sure that I did read them right—and say, "Excuse me. I was looking for Derek Blood. Someone must have been given the wrong room number."

"No, wait," she says. "Is right room."

"Derek's there?" I say, but no answer comes, only the rustle of sheets and the insistent murmur of her voice. It's obvious she's already in the midst of passing the phone—or at least attempting to.

Whether she's a one-night pickup or more, the woman has my sympathy. I've had to rouse my brother-in-law from sleep more than a few times. I smile and wait and wonder where Derek met her. Her accent sounds far more Eastern European than Australian.

Derek finally speaks into the phone. "It's about bloody time," he says. "Do you have any idea how long Cili and I have been stuck in this room waiting for your call?"

I curl a lip at his tone. The man has lived off of my generosity for over two years. At the very least, he should feign politeness. I spit out my words. "If you wanted to talk to me sooner, you could have called me at the house."

"I just thought your man would call you." Derek's voice softens. "But never mind all that now. I have good news."

"You won't need me to pay any more of your expenses?" I say.

Derek ignores my sarcasm. "I wish I could," he says. He pauses for a few moments as if gathering words. "Unfortunately, my circumstances have changed. I'm in, if anything, an even more needful position. I'm afraid I have a mate now, and a child soon to come. You know how that goes, old man."

Even though Derek can't see, I nod. Unlike human females, our kind always conceive on the first try. "So you finally found your mate," I say. "Congratulations."

"Mind you, it wasn't easy. You know how many countries I went to. After the first year, I thought it wasn't ever going to happen. I'd just returned to Germany after a disappointing month in Poland and Lithuania when I caught the first whiff of her. I wish you'd warned me more about how much it would affect me. I was in a beer garden outside Munich chatting up a local *fraulein* when that smell hit me. You should have seen her eyes when the front of my pants started to bulge."

Derek chuckles. "I don't know what damage I would have done if I hadn't run out of there. I'd already started to shift shape by the time I reached the parking lot. Fortunately there were woods nearby. I hid in the trees and bushes until the change was over and then I took to the air.

"I followed her scent the whole night, hid in a cave the next day and searched again the next evening—all the way across Austria and into Hungary before I finally found her."

"And no one else came for her?"

"Just one. He reached her before me. But I thought he was daft. He was just flying beside her, taking his bloody time before they went at it. I hit him with a speed dive and ripped him apart while he was still stunned. Trust me, I wasn't about to waste any time. I was far too hungry and far too randy for that.

"Cili was quite put out at first. Would you believe she knew the chap? It seems these European types all know each other. They don't keep to themselves like we do. She thought I should have given him fair warning." Derek guffaws. "As if I'd do something so silly."

I swivel in my chair and stare out at the marina and the

open bay as Derek launches into a long brag about how wonderful their sex life has been. "And not only in our natural forms either," he says. "I wish you could see her in her human form. She's almost as tall as me, with thick, long, red hair that reaches to the middle of her back, and her body's as curved as a mountain road . . ." The blue inflatable motors into view, and I stand up to watch as it cruises out Monty's channel and turns south once it reaches the open bay.

When Derek pauses for a moment, I say, "So why haven't you brought Cili back here? You know your sister and I would love to meet her."

"Actually, old man, that's why I called. Cili and I wanted to find somewhere where we could have a place of our own. Europe is far too full of our kind, and I have no desire to return to Jamaica and live with my dear parents. My brother Philip is welcome to suffer that fate. And we both know Miami wouldn't do. Don't we?"

I wince at the thought. "You probably would be better off somewhere else."

"Exactly," Derek says. "And now we've found it."

"Australia?" I say.

"I don't think any of our kind live here. We've flown everywhere and hunted almost every night without catching the slightest sliver of anyone else's mindthoughts. Queensland is perfect. There are always plenty of tourists and plenty of boaters to be preyed upon, and in a pinch we can always fly to the Outback and go after the aborigines."

"I really don't think you can expect me to pay for your room at the Stamford Plaza forever," I say.

"Of course not. We wouldn't want to stay here even if you would. We have to think of our son. Cili does say it's a boy. We'd rather go inland. Someplace isolated, rather like what Mum and Pa have. What do you think of that?"

Derek waits for me to say something. I stay silent and watch the blue inflatable motor out of sight. My brother-in-law obviously wants something from me. I have no desire to make it easy.

He clears his throat and says, "Really Peter, you and Chloe would like it here. They have an area, not more than an hour or two drive from Brisbane, called the Bunya Mountains, all tall and covered with trees and vegetation and with deep, green valleys everywhere. It's not as rugged as it is back in Cockpit Country but parts of it are as hard to get to." He pauses, waits for me to say something and clears his throat again when I continue to stay mute.

"We found this place up for sale there called Bowden Ranch. Most of it's on this long, flat plateau, but one corner of it runs into a finger of land that reaches into an area called Bidwilli Valley. The owner built the most incredible stone mansion there. You should see the valley. It's small and overgrown and wonderfully secluded and they're only asking one million, six hundred and fifty thousand U.S. for everything."

"It sounds wonderful," I say. "How do you plan to raise the money?"

"Don't play with me, Peter. You know I'm looking to you for help in this. The realtor told me the ranch can raise enough beef to cover its expenses and pay off the debt we'd have to take on."

"We?" I say.

Derek sighs into the receiver. "You," he says. "But you know damned well—if it covers expenses—it's a damned cheap way to keep me out of your hair."

I grin. Even if it didn't cover all the expenses, I would still consider it a cheap solution to the ongoing problem of what to do with my wife's brother. "I'll have a talk with Ian," I say. "He'll call you later for the realtor's number. If everything is as you say and the figures work out, we'll arrange the deal and send someone over there to help you hire the right people to run the place. Does that sound okay to you?"

"Of course it does, Peter," Derek says.

"Good. Congratulations again. I'll give you a call when everything's set," I say and disconnect the call.

I call Ian's cell phone next and endure fifteen minutes of his objections until he finally says, "Okay. Whatever you say, Peter. It's your money. You can piss it away any way you desire. If you want I'll buy a bunch of kangaroos for your looney brother-in-law too."

Claudia catches up with me just as I'm about to enter the elevator and leave for the rest of the day. "What?" I snap, still irritated from my conversation with Ian.

She backs up and holds her hands in front of her, palms out. "Whoa. I'm your friend here. I've got some news. I think you want to hear it."

"Sorry," I say. "I just got off the phone with Ian. You know what a pain he can be."

"Sure." Claudia nods. "Toba Mathais just called. She and Abby Stiles have been working across the canal from that stupid castle in Gables Estates, the one that belongs to Ouder Raad."

I nod.

"It seems that some visitors just arrived. They came by water—on a large blue inflatable."

13

The warm air envelops me as soon as I step out the door from the Monroe Building's lobby. I stop, turn my face to the sky and let the bright April sun bake the air-conditioning-induced chill from my body. Men in suits and women in business dresses bustle past me on their way to and from the various offices in the building. Not one of them glances at me or looks up to the sky or over to the calm, blue water in the marina across the street.

Their loss, really. Weeks have passed since the last rain and the air carries a dry, clean smell, free of the humidity that will weigh it down as soon as summer comes. If not for the news I heard in LaMar's offices, the clear sky and gentle warmth of the day would put a smile on my face.

But I can't help but think of poor, battered Sarah and our five missing men. I frown. Neither Arturo nor Claudia has yet stated the obvious—a war has been launched against us.

I clench and unclench my fists and start to walk toward Monty's marina. I could care less about business competition, no matter how low or mean it gets. We sometimes play dirty too. But Ouder Raad's actions have made it clear they're as intent on doing harm to my company as they are on making money. Worse, I can't be sure they're not also bent on harming my family. That I can never permit.

When I reach the wide, white concrete sidewalk that runs along the waterfront, all the way from Monty's down through Dinner Key Marina, I glance south. Even three marinas away, the *Anochi Yagdo*'s raked masts tower high enough above all the other boats to be seen and to remind me of the boat's presence.

I suppress a growl. Whoever lives aboard the boat shouldn't think they can come and go and act with impunity. I turn south, take a step and stop. After all, Arturo and Claudia already have surveillance in place and people gathering information. Without any further knowledge at this point I should just turn back, get on my boat and motor home to my island.

But I yearn for more direct action. My heart speeds up as I take another step and then another on my way south toward the *Anochi Yagdo*.

Up close, the blue sailboat towers above its dock. I stop in front of its blue gangplank and look from the bow to the stern. Two small, dark men stand and smoke on the deck near the top of the gangplank, both clad in jeans and white T-shirts emblazoned with the boat's name. They talk and laugh with each other, their eyes on me as I study the boat.

When a few minutes pass with no passengers or other crew showing themselves, I start up the gangplank. One of the crewmen says something to the other and darts over to a narrow stairway that leads to the ship's bridge. He clambers up the steps while the other crewman flicks away his cigarette and steps over to the top of the gangplank. He blocks it with his slight body, his legs spread, his arms folded across his chest.

I stop one step before I reach him. Even with the height

disadvantage of standing below him on the sloped gang-plank, I tower over the small islander. We both know he can do little to stop me from pushing past him. Still, he stands and glares at me as if he can.

"I need to see the captain or whoever's in charge," I say.

The crewman shakes his head and points to the bottom of the gangplank. "*Bai! Warda abou ei,*" he says.

His courage makes me want to smile but I force a glower. "Please move out of the way," I say, and start forward.

"*Mejneer!* Sir! Please, if you would."

The voice comes from above. I pause and look up. A thin, blond man in a starched white uniform stands ramrod-straight, halfway down the stairs that lead from the bridge. "Please to stop and back up a few steps," he says.

I step back and the dark crewman braced in front of me grins and drops his arms down as he relaxes.

The man on the stairs begins to descend to the deck, one step at a time. Once there, he dismisses the crewman with a wave of his hand and strides over to take his place. Unlike the crewman, his height and bulk equal mine. He stares at me with pale blue eyes, nods and says, "*Dank u.* Now what might you want?"

"I want to speak to whoever's in charge."

"Not possible." The man shakes his head. "The *kapitein* is busy."

His rigid posture and Germanic accent grate on me. I glare at him. As large as he seems, I doubt he has the strength to resist any sudden charge I may decide to make. "Either your captain or whoever's in charge of your passengers. I'm afraid I have to insist," I say.

"I am afraid not. Our passengers may not be disturbed. One of my men watches us from the bridge. I have instructed him to call the police if you prove difficult. I am Stil Vanemeer, the ship's first mate. I will have to do."

"I don't know that you will do at all. People have died since your boat arrived. Others have been injured. My daughter was almost abducted . . ."

Vanemeer shrugs. "In Holland they talk all the time, how violent your Miami is. I am sorry for your daughter and the others but none of it has to do with this boat. We are neither killers nor abductors here. We are sailors. We take passengers from here to there and back, whatever the charter requires. That is all."

"Why were you anchored off my island, Caya DelaSangre?"

"If I recall correctly we were near the small islands you call the Ragged Keys. We were more than a mile from any other island. Our berth was not ready. Our ship requires deep water. We anchored in such an area."

"Why has your inflatable been going to Gables Estates?"

The Dutchman shrugs again. "The inflatable goes wherever our passengers wish. We don't question their desires."

This man is too calm, too indifferent to my presence. I want to strike out at him. I want to see terror on his face. Still, any scene I create will surely end in a confrontation with the police. I sigh.

Father taught me not to act on impulse. I knew better than to try to bully my way on board. I should have just gone home. But as much as I know what I should do, I find it impossible to turn away. I just can't disengage without some sort of gesture. "I want you to deliver a message," I say.

The first mate shakes his head. "I am a sailor, not a secretary."

"Wrong answer." I lunge forward, grab his neck with my

right hand and push him back away from the gangplank. The mate gasps for air, flails his arms and struggles to regain his footing. But my momentum carries us both across the walkway. I slam him against the ship's cabin wall and pin him there.

Wide-eyed, he struggles to breathe, his hands on my fingers, pulling, trying to pry them away. His eyes grow wider still when he finds that however hard he tries, he can't.

"Listen carefully," I say. "I can do whatever I want to you and still be long gone before the police get here. Now try to remember this. I am Peter DelaSangre. Tell your passengers there will be hell to pay if they interfere with me again, on any level." I lessen my grip just enough to allow the man to take in a small gasp of air. "Do you think you can deliver that message?"

The man nods.

"Good," I say. "And you understand it will be best for you if you don't bother the police with any report?"

He nods again and I release him.

With an explosive gasp, the sailor doubles over. He barks out coughs and wheezes as he struggles to regain his breath. Finally he glares up at me. "I will tell you one thing about our passengers. They are hard men. I will pass your message to them, but I doubt they'll care."

As nice as the day is, as flat as the water may be, I take no pleasure in my cruise home. I think of attacking the ship at night, ripping every person onboard into shreds and then doing the same to the inhabitants of Ouder Raad's castle in Gables Estates.

It would be so simple. I certainly have the ability to do it. I shake my head. But I doubt I have the means to control the aftermath. There would be too many dead and far too much blood.

My cell phone rings just before I reach the channel to my island. I answer and Claudia says, "Sorry, Boss. I thought you'd want to know. Sarah just died. Her injuries were too much for her."

I suck in a breath. "Shit," I say. "She was just a receptionist. I never should have asked her to go back to the Quarterdeck."

"None of us thought she ran much of a risk," Claudia says.

"Tell that to her."

I hold the phone away from me for a moment, to avoid throwing it in the water. When I put it back to my ear, I catch the end of Claudia's sentence. ". . . missing."

"What?" I say.

"I said, we can't find her friend Maxine either. Her mother say's she's missing."

I find Chloe and Lizzie in the garden. My daughter shouts, "Papa!" and runs to me as soon as she sees me approach. My wife, busy yanking weeds out of the ground under the yellow-and-green leaves of a Dragon's Tear bush, barely nods a greeting.

On another day I would say something about how the garden has thrived under her care. Thanks to her ministrations we have as much Angel Wort, Death's Rose and Dragon's Tear as we could want, more than enough for any drinks or potions we might require. Instead, I sit on the ground near Chloe and mindspeak, masked, {*Sarah's dead.*}

{*What?*} She stops her weeding and turns her head to me. Lizzie takes advantage of the reduced height of my seated position and proceeds to try to climb over me from my back. Ordinarily this would turn into a struggle replete with tickles and much laughter but today I ignore her, let her do as she wishes.

I tell Chloe about Sarah first, and then all about Maxine, our missing people, the black Mercedes coming to the sailboat, the blue inflatable pulling up to Ouder Raad's dock in Gables Estates and Arturo's suspicion that our communications have been breached.

Chloe turns away when I finish and pulls up another weed. {*So what are you planning to do about it?*} she mindspeaks. She digs her fingers into the dirt under yet another weed, loosens the soil, yanks it from the ground and drops it on a pile of weeds that she's already pulled.

I stare at the small mound of soon-to-be dead vegetation and wish that our problem could be solved as easily, with just a few surgical yanks. {*We haven't come up with a plan yet. I'm waiting to find out who's behind Ouder Raad.*}

{*What if it's someone of the Blood?*} Chloe says. {*They would hear us mindspeak.*}

{*Don't think I haven't thought about it—especially about your family. But I doubt your father would have anything to do with another attack on us. He gave his word and I believe him. And Derek's not here.*}

{*How do you know he isn't? This is just the sort of thing he'd get involved in.*}

{*Presupposing someone else had the intelligence to think it up for him,*} I say. {*But he's in Australia right now. I just talked to him this morning. You have a new sister-in-law.*}

Chloe cocks an eyebrow and I tell her everything Derek told me.

{*What about someone else?*} she says.

{*Of the Blood?*}

She nods.

I shake my head. {*Why? What reason would anyone else of the Blood have to come here to attack us?*}

{*Your friends, the Pelk, would have plenty of reasons. We killed enough of them.*}

{*The Pelk live in caves and under the water. They feed on fish and dolphins. They don't have anything to do with people. They only mindspeak. I never heard one of them speak a word out loud.*}

Chloe scowls and spits out her words. {*I notice you didn't deny that they're your friends.*}

{*For God's sake, give it up. There are more important things happening here.*} I return her glare.

{*And you don't think preserving our family's pretty damned important?*} Chloe stands up, slaps the loose dirt from her shorts and walks away, leaving me alone with our daughter and a pile of dying vegetation.

14

Neither of us talk the rest of the day. In the evening we go to bed without a word spoken. To my surprise, as much as anger still vibrates inside me, sleep comes quickly. But a few hours later, Chloe sighs. The sound half wakes me and I make the mistake of shifting my position ever so slightly.

Chloe sits up and nudges me. "I can't sleep," she says.

I resist the impulse to lash out with a harsh, "I can." I have little desire to risk any confrontation that might continue our argument through the night. Instead I say nothing at all, just nestle into my pillow and hope she'll soon tire and fall off to sleep herself.

She nudges me again. "Are you really sleeping?"

A groan escapes my lips. I lift my head and look at her with one half-opened eye. "I've been thinking about everything," she says, as if I'm wide awake and sitting up with her. "I hate that I get jealous like I did today."

With sleep obviously not an option right now, I stretch, open both eyes, roll over and sit up next to my wife. "I hate it too," I say.

She slaps me on the shoulder. "You could say you understand how hard it is for me that you made love to someone else."

"I didn't make love. I was poisoned and forced to do what

I did," I spit out. "The Pelk women know special chants that control their victims' thoughts—you know that. I hate that it happened to me and I hate that it's harmed what we have. And I have said that I understand how hard it is for you more than a few times. I do understand. I'm sure it would be difficult for me if the situation was reversed. But it's been two goddamned years . . ."

Chloe frowns at the tone of my voice. "I know. I'm trying to apologize here."

I draw in a breath. I had expected a continuation of our fight, not contrition. I look at her. Chloe looks away, draws up her knees and hugs them. It makes her seem even younger than she is, and in need of comfort. I would like to take her in my arms and hold her but months have passed since she allowed any such intimacy. Besides, my anger, while diminished, has yet to leave entirely. "You've apologized before," I say.

"And I probably will have reason to apologize again. I'm not saying that everything's okay and that this is the end of it. I'm saying I realize I'm being unreasonable and I'm trying to find a way to make it better. Isn't that what people who love each other are supposed to do?"

I nod.

"So?" she says.

Just enough anger remains to tempt me to say something to continue our fight. I breathe deep, try to will it away and finally say, "Apology accepted."

"That's it?" she says. "You don't want me to make it up to you?"

I look at her and she suddenly gives me a grin that I know far too well. "You're kidding," I say. "That's what all this is about?"

Chloe shakes her head slowly from side to side. "Not all of it. I do think I owe you an apology for how I jumped down your throat today. But before I fell asleep I started to think about all the things we used to do with each other." Her grin stretches into a leer.

"And then I really couldn't sleep. I tried to ignore it, I really did. After all, I *was* mad at you . . . but it's been a long time." She puts her hand on the inside of my left thigh and runs it up toward my crotch. I start to stir and her leer widens even more. "A very long time," she says.

Still she backs away when I reach for her. "What?" I say, "I thought you said you wanted to."

"I do—very much," Chloe says. "Just not here, not like we are." She gets out of bed, goes to the window and opens the shutters. Moonlight floods the room.

Chloe stares out the window, the moonlight turning her face a golden brown. "Oh, you should see how beautiful the sky is, how full of bright stars," she says. "Wouldn't you rather make love surrounded by all of that?"

I could care less what surrounds us. So much time has passed since our last bout of sex that just the mention of the possibility of it makes my heart race and my erection grow painfully hard. I scowl at the thought that any more time will have to pass before I can find relief. "In our natural forms?" I say.

Chloe nods, yanks off her T-shirt and stands naked by the window. The moonlight glows on her skin and casts black shadows under her brown breasts. She touches one of her dark nipples with a finger and it crinkles into a hard nub. "In our natural forms, in the air," she says.

"What about the kids? I thought you didn't want to leave them alone."

"They're asleep. We don't have to hunt. We have plenty of beef here. That way we won't have to go too far. If either of the kids calls for us we can rush home."

She touches her other nipple and sighs when it hardens too. "I'll be outside, Peter. Please don't keep me waiting."

The door remains open after she leaves and I stare at the moonlight pouring through it. I would prefer a dark night and a sky far more crowded with black clouds than bright stars. I shrug. I'd also prefer it if my wife could learn to be less mercurial—if she could find the ability to let the past stay far away from the present.

"*Peter, I'm waiting,*" Chloe mindspeaks.

I sigh, get out of bed and pull off my T-shirt. My father always said that, at best, any relationship consists of accepting a series of compromises. On the whole, tonight doesn't look like it will be a bad one.

Before I join Chloe, I go below to our refrigerated storeroom and take out one of our frozen sides of beef. I carry it up, take it outside onto the veranda and lay it on the oak deck near Chloe's bare feet. "By the time we come back we'll be famished," I say.

She nods, walks over and presses her naked body against mine. Before I can wrap my arms around her, she giggles and steps back. "Your right side's ice-cold from carrying the beef," she says.

I step forward and pull her toward me. "You can warm it," I say and, for the first time in months, I kiss her.

Chloe accepts my kiss and my embrace and she presses her body against me as I hug her close to me.

We stand that way for minutes, ignoring the gentle but insistent tug and push of the night wind as it whispers past us.

Finally Chloe pulls back a few centimeters and looks up to the sky. "I think we should change," she says.

"Why wait?" I grind my erection against her. "We could go back to bed instead."

"Not in our human forms." Chloe shakes her head and pushes away from me. "The way I feel, I need for us to be in our natural forms." Her skin tightens and begins to ripple. *"You go back inside, if that's what you want. I want to fly,"* she mindspeaks.

I watch her until the first outlines of scales begin to show and then I will my body to change too. I let out a low growl as my skin contorts and my back begins to swell.

Chloe groans and stretches and twists beside me, her wonderful, plump lips thinning and lengthening as her snout grows and her mouth fills with fangs. Her tail emerges and her groans give way to growls, which grow louder the farther her tail extends and the more her back swells. Finally her back splits open and her wings burst free. She sighs and snaps them to their full spread.

She turns her eyes to me, flexing her claws and slowly exercising her wings as I continue to shift my shape. But after a few minutes she sighs again and mindspeaks, *"The sky is too beautiful tonight to waste any more time on the ground. Come find me when you're ready."*

A sudden gust of wind rushes over us. Chloe turns into it. She holds her wings open and steps off a few paces before she extends her neck and bounds forward, her wings scooping air, sending blasts of it back over me as she goes airborne.

My wings break free and I half moan and half growl at the pleasure and pain of my transformation. I flex my body, stretch my tail straight out behind me and unfold my wings to their full span. As much as I want to rush forward and take to the sky, I wait for my fangs and claws to reach their full length, and for my scales to harden and thicken to their full depth.

"*Peter,*" Chloe mindspeaks. "*I'm still waiting. Don't you care? Or have you forgotten what it's like to take a female in heat?*"

I growl at her taunt. "*It's been so long that I should have forgotten it,*" I mindspeak.

"*Don't be like that, baby. It won't hurt you very much. I promise. I might even let you catch me.*" Her rich laughter peals in my mind.

No burst of wind welcomes me when I rush forward. No matter. The air could be calm and I would still leave the ground far below me with only a few beats of my wings. I clear the veranda wall by yards and continue to gain altitude as I shoot by, far above the dunes and the beach.

Chloe's laughter peals again. "*Finally,*" she mindspeaks.

I spiral upward and scan the star-studded, moonlit sky and the dark waters all around our island. I let out a sigh. No boat lights show anywhere near. As bright as the night is, an observant boater might be able to make out our forms as we flew overhead.

Still, I catch no glimpse of Chloe anywhere. I flip over and glide upside down—so I can examine the sky exactly overhead—and again find no sign of her.

Before I can call out to her, Chloe zooms up from below and behind me. She flies just above me and passes so low and so close that her underbody rubs against mine, ever so briefly, ever so lightly, and then she dives out of sight.

Just that slight touch of her brings all my frustration, all my lust to a fever pitch. I bellow into the empty air.

"Does that mean you want me to come back?" Chloe mindspeaks.

"Of course I do."

"Fly higher, Peter. I want us to meet over the clouds."

My heart pounds and my breaths come so quickly that my lungs ache—not from any exertion but from my need for her. I spiral upward, each spiral wider and steeper until my island almost shrinks from sight. I search the sky for clouds. Only a few dot the sky this night, most of them too small and too wispy for cover. I look for one large enough to catch Chloe's interest.

Far to my south, a long, fat cloud, made gray by the night, scuds slowly toward the northwest. I nod. No other cloud in sight reaches quite its height or measures half as big. It seems to be headed toward the ocean side of Elliott Key. I turn and fly toward it.

Chloe glides a hundred feet above the cloud, flying long, wide circles as she waits for me. I approach from above her and marvel at her economy of motion and grace in flight. As maddening as she can be, I only need to look at her to know how fortunate I am. I circle above, watch her complete one last, lazy loop and only then mindspeak, *"Chloe."*

She changes direction and scans the dark sky until she sees me. *"It's about time,"* she mindspeaks, and flips over and goes into a shallow dive, her position revealing the pink flush of her swollen sex as she falls away from me.

Rather than waste any time on words, I roar into the evening sky, fold my wings and plummet toward her. The wind rips past me and buffets me, the rush of it against my body only heightening my need.

Just before I crash into Chloe, I open my wings and catch

the air enough to match her speed. I seize her with my claws. She yowls as I draw her to me and bucks as if she wants to break free, but at the same time she digs her claws into my scales and drives her fangs into my throat—enough to hold fast to me and draw blood, but not deep enough to cause any major injury.

In turn I plunge my now-rigid cock into her—the sudden moist heat inside her feeling as if it could almost sear through my skin. I bellow out another roar and fold my wings over hers, collapsing her wingspread, forming a cocoon that enfolds us both.

We plunge toward earth, oblivious to the cloud's wet vapors that coat us as we plummet through it, oblivious to the scream of the wind and the chill of the night, oblivious to almost everything except the feel of each other's bodies. Chloe yowls and writhes beneath me, and digs her claws and teeth into me with every motion of my body, holding me close when I plunge into her, pulling me back when I attempt to withdraw for even a moment.

But we both never lose awareness of the changing pressure of the altitude and the thickness of the air. When both indicate we have only moments before we crash to our deaths, I unfold my wings and Chloe releases her grip and peels away.

I follow her, my snout only inches from her tail as we rocket forward and then spiral back up. The smell of my own blood, seeping from the bites and gashes Chloe inflicted, envelops me but I ignore both it and the pain. I would pay that small price any day for the greater pleasure of sex in our natural forms.

As much as I like sex in my human form—and I do—it lacks the grand, mindless passion that overtakes my kind in our natural forms. With humans, sex is often such a soft thing—soft bodies coupling on soft beds, surrounded by soft pillows. Even when rough, the most adventuresome of humans can never approximate the sensations of airborne sex or the roughness of our sex without doing fatal damage to each other.

Neither Chloe nor I need to exchange a single mind-thought as we soar skyward. As soon as we reach the clear sky above the cloud, she flies close enough for me to seize her again and, once again, we fall toward earth, only to repeat the process a third time and a fourth, our hearts pumping blood so quickly that our ears pound, our breaths rasping out one loud grunt after another.

We orgasm while falling inside the cloud on our fifth descent and hold each other the rest of the way down. This time, when we part, Chloe rockets straight out and descends to just inches above the ocean. I shoot after her, beating my wings just a few flaps more to speed forward and catch up to her, so we can fly alongside each other, wingtip to wingtip.

My body aches but my cock, which should recede to its normal rested state, remains almost as swollen, still throbbing from its recent exertions. I sigh and mindspeak, *"That was good. Want to go again?"*

"I was going to ask if you didn't," Chloe mindspeaks. *"This time, let's go higher."* She shoots ahead and races skyward.

This time, once we pass the cloud, we continue to spiral up until the air grows too cold and thin for comfort. *"Brrr,"* Chloe mindspeaks. *"Come wrap your wings around me."*

We fall again, less frenzied in our movements, less hard

on each other's bodies, but still aware of nothing but each other.

In midfall, Henri mindspeaks, *"Papa? Mama? Where are you?"*

Chloe stiffens beneath me and mindspeaks, *"We're flying nearby. What's wrong?"*

I release her. She snaps her wings open and glides off in a long, shallow arc. I follow right above her.

"Someone's here. Max's growling woke me up. I looked out the window and . . ."

{*Mindspeak masked, Henri.*} Chloe glances over at me and mindspeaks, so only I can hear. {*Just in case.*}

I nod.

{*I didn't see anyone or anything and then one of the shadows moved and got bigger and Max growled really loud. I ducked away. But I don't know what to do now.*}

{*Where's your sister?*} I mindspeak.

{*In bed . . . I think.*}

{*Go get her. Leave Max in your room. If someone's there he'll slow them down. You and Lizzie go downstairs to the small cell where the hidden stairway is. Quickly. Do you understand?*}

{*Sure, Papa. I'm already going.*}

{*Good.*} I look around and frown when I see our mindless flight has taken us south of Elliott Key, almost to the northern tip of Key Largo. Anger rushes through me and I flex my claws and gnash my teeth as I readjust my course north, toward home. Chloe follows suit and we both race forward, as fast as we can.

{*I want you to go into the stairway and pull the cot down, so no one can see you. I want you both to stay there—as still*} *and silent as you can be—with no light on, until we get home,}* I mindspeak.

{On the stairs? Not down by the treasure room?}

{On the stairs. That way if they find the hidden door by the dock and come into the passageway they still won't see you.}

{Okay. I'm in Lizzie's room, waking her up. Rush home, Papá. Please.}

{Just take your sister and hide. We'll be there soon, I promise.}

Chloe mindspeaks, masked to me. *{This is my fault. I was too damned self-indulgent to think what risk I was putting the children in.}*

I shake my head. *{This is the fault of whoever's come to the island—not yours.}*

We pass Rhodes Key, then Adams, then race over Elliott. *{We're in!}* Henri mindspeaks, masked. *{I'm pulling the rope now and the cot's coming down over us.}*

Lizzie mindspeaks, *"Momma! I don't like this!"*

{Masked, honey. You have to mindspeak masked the way all of us are,} Chloe mindspeaks.

{I still don't like it. It's dark and the stair's hard to sit on and Henri keeps pushing me and telling me what to do. He keeps saying things to scare me, too.}

{He's not trying to scare you,} Chloe mindspeaks. *{I know you don't like it when he's bossy but I want you to listen to him now and do exactly as he says.}*

{But, Momma . . .}

{No buts. You have to listen to him.}

{See, Lizzie. I told you,} Henri mindspeaks.

A moment later, he mindspeaks, *{Max is barking. Someone's in the house above us. I hear steps, I think.}*

I glance down as we pass the northern tip of Elliott Key and begin to speed past Sands Key. {*Stay quiet,*} I mindspeak. {*We're almost at Boca Chita. We'll be home in minutes.*}

{*I think it's okay, Papa. The steps are already gone.*}

{*No matter what you hear or don't hear, you stay put exactly where you are.*}

As we pass the Ragged Keys, Chloe mindspeaks, masked, {*I'll take the bay side,*} and angles off over the bay.

I do the same over the ocean. Once I find myself off the coast of Caya DelaSangre, I mindspeak, {*Now!*} and bank left. I glide down, and shoot over the waves and then the beach and the dunes, my heart racing, my claws ready to rip through the flesh of the first foe that I run across. But I see no one, no boat; only the dogs who bark as I pass over them, and Max waiting on the veranda.

Chloe swoops in from the east and lands on the oak deck at the same time as I do. Max thumps his tail and woofs out a greeting. I ignore him and suck in breaths, trying to fill my lungs and calm my racing heart. My wife stands where she landed and does the same.

{*We're home,*} I mindspeak, masked. I turn and stare from place to place as I do so. {*I don't see anyone and nothing looks different.*}

{*I heard them, Papa. I really did.*}

{*I'm sure you did. I still want both of you to stay where you are. We haven't looked in the house yet. After that, we'll come get you.*}

{*Yes, Papa,*} they both mindspeak.

Max pads over to the frozen slab of beef, now partially thawed, and sniffs at it. He knows better than to take a bite without permission. He sits and turns his head toward me and waits for me to nod. I return the beast's stare and mindspeak, {*Henri, I thought I told you to leave Max in your room.*}

{*And I did, Papa. Just like you told me.*}

Chloe walks over to the dog and examines the meat. {*You're not going to like this. Someone's taken some bites out of this.*}

{*Max?*}

Chloe shakes her head. {*Big bites,*} she mindspeaks. {*The kind we'd take.*}

I join her and stare at the empty holes where three big chunks of meat have obviously been ripped from the side of beef. I flex my claws and shake my head. {*I don't get it.*}

{*Why? Haven't you ever been hungry?*}

{*You know what I mean. It has to be one of us . . .*}

{*Or more,*} Chloe mindspeaks.

{*Or more.*} I shrug. {*Either way, he or they would have to know we'd realize they were here.*}

{*Exactly. So he's sending us a message.*}

{*What message? That our children can be threatened and our meat eaten by others?*}

{*No.*} Chloe lowers her head and rips a chunk of beef free with her teeth. {*Sorry, I'm starving,*} she mindspeaks. {*You should have some too. We both need the strength.*}

My stomach growls at the thought, and I join her and tear at the cold, raw meat too, avoiding the areas where someone else has obviously fed. After a few bites, I pause and mindspeak, {*You never answered my question; what message?*}

{*Papa, Momma, when can we come out? I'm bored,*} Lizzie mindspeaks.

{*In a few minutes, honey. Papa and I still have to search the house.*} Chloe tears off another chunk and closes her eyes as she chews it and swallows. Then she mindspeaks to me, {*Two things. I think he wants us to know that we don't scare him and I think he wants us to know that we're the ones who should be afraid.*}

I pause for a moment before I answer. Even the knowledge that someone else of the Blood may be in town answers precious few of my questions. My stomach growls again but fury has dulled my appetite and I ignore it. {*Okay,*} I mind-speak. {*What you say makes sense, but they would have to know we'll fight them to the death. Why would anyone of the Blood want to start that sort of trouble?*}

Chloe shrugs and backs up from the meat. {*All I know is we have two children still hiding in the dark. We should go get them. I doubt that anyone's inside. We got his message. At least, I did. I'm scared to death at what he might try next.*}

15

Brightness and heat intrude on my sleep. I open my eyes and blink at the shaft of light that shines directly in my face. For a moment, I wonder if it's a strong flashlight beam, whether an intruder has penetrated our room. But I turn my head and find the whole room full of light.

I glance at the window and sigh. Neither Chloe nor I remembered to close the shutters she opened the night before. Sunlight pours though the open wood slats. The warmth it brings overpowers the air-conditioning—even with it set low, the way Chloe likes.

Though our naked bodies have become clammy and moist wherever our skin touches, neither the light nor the heat seem to affect Chloe. She amazes me with her ability to sleep on, pressed against me, a brown leg over mine, a brown arm across my chest, her cheek warm and moist on my shoulder. I flex my shoulder and she grimaces, but the slow cadence of her breaths never changes, not when I begin to wriggle my body out from under hers and not when I roll free and get out of bed.

At the window, I peer outside before I close the shutters. The bright daylight and the long shadows stretching west confirm my suspicion that the day has only recently begun.

I clack the shutters closed, and my wife lets out a small groan, rolls over and embraces her pillow.

I look at her stretched across the bed, the sheet barely draped over one bare breast and its opposing leg, her face only half visible above the pillow, and consider returning to bed. Despite our problems, despite the probability that she will grow distant again—as she has before as soon as the memory of the past night's passion faded—I would choose no other.

But as much I would like to lie beside her and wait for her to wake, I can't forget what else happened in the night. The thought that she and I and our children could be threatened by another of our own kind sends a chill through me. Our sharp claws and teeth, our armored scales, our ability to fly, to shift shapes and to heal ourselves, protects us from other species—not from each other. I've fought others of my kind, other Undrae, before and remember how formidable they were and how close to death they brought me.

I shake my head. Whether my wife becomes distant or not matters little when measured against such danger. I throw on a pair of cutoff jeans and go out onto the veranda.

Outside, I squint and hold up my right hand to shield my eyes from the sun's early-morning glare. No morning wind accompanies it. Without the wind, the few white puffs of cloud in the sky seem suspended in place. No leaves rustle in the trees. No waves rush at the shore. Even the water in my island's small harbor lies too still to lap at my dock or budge our boats.

The surface of the bay remains so calm it looks like someone laid a slab of blue-green glass over it. Nothing, not a boat, not a dolphin or a large fish, has broken its surface tension. Far to the south, far inland, a thick column of gray smoke makes a near-perpendicular line in the sky. I study it for a moment, then glance at the nearby grass and leaves, all tinged with brown from three weeks without rain, and nod.

Whenever the area goes too dry for too long, the Everglades begin to burn. Only rain will end the fires and that may not come for weeks or possibly longer.

I know the wind, at least, will soon pick up and all will change as the day progresses, but still I frown at the silence now around me. I walk across the veranda, to the coral stone parapet that rings it, and stare out on the ocean side. A lone fishing boat races south, too far out at sea for me to hear its motors' drone, but at least close enough for me to see the white trail of its wake—the only disturbance in the flat blue expanse of water that, otherwise, so placidly stretches out to the horizon.

At least someone else has risen to face the day. I lean against the coral stone and mutter, "Good," and a dog barks out a muffled answer from its hidden lair in the bushes near the sand dunes. A mockingbird chirps out a response to that from the top branch of the gumbo-limbo tree next to Elizabeth's grave.

Both sounds break the morning's unnatural calm. I smile and turn and study the oak door to the arms room, twelve yards left of my bedroom door. If I must face another Undrae, I see no reason why I should do so armed only with my claws and teeth.

I'm tempted to open the arms room door and stare inside, but I've little reason to do so. I've cleaned and lubricated each ancient flintlock pistol, musket, rail gun and cannon Father stored there more times than I can count. I shrug. While Father may have found them useful during his old pirate days, and they've served me well a few times too, I see no use for them this time.

The small guns lack the power to inflict enough harm on an Undrae, and the big blunderbuss rail guns and cannon are just too cumbersome and limited. Even the modern guns I've stored among them, the Uzi machine guns and the twelve-gauge shotguns, lack the punch to bring down a creature like me for good.

I retrieve my cell phone from the bedroom, return to the veranda and dial Claudia's number. An answering machine picks up after four rings. I disconnect after the first sound of Claudia's recorded voice, wait a few seconds and dial again.

After I make two more calls, she finally picks up. "Jesus! It isn't even seven yet," she says, her voice husky with sleep.

"You should be getting ready for work anyway."

"Boss," Claudia yawns into the receiver. "You know it wouldn't be good for Pops if I showed up for work on time every day. He'd have nothing to complain about. It might even make him feel unneeded."

I grin and say, "Well, I need you to do something for me."

"Sure. Whatever you want."

"How about a gun powerful enough to take down an elephant or a Kodiak bear on a single shot?"

Claudia pauses a moment before she answers. "You planning on going big game hunting?"

"No. But I want something that can knock down anything."

"How about an RPG or an antitank gun? They could do that easy."

I frown. "No. They're too unwieldy. I want something I can carry on the boat or in the car; something smaller. And something with more than one shot. A revolver or an automatic like your Desert Eagle—but more powerful."

"I don't know if I'd want to shoot anything more powerful than that gun. It already shoots fifty-caliber loads . . . and hurts my hand every time I fire it."

"Just see what's out there for me," I say.

"Sure, Boss, but it's on your head."

"What is?"

"You know how I am about guns. You send me into a gun store, you know I'm going to have to buy whatever's new."

I grin. "Then it will give you an opportunity to practice your willpower."

Chloe and I had agreed that we'd all sleep in this morning. Henri could afford to skip a day of school and we'd been up very late. Rather than return to the house and risk waking anyone, I search the island for any sign of whoever visited us the evening before.

I save the beach for last. By the time I finally reach it, the wind has finally begun to stir and small wavelets ripple against the shore. Only the dog pack's paw prints and my footprints mar the smooth surface of the sand. I stare at it and frown.

{*Peter? Where are you?*} Chloe mindspeaks.

{*Down by the beach, looking for signs of our visitor.*}

{*See anything?*}

{*Not a thing.*}

{*Come back up then. I missed having you next to me when I woke.*}

I find Chloe waiting for me, leaning her back against our open bedroom door and looking small and waiflike, her otherwise naked body covered by one of my old Miami Dolphin T-shirts. She smiles when I step onto the veranda and walks toward me as I walk toward her.

We meet in the middle of the deck and she puts her arms around me before I can wrap mine around her. "I didn't like waking up in an empty bed," she says, and presses her body against mine.

"I couldn't sleep," I say, holding her close. "I didn't want to wake you."

She gives me a dirty smirk. "You could have. We haven't done anything special together, in our human forms, for a long time. I wouldn't have minded being woken for that."

"Me neither." I sigh. "But my mind was on the visitor we had last night."

Chloe's face goes somber and she backs away a step. "I've been trying to avoid thinking about it for a little while longer. Have you decided what you want to do about it?"

"Some," I say. I tell her about my conversation with Claudia.

"I don't know," Chloe says. "Even if Claudia finds the guns you want, there's no guarantee they'd help very much."

She turns and stares toward the mainland. "Damn! The Everglades are on fire. Now, if it doesn't rain soon, we'll have smoke everywhere." She wrinkles her nose. "I hate how that smells."

I nod. "Me too. But I think we're going to have to get used to it again. Rainy season won't start for at least another three weeks."

"Yuck." Chloe grimaces. She keeps her eyes on the column of smoke and her back to me. "At least it's another reason," she says.

I wrinkle my forehead. No one could ever accuse my wife of linear thinking. "Another reason for what?" I ask.

"Jamaica. I think we should take the kids there. You know how cruddy it gets around here when everything's burning in the Everglades. We could avoid living with that and keep the kids safe at the same time." Chloe turns around and looks at my face. "What do you think?"

"I don't know," I say. "This other Undrae coming here can't be an accident. He knows who we are and where we live. Why wouldn't he also know about your parents and brother and Morgan Hole?"

Chloe shrugs. "So what do you think we should do?" she asks.

I look down and think over everything that's happened since the morning of *Calle Ocho*. "I'm not sure what's going on," I say. "But it's possible that whoever it is wants Lizzie— to hold her until she reaches maturity and can be taken for a mate."

"But that's against tradition," Chloe says.

"So? It wouldn't be the first time something like that happened. The good thing is that nothing has ever occurred while at least one of us has been with the children. If we do need to fight, I'm sure Claudia will find us guns we can use to have an advantage."

Chloe frowns. She shakes her head, and walks over to the parapet and stares out at the ocean.

I follow and stand next to her and say, "I just can't see leaving. It could give whoever it is the chance to move in here and go after our business. I think we're better off staying here until we learn more about who we're facing. If we can't see any way to win—then we should leave."

"That's fine for you and me." Chloe turns toward me. "But what if we lose before we can go? What will happen to

Henri and Lizzie? If we don't take them somewhere safe, how can we make sure they're protected?"

The concern on her face makes her look older and tired. I want to take her in my arms, to hold her and reassure her, but I know of nothing to say—except one thing, and I know she won't like it. I take a deep breath and look directly at her.

Chloe returns my gaze and says, "Well?"

"There is one place we can take the kids where they can be safe. I doubt any other Undrae could find it."

"And that is?" Chloe says.

I take another deep breath and begin to tell her. Chloe's jaw clenches and she scowls as soon as I mention the name of the location. Her eyes blaze as I try to explain the rest and she turns and walks away before I can finish.

"But . . ." I say, and watch her cross the deck, her bare feet slapping the deck with each angry stride. She reaches the bedroom door, goes in and slams it behind her, and I sigh.

"It's the only way we can be sure," I mutter. But I sigh again when I think of the chasm I've reopened between us. Chloe won't be able to avoid thinking about what I've said. The more she does, the more she'll understand what I've proposed. In the end, I doubt she'll disagree with me. I just worry whether she'll ever forgive me for thinking it up.

16

With Chloe withdrawn and unwilling to speak, I spend most of the morning working on the Grady White, tuning both of its 225-horsepower Yamaha outboard motors. Henri comes out to join me after I finish, as soon as I turn the ignition key and the motors growl to life.

"Going somewhere?" he says.

I shake my head. "No, not yet. I was just making sure everything's okay with the boat—in case I have to take it out on open water."

The boy arches an eyebrow. "If you go, can I come?"

If I go, he will come. But I'm not about to tell him anything until Chloe agrees it's the best course of action. "We'll see," I say. "Why don't you top off the tanks in the meantime?"

"Sure," Henri says. He turns and walks over to the two fifty-five-gallon fuel drums we keep at the side of our house.

My cell phone rings and I answer it. "Okay, Boss, I need your input," Claudia says.

"Ask me whatever you want." I keep my eyes on my son, and smile as he uncoils the fuel line and drags it toward the boat. Henri might complain when he's asked to clean his room and he might balk if he's told to go study, but he's never anything but cooperative when it comes to working on the boats. I stifle a sigh. It will pain me to send him away.

"You have to make some decisions. I'm at the Tamiami Gun Shop. I told them what you wanted. They're calling powerful guns like that hand cannons now. You can't believe how many choices there are."

"So choose one for me."

"Uh-uh. I narrowed it down, but you're going to have to choose. Personally, I like my Desert Eagle. It shoots fifty calibers. But Fernando here insists that you're better off with a revolver. They have a custom Limbaugh that shoots fifty-one calibers, a BFR—they make the Eagles, too—that shoots fifty Magnums and a fifty caliber Smith and Wesson Magnum. All of them shoot five rounds and are more than twice as powerful as a forty-four Magnum."

"Which does Fernando like the most?" I say.

"The Smith and Wesson."

"Done. Buy a dozen for me, some holsters and plenty of ammo. I'd appreciate if you'd bring it all out here."

"Is it okay if I come out tomorrow? Manny Padron had lunch with Thad yesterday. He told him he expected Ouder Raad to submit their final bid today."

"Thad's having lunch with Padron? It's got to drive Ian crazy," I say.

"It does," Claudia says. "But Manny seems to have taken a liking to Thad. He's taken him to lunch at the Versailles a few times and introduced him to a lot of other lawyers and quite a few real estate developers—almost every player in the business. Those contacts could be good for us, too. Anyway, Thad and Ian are with accounting right now, finishing up our new proposal for Buddy Matherby. They should have it done by late this afternoon. Thad said we'll need you to go down there soon."

Matherby Farm and the meeting with Buddy Matherby have been far from my thoughts. I frown at even having to discuss business in the midst of my other problems. "My mind's on other things right now," I say. "I'll give you a call in the morning and let you know when we'll be around. As far as Buddy Matherby—I need to think about when I want to meet with him. I'll let you know about that in a day or two."

After we finish with the boat, Henri and I go inside. We find Lizzie and Chloe in the great room. Chloe has set up Lizzie's new favorite toy, a Barbie Cook With Me Kitchen, and the girl bustles around it, intent on the pretend cooking of plastic food. She looks up, beams at us when we enter the room and says, "Henri come look, see what I'm cooking."

Seated in her recliner, an open Hiassen novel in her lap, Chloe flashes a smile at Henri and ignores me. I leave him with his sister and sit down in the recliner next to hers.

Chloe turns her eyes back to the book. I sit and watch my son and daughter play for a while before I mindspeak, {*Have you thought about what I said?*}

{*I've thought about it.*} Chloe turns a page and stares at the book.

After minutes pass without any further reply, I sigh, get up and walk to the window facing the mainland. The wind has finally risen enough to roil the water and the column of smoke over the southern part of the Everglades has grown thicker, though now it bends and sweeps northward, dissipating and blending into the blue sky the farther it's carried.

Chloe slams her book shut. I turn and Henri and Lizzie

both look at her but she ignores their gazes and glares at me. {*I can't read after you ask something like that.*}

{*All I asked . . .*}

{*I know what you asked. It's what you want that bothers me. The thought that you would be willing to take our children to the Pelk, after what they did to you and how they tried to kill us, disgusts me. How could you ever dare to suggest that I agree to leave our children with her?*}

Sometimes mindspeaking is a poor substitute for speech. If I could I would shout my answer, but Henri and Lizzie already look from me to Chloe and back, frowns on both of their faces. I take a deep breath and mindspeak, {*This isn't about you and me. This is about where the kids can be safe. Neither Lorrel nor Jessai nor any of the other Pelk are the monsters you make them out to be. They have their own ways like we have ours. I'm sure, if they agree to take our children in, they'll treat them well.*}

"Are you guys okay?" Henri says.

"We're fine. Your mother and I are just having a discussion . . ."

"An argument, you mean." Henri glances over at Chloe. "That's what it is, isn't it?"

Chloe nods. "A disagreement," she says. "But we're okay."

He continues to stare at her. "I hope so. You guys have been having a lot of disagreements. Lizzie's been noticing them too. She asked me if you're mad about something she's done. Jeff Lyons and Kara Meyer at my school both had their parents get divorced this year . . ."

"Neither of us are mad at either of you and no one's getting divorced here," Chloe says. She smiles and motions for me to come back and sit. "Why don't you and Lizzie go

back to what you were doing? Your dad and I just need a little more time to talk privately."

After I'm seated, she mindspeaks, {*You can't expect me
to feel good about sending our children to Andros.*}

{*I don't. I just expect you to do what is best for the children.*}

{*And you're not concerned that they'll be harmed in any
way?*}

I think back to my time among the Pelk and shake my
head. {*They may not like the food and they may get bored
but, otherwise, I think they'll be fine.*}

Chloe looks away. {*You told me that Lorrel was good
with potions. When my mum was teaching me how to make
Dragon Tears wine and use Death Rose and Angel Wort and
mix all our other potions, she told me there were other com-
pounds that used to be used—more dangerous ones, some
that could confuse the mind and distort reality.*

{*She said those formulas were lost ages ago. But what if
your precious Pelk have them and use them to turn our children away from us?*}

{*They aren't my precious Pelk. If they had anything like
that I'm sure they would have used it on me. At the very
least, someone would have threatened me with it.*} I shake
my head. {*Anyway, Lorrel has a son of her own and Jessai
to help her have more. She doesn't need to have our children
too.*}

Chloe says nothing else for a while. Finally, she sighs and
turns back to me. {*When were you thinking of doing this?*}

{*I don't even know if we can,*} I mindspeak. {*If you're
willing, I can fly there tonight and ask them if they'll help. If
they say yes we can take them there tomorrow.*}

{*So soon?*}

{*Why wait? If the idea is to make them safe, I would think the sooner, the better.*}

{*What if they refuse to take them?*}

I shake my head. {*I don't think they will.*}

17

Andros Island, the largest island in the Bahamas, lies only a few hours' flight past the Gulf Stream. Since I want to arrive before Lorrel sends Dela to bed, I take to the air shortly after dark. Like the night before, very few clouds float in a clear, black sky ablaze with stars and bright with the golden glow of an almost full moon.

To avoid any chance of accidental detection by a passing boater, I ascend in tight spirals over Caya DelaSangre—until the air turns thin and cold and the island shows as only a dark speck in the water below me. I circle one last time before I turn toward Andros Island and smile at the pattern of light and dark that now spreads beneath me.

At my altitude, it looks like a giant quilt of dotted lights has been laid over the mainland. The dark waters of the bay and ocean, shimmering with reflected moonlight and pinpricked with scattered boat lights, serves as its eastern border. The darker gloom of the Everglades, broken only by one small, irregular patch of angry orange-and-red flames near Homestead, sits to its west.

All the lights together provide a glow that stays behind me as I cross the Gulf Stream and head for Andros—one that still shows on the horizon, however faintly, when I reach Bimini and fly over the sparse lights of Alicetown. With Andros now close enough for communication, I mindspeak, "*Lorrel. It's Peter. I need to speak to you.*"

A few moments pass before she mindspeaks, "*I know it has been a while since you visited your son but is it so long that you would think I could not recognize your thoughts?*"

I growl into the open air. Lorrel presumes a closeness with me that I neither wish for nor feel. Nothing about my stay with her and her people had been chosen by me. Still, as one coming to request a favor, I can hardly scold her for her presumption. "*I was just being polite, in case you couldn't,*" I mindspeak.

"*You are the father of my child. Even if I wanted to, which I do not, I cannot forget that. Jessai and I both wish you would visit more often—for Dela's sake.*"

If not for Dela, I would never have returned the one time I did. That visit had been far more difficult than I expected. Though Lorrel and Jessai had made me as welcome as if I were a member of their family, the cold stares I received from some of the other Pelk made it clear that others were not as glad to see me return. And as much as I found Dela adorable and delightful to hold and make laugh, my memories of my previous forced stay kept me too on edge and wary of being taken prisoner again to fully enjoy my time with the child.

Still, if not for Chloe I would have visited more often. When I returned home, she'd turned away from me as soon as I tried to describe my son to her, and punished me with cold indifference and silence for weeks. "*Well, I'd like to visit now. I have something I need to ask you and Jessai about.*"

"*Where are you?*"

I look at the open water beneath me. "*Past Bimini.*"

"You're welcome to come. It would be good for Dela to see you. But Jessai and the other males are out on a night hunt. So, if you want, we can just as well talk about whatever it is and save you the rest of the trip."

The offer tempts me. I doubt I'll ever visit the Pelk's cave without at least a shudder over what had been done to me there. However, I mindspeak, *"No. I think it would be better if we discussed this in person."*

"I'll leave out a jar of glow-water for you," Lorrel mindspeaks.

No lights show anywhere in the mangrove swamps and overgrown wilderness of South Andros Island. With no roads, no buildings and no landmarks to differentiate between the dozens of brackish creeks and rivers that separate one area of overgrown swamp from another, I search the dark terrain below me for the slightest hint of green luminescence.

As a seagrowing race, the Pelk long ago learned to harvest phosphorescence from the sea and refine it into a powder. Mixed with water, it provides all the illumination they need. Still, it makes for a feeble beacon. I complete two large circles before I finally see the faint green glow from the jar of glow-water Lorrel has set out for me.

I blow out a breath and sweep down toward it, landing near the light in a small clearing bordered by a rock outcrop on one side and ringed by mangrove trees on the other three. As soon as I land, I walk a few paces to an irregular hole in the rock—the only aboveground entrance to the large cavern that serves as home for what the Pelk call their srrynn.

Since the Pelk mostly travel underwater as they come and go, and rarely come above in their natural forms, they've never bothered to enlarge the hole to accommodate anything larger than a human body. I shift to my human shape, take a deep breath and walk through it.

A narrow landing and equally narrow, steep steps leading down to the cavern floor have been carved in the cavern's stone wall. I stand on the landing and stare down at the lagoon below me, and the sandy beach and land beyond it. Dozens of seaweed nests are scattered everywhere that is dry, each with its own glowpool. Enough glowpools have been lit to fill even the furthest recesses of the huge cavern with a faint green light.

Some Pelk have gathered at larger, communal glowpools to share food and conversation. Others have retreated to their nests. Pelk children dart to and fro everywhere. None give me more than a glance as I descend the stairs and change back to my natural form. Most know me, and more than a few turned their backs on me the last time I visited.

"You cannot blame them," Lorrel mindspoke then. *"You and your wife have been responsible for many Pelk deaths."*

"Only because we were attacked," I mindspeak. Fortunately both Lorrel and her mate, Jessai, understood all too well where the fault lay. As I wend my way around one seaweed nest after another, no one offers any threat. Jessai now leads the srrynn and Lorrel heads their healing circle, the lisrrynn. Both have promised that their srrynn will live in peace with my family.

I find Lorrel sharing a meal with six other females and their children, all of them seated on seaweed seats arranged in a semicircle in front of a large glowpool near the back of the cavern. A small Pelk child sits on the floor and leans against Lorrel's tail as he plays with a dried blowfish, rolling it from one side to the other.

"*Hi,*" I mindspeak.

Lorrel turns and looks at me, as do the others. She has grown thicker than she was but still manages to look more lithe than the other females. Not that any of them possess the bulk of Undrae women. Scales barely showing on their black skin, their bodies thin and small and streamlined to help them race through the water, they look more like reptilian otters than my kind of dragons.

"*Welcome to our safehold,*" Lorrel mindspeaks. She motions for me to sit beside her. "*Jessai will be sorry he missed you.*"

I nod and sit. Lorrel gives the other women a look and they all bustle away. She picks up a large chunk of dolphin meat from a platter beside her, holds it out to me and mindspeaks, "*You must be hungry.*"

My stomach grumbles. I nod again and take the meat from her. In truth, I could eat far more. Still, I stop after I devour the one piece. I tilt my head toward the infant by her tail. His shoulders seem wider than the other children's, his black scales more well defined and his body more muscular. "*Dela?*"

The child looks up at the mention of his name. Lorrel leans over and nuzzles her snout against the side of his face. "*Our son,*" she mindspeaks.

Dela grimaces at her show of affection, and pulls his head back, and we both laugh. Unsure at what he did to receive the attention, but glad to receive it nonetheless, the child beams. He looks from his mother to me—and seems to suddenly notice my strangeness. His smile wavers, then fades away. He tilts his head and studies me.

Lorrel mindspeaks, "*It's Peter. You've met him before.*" Still, the child keeps his eyes on me.

I didn't expect him to remember me from my one visit but I still feel a pang of sorrow that he didn't. A sigh escapes my lips. Chloe won't like what I have to do but she'll just have to learn to adjust. "*I won't stay away from him so long the next time,*" I mindspeak.

"*That would be good.*" Lorrel stares into my eyes. "*But this visit isn't really about him, is it?*"

"*No,*" I mindspeak and tell Lorrel about our suspicions that we're under attack from our own kind.

She frowns and shakes her head. "*This isn't good for either of us. Not all Undrae will be as willing to make peace with us as you were. If you have come to ask for our help, I am sure Jessai will agree to give it.*"

The Pelk may lack our bulk and strength, but I've seen how formidable they and their tridents can be in battle. "*We haven't come to needing that type of help yet,*" I mindspeak. I explain the decision Chloe and I have made to send our children to a safer place.

When I finish, Lorrel sits and runs her foreclaws over her midriff as she thinks. Finally, she mindspeaks, "*I understand how hard it must be to have to send your children away. And I understand why you think you should. But Undrae children living in a Pelk srrynn?*" She shakes her head. "*You were fully grown and you grumbled constantly about our strange food and different ways. It may be too hard for them.*"

I picture how wide both of their eyes will grow when they first see the Pelks' safehold. But I know my children. I shake my head. "*They may not like everything, but both of them will do as they're told. They're tough kids—and good. You'll like them.*"

"*I'm sure I would,*" Lorrel mindspeaks. "*But . . .*" She runs a foreclaw over her midriff again and tilts her head, as if to flirt with me. "*Have you not noticed anything different about me?*"

Experience with Chloe has taught me that questions like this have no good answers. Besides, I have no interest in this creature, ever. Rather than say anything, I simply shrug.

Lorrel's nostrils flare and she scowls at me. "*Just once, you should try to say something that might be pleasing to me.*" She places both foreclaws on her midriff. "*Dela will have a sister in five more months. I already feel the heaviness of carrying her. Caring for your children at the same time might be too hard on us, too.*"

"*I promise you, it won't be,*" I mindspeak. "*There is nowhere else I can think of that can be as safe for them as this is. I don't know what else I can say to convince you, but just imagine if Dela were at risk and I refused to take him in . . .*"

"*It is not so easy.*" Lorrel sighs. "*Some of our people still retain enormous anger over the deaths of their friends and relatives. They would not attack an adult like you but your children may have to be protected from them.*"

I start to mindspeak something and Lorrel holds up a single claw. "*No more of this. I will talk to Jessai and some of the others. One of us will come to you within the next two weeks and let you know what we have decided.*"

Few boat lights show on the water when I finally approach Caya DelaSangre, a few hours before dawn. I descend in a long, shallow dive that takes me just above the sand dunes, through the early-morning ground mist, to our oak-decked veranda. It has been a long night and I yearn for the comfort of my bed and the relief of a few hours rest.

As soon as I land, I shift to my human form and make my

way into my bedroom. Chloe barely stirs when I come through the door. I try to slip into bed without waking her but when I move the covers and lie down she turns toward me and opens her eyes. "How'd it go?" she asks.

"Lorrel will let us know sometime in the next few weeks."

Chloe yawns and stretches. "Screw her. Let's just take the kids to Jamaica," she says. "It shouldn't be up to any damned fisheater whether our kids are safe or not."

Two difficult females in the same night seem almost too much to bear. I sigh. "It's fair to be concerned about taking in someone else's kids," I say. "And we are from different castryls. You might want to take some time to decide if someone asked you. I don't think a few weeks is too long."

"I expected you would take her side." Chloe turns away from me and buries her head in her pillow.

"I'm not taking any side. I thought we both agreed that Lizzie and Henri would be safer with the Pelk. Didn't we?"

Chloe keeps her back to me but makes an almost imperceptible nod.

"I take that as a yes," I say. "We'll wait to hear what they say. If the answer's 'No,' then we'll make plans for Jamaica. In the meantime, we'll just have to make sure we do everything we can to protect the kids.

"I already told Claudia to get some new guns for us. I'll get her to bring them out for us later this morning. We can use the time to get familiar with them and practice shooting. That way, if one of us is here without the other, we at least can have the advantage of some serious firepower."

18

Claudia grins widely as she places all four Smith and Wesson 500 Magnum revolvers, one by one, on the oak table in the great room. "Big suckers, aren't they?" she says.

Chloe nods, picks one up and grimaces. "Heavy, too. I think you could kill someone just throwing one of these at them."

We all laugh and Claudia picks one of the other revolvers up, holds it with two hands and aims it toward the bayside window. "Four and a half pounds, five loaded. Fifteen inches long, all stainless steel, double action so you only have to pull the trigger to shoot all five rounds."

I pick up one by its black rubber handgrip and aim it one-handed in the same direction as Claudia has pointed hers. She shakes her head. "Trust me, Boss. These are two-handers for sure. I tried one at the range before I bought them. Remember you're shooting fifty-caliber Magnum bullets. Fernando at Tamiami says they're strong enough to take down any animal living on earth today—even an elephant."

"That's what I wanted," I say. I readjust my grip and hold the revolver with both hands as Claudia suggested. I sight it out the window and nod. "It does feel better."

"Personally, I prefer my automatic. I think something this powerful is overkill," Claudia says.

"Sometimes," I say, and glance at my wife, "overkill is just what you need." Chloe nods her agreement.

Later, after all three of us have taken turns at blasting away at six makeshift wooden targets I've nailed to trees in the center of the island—reducing all of them to splinters and even breaking a four-inch-thick sapling in half with an errant bullet—Claudia turns to me. "Thad asked me to bring up the Matherby meeting again. He really thinks we need to move on this soon."

I sigh. "There are other things that are more important right now," I say. "I really think I should stay here on the island with Chloe and the kids."

"But he'll accept Ouder Raad's bid if he doesn't hear from us soon."

"Can't you just give it to him without me?"

Claudia shakes her head. "Buddy's weird. You know that. He wants to hear it from you personally."

"Really, Peter," Chloe says. "If you need to go take care of business, do it. We're only waiting for an answer on the other matter. There's nothing to make you stay on the island twenty-four hours a day. The kids and I will be fine if you're gone for a few hours. After all . . ." She grins and holds up her revolver. "How much more protection do we need than a few of these?"

Two days later, I leave the island late in the day and motor to shore. My dinner with Buddy Matherby has been scheduled for eight, at his place. Since I won't arrive at the docks until after business hours, Thad has volunteered to meet me with directions to Matherby's and hand me our written offer.

I see him as soon as I cruise past the NO WAKE sign at the entrance to the marina. The man has taken no chance on offending me with any hint of tardiness. Already on the dock, he waits by my slip, still dressed in his suit, holding his leather briefcase in his right hand for a few moments, then shifting it to his left and then back as he studies each boat that cruises in and out of the marina.

When he sees me behind the wheel of my Grady White, he smiles and waves his free hand—a little too enthusiastically. I grin at his obvious discomfort and return the wave with a nod.

Thad's eyes stay on me as I approach. Obviously no boater, when the Grady White glides up to the dock he steps back a few steps and offers no help. Instead, he watches me tie up and waits for me to finish securing the boat. After I've done so, he holds up his briefcase and says, "Good evening, Mr. DelaSangre. I have our written offer for Matherby Farm right here—and directions for you."

"Fine," I say, and step off the boat. I hold out an open hand. Campbell nods. The day has cooled and the late-afternoon sun gone feeble, but still a sheen of perspiration covers his face. He opens his briefcase and fumbles through the papers inside. He takes one sheet and holds it out to me. "Directions," he says.

I take it, glance at it for a moment, then fold it and put it in my pants pocket. A moment later he holds out a thick sheaf of papers.

"What's that?" I say.

"The offer," Thad says. "The whole contract, actually. I thought, if you could get him to sign, it would make everything go all that much easier."

"I'm sure it would," I take the papers from him and leaf through the pages. "Good work," I say.

Thad grins and says, "Thanks, it's nice to hear someone say that. The best I can get out of Ian is a grunt."

"Ian's not the type to give you anything more than that," I say. I read the figure typed on the first page and whistle at the size of it.

Thad nods. "It *is* a very nice offer, sir. I can't see how Mr. Matherby could turn it down."

"We'll see," I say.

Glancing at his watch, Thad says, "It's almost seven, sir."

I grin. I doubt that someone like Buddy Matherby will either notice or care if I'm a few minutes late. "I'm on my way," I say.

Monty's parking lot lies a few dozen yards from the waterfront, inland just enough that the cleansing breezes that blow across the bay do little to minimize the faint odor of smoke that I now notice in the air. I wrinkle my nose. The smoke carries the rank smell of burnt vegetation—a sure sign that the Everglades' swamp fire has grown.

I look up at the clear sky and frown. No sign of rain. Without it, the fires in the Everglades will continue to expand and strengthen. It seems silly to wish for bad weather, but the longer we remain dry, the worse it will get. I would far rather have a few weeks of rain and storm than days and days of gray, smoke-laden skies—not that I have any choice in the matter. I shrug and go to my car.

Fortunately, once inside the Cayenne, its air-conditioning and the fresh, sweet smell of its leather upholstery overwhelm any trace of smoke that might have penetrated into the car's interior. I turn on the stereo radio and throw the car into gear. Weeks have passed since I last drove it. I grin. Homestead's a long drive from the Grove. I'll have an hour alone with nothing to do but drive and listen to music.

By the time I reach the western end of Homestead and turn south on Southwest 312th Avenue, the night's dark has almost taken over the sky. Few homes or other buildings sit in view of the street. Areas of overgrown vegetation, bushes and trees intersperse with open fields, some cultivated and some not. I flick on my headlights and slow at each intersection. Traditional metal street signs mark some roads, hand-painted wood signs identify others and a few seem to have no markings at all.

Even Thad Campbell's meticulous instructions do nothing to help me here. I begin to wonder if I will ever be able to find the turnoff, but finally my headlights glare on an old round chrome hubcap nailed to a short wooden stake on the right-hand side of the road. Hand-painted red letters on it read MATHERBY LANE. I smile and turn.

Age and lack of maintenance have turned the two-lane road's asphalt gray and rough. I begin to let the car speed up, the overgrown brush on each side of the road whizzing by, the tires humming on the road's irregular surface.

After a little more than quarter of a mile, my headlights shine on a faded yellow sign, large enough to block the road a few hundred yards in front of me. It reads MATHERBY FARM and shows a large arrow pointing to the right. I downshift and put my foot on the brake to slow my approach.

As I get closer I see another sign, a small wood one, shaped like an arrow, the name MATHERBY painted on it. It points to the left.

The road ends at a T-shaped intersection right in front of the signs. I stop and look to the right at the paved road that runs straight as far as I can see, then look left at the one-lane dirt road—just wheel ruts really—that curves quickly out of sight, behind trees and bushes that seem on the verge of overgrowing it.

I stare at the dirt road. I've never taken the Cayenne off-road before and wonder how well it will cope with it. From the look of it and the surrounding brush, there also may be no room for me to turn around for quite some distance. I click on the map light and recheck Thad Campbell's instructions. They call for me to follow the MATHERBY sign.

After one last glance at the paved road to my right, I shrug, throw the car back in gear and turn left. By now the last vestiges of daylight have disappeared and no lights but my headlights show anywhere. The Cayenne lurches, dips and sways along the roadway. I tighten my grip on the wheel and stare ahead as the dirt road curves and grows even more irregular. Insects fly in and out of the headlights' glare. Shadows grow and loom and fade as trees and bushes come into view and then disappear.

With a sudden jolt, the front tires splash through a deep puddle and the car's undercarriage scrapes for a moment against the raised mound of dirt that runs in the middle of the tire ruts. Other puddles follow, and more scrapes and for a long while a green, waving wall of saw grass borders both sides of the road.

Then only water shows, the road now a narrow dirt causeway, raised less than a foot above it. I begin to wonder if this whole drive could be a joke. Had Buddy Matherby planned it as some sort of test? I wouldn't be surprised if he had another road nearby, a paved one, that he used as his real main entrance.

But the tires bump up onto a narrow wood bridge and the

road finally begins to smooth and rise. Trees come into view
and a campfire flickers somewhere in the distance behind
them. I grin and relax my grip on the wheel.

The bridge ends and the tires bump and then crunch as
the road turns to gravel. It curves and winds through stands
of trees—gumbo-limbos, wide oaks and tall mahoganies—
and then angles across a wide lawn and past a ramshackle
building, all its windows dark and unwelcoming, that, from
its shape, has to be Matherby's house.

I follow the road as it curves behind the building. It ends
shortly after that, next to a palm-thatched, open-sided,
Seminole-style chickee hut—an old, faded, red Ford pickup
truck parked on the grass near it. I pull in next to the truck,
turn off the ignition and look around for Buddy Matherby.

Two kerosene lamps suspended from the chickee's log
rafters illuminate its interior. Moths and other unrecogniz-
able, but far too large bugs, fly around them and dart in and
out of their yellow glow. But except for them, a makeshift
table, a folding chair, a camp chest, some scattered clothes,
a large red Igloo cooler and a sleeping bag, the chickee
seems empty.

The campfire I'd first noticed on my approach throws off
its own light on the other side of the hut. The shadow of a
large man looms out of the dark near it as he comes into the
fire's light, crouches near the flames and pokes the burning
logs with a stick until the flames flare higher and bright
sparks swirl upward into the air.

From my distance, in the wavering light of the flames, I
can't be sure if his bulk comes from fat or muscle, but either
way, he measures more than a few inches wider and taller
than I do. The man has to be aware of my arrival, but he
makes no move to greet me.

No matter. I get out of the car and give myself a few moments to get a sense of whether I truly want to use this place as a weekend retreat. Fortunately the swamp fire in the Everglades burns far enough away that the smell of its smoke is still too weak to overpower the mixed aromas of fresh water and growing plants that pervade the air.

The area has a sense of calm, like on my island. Not that silence rules here any more than there, but no motors, no electronic sounds disturb the night—instead, the air carries the monotonous songs of countless frogs and crickets out somewhere in the dark, the gentle whisper of the wind through the trees, the pop and crackle of Buddy's campfire.

I have to force myself to speak loud enough for my voice to carry. "Buddy?"

He doesn't stand, doesn't stop what he's doing. "Hey, Hoss," he says. "Good timing. Dinner's 'bout ready."

Hearing a genuine South Florida drawl makes me smile. I can't think how many years have passed since I last heard one like it. I walk toward the fire.

Just as I reach him, a loud, harsh screech pierces the night's calm. I freeze in place. "Goddamned piece of shit!" Buddy shouts. He grabs on the ground for a small rock and throws it into the dark. "Shut your goddamned racket!"

Then he turns in my direction. "Sorry 'bout.that. Just one of our stupid peacocks. Got them all over the place. Could wake a dead man with their noise but they're better than guard dogs. My granddaddy brought the first ones here. Had them ever since."

He stands, unwinds really, to his full height and I find myself at eye level with his Adam's apple. Buddy brushes his hands on his jeans, offers his right hand and says, "Glad you came. Don't much care for those other guys."

"I don't either," I say, and shake his hand.

"Seat?" he says, and motions toward one of the two small blue rectangular coolers near the campfire. I nod and sit down.

Buddy towers over me for a moment, stares at me. "Got to say, you don't look much like I expected."

"How's that?"

"My dad said all of you were dark and sort of foreign-looking. Except for the way you're dressed, you could pass for a good old boy."

"My father looked like that," I say. "I don't take after him."

"Me, I look just like my old man," Buddy says. He goes to the other cooler, opens it, takes out a can and holds it out, toward me. "Bud?"

I shake my head. "I don't really drink," I say.

"No fooling?" He studies me and grins. "Can't handle it, huh?"

"Sort of." I shrug. If the man wants to think I'm a problem drinker, let him. I certainly can't tell him that alcohol wreaks havoc on my kind's metabolism.

"Oh, well." He pops the tab on the beer can, drains a good half of the can in one long swallow, then grins again. "Just leaves more for me."

I nod. Buddy chugs another drink, then turns his eyes toward a large cast-iron pot in the middle of the fire. "Hungry?" he asks.

Not really, but to be polite I nod anyway. A thick, brown liquid tumbles and forms bubbles as it boils in the pot. Chunks of something show and disappear. I study it as if staring will help me decipher what meat is having its flavor cooked away. Fortunately, I ate before I left the island. If I hadn't, I'd be far more interested in devouring Buddy than what he has in his pot.

"Do me a favor, Hoss," he says as he picks up a long, thick stick with a forked end. "There are some plates and silverware on the edge of the chickee over there." He motions toward it with his head. "Why don't you go get them while I get this pot out of the fire?"

By the time I return with the two white ceramic plates and the plain metal tablespoons that Buddy had left out on the elevated chickee floor, he's lifted the pot from the fire and placed it on the ground between the two coolers.

Buddy takes a long-handled metal ladle and stirs the contents of the pot, steam rising as he mixes them. "Don't ask what this is. We're under potluck rules," he says after I sit. "My daddy started it. You got to eat first, and you can't get seconds until you finish what's on your plate and guess what it is. And you got to guess even if you think you can't figure it out for shit."

He stirs the pot one more time, then lifts a ladle full of the viscous substance. "Hold out your plate," he says.

I hold back a groan. Whatever he's cooked, my preference would have been to eat it raw, but I hold my plate out and watch as he plops the brown mixture on it. Large wings whir by behind me, just overhead, close enough for me to feel the wind of their passage. I jerk my head around to see what has just passed, neglecting to hold my plate level.

"Whoa, Hoss." Buddy laughs, catches the bottom of the plate with one hand and corrects the tilt. "You ain't gonna see him unless he wants you to. We're on the edge of the Everglades here, man, remember? That's most probably just a big old hoot owl. Nothing to cause you to spill old Buddy's good home cooking over."

He fills his plate with two full ladles and attacks his meal as if it will run off if he stops. I watch him eat spoonful after spoonful, stare at the brown glop on my plate and finally venture a bite. The thick brown gravy tastes of starch and grease and salt and pepper, but the meat surprises me. White and still firm, it carries no trace of the blood that once pumped through it but it has a sweetness to it that pleases my tongue. I find it no hardship to eat.

Buddy finishes his meal before me and watches me eat the last of mine. When I'm done, he grins and says, "Like it, huh?"

I nod. "It's good."

"No shit." He leans forward. "Now guess what it was."

"I don't know," I say. I hold back a frown. In the interest of business, I'm willing to humor this man just so far. But I didn't come to play guessing games or keep him company on a lonely night. I put my plate down on the ground in front of me. "Listen, I have the offer in my car. I can go get it and we can start going over the contract."

"Relax. The night's early." Buddy gets another beer and pops it open. "Besides, I told you; potluck rules."

I sigh. Had the meat been raw I might have had a clue. "Chicken?" I say.

Buddy laughs. "Sort of tastes like that, doesn't it?" He shakes his head. "Never ate any chicken that tasted that good. You just had cat. One hundred percent, grade A, prime house cat."

My eyes widen and Buddy laughs again. "Your pet?" I say.

"No, of course not. What do you take me for?" He scowls. "Damned cat belongs to some Mexican laborers that live on the farm up from here. Assholes let it out every night and every night it made a beeline for my place, attacked my damned peacocks, raised all kinds of hell with them. I caught it three times. Got scratched up every time . . ." He holds out his arm so I can see the red furrows gouged in his forearm.

"Last time I brought it back to them, I told them I'd blow the piece of shit away if it ever came back again. Last night it did." He shrugs. "My daddy brought me up to respect all life. Anytime we'd kill anything we'd have to eat it, except for rats and stuff like that. Pretty good eating though, anyway, huh?"

"Pretty good. Now, really, about the offer . . ."

"Hey, you want to go. Okay, I get it. So talk." Buddy drains his beer can and grins. "Think you can do it without leafing through a stack of papers?"

"Sure," I say.

"You ever met that Holden Grey?"

I shake my head.

"What a stuck-up ass that one is. You should have seen him when he came out here today. I bet he ran to take a bath after he left."

"Grey was out here today? I thought they made their offer a little while ago. Your lawyer said we could make the last offer."

Buddy leans toward me, his eyes suddenly hard, his lips tightened so they press against his teeth. "Don't think my daddy raised any fool. Grey came out to raise those foreigners' offer. You think I'd turn that away? I'd rather this land stayed in local hands, but I can think of a lot others who my daddy talked better of than he did you DelaSangres.

"He always said you were a bunch of thieves and murderers. Don't know if he was right." Buddy shrugs. "Don't much care. I just want to get out of here. Too damned many Cubans and Mexicans talking their language around here. Haitians too, with their gobbledygook. Hell, I went down Krome Avenue to Heritage Restaurant in downtown the other day. I was in the mood for some of their fine country cooking. And I found they had put quiche on their menu! Time for this good old boy to move on out.

"There's a place up in Ochopee, by the Big Cyprus, near where the free Seminoles camp. Going to buy it and settle down there. My daddy always was friends with those people, raised me so I could talk Hitchee, find my way around the Glades like I wasn't white, and hunt with the best of them. Plenty of good hunting up there. Saw a panther once and even stared eye to eye with a skunk ape." He looks at me. "Know what that is?"

I nod. I've heard the legend all of my life. Every so often the news would report a sighting of an overlarge, humanlike creature shambling through the swamp. Invariably the eye witness would report on its intense stench too. "It's like our area's Bigfoot," I say. "I thought it was a myth."

"Think what you want. I know what I saw—and smelled," Buddy says. "The Seminoles call them giant people. They say they're smart. Then again they have all other types of myths too. Like the one about the night bird. You heard that one, Hoss?"

"No." I shake my head.

"Thought you might of. They say there's this big bird that comes out only at night. If it finds anyone out alone, especially children, it swoops down and takes them away, never to be seen again." He stares at me, as if to watch for my reaction. "My daddy said some of the older Seminoles believed that bird was your daddy's personal pet."

I force a laugh, though I know far too well of that legend. In the early days, before the main population grew, my father hunted Seminoles more frequently than any other humans. "That one's certainly a myth," I say. "My father kept dogs, just like I do."

"Sort of figured that," Buddy says. He points to the chickee. "But you can see I like Seminole ways. Nothing wrong with the house, mind you; just prefer living more natural. Hope to find a Seminole woman after I go up to Ochopee, make babies and live free, without any of the rules you all like so much down here."

He goes silent and stares at the fire. I stare too, and listen to the logs pop and crackle, the sounds of the swamp around us. I wonder if Buddy really saw something in the swamp or was just doing some old-fashioned yarn telling. Certainly my father never confirmed the existence of the creature—or denied the possibility it existed.

When minutes pass without my speaking, Buddy turns and says, "So, what's your offer?"

I tell him the figure.

He shakes his head. "Would of been good this morning, but not now."

"You could have called and let us know things had changed," I say.

"You could have come earlier before they upped their offer."

"Now what?"

Buddy stares into my face. "They didn't offer that much more. Just enough that I'd be stupid to turn down their increase. Make another offer, Hoss. That's how these things work."

I blow out a sigh. "Look, I'm no negotiator. People at my

company do things like that for me. If you want to come to the office tomorrow we can all sit down and see what we can work out."

"Shit, we're both over twenty-one and free to do whatever we fucking please. Don't make me give this deal to Holden Grey and those foreigners. Offer me something."

"Just forget the games and tell me what you want," I say.

Buddy shakes his head. "Hoss, you are no fun at all." He sits and thinks for a while, then stands and brushes his hands on his jeans. "Another million and we'll shake on it right now." He holds out his right hand. "Deal?"

I stand too. Our offer already will strain our credit line. Ian will howl if I commit more. I look around. But this place feels good to me. The causeway and surrounding waters ensure that no matter how we develop the rest of the adjoining property, nothing need disturb this area. It will make for a welcome change from island life for my family, without any sacrifice of our seclusion.

Fortunately, there are sound business reasons to pursue this deal too—not the least of which is that Matherby Farm is the last large tract of undeveloped land in the county, a place where we can sell homes and condos to thousands of people.

Ouder Raad's interest in buying this property only confirms that we were right to look at it as a good investment. After all, even with the expense as high as it will be, I can't think of any reason why LaMar shouldn't be able to make it as profitable as Ouder Raad thinks it can. I shake his hand and say, "Deal."

"You could have had it for less!" Buddy laughs. "They only offered a hundred thousand more."

I open my mouth and he wags a finger and says, "No. Too

late. We shook on it. It's not my fault you can't bargain for shit. I'll have Manny go to your office tomorrow to work the contract out with your people." He puts an arm around my shoulders and walks with me to my car.

"It's been a pleasure, Hoss," he says.

I nod and say, "Me, too," and realize I mean it. I open the car's door, then turn. "What if Grey makes another offer before you sign?"

Buddy shakes his head. "We shook on it. Doesn't matter what he offers now." He fishes in his right front pants pocket and pulls out a key ring holding two keys. "Here," he says, and holds the keys out to me. "This way you won't have to wait for the lawyers. Use the house whenever you want."

"What about you?" I say.

He grins. "I haven't slept inside in years. If I'm here, just leave me be in my chickee and go about your own business."

I nod and take the keys. "I just may take you up on that."

"Hope you do, Hoss. Got a piece of advice for you too."

"Yes?" I look up at the big man's face.

"If I were you, I'd question how Holden Grey managed to overbid so close to your offer. You just might have a skunk somewhere in your works."

19

In the morning, I call the office as soon as it opens. Marcia Voss, who's been given Sarah's job full-time, answers the phone. When I ask for Arturo or Claudia, she says, "Neither of them are in yet, Mr. DelaSangre. Mr. Tindall hasn't arrived yet either. Mr. Campbell's in his office, though, if you care to speak to him."

"Good enough," I say. As far as I can see, the man has done everything he can so far to prove his worth. He certainly knows the Matherby deal inside and out. He'll be able to pass the information on without garbling it. I wait for Marcia to forward the call and cut Thad off when he tries to make pleasantries. I tell him about the new offer, instruct him to tell the others and to have Arturo call me.

The phone rings forty-five minutes later. "Thanks to you, it's been a busy morning," Arturo says. "Ian's angry with Thad for hearing the news first. And he's moaning that you may have bankrupted us . . ."

"Wait a minute," I say. "I didn't have any choice. If I didn't respond to Holden Grey's offer . . ."

"Relax, Peter." Arturo chuckles. "Ian can moan all he wants. You did just fine. We left some room for negotiating when we gave you that figure. We can afford it."

"Good. I just wanted to get it settled."

"Good thing you did, too. I just got off the phone with Manny Padron. Holden Grey called him a little while ago with another offer—higher than yours. He said Buddy wanted you to know it was turned down. That with him, a handshake deal is as good as any contract. He said Buddy likes you. Though considering the way you upped our offer, I'd be amazed if he didn't."

I frown at the phone but resist reacting to his teasing. "Handshake or not, I'll feel better when the deal's signed."

"Me too, but it will be a little while. Padron wants to see all our financing lined up before they sign on the deal."

"Whatever," I say. "I'll be there whenever you need me." Then I tell him about Buddy's warning.

"We've already had the offices swept for bugs, so we can rule that out. Anyway, you say skunk to me and I think Ian," Arturo says. "It's been a while since we've had surveillance on him. I'll assign some operatives right away. We'll check his bank accounts for any strange deposits, too. But I wouldn't count on us finding much."

"There might not be anything to find."

"That would be my hope," he says.

Chloe and I continue to keep Henri home. He objects to that and objects louder when we no longer let him venture out alone on either of our boats, or even on the island. "No fair," he says. "It's not like I'm a little kid like Lizzie. I can take care of myself."

"I'm not little. I'm four," she says.

Chloe shuts any further conversation off with a stern look. "We have to make sure you're both safe. Right now that means that neither of you can be anywhere without at least one of us. Is that clear?" she asks.

Neither of us tells the children of our plan to send them away. "We can tell them that," Chloe says, "when we know for sure just where they're going."

Days pass with Chloe and me both on edge, alert for any sign of an attack. Nothing happens, but still neither of us feel any desire to leave the island—even to fly and hunt. We continue to share our bed, take our meals together with the children and discuss those things we need to pay attention to, but Chloe grows more distant than ever. In turn, I withdraw further from her until it's like two strangers sharing their lives.

With the children sure to be sent away, either to the Pelk or to Chloe's parents in Jamaica, both of us try to spend as much time as we can with them. So much so that Henri scowls and says, "Don't you guys have anything else to do? Sometimes I'd like to just watch TV by myself, you know."

Still, a few days later, it's his idea that he and I go fishing late in the afternoon, just before the sun goes down. "Claudia told me fish like to feed just before it gets dark," he says. "Can we try it, Pops?"

We carry our rods and some frozen pieces of fish onto the dock. Henri takes the frozen strips of fish, puts them in a bait bucket and lowers it into the water so the pieces will warm enough to be useful as bait. "Look, Papa, a dolphin!" he says, and points to our small harbor's mouth.

I glance over at the entrance and study the gray dorsal fin slicing through the water. Dolphins ordinarily dislike confined spaces like our harbor. Pelk, however, have no such problem and often find it convenient to travel in that form. I smile and mindspeak, *"Lorrel?"*

No answer comes. I wait a few moments more, while the

dolphin circles the harbor and then mindspeak, "*Lorrel?*" again.

Henri looks at me, says, "Really? You think so?"

"*Undrae. Why must you assume my mate would come to you?*" Jessai mindspeaks before I can answer my son.

A wide smile spreads over Henri's face. "All right!" he says.

I nod and turn my attention to Jessai. "*Can we mindspeak masked?*"

{*If we must.*} Jessai swims toward the dock, his gray form thinning, turning lighter.

{*There may be others who shouldn't hear what we have to say,*} I mindspeak.

Jessai reaches the dock, his transformation to human form already complete. He pulls himself out of the water and stands near my son, only a few inches taller than he.

Henri gapes at the man's naked, ghost white body—muscular and sleek and devoid of hair everywhere except for his head. "Whoa!" he says. "Can he teach me to change shape like that?"

"He can't, but Lorrel can," I say. I send Henri to go get some towels and—since Jessai would find my clothes far too big to wear—to ask Chloe for one of her sweatpants outfits.

After Henri runs off, Jessai mindspeaks, {*He looks like a good son. I am sure it will pain you to send him away.*}

I look at him. {*So it's your decision to take them?*}

Jessai nods. {*There were many in our srrynn who objected, but they won't go against our wishes. Your children will be safe with us.*}

{*Good,*} I mindspeak masked. {*My wife, Chloe, will be*

glad to hear it. I'm sure she'd like to meet you. Please come inside and join us for dinner.}

Even dressed, Jessai's small frame, pale complexion and almost Oriental face, coupled with his lack of eyebrows and eyelashes and the way his small ears lie flat against his skull, looks different enough that Henri and Lizzie and Chloe stare at him all through dinner. "He lives underwater?" Lizzie asks.

Chloe nods and I mindspeak, so Jessai and my family can hear, {*He spends a lot of time underwater but he lives on dry land in a cave they call a safehold. In the old days they built them all over the Caribbean. There's even one underneath our island.*}

"Really?" Henri says. "Do you know where it is? Can we get into it?"

I smile at him. {*There's an entrance to it hidden by the mangroves in the harbor and another underwater in the Wayward Channel. I'll show them to you one of these days. I promise. And it would be nicer if we all mindspoke, so Jessai can join in the conversation.*}

But Chloe mindspeaks so only I can hear, {*They look so odd. How could you find that Pelk woman attractive?*}

I sigh. {*I'm tired of this. She was attractive—in a different sort of way—but I didn't want her. I only wanted you. I still only want you. When will you get that?*}

{*When you tell me in a way that makes me believe how you say you feel.*} Chloe turns her attention away from me and runs her fingers through Lizzie's hair, untangling a few knots, smiling as the children pepper Jessai with questions about Pelk life.

He manages to maintain a grin as he fires back answers

in rapid succession. {*Yes, the meat tastes fine, but I prefer fish and dolphin. No, Pelk don't fly, but we're far better swimmers than you Undrae. We are smaller but we use very sharp tridents for hunting and battle. No, we don't miss having TV or electricity. Yes, I swam all the way here, but, stopping only at night, it only took three days. No, I am not tired. We Pelk are used to traveling long distances.*}

As their interrogation continues, Chloe mindspeaks just to me. {*I hate hearing all this. Our children are going to have to live with these creatures for God knows how long. If they're going to go, I want to get this over with as soon as possible. I think we should tell them now and I think you should take them tomorrow.*}

I look at her. {*Aren't you going to come too?*}

She shakes her head. {*I don't want to meet that woman. I don't want to have to be polite to her and I certainly don't want to have anything to do with her child. You can take Henri and Lizzie without me. Just do it soon. It hurts too much already.*}

Lizzie wails when she hears the news. Henri goes stone-faced. He shakes his head and says, {*No. You can't make me. I won't go.*}

{*It's for your own safety,*} I mindspeak.

{*What about your safety, and Mom's? I know I'm too young to be a warrior yet, but I could help. If you'd only let me, I could show you.*}

I want to smile at the boy and tell him how proud he makes me but I doubt he wants to be treated like my young son right now. I keep my face as expressionless as his. {*You'll have plenty of time to show me and your mother what you can do. We need you to watch Lizzie and make sure she doesn't feel too lonely. Your mother and I will be fine. It just will make it easier for us if we don't have to worry about you two.*}

{*No,*} Henri says. {*I want to stay right here.*}

Chloe looks at him. {*Please, Henri, we need you to go with your sister.*}

Henri shakes his head and Jessai mindspeaks, {*It is good to want to be a warrior, but warriors have to learn to obey orders too.*}

My son frowns at him but Jessai ignores the expression and continues. {*Besides, a good warrior would want to learn new ways to hunt and fight. If you stay with us I can teach you how to use a trident and Lorrel can teach you how to shift yourself into a dolphin. You are old enough already. After you learn our ways, you can join us on our hunts.*}

I nod at Jessai's words. The Pelk's right. My son is more than old enough to be treated like one of the Blood. As much as I'd prefer he kept that part of his childhood a little longer, it's time already that he experienced his first kill. {*Those are good things to learn,*} I mindspeak. {*And when you come back we can finally go on your first hunt.*}

Henri's eyes widen and he swivels his head toward me. "Really? You promise?" he says out loud.

"I promise," I say.

In the morning, after breakfast, Henri rushes off to gas up the Grady White. Since it cruises fast enough and carries enough fuel to reach Andros in less than a day, Jessai has agreed to travel with us, so we won't have the awkwardness of arriving before him.

Chloe busies herself packing a small bag for each of the children. While they'll live mostly in their natural forms among the Pelk, she wants them to have a few of their favorite outfits and a couple of their favorite toys.

I have other concerns. I go to our room, take out all of the Smith and Wesson revolvers and load each one. I place one on Chloe's nightstand, one on mine and the third on the dresser. I take the fourth up to the great room and leave it on the dining room table.

Before I go to the boat I show Chloe where each has been left. "Are you expecting something?" she says.

"No." I shake my head. "But I haven't left you alone out here in a long time. I'm going to be gone for the day and a good part of the night. It will make me feel better to know you have some extra protection—just in case."

Chloe nods. "Don't worry," she says. "I'll make sure to keep one near me."

"I should be back sometime late at night," I say.

"Just make sure the kids are settled in and comfortable before you leave them."

Fortunately the weather remains unnaturally calm. Except for a few skimpy white clouds and the pillar of dark smoke out west, over the Everglades, caused by the ongoing swamp fire, the sky remains an unbroken expanse of pale blue. Undisturbed by wind or storm, the ocean lies flat as far as I can see; light blue near shore, much darker where it grows deeper, barely ruffled anywhere by anything more than small swells.

The Grady White shoots over its calm surface and we arrive at Andros Island far before nightfall. Jessai guides me to the mouth of Lusca Creek and we follow its winding course through the mangroves until the water grows too shallow to allow us to venture any farther.

Jessai waits for me to set anchor, then strips off his clothes and shifts to his natural form. Since we are far past mindthought range from Miami, he mindspeaks, unmasked, *"Undrae. My safehold is only a short swim from here."*

I nod. *"I know, but my daughter is too young to swim with us. She lacks the lungpower to stay underwater as long as we would have to. We're better off waiting for dark and flying to you."*

"As you wish." Jessai nods. *"But I am anxious to be home. I will tell Lorrel to put out a glow-jar for you. We will wait to see you then."* He walks to the side of the boat.

"Wait!" Henri mindspeaks. *"I can hold my breath real long. Papa, you know that. You've seen me do it. Can I go with Jessai?"*

I shake my head.

"Why not?"

"Because we don't have very much time left to spend together," I mindspeak. *"I'm going to leave as soon as I'm sure you're both settled in. So, whatever time is left, I'd like to spend with both of you."*

"I will see all of you tonight," Jessai mindspeaks and dives off the boat. He barely splashes as he cuts into the water.

Neither Henri nor Lizzie have ever been to Andros before. Ordinarily, when in a new situation, their eyes would dart in all directions and they'd pepper me with questions. At the very least, they'd plead for permission to go swimming and maybe explore just a little of the surrounding area.

But today both sit still and stare at the water. Neither of them respond to anything I say with more than a grunt or a monosyllabic word. For my part, I can't keep my mind away from imagining how quiet it will be at home without them, how empty the house will seem.

While it feels like it takes forever for the sun to set and the night to grow dark, I still sigh when Henri says, "It's night, Papa. Can we go now?"

20

I push both throttles to full power as soon as I maneuver the Grady White out of Lusca Creek and into open water. The roar of the motors, the speed, the wind in my face, the way the boat skims over the water, all usually bring a smile to my face, but tonight nothing pleases me.

Lorrel and Jessai did all they could to make the children comfortable. They had built a new seaweed nest just for them, adjacent to their own nest, and they made sure to have a first meal of dolphin meat, rather than fish, waiting for them. Still, Henri and Lizzie's eyes had been wide the whole time, both children staying close to me, neither talking to the smaller, black-scaled Pelk children who gathered around to gawk at them.

Lizzie cried when I kissed her good-bye and Henri permitted me to hug him much longer than he ordinarily would. I shake my head. It was right to take them to safety but I hate that I had to do such a thing. I want to find whatever being brought this threat into our lives and rip its flesh apart—until nothing remains of it.

If only Chloe had come. With the children gone and no one else on the boat, I find my new solitude almost painful. Since Andros lies far outside mindspeaking range of Miami, I can't even contact her until I reach Bimini. I sigh and search the dark waters around me for boat lights, for any signs of other life, but nothing shows anywhere I look.

At Bimini, I interrupt my journey long enough to cruise into the harbor and pull into Blue Water Marina—both for gas and for the opportunity to talk to a living being face-to-face. But my short conversation with the dockman does little to diminish the pangs of loneliness I feel. As soon as he tops off my tanks, I race back to sea.

Since Chloe is finally within range, I check my watch. It reads 2:45 A.M. She'll surely be asleep. But I doubt she'll object to being woken. She'll understand how I feel about leaving our children behind. I mindspeak, {*Chloe. I know it's late, but I need to talk.*}

No answer comes. I shrug. Sometimes my wife sleeps so deeply that almost nothing can wake her. Or I could still be slightly out of range. I wait fifteen minutes more and mindspeak again. {*Chloe? . . . Chloe?*}

No answer comes and I try another time, and another.

When another fifteen minutes and three more attempts pass without any response, I frown and shake my head. Though she's most probably just lost in sleep and though she's never taken kindly to being pestered awake, I need to know that she's all right. I call, {*Chloe?*} again and again and still receive no answer.

I check my watch again. I should reach the Gulf Stream soon. Home can't be more than another hour away. {*Chloe?*} I mindspeak and she still doesn't answer. I wonder if she could have decided to leave—to go to Jamaica without telling me. I shake my head. Chloe wouldn't do something like that to me, no matter how angry she was.

Even if she were injured or ill, she would surely answer me. She would have to be unconscious or worse not to. A groan escapes my lips. The boat suddenly seems far too slow. I can't bear the thought that something may have happened to her. I need to know she's okay now. From here, if I take to the air, I can reach home in twenty minutes.

The motors grow quiet as soon as I pull back on the throttles and turn off the ignition. I check the depthfinder as the boat coasts to a stop and nod. Thirty-five feet. Deep, but not too deep to anchor. I call Chloe again, and go forward and throw the anchor out.

Rather than wait to make sure it's set, I rush back to the cockpit, strip, shift into my natural form and take to the air. {*Chloe!*} I mindspeak. {*I'm almost home.*}

From the air, nothing looks awry. I circle Caya DelaSangre twice and shoot down, so I can approach from the bay side, over the harbor—just in case a strange boat lurks in the shadows. But all seems clear.

I land on the veranda and pause before I rush to our bedroom. As usual, some of the dogs out in the bushes bark a greeting to me. No strange scents invade my nostrils. Still, I remain in my natural form—just in case—as I approach my door.

When I grab its latch, the door swings free, as if it hadn't quite been closed. I jerk it open, and gasp at the thick aroma of blood and the rank, burnt-sulfur smell of spent gunpowder that floods the room's air. A jolt of adrenaline courses through me and my heart begins to race. I clench my jaws and flex my claws open and closed and open again. Though I can see well enough in the dark to know that the sheets and blankets and pillows have been tossed and turned and jumbled and the lights on the nightstands knocked over and that Chloe is nowhere in view, I flick the light on.

I bellow out a roar. Blood soaks the bed linens crimson red and pools on the floor near me. Streaks of it form a path that leads to the interior door. One of our new Smith and Wesson Magnums lies in the pool of blood in front of me, another has been left on the bed.

{*Chloe?*} I mindspeak, {*Chloe, please,*} as I rush into the room without any care as to where I step or what I touch. No police can be called anyway, and no investigation other than mine will ever be performed, no matter what has happened. I snatch up the large revolver from the floor, sniff at the end of its barrel and nod. The gun has been fired. I smile. At least Chloe had a chance to defend herself. At least there's a chance that not all the blood is hers.

{*Chloe, please, where are you? Answer me, please!*} No answer comes. I moan and mindspeak, {*Chloe?*} again and again—and again and again no answer comes. I shake my head and fight the thought that she might be dead, fight the images of her lying bloodied and still that try to flood my mind. Such things can't be. I ignore my pounding heart and shake my head again. I refuse to think such things. Chloe could just as well be only hurt or in hiding.

{*Chloe?*} I mindspeak. {*Chloe?*} Again no answer comes. I snap the cylinder open and eject the cartridges. They fall to the floor, each one of them an empty brass casing—all five fired at something. A quick check on the gun dropped on the bed reveals that all five of its bullets have been fired too.

But I take little solace from that. The red streaks on the floor look like someone dragged something large and bloody out of the bedroom, onto the landing in the interior of the house. I groan, suck in a breath, throw that door open, step onto the landing and throw the interior light on.

All traces of blood end a few feet from the front of the door. No blood, not even a drop, shows anywhere on the steps leading up to the great room. But still I smell more blood. It maddens me that I can't tell whether it's Chloe's or not. I let out a long, sad yowl.

A faint whimper answers me.

I look around the landing and see nothing. Another whimper comes. I go to the rail, look down to the bottom floor and gasp once again. Two creatures, Max and one of my kind, too large to be Chloe, lie still in a large pool of blood—their bodies askew as if they'd been thrown over the railing.

Taking the stairs two and three at a time, I rush down and throw on the lights. Max whimpers again but, from the eight bullet holes I count in its carcass and head, the other creature has clearly lost its ability to make sounds or do anything else ever again. I would like to study it further but I shake my head. My dog needs help and I've yet to learn what may have happened to my wife.

Other than a few small gouges in his fur, Max shows no visible injuries. Still, he howls when I attempt to move him. I see no choice but to leave him while I try to find what became of Chloe. Since I'm still in my natural form and can't speak to him, I make what I hope he'll find are reassuring sounds and rush off to search the rest of the house.

But I find no further signs of Chloe or of any struggle anywhere else—not in the cells and storerooms on the bottom floor, not in the bedrooms on the second, or the great room on the third. By the time I finish my search, I want to sit and wail, to give myself over to the sorrow and worry and despair that have been building inside me. At the same time, my heart pounds so heavily that it aches with each beat and the sound of it reverberates in my head.

I clench and unclench my claws. I want to—I need to rip into flesh. My father called it blood anger—the kind of fury that requires that an opponent's blood must be spilled. More than one of my kind had to have been involved in this attack. At least Chloe had the satisfaction of killing one of them. But I will not rest until the other or others suffer the same fate.

As much as it pains me to leave Max, I dare not let any more time lapse before I search more for Chloe. I race back to the veranda. Fortunately, the sky has at least two hours to go yet before it will begin to turn light. Time enough for me to search all over the nearby sky and waters for any sign of my wife or the creatures who attacked her.

After three circuits of the bay and coastal waters near Miami, I bellow out a roar. No one suspicious, nothing peculiar shows anywhere. Even though I risk exposure, I bank over Homestead and fly low along the bay shore heading north. Nothing odd shows at Ouder Raad's castle in Gables Estates either—no late-burning lights, no strange boats, no massive gathering of cars—just the large blue inflatable, docked in the customary place. I continue north toward Dinner Key.

As I near the marina, I look for the large blue sailboat's masts. Ordinarily the three tower over all the rest, but tonight they either have grown invisible or are no longer in the marina. I growl and fly lower—no longer caring if I'm seen—until my underbelly almost grazes the highest masts. The slip that held the large blue sailboat, the *Anochi Yagdo*, now sits empty.

I climb and circle. Whatever happened, it occurred long

enough ago for the ship to cruise out of sight. I have no way of knowing where it is. It could already be anywhere within hundreds of miles of ocean—or just docked a dozen miles up the bay or in a dockyard up the Miami River. But at least I know its inflatable is docked at Ouder Raad's castle.

The wind rushes by me as I race south. I have no idea whether the inhabitants of the house have anything to do with my wife's disappearance but I'm willing to risk savaging them to find out. I growl into the air. Even if they have done nothing, it will at least give me some relief to rip into their live flesh.

"DelaSangre, go home. Your wife is elsewhere."

I growl and wheel in midair but I see nothing. *"Who are you? What do you know about my wife?"* I mindspeak.

"More than you do." His chuckle reverberates in my mind. *"Your Chloe, she is well, though—thanks to her—one of my comrades most definitely is not. As you no doubt have already discovered."*

"Where is she?"

"In time, DelaSangre, in time. For now I advise you to return home. It is most untidy there and in need of your attention. I will be glad to meet you later today, for lunch I think, at one, at Monty's, outside on the patio."

"How will I recognize you?"

"No need, DelaSangre. We know what your human form looks like. If you would be so kind as to take a table, we'll find you."

"What do you want?"

"Patience, DelaSangre," he mindspeaks. *"You Americans, you really must learn patience. All your answers will come in due time if you wait . . . and if you do as we ask."*

21

Chloe is well. I dwell on those words all the way home. I don't know if I could bear her death. The knowledge that she lives leaves me hope that I may find some way for us to be together again. But it does little to dull the fury that burns inside me. I shake my head. Revenge can wait. First, I have to do whatever I must to bring my wife home.

When I swoop down and land on the veranda outside my coral stone house, I look out toward the ocean's horizon and groan. Not a hint of morning light shows anywhere in the sky yet. I'll learn nothing more about my wife's disappearance until lunch. I sigh. The morning will take an unbearably long time to pass.

Once again, I stay in my natural form. In my human form I may not have the strength to handle Max's weight and bulk without doing injury to the poor dog. He whimpers when he sees me, the sound so slight I doubt it could be heard six feet away. But I smile. If he still has enough strength for that, I may still be able to save him.

I go to the storage room where I keep my carpentry tools and spare scraps of lumber. Part of a sheet of one-inch-thick plywood, left over from a repair project a few months ago, leans against the far wall. I grab it, study its size and nod.

Max barely grunts when I push the plywood partway beneath him. But he yelps when I grab him and yank him the rest of the way onto the board. I try to disturb him as little as possible as I carry and drag him and the board up the steps to the second level, through my bedroom to the veranda and then down the steps to the dock.

He whimpers the whole way, his discomfort only growing as I wrestle him onto Chloe's Donzi and lay him down in its cockpit. Once he's secure, I shift to my human form, kneel beside him and stroke his head with the palm of my hand. "Sorry, boy," I say, "I had to get you out here. Now we can take you for some help."

I race back into the house, throw on a pair of shorts and a T-shirt, pick up my cell phone from my nightstand, turn toward the dresser and stop. Chloe has left her keys there as usual, but something seems off. I walk over and pick her key chain up while I dial Claudia's number with my other hand. Her phone begins to ring and I start toward the door—and then stop again.

When I left the revolvers out for Chloe, I'm sure I placed one on top of the dresser. It is no longer there. Still listening to the cell phone ring, I walk back, look on the floor under and nearby it—and find nothing. I shrug. It could be anywhere and I certainly don't have the time to waste searching for it.

I've already redialed twice and reached the boat by the time Claudia finally answers my call. "What?" she slurs, her voice heavy with sleep.

"Wake up. It's me, Peter. I need you to get a veterinarian to rush to my dock at Monty's. He has to be able to handle Max."

"Max is hurt?"

"Badly."

"My God, it isn't even light out. You don't ask for much, do you?"

"You know better than to say something like that," I snap. "Don't we donate a ton of money to Metrozoo?"

"It's one of Pop's favorite charities."

"Get him to call the zoo director and have him send one of their vets and a truck to my boat slip. I don't know how much longer Max can hold on but hopefully we'll both be waiting there." I untie the boat's dock lines one-handed and jump on board.

"What do I tell him about Max?"

I put the key in the ignition, turn it and the motors grumble to life. "Tell him I'm a kook who likes to breed big, dangerous guard dogs. Tell him they sometime happen to hurt each other. Tell him I think this one fell. And tell him I like my privacy and that I'm too big of a donor to risk offending with any loose talk." I disconnect the phone, throw the motors in gear and shoot out the channel.

Since the wait for the vet will probably take longer than the time it takes to race the Donzi across the bay, I choose to travel at half speed, so I can minimize the amount of pounding Max will have to endure. By the time I reach Monty's channel and motor into the harbor, the sun has finally broken into the sky.

Dressed in only a rumpled T-shirt and short cutoffs, her hair tousled and unbrushed, Claudia's already at the dock. She waves as soon as she sees me. When I come within shouting distance, she calls out, "Pops said they're on the way."

I nod, say, "Good," and guide the Donzi into my slip.

Claudia jumps onto the bow as soon as it's near enough and ties off the boat's lines. Then she kneels next to Max and strokes the black fur on his neck. The poor dog's tail thumps only once. He tries to raise his head but only manages to move it a few centimeters.

Claudia looks at me. "Jesus, Boss, what happened to him?"

"Nothing good," I say. I turn the motors off and all goes quiet around us.

"Chloe and the kids must be upset," she says.

I shake my head. "They're away right now."

"Away?" Claudia frowns.

Before she can ask anything else, I hold up a hand. "No more questions. Some things are going on. That's all you need to know for now."

"Chloe *is* my friend." Claudia glares at me.

If my father were here he'd say, "*See, this is what happens when you let humans come too close to you. You can never afford to have a true friendship with any of them—not even the Gomezes and Tindalls. Never let them any of them assume they have a right to treat you as an equal.*"

I return her stare. "And she *is* my wife and you *are* my employee. We both like you and value our relationships with you, but there are limits to that relationship. Are you the first Gomez in four centuries who can't understand that?"

"I understand." Claudia looks down. "I care about you guys. Sometimes it makes me forget."

"Sometimes we do too," I say. "But you know as well as I do, there are things in our lives you're better off never knowing about."

A white Metrozoo van pulls into Monty's parking lot. Both of us look in its direction. Three men, all dressed in jeans and Metrozoo shirts, rush to the dock. The tallest carries a black medical bag. They stop by the boat and gawk at Max. The dog just lies on the sheet of plywood, where I first placed him, and pants rapid, shallow breaths. He does nothing to acknowledge their presence. "What the hell is that?" one of the men mutters.

I frown at him. "My dog."

"Mr. DelaSangre?" the man carrying the bag says. "They told me your dog fell. Could you say how far?"

"About twenty feet . . . I think. I wasn't there when it happened. But whatever injuries he has don't show. They have to be internal."

The vet nods. He gets in the boat, crouches by the dog and examines him. Then he looks at me. "I won't know what we can do until I get him to an X-ray machine."

"That's fine. Just be careful. He's a good dog, but when he feels better he might get a little tough to deal with."

"Don't forget we deal with lions and tigers and bears out there." The vet stands and smiles. "I think we can deal okay with one broken-up dog."

Claudia hands him her business card. "I handle things for Mr. DelaSangre. Call me when you find something out."

The man takes her card, studies it and then turns his gaze on her. "Sure." His eyes goes back to the card for a moment. "It's okay to call you Claudia, right?"

A flush rises on her tan cheeks and her hand goes to her tousled hair in a vain attempt to straighten out some of the knots. She nods.

"Cool." His smile widens. "I'm Benito Luz. Benny. I'll be calling you soon."

I watch it all with a grin. The man looks to be around her age. He's a little too skinny, but otherwise he has the rugged good looks of an outdoorsman; certainly features that would tempt someone like Claudia. Once they've carried Max away, I say, "So you liked him, huh?"

She shrugs and then nods her head just the slightest bit.

I spend the rest of the morning back on my island, cleaning the blood from the floor in my bedroom and on the landing, throwing away the ruined linens, straightening out the mess left from Chloe's struggle. I leave the disorder on the bottom floor for later, after dark, when I can move the dragon's carcass without fear of discovery.

Nothing has been disturbed in the great room. The fourth revolver still lies in open sight, on the table where I left it. But no matter how I search, where I look, the third revolver, the one I'd left on my bedroom dresser, remains missing. Unless it somehow ended up under the dead dragon on the bottom floor, I can only assume Chloe's attackers either discarded it somewhere outside or took it with them.

After a long, hot shower, I throw on a fresh pair of shorts, a Tommy Bahama knit shirt and a pair of boat shoes. I study myself in the mirror and shrug. That's as dressed up as I care to get for lunch with an abductor.

Without an injured dog to worry about, I jam the throttles on Chloe's Donzi as far forward as they go. The motors yowl and the boat shoots ahead, the hull rising and leveling off as the Donzi reaches planing speed—barely any of it in contact with the water except for the props and a few inches of the boat's bottom.

The boat skitters across the bay at over sixty miles an hour, delivering me to Monty's channel in less than fifteen minutes. Another time, without my wife to worry about, such a quick ride would bring a huge smile to my lips. Today, I look at my watch and frown. I may have saved time on my trip across the bay but now I have twenty minutes to wait until my luncheon appointment shows up.

Rather than occupy my time with meaningless activity or sit and wait in boredom, I go up to Monty's outdoor patio. Most days people crowd almost every available table, but today only a third have two or more patrons sitting on their wood benches. I take a seat at a table facing the marina, looking over to where the *Anochi Yagdo* had been berthed only a day ago. A waitress appears almost immediately—another unusual occurrence for Monty's.

She's young and small with a pointed-up nose, freckled cheeks, wide, bright blue eyes, blond hair braided into two long ponytails and breasts barely large enough to disturb the lines of her blouse. Her diminutive size makes her look even younger than her features do and I wonder if she's old enough for the job. She flashes me a bright smile. "Dining alone?" she asks.

I shake my head.

"Too bad," she says. "I sort of like it when I have a good-looking guy like you all to myself."

Whether she's saying it to build up her tip or flirting for real, I have no interest in engaging in banter with her. Even if I were interested in sex with a human female, this one looks too young to tempt me. And even if she were old enough to consider as a meal, she's too slight to make for much more than a late evening's snack.

Still, just the thought of food makes my empty stomach growl in protest. "Please bring me a glass of water and two blood-rare hamburgers while I'm waiting," I say.

"Sure, mister," she says and wanders off.

I watch the water and the docks while I wait, and hope the sounds of the marina and the murmur of the conversations around me will relax me and dull the edge of the adrenaline rush I've been on for so long. While I've only lost one night's sleep, I feel as if I've been going much longer. My body needs sustenance and rest. I close my eyes. But I ache so much to see my wife again—to hold her close—that my body refuses to relax.

"Mister, you okay?"

"Sure," I say, opening my eyes, finding the waitress back with my glass of water. "Just tired."

She makes a face as she puts the water in front of me. "I know how that goes. Damned Everglades. With all the smoke in the air, people are eating inside most of the time now. I have to work double shifts just to make the money I was making before."

I sniff the air and nod. "It is getting worse, isn't it?"

"You betcha. They said on the news that the fire's already doubled in size. If it doesn't rain soon I'm going to have to start looking for another job."

After she leaves, I study the sky. For the first time, a slight gray haze seems to be everywhere. If the fires continue much longer the whole sky will go gray.

"You are looking up like that to watch for me? You couldn't possibly think I would come in my natural form, could you?"

The German accent leaves no doubt in my mind who I'll encounter when I turn toward the voice. I swivel my head and stare at the man, his long, dark hair as greasy as ever. "Hardly," I say.

"Good," he says. "You know I am teasing you," and sits across from me.

"Tell me about Chloe," I say.

"Really, DelaSangre. In time." He takes off his sunglasses, stares at me with hard, emerald green eyes and smiles a false smile. "We have much to discuss. You must understand, none of us desired any of this. We would not be here had we not been forced."

I take off my sunglasses and return his stare. His eyes don't waver. His lips remain frozen into a smile. I grin back. I have no more fear of this creature than he has of me. If not for Chloe, I would invite him to meet me in the sky as soon as it turns dark.

"Wow, you guys both have great eyes. Are you brothers or something?" The young waitress places a platter with two hamburgers in front of me.

The German shakes his head. "*Vetters,*" he says. "Cousins, I think, distant cousins."

"Care for a menu?" The waitress holds one out to him.

"*Nein* . . . no." He reaches across the table and takes one of my burgers. "I will have one of his." The German smiles at me. "You see no reason to object, do you cousin?"

I do object. Still, I suppress a frown or any other show of emotion. "*Fighting is more than claws and teeth and blood. Never show anything to your enemy, certainly not your rage or fears,*" Father taught me. "*Keep him uncertain at all times—especially as to when you will attack or what will provoke you. But keep him sure that once you do engage, the fight will be to the death.*"

"Bring four more," I say, and grin at the waitress. "That way neither of us will have to worry about sharing."

She nods, jots it down on her pad and walks off.

The German eats his hamburger patty from between the two halves of the bun as he watches her walk away. *"She has the look of a convenient girl,"* he mindspeaks. *"I have not been able to hunt here as much as I would like. I could use someone like that. She could satisfy me under the sheets and dull my hunger afterward."*

"I try to avoid killing the young of any kind," I mindspeak.

"Ah, but their flesh tastes so sweet." The German makes a face and drops his uneaten bun on my plate. *"Far better than this ground, dead cow you content yourself with."*

Though ordinarily I would eat just the patty too, I pick up my burger, bun and all, and eat it, one bite after another. *"You didn't come to discuss human girls with me,"* I mindspeak. *"I don't need for us to make conversation. I need my wife back."*

The man leans back, and rearranges his long hair with a toss of his head. "And we will be glad to arrange that as soon as you arrange something for us," he says, out loud. He leans forward and lowers his voice. "We need someone returned too."

Could all of this has been caused by some misunderstanding, some grand mistake? I stare at the man. "What the hell are you talking about?" I say. "We're holding no one here—certainly not anyone of the Blood."

"We're not fools. We know that. But the council can't—how you say—look the other way again. Your father violated its prime rule the last time. Now you are responsible for violating it again. I am part of a host the council has sent against you."

I hold back a gasp and fight to keep my face devoid of emotion, of any show of surprise. None of what he says makes any sense to me. My parents taught me how few People of the Blood were left. How scattered and private they were. If this is true, his talk of a council and a host of my kind means there are far more of us than I ever thought.

"A host? What council? What rule?" I say.

The German dismisses my questions with a toss of his right hand and says, "We want Cili back."

22

"Cili?" At first I draw a blank on the name. Then I remember the accented voice of Derek's new wife. My brother-in-law Derek, who I supported the whole time he searched for his wife. I groan.

Our waitress returns with two plates of hamburgers. "Is this a family argument or business?" she says, and places one in front of the German and the other in front of me. "You guys look so serious."

The German smiles at her. "Actually we've been fighting over which one of us should ask for your phone number. Since my cousin here is married, I thought it should be me."

She glances at me and then looks at the German. "I'll think about it. My name's Mickey. It's short for Michelina."

"I'm Aric," he says. "And that's Peter."

"Cool." She smiles. "I'll be back to check on you in a little bit."

Once she leaves, I look at the German. After referring to him as Samson for so long I find it strange to hear his real name. "Aric?" I say.

He nods. "Aric Blut."

"And this is about Cili? My brother-in-law Derek's mate?"

"Istvan Ver's daughter. She was promised to Burian Krovyanoy. Derek killed him."

As much as I try, I can't keep the look of confusion from my face. "So? Isn't that what happens when a female's in heat? Don't males fight for her?"

"Not among us." Aric Blut laughs and picks up one of his hamburgers. "Burian's death only shifted the promise to his younger brother, Danya." Aric takes a bite from his burger, chews and swallows it, and then says, "Do you really know as little as you seem to?"

"Except for Cili, I don't have the foggiest idea what you're talking about."

He takes a few bites from his burger and studies me. "Derek never told you of his problems?"

I shake my head. "But he'll damn sure explain to me after this," I say.

"And neither your father nor mother ever warned you about the Council of Elders?"

I shake my head again.

He sighs. "In Europe, our kind lives differently than you do. We have not as much land and many more families. In the old days, before the council was formed, any time one of our females went into heat, dozens of our young males would die fighting to have her. In the early eighteen hundreds, the Van Bloed family in Holland lost all five of their sons in one year.

"Henrik Van Bloed, their father, contacted all the other families of the Blood in Europe, including Russia and Turkey, and arranged for the eldest member of each to come for a meeting. When all were gathered together, he argued that it made no sense to continue a tradition that caused so many of our young males to kill each other. He proposed arranged marriages instead, and a council to oversee the arrangements and enforce their provisions."

The German pauses to finish his burger, then continues. "The Council of Elders adopted all of Van Bloed's proposals on marriage and added one other provision—no outsider may be permitted to take one of our females."

"My father must have. He told me he met my mother in Paris."

Aric raises an eyebrow. "And you know nothing else about that?"

"Not very much. My mother died when I was young and my father didn't like to talk very much about her after that."

Mickey walks by and Aric's eyes follow her as she goes from table to table. He goes silent for a few moments, obviously thinking something over, then says, "I will tell you something as a gift—a gesture of our goodwill. It will not help you against us . . ." He looks at me, his eyes no longer hard. "Have you never looked under your father's log books and charts?"

"I've been through that chest dozens of times," I say.

"We only had to search through it once." The German shakes his head. "I don't understand your father. How could he never teach you about the false bottom?"

My mouth starts to drop open. I freeze my face.

Aric nods. "What need would you have for such a thing when you have safe deposit boxes? In Europe many of our elders still keep their personal papers and favorite baubles hidden in such false compartments. As soon as we saw that old chest on your third floor we knew. We found their writings about their meeting."

"Their? My father's and my mother's?"

"I scanned through both. The story may interest you—if you can find a way to have them translated."

I nod.

Aric's eyes go hard again. "Your father and mother may have escaped us but, over the years, our hosts have killed dozens of others who tried the same thing."

"I might be impressed if I knew what a host was," I say.

"A war gathering," Aric says. "In the old days, during the Great War, our fighters were organized in groupings of twelve called hosts. When the council decided to ensure that no one person of the Blood could prevail against its wishes, they adopted the same fighting units—twelve warriors of the Blood, one host for each quadrant of Europe. Since the council was established, only your father and Derek Blood have managed to violate its rules and live."

"Look," I say. "I can't give you Cili. She isn't here. She's with Derek. She's pregnant anyway. Danya, whatever his name is, will have to find someone else . . ."

Aric curls his lip. "Danya's dead and lying on the cold stone floor at the bottom of your house. Your wife killed him with those big guns she had. Cili will go to someone else. The council has already dictated who. I assure you no one will object to her swollen stomach."

"I don't get it. None of you followed my mother here."

"A claim had been placed on your mother but she had never been promised. Trust me, she and your father did not leave easily." Aric picks up his other burger and looks at my plate. "Have you no more hunger?"

I glance down at the burgers. In truth, my hunger has deserted me. But I know better than to deny my body nourishment. This creature and I may be sharing a gentle conversation right now but that's no guarantee that we won't be locked in mortal combat in the near future. I take the now-cool patty from one bun, add it on top of the other and gulp the whole thing down. Then I look at the German. "So where do we go from here?" I say.

He leans back and stretches. "Always trying to rush to the point." Aric shakes his head. "It's so American of you. We are taking your wife and you appreciate none of the subtlety of what we do. Surely you know chess?"

I nod. "My father taught me."

"As he should have," the German says. "Another decision of our council was to pool our fortunes and invest them together. It has given us much power in Europe and the ability to launch efforts like the one Ouder Raad has been taking against your LaMar Associates."

He leans closer to me and snarls, "Now to the point you have been so anxious to hear. We have your wife—your queen. We are in position to financially destroy your company. In time we can find where your children have been taken and take them too. We have done all this to convince you to cooperate with us. At the minimum you are in check—if not checkmated."

"And you're going to kill Chloe if I refuse?"

Aric sits back as if shocked at the thought. "We have no need to kill your queen. If need be, we'll kill you. Once your wife knows you're dead, she'll become as available again as if she was in her first heat. You do know that?"

I nod. We may mate for life but if the male partner dies, the female's body goes into heat and she has no choice but to mate again with whoever comes to claim her.

"We know you know where Derek is. You must call him and have him bring Cili here."

In all the time I've known Derek, I've never seen him

agree to anything that might inconvenience him without a much greater promise of pain or reward. "And what if he refuses?" I say.

Aric shrugs. "We kill you. If any of your people oppose us—we kill them too. We take over all your companies and all of your properties." He grins at me. "I wouldn't mind if I was chosen to stay here to oversee all of it." And then his face turns grim again. "One of us takes your wife as his mate. Once we find your children, we give your daughter to one of our families to raise. If your son proves intractable, we kill him. And, of course, we send another host to Australia and kill your brother-in-law. Cili we bring home for her next mate . . ." The German pauses and sighs. "But wouldn't it be so much more pleasant if we didn't have to do all of that?"

I glare at him. "Don't assume it will be so easy. My wife already eliminated one of your precious host."

"Which leaves us with eleven warriors to your one."

I open my mouth to respond but Aric holds up a hand. "I know. You have many big guns. Ach, and they are such terrible things—so powerful, so American of you—like one of your cowboys. Fortunately they have laws against weapons like that in Europe." Aric's grin widens. "Did you notice one was missing?"

I nod.

"Such big bullets. You should see what they do to a human—your friend Buddy Matherby, for instance. Far worse than what they did to Danya."

Before I can say anything, our waitress appears with our check. Aric takes it. "Please, allow me," he says to me and produces a few large bills, which he hands to Mickey.

Her eyes go wide and she grins when he tells her to keep

the change. She presses a piece of paper into his hand, says, "Call me," and rushes back to work.

He examines the phone number she wrote on the paper and says, "At last, a decent meal."

"What about Buddy Matherby?" I say.

"Forget him. He's just one more human. You have other worries. Call Derek this afternoon. Tell him, he must bring Cili here."

"And if I do?"

Aric stands and smiles like an old friend. "I'll contact you later. We can discuss that after you tell me when Derek and Cili will arrive."

He turns and walks away. I stay seated, sip on my water and watch him leave. If Father were alive I'd rush to consult with him. All my instincts tell me not to trust a word this creature has uttered. Still, I have to find a way to bring Chloe home.

Mickey comes by. "Need something else?" she says.

If Aric's words are true, I need enough help to fight eleven others of my kind. Certainly nothing she can provide assistance on. "No." I shake my head and get up. Fortunately LaMar sits just across the street. I can call Derek from there.

She flashes a waitress smile. "Later," she says, and starts to turn.

"No. Wait," I say. "That guy you just gave your number to."

"Your cousin?"

"Yeah. Listen, take some advice. He's a bad guy. If he calls, please don't go out with him. He's one of the ones who like to hurt people."

Mickey's eyes go wide. "You're not just saying that because I gave my number to him instead of you?"

I shake my head. "If you ever go out with him, you will regret it. He's worse than you could ever imagine. Believe me, I know."

23

"Who the bloody hell told them we're in Australia?" Derek says.

I shake my head. I'm in no mood to listen to attitude from my brother-in-law. Had I not sponsored his trip to Europe, my wife and children would still be with me. "I have no god-damned idea." I spit my words out. "If you had half the brains of either of your sisters, you would have told me what was going on."

"Listen, old man, you ring me up and wake Cili and me in the middle of the night and then you tear into me about this mess you're in. I appreciate your money and the help you've given us—but it gives you no right to scold or insult me. Cili grew up with these creatures. She knows how they operate. She and I had everything under control. We killed seven of them altogether—eight, if you count the chap I did in to win Cili. By the time we got to Turkey, they were so wary of us they barely cared where we went—as long as we were gone."

I want to shout and curse, to bang my receiver on the desk, to do anything that might penetrate my brother-in-law's thick skull. But I take a long, deep breath instead and then say, "It never occurred to you that they might come here instead?"

"Not really. Cili said they all know the name DelaSangre. Apparently your father made quite an impression on them a long time ago. She told me the European families have very little appetite for dangerous conflict anymore. They only attack when they feel they have an overwhelming advantage."

Claudia looks in from the doorway of my office. "Marcia said you stormed in without saying anything. Is everything okay, Boss?"

I mouth "Later," to her and send her away with a quick hand motion. Then I say to Derek, "Would you think twelve to one is good enough odds for them?"

Derek lets out a long, quiet whistle. "They sent a complete host after you?"

"Not as complete as it was. Chloe eliminated one of them."

"Good girl," Derek says. "See, old man? They're not invincible."

"You come and face eleven of them by yourself."

He barks out a laugh. "Hardly. I find life here with Cili to be more my cup of tea. Once we can move to our ranch things will be perfect."

"Derek, haven't you been listening?" I say. "They've taken Chloe and won't return her unless we give them Cili."

"That will never happen," Derek says, his voice suddenly harsh.

"I know. I wouldn't expect you—or her—to agree to anything like that." I sigh. "But I need your help. I've already had to send my children into hiding. I don't think I can defeat eleven of them by myself. Remember, if you refuse to help, there won't be any more support money from me or any possibility of buying that ranch ever again—no matter whether I beat them or not. And if they're successful here they'll still send a host to attack you."

Derek's voice goes monotone. "I understand you perfectly well. You ask a lot, old man. Let me chat with Cili a bit. It does concern her too, you know. I'll ring you back within the hour."

"I'm at the office," I say.

"I thought that," Derek says. "I'll ring you back in a bit."

After I hang up, I swivel around and stare out the window at the marina and the empty slip that housed the *Anochi Yagdo* so recently. Though I know it's futile, I mindspeak, masked, yet one more time, {*Chloe, it's me, please answer,*} and receive only silence in reply.

For her to not answer me, she has to be either drugged or outside mindspeaking range. I let out a low groan. From the look of its length, lines and rigging, the large blue sailboat has to be capable of some major speed. If they took Chloe soon after I left for Andros, they could easily have been hundreds of miles away by the time I first tried to contact her.

I turn back to my desk and buzz Claudia. "I want everyone in my office. Now," I say.

Claudia and Arturo rush in almost immediately. Ian follows a moment later. I motion for them to be seated, shake my head and wave away any inquiries. "I don't want to have to repeat myself," I say. "Let's wait for Thad and do it all at once."

He rushes in a few minutes later, fumbling with the top of his zipper. "Sorry," he says. "I was in the toilet when Claudia called."

After he sits, I look at each of their faces and then say, "I have some problems—and so do we." Claudia and Arturo lean forward, their faces showing their concern. Ian, on the other hand leans back, his face as impassive as stone. Thad leans forward, his forehead furrowed.

"Chloe has been taken . . . kidnapped."

"*What?*" Claudia says.

I frown at her. "In a minute. Just listen for now. I just came from a meeting with Aric Blut—he's the greasy-haired one with Ouder Raad we've been referring to as Samson. He's presented me with some difficult demands that must be met before they'll return Chloe."

Ian says, "Over a business deal?"

Arturo shakes his head. "This is obviously over more than business, Ian."

"What about Henri and Lizzie?" Claudia says.

"They're safe—for now," I say. "And Arturo's right. This is over more than business. But you have to understand that our friends at Ouder Raad are willing to use some pretty hardball tactics to further their business goals too."

Ian makes a contemptuous face. "Nothing we can't handle."

"Oh." I look at him. "Have you heard from Manny Padron recently?"

"No. There's no reason for him to call today."

"He will," I say. "Buddy Matherby's dead. Aric told me they used a Smith and Wesson 500 Magnum on him."

Claudia gasps.

I look at her and nod. "One of the ones you bought. You made sure it wasn't traceable, didn't you?"

"As always," Claudia says. "Tamiami knows what we expect."

Arturo sighs. "So much for your handshake deal. Now, without anything on paper and signed and witnessed, it will all be thrown into probate. Top bidder will take it once the court makes it available again."

"It won't be Ouder Raad, if I have anything to do with it," I say. "Now I need some answers." I turn my eyes to Ian and Thad. "What have you found out about Ouder Raad from the Ramirez brothers' contact at DEA?"

"That's Thad's deal," Ian says. He looks at his assistant.

The man's face flushes red. "I haven't exactly received an answer yet."

Ian glowers at him. "Have you exactly asked the question yet?"

"Of course." Thad shakes his head to emphasize his words. "But the brothers went back to South America right after I called. We've been playing telephone tag since they got back."

Fortunately for the man, his other work has been exemplary—good enough for me to think that, should need be, he'd make an excellent replacement for Ian. Otherwise, I would be tempted, at the least, to lash out at him. "That's not what I wanted to hear," I growl. "I suggest you get on the phone with the Ramirez brothers right now."

Thad nods but doesn't get up. "Leave!" I bark. He jumps from his chair and rushes from the room.

I look at Ian. "I want you more involved in this. If necessary, *you* call the Ramirez brothers. Just make sure we find out everything the DEA knows about Ouder Raad and do it quickly. Do you understand me?"

The thin man nods.

"Good," I say. "Now. I know how you are, Ian. I'm about to talk hardball with Arturo and Claudia. You're welcome to stay . . ."

"No." Ian waves his hand as if to dismiss the thought. "As

your attorney, I shouldn't know anything that might compromise my ability to defend you." He gets up and backs out of the room murmuring words of regret that he can't participate in such things, and promises of his loyalty and support.

Once he's gone, Arturo arches an eyebrow and says, "Yada, yada, yada."

We all laugh and then I turn to Claudia. "You sent someone to Curaçao and Bonaire, didn't you?"

She nods and holds up two fingers. "I sent two someones. Arty Levine went to Curaçao right after you asked me to send someone down there to check out Ouder Raad and VastenZeilen." Claudia shakes her head. "Arty's usually good, but something must have happened. We stopped hearing from him weeks ago. So I sent Sammy Dal down last week."

"And?" I say.

"So far Sammy has reported in every day. But all he knows about Arty is that the man can't be found and that all of his stuff was left in his hotel room. He did find Ouder Raad's office—near the harbor in Willemstedd. But none of the employees will talk to him about anything."

I swivel in my chair, my back to Claudia and Arturo, and stare at the marina, the blue sailboat's empty slip. "The *Anochi Yagdo*'s gone," I say. "I think Chloe may be on board. What's the chance of finding it on the open sea?"

"Not much," Claudia says. "We can put out word to be notified if it sails into a port and we can hire some planes to search for it, but there's a whole lot of water out there."

"I know. But I still want you to try."

I continue to stare at the empty slip. Aric seemed so confident of his power that I doubt he and the rest of his host have much concern about my ability to threaten them, certainly not enough to have their boat go into hiding. "Isn't Bonaire the *Anochi Yagdo*'s home port?" I say.

"Sure, Boss."

My phone buzzes. I turn back to my desk and pick up. "You have a call from Derek Blood," Marcia says. "He said you're waiting for it."

"In a minute," I say. I put the phone on hold and look at Claudia. "I think there's a good chance the damned blue sailboat is headed for Bonaire. I want Sammy sent there to wait and see if it shows up. And I want to know as soon as it does."

Claudia nods.

I wait until Claudia and Arturo leave and then pick up the phone. As soon as Marcia connects Derek's call, he says, "Okay, Peter, there are some matters we need to go over before Cili and I can give you any answer."

"Okay."

"You said one of them was killed. Cili asked if you can describe him."

I picture the dead creature lying on the bottom floor of my house, the pool of coagulated blood around him, and shake my head. "I can't really describe him but I was told his name was Danya something."

Derek talks away from the phone, his hand over the receiver, so all I can make out are the muffled sounds of a conversation. It continues for a few minutes and then Derek abruptly says, "His last name was Krovyanoy. I killed his bloody brother. Do you know if any member of the host is very old?"

"We think there's one. But he's only been seen by my people once."

A hand covers the receiver again and I endure another minute of muffled sounds before Derek returns to the line. "All right, old man, that takes care of it. Cili won't come."

"What? Wait a minute here," I say.

"No, you listen to me," Derek says. "You don't know what you're facing. That old one is Anatoly Krovyanoy, Burian and Danya's father. Cili says if he's with the host, it's for only one reason—the bloody bastard wants revenge. Their tradition calls for my death and the death of my child. Cili won't come if it puts our child at risk. . . ."

"So that leaves me facing them alone for something you did."

"No, I'll come. I certainly don't want to. You'll probably get us both killed, but I'll be in it with you—not for you or your money but because I want Anatoly Krovyanoy dead. Neither Cili or I want to spend our lives waiting for his next attack."

"I understand," I say. "I still appreciate your help."

"Appreciate what you want. You should want Krovyanoy dead too. Your wife killed his other son. He will want her to know how it feels to lose her family. He'll never allow her return to you. The council won't ever permit anyone to take a female's life, but they'll allow him that. They'll also be perfectly happy to allow him to kill you and Henri."

I suck in a breath at the thought that my son might be targeted too. "In that case, Krovyanoy's dead, no matter what."

"Good go, that," Derek says. "But, if you don't get us killed, I'll be most pleased to take care of the old codger myself. If you could get someone to arrange my travel plans, I'll be glad to get on the way."

*   *   *

Arturo and Claudia come back as soon as I call them. "Derek's in," I say. "But his wife is staying behind."

"Isn't she the whole reason they're doing this?" Arturo asks. "I know you don't want to hand her over, but we could use her here."

I frown, as much at myself as at him. Even with Derek's help, I can see no clear way we can defeat eleven of our own kind and rescue Chloe. "So what do you think we should do?" I say to Arturo.

He sighs. "Claudia and I were talking about it while you were on the phone. You know me. I like direct action. But you haven't told us the whole story here. . . ."

"There's only so much I should tell you . . ."

The man shakes his head. "I know. You don't have to bother to explain, Peter. Claudia and I both understand there are things that are best left unsaid." He stands and stretches, then walks toward the window and stares out at the harbor. "Is it safe to assume that you're not going to agree to their terms?"

"I don't think I could if I wanted to."

"Where does that leave Chloe? Do you think they're prepared to kill her?"

"No. They may make her unhappy but they have no desire to kill her," I say and then smile. "They did threaten to kill me, though—and all of you."

Arturo shrugs. "So let them try. They won't be the first who did. At least if we don't have to worry about Chloe's life—that makes things easier. Tell me as much as you can about what they want from you."

"They want my brother-in-law and his wife."

Both Arturo and Claudia look at me. "And they're like us, not you," I say.

"All of the ones in our surveillance pictures?" Claudia says.

I shake my head. "None of the crew but all the rest—except for one, who's no longer a problem."

"How many altogether?" Arturo says.

"Eleven."

"Wow," Claudia says.

Arturo walks from the window toward the door and back. He continues to pace, and finally stops after his fifth circuit of the room. He turns to me. "When do you have to answer them?"

"Tomorrow."

"Do you know what Derek's wife looks like?"

I let out a breath and think back to what my brother-in-law told me. "I don't know that much," I say. "She's tall—around six feet—and curvaceous, I think. With red hair down to the middle of her back."

The man exchanges a glance with his daughter. She nods. "Great," Arturo says. "When do you expect Derek to leave?"

"As soon as we arrange a ticket for him."

Arturo shakes his head. "Is there any reason we can't delay him a day?"

"I suppose not," I say, studying him.

"Good." The man grins. He looks at his daughter. "Then we'll buy two tickets, right?"

Claudia nods.

"And what are you both thinking?" I say.

"Just about buying us some time to put things together," Arturo says. "Didn't your father have a saying about how to react to a threat?"

I smile. "My father had sayings for everything," I say. "He said, 'If you know that someone's going to hit you, you would be a fool not to hit them first.' Is that the one you're thinking of?"

"Exactly." Arturo nods. "Which is what I think too. We have to discuss plans, and decide what you think Claudia and I and our operatives can accomplish, but I think we should hit them hard while they still think we might cooperate." The man looks at me, his face somber. "You do understand that as soon we take any action, the game is on?"

I nod. "Of course," I say. "To the death."

24

Arturo, Claudia and I spend a good deal of the rest of the afternoon discussing plans. Manny Padron calls somewhere in the middle of our discussions to inform us of Buddy Matherby's unfortunate demise and the cessation of any negotiations until his estate's settled—which drags out our meeting even longer. By the time I leave the Monroe Building, Bayshore Drive has already begun to fill up with early commuters trying to reach home before traffic clogs the road, and a pleasant drive turns into an irritating game of wait and crawl.

I pay little attention to the cars stopped at the light as I cross the road and walk toward the marina. Even if Claudia and Arturo do what they propose, I have no confidence that their plans will work. Like most humans, they have too much faith in their weapons. They heard that Chloe killed one of my kind with a 500 Magnum and they took it as a sign of our vulnerability. I remember the eight holes Chloe blasted through Danya Krovyanoy's armored scales and think how difficult we are to kill.

At my boat slip, I stare at the Donzi and sigh. The boat reminds me of both my missing wife and my Grady White, left anchored in open water, just east of the Gulf Stream. I look up at the late-afternoon sky, clear except for a slight tinge of gray from the Everglades fires, and see no hint of pending bad weather.

As fast and well built as the Donzi is, I usually only trust it for the calm waters of the bay. I have been in the Gulf Stream on days when the swells rose so high that nothing could be seen except for walls of water rising on each side of the boat and the sky directly overhead. While the Grady White can handle seas like that, I doubt the Donzi can.

I get on the boat, cast off and motor out of the marina. Everywhere I look, the water lies flat and calm. I shrug and turn the boat toward Key Biscayne and the channel that runs alongside it and out into the open ocean. On a calm day, the Donzi's as good as any other—and quite a bit faster than most.

When I reach about halfway across the bay, the blue inflatable comes into view, far south of me. I hold my course and watch it motor north, its nose forced out of the water by its speed, its motors spewing white foam behind its stern. Even though the boat could be out on the bay for reasons having nothing to do with me, I frown.

While the distance makes it impossible to identify their features, I can see that the boat carries four passengers today, including the one at the wheel—far more than I care to confront alone. I tap the Donzi's throttles back a bit. The boat slows and I adjust course toward the western end of Key Biscayne and grin. Should the inflatable choose to follow me, they'll learn a lesson about our local waters.

The inflatable maintains its course for a few minutes and then begins to angle toward me. I slow the Donzi even more and hold my course, as if I were out for a late-afternoon cruise. If anything, the inflatable appears to speed up.

By the time it nears, Key Biscayne looms large before me—one mansion after another lined up along a long, arcing shoreline that forms a wide, shallow C-shaped harbor bordered on its southeast by Mashta Island, a smaller island crowded with even grander mansions. I glance back at the inflatable and recognize the long, greasy hair of the person standing next to the man at the wheel. Aric Blut waves his hand. It could be an invitation to slow down to talk or a simple greeting.

I choose to treat it as a greeting. I wave back, turn my wheel and point the Donzi's bow toward the westernmost mansion along the island's waterfront. Behind me, the inflatable turns too. I nudge the Donzi's throttles forward—just enough to prevent it from catching up to me. But the inflatable's helmsman nudges his throttles forward too and we both race toward the mansion's concrete seawall.

The inflatable continues to gain on me and the mansion's seawall continues to draw nearer. Still I hold my speed and my course—my eyes on the rapidly diminishing distance between my boat and the seawall.

I nod when the inflatable finally draws close enough that the roar of its engines commingles with mine. With the mansion's seawall only a few dozen yards away—far too close at our speed—I throw the wheel to the right. The Donzi heels so hard that its port side rises in the air and its starboard almost buries itself in the water, and the boat skitters into a long, wide turn.

Behind me, the inflatable turns too, its turn wider, almost grazing the seawall before it follows completely in my direction. I slow again and let it gain on me while I straighten the wheel and aim for the western tip of Mashta Island. We shoot across the harbor, the inflatable drawing near me again just as we approach Mashta Island's shore.

"*Enough, DelaSangre,*" Aric Blut mindspeaks. "*We have much to talk about.*"

"*I thought we were going to talk later,*" I mindspeak and turn my wheel a hair to the right, so the Donzi will pass a dozen or so yards to the south side of the island. The inflatable, its bow almost close enough to touch the motors at my stern, once again turns with me.

"*We know you ordered tickets for them. Don't you think we should now discuss what will happen when they arrive?*"

I search the waters in front of me and grin when I locate the white diamond-shaped marker posted in the water only a hundred feet in front of me. "*I think you should learn to read markers,*" I mindspeak and slam my throttles all the way forward. The Donzi leaps ahead, its hull rising as it reaches its plane. It shoots across the shoals, just far enough out of the water to pass safely over the sharp rocks and shallows the white marker warns about.

Unable to go as fast or plane as high, the inflatable bumps over the shoals, its outboard motors bouncing at each impact with the bottom, sharp rocks shredding its tough fabric. It only manages to travel a few lengths before both motors stall and the boat begins to settle in the water.

"*DelaSangre!*" Aric mindspeaks.

I slow the Donzi as soon as it clears the shoals and turn to look back at the four men and their sinking inflatable. "*Sorry I can't stay to chat,*" I mindspeak. "*I have things to do. But I wouldn't worry if I were you. You're in shallows. You can walk to shore. We can talk tomorrow and make our plans then.*"

Aric mindspeaks, "*DelaSangre!*" again. I grin, turn the boat toward sea and throw the throttles forward.

By the time I return to my island in my Grady White, Chloe's Donzi in tow behind me, the sky has gone dark, its black expanse sprinkled with bright stars. I pause after both boats have been tied up at the dock and stare upward.

The dark sky tempts me. Too many weeks have passed since my last hunt. My empty stomach growls at the thought of fresh prey. But too many hours have passed since I last slept, too, and I already have to concentrate to keep my eyes open. While I prefer the excitement of the hunt and the taste of fresh human blood and meat, tonight I find the thought of a quick steak meal and then bed much, much more tempting.

And no matter all of my worries about Chloe and my children and the creatures that threaten us, sleep comes as soon as I rest my head on my pillow.

The twin mutters of matched outboard engines idling in my harbor penetrate the quiet of my bedroom. I open one eye, see the light in my room and glance at the clock on my nightstand. Almost noon. I groan. With no one to disturb the bed next to me, no children to make noise and no dog to come bounding into my room, I've slept half the day away.

I lie still, listen to the motors until they go quiet and then turn onto my back and stretch. Besides Chloe, Henri and me, only Claudia and Arturo know how to navigate the tortuous twists and turns of my island's channel. Most probably the outboards belong to Claudia's boat. Arturo's SeaRay's inboard motors make far less noise. Still, I make sure to stay within reach of at least one of the Smith and Wesson Magnums while I get out of bed and throw on a pair of cutoffs.

Claudia knocks on the door moments after I dress and says, "Boss? Are you in there?"

"Where else would you expect me?" I say, and open the door.

"With you, I'm never quite sure." She walks past me, studies my rumpled bed and turns. "Didn't think you'd sleep in with all that's going on."

I shrug. "I didn't either. I was up late doing some stuff with the boats. I guess I was just too tired to stay awake." I look at her. "Now why are you here?"

"When we didn't hear from you this morning, Pops asked me to come out. He's kind of leery about cell phones right now anyway. Thinks your friends from Ouder Raad are finding out too much too quickly."

"He's right to be concerned," I say. "After I left the office, I sort of ran into Aric Blut—or he ran into me." I smile at the memory of leaving him sinking into the water. "He already knew that we'd ordered the two tickets for Derek. . . ."

Claudia's eyes go wide and she sits on the corner of my bed. "How?" she says.

"You tell me."

She shakes her head. "Believe me, we're looking. So far Ian comes up clean."

"He's not the only one in the office. Who else would know about the tickets?"

"Pops and me, of course," Claudia says. She looks away, thinks for a few moments and turns back. "I had Marcia place the call to Hadley Travel for me, but I made all the arrangements with them. If the office phones were bugged they could have heard me . . . But we just had everything checked. It doesn't make sense."

I frown. "No, it doesn't."

"Fortunately, Pop insisted that the other arrangements—the ones for the redhead—had to be made away from the office and outside our usual channels."

"She's on the way?"

Claudia nods. "It wasn't easy finding someone to meet your description—a six-foot-tall, curvy redhead—but we did." She grins. "Though your brother-in-law might not be too thrilled when he finds out he's a female impersonator."

"What?"

"None of our female operatives are anywhere near that tall. Jimmy's done work for us before. He's a real redhead and gorgeous—and a great sailor too. Don't worry, he'll do fine. He'll arrive in time to join Derek at the airport and fly back here with him. He understands she's supposed to be Hungarian. Once he gets back here, he won't speak English anywhere in public."

"I'm not sure what we're going to do with him, once he gets here. He knows it's risky?"

"He knows he's getting a ton of·money," Claudia says. "He's not stupid enough to think we'd pay that much for anything safe."

"Good enough." I glance back at the clock. "What time will they be in?" I say.

"Ten. Tomorrow morning. At MIA."

"And Jimmy understands he's to listen to me and do as I say?"

"Of course." Claudia stands. "I brought out the extra ammo and guns and the other stuff you asked for. It's outside in the boat."

"Good. What about the rest?"

"Everything else we discussed has been put into action." Claudia walks toward the door and I follow her. "Toba's placing her package today. We already have a crew ready, working as valets at the Biltmore. Ian promises to have a report on Ouder Raad by tomorrow. And Sammy Dal's moved over to Bonaire. Pops says he thinks this whole thing may end up being kind of fun."

Just the thought of confronting eleven others of my kind makes me shudder. "Hardly," I say.

After Claudia leaves, I put everything in my bedroom and go out on the veranda. Like the day before and the day before that, barely any clouds float in the sky. I stare toward the mainland across the bay and frown at the multiple pillars of smoke rising in the west and the gray haze hovering over the land and the waters near it.

I sniff in a breath of air, and a second, and then nod. At least the smoke has not yet traveled far enough from the mainland to begin to taint the air out here. But I have more important things to do than worry about air quality. I suck in a breath and mindspeak, *"Aric. It's time to talk."*

A moment passes and then he mindspeaks, *"Yesterday it was time to talk. Today it is past time. My comrades and I did not find your little water joke to be very entertaining. If not for Cili, you would already be dead, DelaSangre."*

My lip curls. I am tired of this creature and his threats. *"You seem to assume that my death will be easy to bring about,"* I mindspeak. *"Maybe you should think that, if not for Chloe, you would be dead or dying right now."*

"In time perhaps we'll learn which one of us is right. For now you owe me some information."

"But you already know about the tickets," I mindspeak and walk farther out, across the veranda's oak deck to the short coral wall that rings it. *"Don't you know the rest?"*

"I will be glad when all this is done. I find you tiresome. What we already know is not your concern. Tell me, please, when and where they will arrive."

"First tell me about Chloe."

"DelaSangre, I have told you she is well. That is all you need to know. Trying my patience will not bring her home sooner. Please to answer my question."

I sigh and mindspeak, *"They're coming into Miami International at ten, tomorrow morning. I'm going to pick them up and bring them to my island."*

"Then we will visit you there after dark," Aric mindspeaks. *"It would be helpful if you could arrange to have your guests outside."*

I wish I could be in the creature's presence, just so he can see my glare and understand my sarcasm. *"That's just what I'm concerned with,"* I mindspeak. *"Being of help to you."*

25

Per usual, nothing happens on time at Miami International. I stand and pace and wait by the doorway at International Arrivals. Dozens of others wait with me, some chattering in Spanish or Creole, others conversing in English. Two dark-haired men, their eyes shielded by dark sunglasses, both about as tall as me, one's wide-shouldered body only a little thicker than mine, the other's thinner, wait toward the back of the room and speak to no one.

Visitors dribble through the doorway, sometimes one or two at a time and, at other times, in a steady stream, but Derek doesn't come through the doors until after eleven. Tall, blond and athletic-looking, except for his rumpled shirt and pants, he hardly shows any strain from flying halfway around the world. A statuesque and very attractive redhead, made even taller by her high heels, follows right behind him. She attempts to hold him by his arm but he shrugs her off.

{*Careful,*} I mindspeak to him. {*I think you're being watched. Treat her like Cili.*}

Derek looks around the room, sees me and smiles in my direction. He slows his pace and offers his arm to the red-head. {*Cili isn't a bloody ponce,*} he mindspeaks.

I step out of the crowd and grin at both of them. "Welcome to Miami," I say, shaking his free hand and kissing the redhead on her cheek. In the back of the room, the two dark-haired men turn and walk away.

In the car, Derek sits beside me and the redhead takes a seat in the rear. "You could have given a chap a break," he says and points to the rear seat, "and let me know what that one was."

"How many times do I have to tell you? My name's Jamie," the redhead says, her voice deep and sultry. "No one told him to come on to me. Believe me, I would have shut him down if he wasn't such a hunk. I mean, that wasn't what you were paying me for, was it?"

I grin and shake my head, pull out of my parking spot and begin to wend my way through the maze of garages that masquerade as a parking system at Miami International.

"So how was I to know no one told him about me?" she says. "So when he asked me to go to the restroom with him, I just assumed he was either into it or curious about it. You know?"

"I just wanted to pass some time," Derek says. "I mean, Cili wasn't around, and I thought she was a looker. At least, I did until I got her underpants down."

Jamie breaks out into a most unfeminine guffaw. "You should have seen his face! It was priceless." She regains her composure. "Fortunately he's not one of the ones that hits a girl when he finds out she's a little funny."

"A little funny?" Derek says. "Not bloody funny at all."

The redhead guffaws again.

I leave the last parking garage and pull behind a group of cars lined up to pay their parking fees at one of the parking attendants' stations.

Derek looks back at the redhead and shakes his head.

"Besides, old man, I don't know what you expected to accomplish. She doesn't look barely anything like Cili at all."

"Is there any reason they'd all know her human form by
sight?"

"Only the ones close to her family."

I shrug. "Then either they realized it wasn't her, or they
didn't. Personally, I think the ones watching in the waiting
area bought it."

"Maybe," Derek says.

A black Mercedes 500C pulls into the line two car
lengths behind us. "See the black Mercedes behind us?" I
grin. Derek swivels in his seat and stares at it. "They bought
it," I say. "No maybe to it."

The black Mercedes stays one or two car lengths behind
us all the way out of the airport. When I turn onto Ponce
DeLeon Boulevard heading south, it turns too. "I hope
you're hungry," I say. "We're going to the Biltmore for
lunch."

"Why don't we just go to your island? I'd be just as
happy with one of your steaks," Derek says.

Jamie slaps him on the shoulder. "Don't be silly. No one
turns down lunch at a place like the Biltmore."

We see the coral-painted main tower of the hotel, towering over the large trees that shade most of the roads in Coral
Gables, long before we see the rest of the hotel's buildings.
Built in 1926 and renovated recently, the Biltmore has the
look of a classical hotel and a deserved reputation for fine
lodging, fine food, excellent service and high prices.

Uniformed valets rush to the car's doors when we pull up
to the front. Derek and Jamie get out as soon as their doors

are opened. I pause and watch the Mercedes pull in, once again, a few car lengths behind us. Valets mob it too, and the two dark-haired men get out and walk quickly toward the entrance, without a glance backward.

I get out of my car and accept a claim check from the valet. He's a short dark-skinned Latino with a shaved head and a broad smile. "Thank you, sir. Don't worry, we'll take good care of it," he says, and winks. "Almost as good as we take care of that Mercedes back there."

We don't see the dark-haired men during lunch, but they come out of the hotel's front entrance just a few moments after we do. We leave before they get their car. Still, after only a few blocks, the black Mercedes pulls into the lane behind us. They stay with us all the way to Monty's marina and only drive away after they see us get on my Grady White.

But, near the end of the channel, we approach a white, twenty-five-foot Mako open fisherman anchored just yards outside the channel. One of the two men aboard rushes forward as we near and begins to pull up the anchor, while the other starts the boat's outboard engines.

Ordinarily I would pay no attention to a boat getting under way, but both men are tall and wide-shouldered, like the men in the Mercedes. I glance back after we pass them. The Mako begins to move, turning toward open water and then pointing in our direction and speeding toward us. I groan, nod my head in its direction and say to Derek, "I think it's two more of them. They seem to just want to be sure we're where we promised to be."

"Damned cheeky of them," he says.

At least the Mako makes no attempt to catch up with us. It stays back a few hundred yards and anchors well away from my channel when we motor in to my harbor. As soon as I pull up to the dock, Jamie gets out, high heels and all, and proceeds to tie off the boat's lines like a seasoned boater. Both Derek and I watch and when she finishes the last line she turns to us, hands on hips and says, "What? Can't a girl do something butch without everyone staring? I grew up down here. You name a boat and I can handle it. I've been sailing since I was a kid."

"Really?" I say.

"Who cares?" Derek says and steps off the boat.

I follow and mindspeak, masked. {*I care. I've been worrying about what to do with him. They've seen him arrive and come out here with us. We don't need him for anything else. He wouldn't last a minute in front of any of them . . .*}

Derek studies the redhead. {*There's plenty of meat on those bones. Why not throw him in one of your cells until we grow hungry? That would be a proper use for him.*}

{*I try to make a habit of not eating the help,*} I mindspeak. {*With the boat watching the channel I have no way of taking him to safety. And I'd rather not have him hide in the house, if possible.*}

"Jamie," I say, and glance over at the two Mistral windsurfers we keep on the dock. "Ever use one of them?"

Jamie looks at the Mistrals and shakes her head. "Do I look like a tourist?" she says. "Believe me, those are too slow. I own an Exocet. On a decent day I can blow those things away."

"Well one of our Mistrals will have to do today," I say, and explain what I want from him.

Except for the long red hair and fingernails, Jamie only has to remove his makeup and clothes to transform himself into Jimmy. He clips the fingernails himself but asks for help in cropping his hair. "I can't bear to cut it myself," he says. "You tell Claudia I expect something extra for this."

"Bloody rubbish," Derek says. He walks out of my bedroom and goes up to the great room to watch TV while I cut the man's hair and help him select one of my bathing suits.

Jimmy asks for a pillowcase and uses it to store his shorn hair. He places the pillowcase on top of his clothes and shoes and says, "Please make sure Claudia gets all this to me. I'll die if I lose it."

I walk with him to our island's beach and wait while he makes sure the Mistral's been set up correctly. Once the windsurfer's ready, he turns to me. "I'd be glad to stay and help with whatever's going on," Jimmy says.

"No. You did your part. Now we have to do ours," I say.

I call Derek downstairs as soon as I get back in the house and show him the guns. He shakes his head. "My claws and teeth are good enough for me," he says.

"We don't know how many are going to come out here tonight," I say. "The guns are just extra insurance."

Derek picks up one of the massive revolvers and spins its cylinder. It makes a ratcheting sound as it spins. He grins and shrugs. "What the hell. We might as well make some noise before we die."

26

Derek grumbles as soon as we take to the air. {*I feel like a fool,*} he mindspeaks. {*If we were meant to dress up like bloody cowboys, we would have a better way of wearing these damned things.*}

I nod and beat my way skyward, four Magnum revolvers in leather holsters suspended from crossed leather straps at the base of my neck. The holsters flap in the air and slap against my scales at each beat of my wings, and irritate me too. I only have to glance at Derek to remind me how ridiculous I must look, like a dragon imitating a Mexican bandito. Still, I mindspeak, {*Let there be more than two of them and you'll be glad you have these.*}

{*You forget. Cili and I had to fight against a host of them. There will be more than two and they will attack from more than one direction. They train high up, in the thinnest air possible. We need height more than we need to carry your heavy guns.*}

Neither of us say any more as we climb in tight spirals over Caya DelaSangre. On another night, I would ascend more slowly and savor the beauty of the dark, clear sky, the panoply of lights on the mainland and the awesome red-and-orange display of the flames now raging over the south-western corner of the Everglades. But tonight I climb as fast as I can, alert for any glimpse of a dark form gliding above or below us, and concerned about what might lie past any of the few dark clouds scattered in the sky.

Once the air turns frigid and almost too thin to breathe and my island has grown so small beneath us that it's hard to differentiate from the others, we level off. {*Do you think we should go lower?*} I mindspeak to Derek.

{*I wonder if we've gone high enough,*} Derek mindspeaks. {*In Greece, three of them fell on us from an altitude higher than this. If Cili hadn't finished hers quickly, you would have had a very dead brother-in-law.*} He shakes his head. {*Bad thought, that.*}

I say nothing and he adds, {*At least, I think so.*}

We say nothing more, just circle and wait and watch. Hours pass. The cold seeps into my scales and the thin air makes me feel light-headed and still we circle. I think of Chloe held somewhere far away, and my children living an alien life among the Pelk, and Cili living alone and with child in Australia and I wonder about my kind. We have so much wealth and so much power and still it does us so little good.

Derek adjusts course, just a bit. {*Below,*} he mindspeaks. {*Do you see something?*}

I alter course too and stare through the dark air, at the dark water and the dark islands beneath us. At first I see nothing. Then I catch a glimpse of something darker moving through the air far below me and then another form behind it and another. They fly in formation, a dark V soaring through the night. {*I count seven,*} I mindspeak.

Derek shakes his head. {*Too many. There's no shame in waiting for a better time.*}

{*And where would you run to now? They'll be at my island soon.*}

One wing of the V separates and spreads out, all four members of it flying in wide circles as they gain altitude. The other wing of three reforms into a small V and continues forward. {*Shit, bloody shit, they're flying higher to take a defensive position. It's going to bring them right into us,*} Derek mindspeaks.

The small V reaches Caya DelaSangre and I lose sight of it over the black mass of the island. Moments later, Aric mindspeaks, "*DelaSangre, my friend, have you forgotten our agreement?*"

"*How could I forget?*" I mindspeak.

"*Then where are you and your brother-in-law? Where is Cili?*"

Below me, the four warriors from the larger V climb closer. I growl into the thin air. I want no more talk. I want the smell of blood in the air. I want the yowls of injured foes to fill my ears. "*First you tell me—where is Chloe?*"

"*If this is a betrayal, you will never see her again.*"

"*As if you would have allowed it anyway,*" I mindspeak. I fold my wings and plummet.

{*Are you daft?*} Derek mindspeaks. {*There are four of them below you.*}

{*That makes it just two for each of us.*}

{*You are daft,*} Derek mindspeaks, and dives after me.

The wind whistles past me as I drop. It buffets me and batters all four holsters from one direction to another as if they held no guns at all. I reach with both front claws and attempt to grab two of the revolvers at the same time. Only the right one draws easily. The wind pushes the holster on the

left into an angle that makes the sight on the gun's barrel dig
into the leather and freeze it in place. I growl into the air and
tug on the revolver. With the lead warrior at best only two
thousand feet below me and approaching fast, I have little
time to waste on such things.

But no matter what angle I pull from, the gun remains
stuck in its holster. I sigh, and point the other revolver at the
lead warrior as I dive toward him—the creature's eyes so focused on the sky below him that he's unaware of my approach. I gasp at the breadth of his wingspan—the warrior
far longer, wider and bulkier than either me or Derek. Within
seconds my fall brings me close enough to fire.

The trigger barely resists when I pull on it and the gunblast shatters the night. The lead warrior bellows. I fire again
and again—four more shots in rapid succession before I
speed past him too fast to smell any blood or tell whether his
roars are from pain or surprise or both. Below me, the other
three warriors break formation and scatter.

{*Bloody lot of good you've done us,*} Derek mindspeaks,
masked. {*That's the end of any chance of surprise for me.*}

{*At least I got one of them . . . I think.*} I snap my wings
open, catch the air and rocket forward in a wide, shallow
turn to stop my descent.

{*Actually, I think you may have just irritated him.*} Derek
shoots pasts me, levels off a few dozen yards below me and
heads toward one of the other warriors. {*Look up.*}

I glance skyward just in time to see the lead warrior
hurtling toward me, his wings folded and his claws extended. Rather than waste time fumbling to put the spent revolver back in its holster, I drop the gun and grab the second
pistol with one claw while I wrestle it free from the holster

with the other. Once I have it out, I turn in midair and point it at my approaching foe.

"DelaSangre, why not fight with what nature gave you?" the lead warrior mindspeaks. *"Do you think a few more bullets will stop me?"*

From the look of it, obviously not. *"No,"* I mindspeak. *"But I think a lot of them might."* I hold my course and wait for the creature to close. Just before he reaches me, I fire all five bullets as rapidly as possible.

The creature yowls. He slams into me, and grabs for my throat with his teeth and my body with his claws. A gun barks somewhere near me, followed by bellows and growls and moans. I want to break free and help Derek but the lead warrior has the advantage in both size and weight. I block his fangs with my left forearm but he sinks his talons into my scales and hangs onto me, his full weight a sudden burden.

He drives his teeth through the scales on my forearm— all the way to the bone—and I bellow into the night air. My wings begin to ache from the effort of keeping both our bodies aloft. I know if I don't break free of his grasp soon, they will fail me. I growl and twist and turn, dropping my now empty gun, gouging at the creature's armored scales with my free claws, trying to find an opportunity to sink my teeth into him, the smell of our blood all around us.

"At least you're fighting like one of the Blood now," the lead warrior mindspeaks. *"Don't worry. It won't be long until this ends."* He opens his jaws, pulls his head back and thrusts it forward, toward my neck again. This time I block him with my mouth and lock my fangs against his, each of us bleeding, blood spraying into the sky.

More gunshots blast the air above us and a dark, still

form falls past us. {*Damn it, Peter. I could use some help up here,*} Derek mindspeaks.

{*Me too.*} I ignore the throbbing puncture wounds in my left forearm and reach with both front claws for the other two holsters holding the remaining loaded guns. But the creature presses his body against mine, as close as he can, and pins them beneath his bulk. To do anything, I have to break his hold on me—if only for a moment.

I fold my wings and let us drop. Even though our speed increases with each passing foot and the earth looms closer every second, the warrior continues his relentless attack, readjusting his mouth and bearing down on mine until my teeth ache and our blood runs down my throat and threatens to choke me. As much as I rip and bite back, his teeth and claws never stop moving. I roar and gouge with my hind claws in return, but it does little good. All I can do is push against him and hope our fall ends before he reaches any of my vital organs.

We plummet past the remaining three warriors as they make their way skyward to join the fray. {*Derek, there are more coming,*} I mindspeak.

Two more gunshots sound out far above me. {*And what do you expect me to do about that?*} he mindspeaks.

Before I can answer, the lead warrior mindspeaks, "*Fool, there is only water beneath us. What good will our fall do you?*"

A lot, I think. I look down at the dark bay only a few hundred feet below us and rushing closer. "*Obviously you've never hit water at high speed,*" I mindspeak. An instant later we slam into the water at over a hundred miles an hour, the lead warrior beneath me.

He hits first, the water unyielding at first, turned hard by our speed. The impact makes him blast a giant huff of air from his lungs and lose his grasp on me. Shielded from the impact by his body, I gasp in a final breath and shove him away before our momentum carries both of us down, beneath the surface.

The warrior ignores the water around us, grabs for me and seizes me again even as we shoot toward the bottom. I push against him, kick and gouge with three of my claws while I search for a full holster with the other. He only tightens his grip and lunges for my throat again. I throw up my wounded left forearm to block him but lack the strength to hold him back.

His teeth pierce my throat's thick scales and pain shoots through me. My muscles ache with exhaustion. To slow my bleeding, I force myself to think past all of it and tighten the veins and arteries and capillaries that lead to my wounded areas. But I need more energy, more nourishment, to heal any of my wounds. Even worse, if we continue to struggle like this, my lungs will soon begin to burn from their need for fresh air.

We strike bottom, soft sand breaking our descent. The softness tempts me. I don't see how I'm going to defeat this creature. I've already fired ten bullets at him. At least half had to have hit him. He is simply too big and too powerful for me. If not for Chloe and the children, I would be tempted to surrender. How easy that would be, how simple to lie down, breathe in water and be done with the pain, the worry and the struggle.

Despite his wounds, the warrior seems not to have weakened at all. He maintains his hold on me—as tight as before—and pushes off from the bottom as hard as he can. But, instead of just letting our natural flotation raise us, he thrashes his tail and kicks frantically to speed our ascent. I wonder how desperate he must be for air. After all, he had no opportunity to gasp a breath before we sank like I did.

To slow our rise, I spread my legs out and let my weight go dead. Rather than fight my movements or tighten his hold on me any further, the warrior kicks even harder to compensate for my resistance—a small space opening between our bodies. I jam a claw into the space and squeeze and push it upward in search for one of the revolvers.

I touch leather first and then an empty holster before I feel the hard rubber surface of a gun grip. I squirm and twist and work my claw around it until I finally take hold of the entire grip. I tug on it. Nothing happens and I groan. His bulk still blocks me from drawing the revolver. I can only hold on and wait for an opportunity to occur while we rise toward the surface.

None comes. We break through the surface together, the fresh air suddenly cool on our wet scales. The lead warrior releases my throat and gasps in a huge breath. As much as I yearn to fill my lungs too, I shove against him instead—as hard as I can.

The warrior seems not to notice. He gasps in another breath and then another. I butt him again and yank on the revolver at the same time, freeing it from the holster. He gags, as if his deep breaths have taken down some water along with the air, and he whoops out a cough, his body convulsing as he hacks out another cough and another. I shove against him again. It barely moves him but it frees just enough space for me to turn the gun, where it's wedged between us, and point it upward.

He coughs again and I shove the revolver further up, pushing and working it from side to side until the tip of its barrel presses against the soft underside of his jaw. The warrior finally calms his lungs and sucks in another breath. I pull the trigger.

The gunblast deafens me and vibrates through my body—as if an explosion has gone off between us. The warrior stiffens, but still he tightens his hold and drives his teeth and claws deeper into me, his teeth perilously close to the arteries in my neck. I fire again and his bite weakens. I fire again and again and again.

He finally goes slack. I growl and shove at his body again. This time it floats away and I sigh and drop my empty gun. Finally free of the warrior's grasp, I tilt my head and breathe in the sweet night air, the fresh, sweet night air. The dark sky above me seems devoid of any sign of Aric or the rest of his host. I gasp in one breath after another, tread in place and stare at the empty sky.

Its apparent emptiness hardly reassures me. As best as I can tell, Derek and I have eliminated only two of the seven warriors so far. I have one gun with five shots left, obviously not enough to take down even one of my kind, and I have no idea how many guns Derek has or what condition he's in.

{*Derek, are you okay? How are you doing?*} I mind-speak.

{*How do you think, with five of them out there? I'm hiding under some trees on some tiny island south of yours. You took your bloody time, didn't you now?*}

The irritating creature wouldn't think to ask after my welfare. I slap at the water. {*Look, it's not like I was holding back. You should have seen the size of the one I was fighting. For a while, I didn't think I was going to get out of it at all.*}

{*He was big, but at least you had just one of them. I had all the rest. Fortunately, after I shot the one out of the air, the*} *rest kept a wary distance. But when the other three joined them, I decided that retreat was the only sensible option.*}

{*You're probably right,*} I mindspeak.

"*DelaSangre? Are you out there or has Sorin already killed you?*" Aric mindspeaks.

"*Sorry, but I'm afraid you have that backward.*"

"*I am truly impressed. Even with your guns, I didn't think that we would lose two of us. Certainly not without Cili in the air with you. I understand Derek defeating Hagop. He was the least of us. But Sorin was formidable. There will be sorrow in Romania when they learn of it.*"

My wounds throb. My body aches for sustenance and time to rest and heal. A moan begins to escape my lips. I cut it off and look up at the dark. Only moments later, something dark flits by, just at the edge of my peripheral vision. I suck in another breath and dive beneath the water.

Something strikes the surface just where I'd just treaded water and I dive deeper. Two other splashes follow. "*Your brother-in-law has run away and gone into hiding, but we can take turns diving here for you,*" Aric mindspeaks. "*How long do you think you can stay down there before we find you or you run out of air?*"

As weary as I am, as in need of healing, the last thing I want is to change shape. But I see no choice. I concentrate on the lessons that Lorrel taught me and pull in my arms and legs and smooth my scales. "*Two of yours are dead and floating in the water. How long do you have before daylight comes and humans discover them?*" I mindspeak, my legs fusing into a powerful fluke, my arms turning into fins, my skull growing bulbous.

Without a thought, I send out a series of clicks and sense their return and read my surroundings as any dolphin would, the nearest of Aric's warriors swimming only a few dozen yards away. As much as I would like to butt him with my hard snout, I know such strange behavior from a dolphin would prove too suspicious. I dart away with a flick of my tail.

"*DelaSangre!*" Aric mindspeaks.

My change in shape has used up precious energy and done nothing to heal my wounds. I need to sound and take in fresh air. I need to rest. I ignore Aric and concentrate on making my body function well enough to swim far away from him and his warriors.

{*What about me?*} Derek mindspeaks. {*How long am I supposed to crouch under these bloody trees?*}

I suppress a growl. {*No one is making you stay there. Hide as long as you want or don't hide at all. I'm sure Aric would love to see you.*}

{*Really, Peter. What can I do?*}

{*If you think you can find your way and you stay mostly underwater, you can swim to the island . . .*}

{*What bloody good would that do? They could have warriors waiting for us.*}

{*On the land or in the sky, maybe. But not underwater. You remember the Pelk safehold under my island, don't you?*}

{*I remember your saying there was one. I never saw the damned thing.*}

{*It's not anything like as large as the one on Andros but we can stay there in safety—even if Aric and his warriors are at the house. I doubt they know that safeholds or the Pelk exist anymore at all. We can raid the food stored there and rest and heal as long as we need.*}

{*You mean as long as we can stomach their awful dried fish.*}

My stomach growls at the thought of any type of food at all. Even something as rancid and unpleasant as the Pelk's dried fish will give me the nourishment I need to replenish my energy and heal my body. I stop swimming for a moment and let my body glide through the water. {*Look, Derek, I don't care if you eat it or not. I don't care if you come or not. The entrance is underwater, near the rock jutting into the Wayward Channel.*} I flick my tail again and pain shoots through my body. {*I can't go on much longer without food and rest. Once I get there, I'll wait for you for a half hour. After that you're on your own.*}

{*Awfully cold of you, old man.*}

I sigh. {*That's the best I can do for now.*} I angle up to the surface, blow the spent air out my blowhole and suck in fresh air. Something large, one of the warriors I assume, splashes into the water a few hundred yards behind me. Aric mindspeaks, "*It won't be long, DelaSangre. We see you now.*"

"*Aric, trust me, you don't. Neither you nor your warriors will find me tonight,*" I mindspeak. I turn toward home and wince at the pain the movement brings. "*But I promise, I will come for you soon enough.*"

27

{*Found it,*} Derek mindspeaks, while I'm still at least a mile from my island.

I nod in the water, glad to know I won't have to wait for him once I finally get there. An incoming tide has already made my slow journey even slower. {*I won't be there for a bit longer,*} I mindspeak. {*No need for you to wait for me.*}

{*Who said I would? I'm already inside the bloody thing, banging around in the dark, looking for some glow powder.*}

{*Feel your way to the back wall. There are wood chests there. You should find some inside a few of those.*}

{*Right-o.*} Derek goes quiet and, as much as I ache to rest, I continue to force myself forward. With an incoming tide at my nose, any attempt to stop will only result in my being carried back, away from my destination.

{*Ah, good, found it right where you said. I'm mixing it in the glowpool now. Adding a little bit more . . . This is small, isn't it?*}

{*There's an alcove farther on. That's the one that leads to the harbor entrance.*}

{*Still, it's all fairly basic—nothing like the safehold on Andros. Where did you say they keep the dried fish?*}

I growl into the water. {*I didn't say,*} I mindspeak.

{*No matter. It has to be in one of the other chests.*} Derek goes silent again for a minute or two and then mindspeaks. {*You certainly don't have to rush here before I eat your share of food. They have chests full—slab after slab of dried fish here.*}

My stomach growls, but I ignore it and Derek's words. I only have the strength to focus my mind on one thing, and the incoming tide is more than enough for me right now. It tugs at me, tries to force me back, and I fight to move my flippers and tail enough to make headway against it. To make matters worse, each movement I make seems more difficult and painful than the last.

{*What is keeping you so bloody long anyway?*} Derek mindspeaks.

I ignore him and continue with my struggle against the tide.

{*I thought you'd be here already. You wouldn't have figured out somewhere better to go than this hole in the ground, would you have, old man?*}

Right now, just the image of sharing a small space with such an irritating creature as my brother-in-law seems more than I can bear. If I could, I would surely go to any other place possible. {*There is no other place, you asshole,*} I mindspeak. {*I'm going slow because that oversize warrior of Aric's tore more holes in me than I thought I could handle—and because I used up whatever energy I had left changing from my natural form into a dolphin's . . . and because there's an incoming tide which, in my current state, seems bent on carrying me all the way back to the mainland.*}

{*No need for you to get personal, old man. I've never called you any names.*}

{*True.*} I sigh. {*I just can't chat with you right now.*}

{*I understand, old man. I really do.*}

To my relief, Derek says nothing more. Rather than think of the whole distance remaining, I ignore everything around me and concentrate on swimming the next yard and the yard after that, keeping a count of one completed, then two, then three—almost hypnotized by the endless rhythm of flipper stroke after stroke after stroke.

At two hundred and twenty-seven yards, my snout bumps into a large slab of dried fish made moist by the salt water. I almost let it pass by me and Derek mindspeaks, masked. {*Eat the vile thing, you bloody fool. Do you think I came out here to dine in front of you?*}

His words shock me back to awareness. I lunge at the slab and take the largest bite I can. It *is* vile, old and rancid and still stiff, despite its recent immersion in water, but I still gulp it down.

The tide begins to carry me back and Derek grabs me by a flipper. {*No need for you to fight against the tide so much,*} he mindspeaks, and pulls me forward. {*When I'm here to help you.*}

With Derek's help and the small energy boost provided by the slab of fish, we travel the rest of the way to the Wayward Channel, on the north side of Caya DelaSangre, in less than fifteen minutes. I sigh when we reach the irregular zigzag hole cut through the island's stone side, twenty feet below the surface. Tonight I find it as welcoming as the lights I usually leave shining through the great room's windows.

I ignore my pain and exhaustion and jet forward in front of Derek. {*No need to rush, old man,*} he mindspeaks. {*The*} *same amount of food will still be there no matter how quickly we arrive.*}

{*Sure, but it won't be in my stomach until I get there.*} I speed through the narrow stone tunnel and the square shaft rising from it, scraping my hide against the irregular stone, opening wounds that have just recently closed. None of it matters to me—only thoughts of food and rest.

I break through the surface of a small, circular underground pond, blow my lungs clear and suck in air. The green glow of a glowpool illuminates the cave and I balance on my fluke, my head out of water and examine the area. Moments later Derek pops up next to me. {*Time to change form, old man,*} he mindspeaks, clambering out of the water onto the cave's rock floor. {*Or would you rather I toss fish to you here?*}

He may have said it sarcastically, but I worry whether I have enough energy left to shift form again. {*It wouldn't be a bad idea to let me eat a little more fish before I change,*} I mindspeak.

Derek shrugs and ambles back to the wooden chests by the cave's rear wall. He returns with two translucent slabs of dried fish, tosses one toward me, dunks the other in the water and then begins to eat it.

I finish mine as quickly as I did the last and then, just as quickly, I concentrate on my body, growing scales and shifting to my natural form before Derek finishes the last of his fish. Though it hurts more than I care to admit, I pull myself from the water and stand in front of him, blood-pinked water dripping from my scales, my body wavering from the effort.

My brother-in-law pauses his meal and studies me, his eyes going from wound to wound. Finally he shakes his head and mindspeaks, {*What? No dolphin tricks?*}

{*Not a one.*} I stumble past him, go to the wooden chests and pull out seaweed blankets and slab after slab of dried fish. I carry all of it back by the water and form a nest out of the blankets. After it's done, I pile the slabs of fish next to it and lie down in the nest and rest on one haunch.

As desperately as I'd like to sleep, I force myself to pick up a slab of fish and immerse it in the water. After only a few seconds, I pull it out and take a huge bite from it.

{*It takes more time than that to soften,*} Derek mind-speaks.

I nod and swallow and crunch out another bite. {*That's all the time I'm willing to give it for now.*} It takes me only four bites to consume the slab, and I gulp down three more slabs just as quickly. Exhaustion washes over me and I find it impossible to resist lying down and curling my body so it nestles into the seaweed blanket nest. {*I'm going to sleep now and try to heal. Please let me rest,*} I mindspeak. {*I'll wake when I'm ready.*}

Sleep comes so quickly that however Derek answers, whatever he says is lost to me.

28

At first, I dream of long fruitless hunts that leave me hungry and exhausted, and of disastrous battles that leave me racked with pain and unsure of my abilities. Worse nightmares come after that—my wife and children taken away before my eyes, my house and company destroyed, Derek ripped open and left to bleed to death, Arturo and Claudia murdered.

Sometimes Aric mindspeaks to me—or I dream he does—his words garbled by my sleep. I never answer. I groan and twist and turn in my bed of seaweed. Reassuring sounds murmur near me and someone rearranges the blankets.

Later, my sleep calms and turns dreamless. I have a sense of Derek at sleep near me at times, and of the cave going dark and empty at others. I move and feed when necessary, never fully wakening, my pain lessening, my wounds closing as my continuing nourishment bolsters my power to heal.

When I reach for another slab of fish and find none there, I sigh and open my eyes. The glowpool has gone dim, its feeble green light barely illuminating the cave. I sit up and look around.

A jumble of seaweed blankets, arranged not far from my

own seaweed nest, has to be Derek's but I neither see him in the cave nor hear him in the alcove. I could mindspeak to him, but my empty stomach growls. I shrug and look around for a bag of glowpowder. If my brother-in-law doesn't show himself before I grow too bored with my solitude, I can contact him then. In the meantime, I'm far more interested in finding another slab or two of dried fish.

The glowpool has turned bright and my stomach has been filled by the time I hear Derek clamber into the cave's alcove. {*Using the harbor entrance, are you?*} I mindspeak.

{*No reason not to. Not another bloody soul on this island except for you and me.*} Derek pokes his head through a crevice at the far end of the wall and squeezes his body through, a Pelk trident grasped in one foreclaw. {*Good thing that. I don't know how much longer I could sit in this damnable hole watching you sleep.*}

I look at him. {*How long has it been?*}

{*Over three days,*} Derek mindspeaks. {*Three days of watching you toss and turn—moaning and groaning like you were near death.*} He shakes his head. {*I never saw a grown being carry on so over a few wounds.*}

{*A few wounds?*} I glare at my insufferable brother-in-law. But then I remember the reassuring sounds I'd heard and the constant rearranging of my bed during my long sleep. {*And yet you helped me,*} I mindspeak. {*Why?*}

{*I didn't have much choice, now did I? For all I knew Aric and his bloody host were all waiting out there, ready to slice us to pieces. As long as I was stuck here with you, it was the only way I thought I could get you to quiet down. A chap has to get some sleep, doesn't he?*}

{*Of course.*} I grin at him. {*You looked after me just so you could sleep.*}

Derek looks away, as if he were caught doing something wrong. {*I didn't chance going topside until after dark yesterday. I've been up a few times since.*} He turns his eyes toward the cave roof. {*It will be dawn soon. It would be nice to go up in time to see the sun rise.*} He toys with his trident, spearing the seaweed blankets in his nest with its three sharp tips and flipping them over.

{*And the trident?*}

{*I found a good half dozen of them propped up against a wall in the alcove.*} Derek turns, grins at me and cuts an arc in the air in front of him with the trident—the way a Pelk warrior would. {*I rather liked taking it with me when I went up top. I didn't have any of your guns left and, even if I did, I had no bullets.*} He points the trident toward me. {*See how proper sharp these tips are? I think if any of Aric's warriors had been up at your house, this would have done at least as good a job on them as your bloody guns did.*}

I nod. The Pelk use tiger shark teeth inlaid in each tip of their tridents. I know all too well how easily they can cut through my kind's armored scales, how sickening it feels to be sliced open with one simple sweep of the weapon. Certainly it would give any of Aric's warriors a very nasty surprise.

{*Good idea,*} I mindspeak. {*I'll take one with me too.*}

As soon as we emerge from the cave's harbor entrance in the mangroves at the far side of the harbor, I wrinkle my nose at the bitter smell of smoke that permeates the air. {*The swamp fires in the Everglades must be intense for the smoke to reach out here.*}

Derek shrugs. {*There are other things that might upset you more.*}

{*My house?*}

{*No problem there, old man. I mean, they were obviously inside. But they only tussled things up a bit in the great room—drank some of your Dragon's Tear wine and ate some of your steaks. They did go through your bedroom though and muck around with all of your and Chloe's clothes . . .*}

{*So? I can always buy new clothes,*} I mindspeak.

{*True—and you can always buy new boats too.*} Derek points across the harbor to the dock. {*But I don't think you'll be very happy about it.*}

I gape through the predawn dark at the empty dock, my Grady White and Chloe's Donzi nowhere in sight. {*What the hell?*} I mindspeak.

Derek grasps my forearm and tugs me toward the house. {*Come. Let's go inside. Just because none of Aric's warriors are in sight doesn't mean that one might not fly by at any moment.*}

I shift to my human form as soon as I enter the house, and allow myself the luxury of a long, hot shower before I do anything else. The sun has risen and spread its light across the bay and the mainland by the time I dress and go up to the great room.

Derek has yet to come up. I walk to the bayside window, look out over the water and frown. A light layer of foggy smoke mutes the customary brightness of the morning sunlight, but I still have no trouble spotting my Grady White where it lies, half sunk, sitting on the submerged rocks outside the middle of the channel to my island.

"I told you, you wouldn't be happy," Derek says. He walks up and stands beside me and points to the water a few dozen yards from the end of the channel. The sharp bow of Chloe's Donzi juts only a few feet into the air—the rest of the boat is submerged below the surface.

"I don't get them," I say. "They could have trashed the house but they just took some of my clothes and most of Chloe's. So why the hell did they have to sink the boats?"

He shrugs, goes to the freezer and takes out four steaks. "Now what?" he says.

Just the sight of real meat brings saliva flooding into my mouth. After nothing but dried fish I could care less whether it's frozen or fresh as long as it tastes of real flesh and blood. "For now, why don't you warm the steaks?" I say. "Afterward we can discuss how we plan to teach our European friends how inhospitable we can make things for them."

Derek arches an eyebrow. "That said by one who just spent three days hiding in a cave while they slept in comfort," he says.

"Just put the steaks in the microwave," I growl. I pick up my cell phone, turn it on and stare at the blinking messages icon. "I have a call I have to make."

Claudia picks up her phone on the third ring. "Boss, am I glad to hear from you," she says. "I haven't been able to sleep worth a damn. After you didn't return our calls, Pop and I weren't sure whether something happened to you or not."

"Something happened, but nothing I couldn't handle." Derek punches a button on the microwave and the aroma of warm meat and blood fills the great room. I swallow hard before I continue. "And you and your father have everything ready?"

"Everything's been ready. You know that."

"Good," I say. I check my watch and nod when I see it's not yet seven. "Can you handle the first part now?"

"There's a lot more we need to go over. Pop had some of our people run financial reports on everyone at LaMar who would have known about both the Matherby deal and the plane tickets for Derek and Jamie. Ian came back clean. Thad did too, though he's recently accelerated his payoff of his student loan and credit card debt. It's nothing he can't afford on his current rate of pay and Pop likes him—at least, he likes him a hell of a lot more than Ian—but he's uncomfortable with the guy's recent rate of payoff. He wants you to come to the office to go over that and a bunch else as soon as you can."

"That's another problem. I'll need you to come get us." I tell her about the boats.

"I'll pick you up by nine," Claudia, says. "And I bet we can have a new Grady White at your dock before you go home."

Even though she can't see, I nod. "Now tell me," I say. "Can you do the first part this morning?"

No answer comes for a few moments and then Claudia says, "You sure you don't want to talk to Pops first?"

I scowl and spit my words. "Claudia, I want to send a message. The rest can wait until we all talk but for now—tell me if your people can pull it off this morning."

"I think so . . . if he didn't go in early to his office."

"Then do it."

"Then what about the rest?"

I sigh. "Not yet. We can discuss it at the meeting."

*   *   *

My cell phone rings just as I'm about to eat the last piece of my second steak. I answer it and Claudia says, "Put on Channel Seven, quick. The game's on."

I grab the remote, click on the TV and put it on seven. An overhead shot, obviously from a helicopter, fills the screen—the camera focused on three police cars and an ambulance parked in the circular drive of a large, very expensive home, their doors ajar and their lights still blinking. The policemen themselves are gathered around a long-haired woman wearing a long, white robe. Two white-uniformed men kneel by a body lying in the driveway, a sheet already spread over it.

". . . when Grey didn't return with his morning *Herald*, his wife went outside to look for him," the newscaster says. "She found him lying in the driveway next to it. The police report he died from two gunshot wounds to the head. They say that, as of this time, there are no suspects."

The newscaster goes on to talk about Holden Grey's legal reputation and his many courtroom triumphs. At the end of the report he says, "Channel Seven has heard from our sources that this has all the marks of an underworld hit. Though Holden Grey has a sterling record, he has represented a number of less than sterling clients. Our sources say that Mr. Grey may have displeased one of them."

Claudia makes a satisfied grunt into the phone. "Good," she says. "Pops wanted them to put that in. He says it might make his partners worry, make them a little suspicious of their new clients, like Ouder Raad."

"Under any circumstances it should slow down all of Ouder Raad's deals for a while," I say.

"I don't know for how long, Boss," Claudia says. "Remember what your dad said."

I smile and nod. My father never hid his disdain for the legal profession. *"They're like cockroaches,"* he said. *"You can never be sure, whether you step on one or a hundred of them, that you got the last of them."*

After I disconnect the call, I walk over to the bayside window and stare across the water, toward the mainland far to the west. I frown at the gray haze that hangs over all of it and limits my view of even the largest condos and high-rises. Without them to use as landmarks, I find it more difficult to locate Gables Estates on the horizon.

"Aric," I mindspeak.

"What the bloody hell are you doing?" Derek rises from his seat at the table. "Haven't you heard of letting sleeping dogs lie?"

I shake my head. "My father believed in destroying those things that threatened him, not ignoring them," I say. "He also said it's best to confront threats before they confront you."

I mindspeak again, *"Aric. Answer me."*

"DelaSangre. So sorry about your boats, but at least we didn't leave you sinking in the middle of the bay—like you did to us, no? I'm so glad you've decided to come out of hiding."

"I've decided it's time for us to meet again."

"Oh? Tonight, after dark, in the sky by your island again? Or did that not work out as well as you liked?"

"This afternoon at Monty's would be fine. If you haven't heard, you've lost your attorney."

"We were notified. It is a small inconvenience, no more. He will be replaced by another human. Really, DelaSangre,

would it be of much consequence to you if we killed your Mr. Tindall?"

I smile at the thought. If only Aric knew how many times I was tempted to order such a thing myself. *"You've lost three warriors so far,"* I mindspeak. *"We've lost no one. I would count that as more than an inconvenience for you."*

"You forget. We have your wife."

Just Aric's reminder of Chloe's situation makes me clench my fists. *"I haven't forgotten for a moment, not for a second,"* I mindspeak. *"I expect her to be returned unharmed as you promised."*

"You misunderstood my words. You must learn to listen, my friend. I said she would not be killed. Whether she's harmed or not rests on your head. No, I will not meet with you at Monty's or anywhere else. I will not tolerate any more of your arrogance and foolishness.

"You were fortunate in our last encounter. Do not expect to survive the next. You will bring to us our Cili and we will return to you your wife. Do anything less, fight us in any other way, delay too much longer and I promise you—your wife will suffer more pain than she ever thought she could survive."

Aric says no more, nor do I answer him. I stand still and stare at the bay and the smoky sky, and try to push away images of my wife ripped open and bleeding and in agony. I shake my head. I can't allow such a thing to happen and I have no idea how to prevent it.

"Bollocks!" Derek says. "It's an empty threat. They won't torture someone who may become one of their mates."

I turn and look at him. "What makes you so sure of that? Would you risk that for Cili?"

He looks down and speaks, his voice no longer quite as confident. "It doesn't make sense for them to hurt her. Even if they do, Chloe's a strong girl. I'm sure she can handle it."

"I don't want her to have to handle anything," I growl. "I want this over. I want my family back."

"I understand, old man. Remember, I have a wife I want to return to myself."

"I know," I say. "But how do we finish this?"

Derek shrugs. "You should know better than to ask me something like that. Thinking has never been my strong suit."

29

Claudia stares up from her blue speedboat at the tridents that Derek and I both carry. "Aren't those a bit primitive?" she says. "What happened to the guns I brought you?"

I think of all the revolvers that Derek and I used and dropped during our battle with Aric's warriors, and the watery resting place they've found. Claudia would be horrified with the waste. "Don't ask," I say, and step into her boat. "For now, we just think these may be of some use." Derek nods and follows me onto the boat.

"Any word on the *Anochi Yagdo* yet?" I say to Claudia.

"Nope. I talked to Sammy Dal this morning. No sign of it yet in Bonaire," she says, pushing her boat's throttles forward, turning the craft toward the channel. I sit next to her while Derek sits on the boat's stern bench.

"Too bad." I sigh. "The boat should have been fast enough to reach port by now."

"Don't know what to tell you, Boss. All we can do is wait."

"Which has never been my favorite thing," I say.

Claudia grins. "Not mine either."

"Will everyone at least be at the office?"

She nods.

"Can you get Jamie to come in too?" I ask.

Derek groans. "Not that ponce again."

I grin at him. "Decked out again, too. Remind her she's a Hungarian woman who can't speak English."

"No problem, Boss," Claudia says. "Though thanks to the way you butchered his hair, he'll have to wear a wig." She pulls her cell phone out of her bag with one hand while she steers with the other.

I ignore Claudia's phone conversation and study the water and the sky. The thin layer of smoke that blankets the bay obscures any vision of anything more than a half mile away and blocks much of the sunlight warming the day. I wrinkle my nose at its rank aroma. If not for the smell, it could be taken for fog. Unfortunately, no sun can burn through this gloom.

Far off in the distance, at the very edge of where the smoke closes off any further view, the shadow of a boat appears. It grows in definition as we draw closer to each other, the metal struts of its fishing tower finally coming clear just moments before the boat passes only a few hundred feet from us, the drumming of its diesel motors filling the air. It slowly fades from view again as it draws away, the boat disappearing into the smoke before the sound of it fades from our ears.

"Spooky, that," Derek says.

I nod and stare toward the mainland and wait for the first glimpse of its buildings to loom into view.

Claudia puts away her phone. "Jamie's on," she says. "She should be at the office in about an hour." The girl grins. "She said you should remember—a girl usually needs more time than that to get ready."

"Remember my ass. I don't see why we need her anyway," Derek says. "It's not like she can be of much help."

"I don't know," I say. "I'm not sure if we can use her or not. But, for the time being, if Aric still thinks she's Cili, then she might be useful."

Another boat's shadow emerges from the smoky air at the far edge of our vision. This time its features take longer to come into view. "Probably anchored and fishing," Claudia says.

I nod, but I wonder what type of fool would anchor in the midst of such unpleasant conditions. Not that I haven't seen fishermen endure rain and storm and cold before—just for the possibility of hooking some unwary fish. Still, I have trouble turning my eyes from the boat. I watch it come more fully into view as we near it.

Much smaller than the craft that passed us before and anchored as Claudia suggested, it holds three men. All of them seem oblivious to our approach, more concerned with the rods in their hands than anything else around them. But the boat looks as if it's white and I find it disturbingly familiar.

"Is that a Mako?" I say.

Claudia stares at it for a moment, then says, "Could be. We're still too far to see its logo."

"You have your gun?"

The girl turns and looks at me, her eyes wide. "You sure? There are a hell of a lot of Makos on the bay."

I glance back at the boat and the three fishermen, and shrug. "I don't know," I say. "But it can't hurt to have it out."

"In the purse," Claudia says. "My Desert Eagle. Be careful where you point it. It's not quite as powerful as your revolvers but it's still a fifty cal. Don't want you blowing any holes in my hull."

"If I use it, it won't be your boat I'll blow holes in," I say.

I reach into her bag, pull the semiautomatic out, pull its slide back and rack a bullet into the chamber.

The three fishermen should have begun to hear our motors but none even glances in our direction. I stare at them for a few minutes, then say, "Maybe I'm being a bit too cautious here."

Claudia shrugs. "Like you said—it can't hurt. If you want, I can call Toba and see if Ouder Raad's white Mako is at their dock in Gables Estates."

"She's there now?" I say.

"Every day, until we change her assignment." Claudia picks up her cell phone. "Should I?"

I nod.

The girl dials, talks for only a moment and disconnects. "Not there," she says. "That doesn't mean this one's it." Still, she taps the throttles forward and adjusts course so we'll race by further off the Mako's beam.

Almost immediately after we change course and speed, the three fishermen drop their rods. One bends over and fumbles with a tackle box while another rushes to the bow and cuts the anchor line. The third man goes to the wheel and starts the boat's two outboard engines. He throws them into gear and jams the throttles forward as soon as the second man scrambles back from the bow.

The first man, the one who reached into the toolbox, pulls something out and stands, his legs spread to brace himself against the boat's movements. He points toward our boat with the thing in his right hand and the Mako turns and speeds at an angle to intercept our course.

"I'm not sure we can outrun them," Claudia says. "But we can make it a good try. What do you want me to do, Boss?"

The Desert Eagle feels as heavy as one of my revolvers. I hold it out in one hand and sight it at a point a few dozen feet from the boat. "How many shots do I have?"

"Six."

I stare at the three men on the boat. If they're who I think they are, six well-placed bullets might take care of one of them; certainly not all. "Do you have any extra ammo?"

"The gun makes my purse heavy enough as it is."

"Why don't we run?" Derek says. "We can always fight if they catch us."

I shake my head. "I don't want to run."

"You can't kill them all with just that one gun."

"Not all of them." I nod. "But if we don't keep reducing their numbers we'll never have a chance to win. My father taught me in chess that games can be won and lost over how many pawns are removed from the game."

"I'm more worried about them removing us," Derek says.

"You don't have to shoot anyone, if you don't want," Claudia says. "Those bullets can shoot through a car engine. Think what they'd do to an outboard. You don't even have to hit both of them. With one gone they'll never catch us."

By the time our boats draw a little closer, it becomes clear that the object in the first man's hand has to be a pistol. "Probably the one they took from my room," I say. "The one they used to kill Buddy."

"That might be a perfectly good reason for us to avoid them," Derek says.

Claudia shakes her head. "It's one thing to have a gun. It's another thing to know how to use it." She tells me her plan.

*   *   *

Close up, I have no doubt that the Mako is the same boat that followed me back from Monty's a few days before, or that the wide-shouldered men in the boat are of my people. The man holding the revolver points it at us, one-handed, as our boats race toward each other.

"That's his first mistake," Claudia says. She turns her boat so it aims directly at the man and throws her throttles all the way forward.

Rather than wait for us to close the small remaining distance, the man adjusts his stance to cope with a passing swell, aims and fires. A bullet slashes past us, close enough for us to hear the vicious whir of its passage an instant before we hear the loud clap of the pistol firing.

The recoil throws the man's arm up and knocks him off his balance. He tries to recover his stance, but by then we're already just yards from colliding with the side of his boat. Claudia throws her wheel hard to the side and our boat heels over and digs into the water as we turn, throwing a wave of water at the Mako.

The wave hits and pitches the Mako around like a cork just as the man points the revolver again. His feet fly out from under him and he fires and falls at the same instant. The bullet passes so far over us that its sound is lost in the engine's roar.

"Now!" Claudia says. She turns the wheel again and pulls back on the throttles and we slow as we pass by the Mako's stern.

I fire four bullets into the starboard engine and grin when smoke pours from it and it shakes to a stop.

"What about the other one? You have more bullets," Derek shouts.

Claudia turns the wheel again and throws her throttles

forward, and we accelerate along the other side of the Mako. The first man, who has just recovered his footing, begins to raise his gun. I point the Desert Eagle at him, wait until he points his gun at me and fire twice, both shots aimed at his midsection, where I have the best chance of hitting him.

Two red spots blossom on his shirt, and he drops his arm and falls to his knees. "Good go, that," Derek says.

"You know they can still follow us with one engine," Claudia says.

"They can, but they won't waste their time. They know they can't catch us," I say. "They'll take their wounded comrade home to Gables Estates and regroup."

The girl looks at me. "And that's okay with you?"

"Toba has everything ready down there, right?" I say.

A grin starts to spread on Claudia's face. "Oh," she says. "I see."

I nod. "Call her. Tell her to call you back the instant the Mako turns into the channel behind the house."

"It'll be my pleasure entirely," Claudia says. She makes the call, then jams the throttles forward and we race away toward the mainland and the smoke-filled air that will soon hide our movements.

30

At the office, I stare out my window at the marina and the smoke-obscured view of the bay. Derek stands next to me and gazes out too. "Terrible, that," he says. "Don't know how you put up with it."

"Doesn't happen that often," I say. "As soon as the rains come, it will all go away."

"Can't be soon enough for me. Bloody disgusting smell."

I nod, but the smoke hardly concerns me at all. All my worries focus on Chloe. If Aric means to harm her, as he threatened, and if he hasn't moved to punish her for my actions on the bay, he certainly will extract revenge for what's about to occur. But as hard as I think, I see no other choices.

Claudia walks into the room. "Pops will be here in a minute. Marcia says Ian won't be much longer."

"What about Thad?" I ask.

"What? I told you Pop's uncomfortable with him," Claudia says.

"I know. So am I. But I still want him to sit in at the beginning of this one. I think he can be of use."

She gives me a wary look and goes back out of the office.

"Your girl didn't seem too confident with that decision. Do you have any idea of what you're doing?" Derek asks.

"Besides ordering up ponces in dresses and finding ways to put us at risk?"

I smile at my brother-in-law. "I'm beginning to," I say. "Just bear with me. There is a chance we might pull this off."

He grunts. "I'd feel better if there was more than just a bloody chance."

Claudia returns with Arturo. Thad rushes in, pad in hand, a moment later. I sit behind my desk and the rest take seats in front of me. "I heard you had an interesting ride across the bay," Arturo says.

I nod. "Everything should get more interesting soon."

Arturo grins. "And about time, too."

Ian walks into the office and frowns when he sees Thad. "I didn't invite you," he says.

"I did," I say.

"But—" Ian says and Claudia's cell phone rings. He glares at her but she ignores him and answers.

She looks at me, cell phone to her ear. "It's Toba. What should I tell her?"

I take in a breath. {*And you're sure they won't kill Chloe?*} I mindspeak, to Derek.

{*That's what Cili said. I don't think she'd be mistaken on something like that, old man.*}

{*But if she's wrong I could be signing my wife's death warrant.*}

Derek sighs. {*I believe Cili believes it. But I can't swear she's right.*}

"Boss, their boat's getting near to the dock. Tell me what you want."

I look at Derek and he holds up both hands to show he has no further input to give. "Do it," I say.

Claudia grins and says, "Do it," into the cell phone.

Ian opens his mouth and I hold up a finger to silence him. We all wait while Claudia listens. Finally she nods and says, "Done."

"What the hell is going on?" Ian says.

Arturo smiles at him. "You don't want to know."

"Please." Claudia holds up her hand to silence the room and continues to listen. "One pulled out of the water," she says. "Badly burned but able to move. Two blown to pieces along with the dock and boat." She disconnects and closes her phone. "Mission accomplished."

Thad goes pale and Ian frowns, but Claudia and Arturo both grin like they just won a major bet at a racetrack. "Good, now we can get things moving," Arturo says.

"Good?" Ian says. "Blowing a boat up in Gables Estates? The police are going to go crazy."

Arturo shrugs. "Let them. We have enough members of the force on our payroll to make sure they don't look in our direction. And to keep the heat off of them, we've already arranged for an article in the paper tomorrow suggesting that Ouder Raad, as a Netherland Antilles trading company, may well be linked to the drug trade."

"And those guys always go around whacking each other. Just business as usual," Claudia says.

Her father nods and turns to me. "We have things we need to discuss now, Peter."

"Not quite yet," I say. I open my desk drawer, stare at the small ring of keys that Buddy Matherby gave me and look up at Thad. "Thad, do you think you could find your way to the Matherby house?"

His eyes widen. "Sure, sure, I think so," he stammers.

"Good." I hold out the keys to him. "Derek's wife, Cili,

will be here soon. I need you to take her down there and open the house for her, and stay with her until Derek and I come down. We'll leave here a bit later on with the baggage and everything."

Derek frowns. {*We will?*} he mindspeaks.

{*Remember, patience.*} I give my brother-in-law a hard look. {*Let me set things up. I'll explain later.*}

Thad takes the keys and says, "No problem. I'll try and make her comfortable."

"Don't worry about entertaining her. She's Hungarian and doesn't speak English," I say, even though Derek and I both know the real Cili can. The less Jamie has to do to maintain his charade, the better. "You can wait for her in your office. I'll have Marcia buzz you when she arrives."

After Thad leaves, I look at Ian. He nods, hands me a manila folder and passes identical ones to Claudia and her father. "This is the information on Ouder Raad that the Ramirez brothers helped us get from the DEA." He grins. "You're going to love this."

I nod and open the folder, and glance at the top page as Ian says something about ownership of Ouder Raad. But Aric mindspeaks me at the same time, "*DelaSangre. For what did you do such a thing? Such foolishness.*"

"*Did you think it foolish when you sent those men to attack me? Do you think it's foolish to lose two more of your warriors?*"

"*We still have more than enough to overpower you and your brother-in-law. Please, DelaSangre, stop this nonsense and turn Cili over to us now.*"

"*Bring Chloe back unharmed and well, and then we'll talk,*" I mindspeak.

"*Your actions have already ensured that she'll be*

harmed," Aric mindspeaks. *"She will not be returned until we have Cili. If we must, we will take her from you by ourselves."*

"You won't find her."

"That remains to be seen, DelaSangre. Just remember— you are responsible for whatever pain your wife suffers."

"Peter, do you have any questions so far?" Ian says.

I ball my fists, look up and glare at the man as I mindspeak to Aric, *"No. I will hold you responsible. And I will make sure you suffer far more than she ever does, before you die."*

Ian's eyes go wide and his hands tremble slightly at the anger in my gaze. He says, "Peter?"

"Enough. You will hear from me again soon. And you will not be happy," Aric mindspeaks.

"Sorry," I say to Ian. I open my fingers, suck in a breath and exhale, the anger that rages inside me abating enough for me to regain my composure. "My mind was elsewhere." Forcing all thoughts of Aric and Chloe from my mind, I stare at the page in front of me and read the first paragraph.

My mouth drops open. "Wallenstein, Bearce? The same Wallenstein, Bearce that bought our banks and choked off our credit, owns Ouder Raad Investering?" I say.

Ian nods. "Lock, stock and barrel," he says. "And Ouder Raad Investering owns VastenZeiling. Now take a look below that."

I read the next paragraph and shake my head. "So there's another Ouder Raad?" I say.

"In Europe. Ouder Raad Wereldwidj. They're a Dutch trading company."

"And they own Wallenstein, Bearce?" I ask.

"Not all of it; just enough stock to ensure control of the

board," Ian says. "That way our government still looks at it as an American-owned corporation, not a foreign subsidiary. They've held it that way for years. It looks like they've used it and Ouder Raad Investering for investments all over the country—just not down here until this."

I shake my head. "It looks like a lot of duplication to me."

"The Ramirez brothers and their friends at the DEA say it all has to do with smuggling and money laundering. VastenZeiling owns a lot more ships than just the *Anochi Yagdo*. They specialize in carrying cargo from South and Central America to the U.S. and Europe. All their ships are financed by Ouder Raad Wereldwidj. All three companies have loans and payments going back and forth to each other continuously. No one's been able to break it all down yet."

"Too bad we can't do something to harm them at that level."

Arturo grins. "Who says we can't?"

"Like what?" I look at him.

"Ian said they have a controlling interest. I looked at their shareholders' list. They don't hold anywhere near a majority of the shares. Everything's privately held. I've already had people contact the other shareholders. With enough money and pressure, we can pick up the majority."

"Which would put us in control of Ouder Raad Investering," Claudia says. She smiles. "And in position to play hardball with Ouder Raad Wereldwidj in Holland."

"Not to say it won't be a strain . . ." Ian smiles too, his grin almost cruel as he says, "But we can afford it. Thanks to Ouder Raad's interfering with our spending on new investments, we have plenty of cash and unused credit sitting around to use in the takeover."

I smile too and say, "Put it in motion."

"It already is," Arturo says. "We'll have papers ready for you to sign before you leave today."

"Good." I look down at the papers again and leaf through the pages until I come to a list of Ouder Raad Investering's holdings. I nod at the familiar ones—Hoffsinger's castle in Gables Estates, Flagler Station in Miami, the Young Circle condominium project in Hollywood—and glance past others that I don't recognize.

But a few entries above the bottom of the page I see the name Weir Point Lodge and Marina and stare at it. A marina. My heart beats a little faster at the possibility it brings to my mind. I put a finger on the line and look up. "What does anyone know about this Weir Point Marina?" I say.

Ian and Arturo return my stare with blank looks. Claudia looks at the page in front of her and says, "If it's the place I'm thinking of, Wier Point's sort of off the causeway between Everglades City and Chokaloskee Island, up on the west coast, south of Marcos Island. I weekended at the rod and gun club near there last year. I think I remember driving by the sign then. It was pretty faded."

I turn my eyes back to the page and stare at the name again. Everglades City can't be more than a two-hour drive from Coconut Grove and hardly a longer flight for me than to Bimini—just far enough to be out of mindspeaking range. "Do you think the marina has deep enough water for the *Anochi Yagdo*?" I say.

Claudia thinks and shakes her head slowly. "Doubt it, Boss. We rented a fourteen-foot skiff up there and, even with that, we ran aground six times. That's Ten Thousand Mile Island territory, right next to the Everglades. Most of the water around there is shallow enough to wade in."

I nod. "Still, how can we check it out for sure?"

My phone buzzes and I pick it up. Marcia Voss says, "Mr. DelaSangre, there's a large redheaded woman here. She'll only say your name."

"She's expected," I say. "Claudia will be there in a few moments."

I look at Claudia. "Jamie's here. Will you put her together with Thad and get them on their way?" She nods and leaves the room.

"We have a relationship with a Watson Realty up there. They're commercial realtors in Naples," Arturo says, getting up. "Hal Watson's pretty plugged in to everything that goes on in Collier County. I can call him and see what he knows about Weir."

"Good," I say.

Ian remains in his seat. I look at him and he says, "Don't worry, I'll get up in a second. I have to make sure all the paperwork's been set up properly on the Wallenstein and Bearce thing—so you can sign it before you go." The thin man pauses and looks directly at me. "I need to be on the record with you about something."

I arch an eyebrow.

He puts his hands together and stares at his long bony fingers. "As far as Thad—I'm pretty frosted that he dropped the ball on the Ramirez brothers' thing. He may be my nephew but that doesn't mean a thing to me if he's screwed up in any way here. I want you to know, I understand there are things that have to be done for the sake of your family and LaMar Associates. If that means Thad suffers, so be it."

"You understand it could go badly for him?" I say.

Ian raises an eyebrow, then shrugs. "If so, I gave the boy a chance. He should have valued it more."

* * *

After Ian leaves, Derek stands and walks over to the window. He stares out at the gray sky and sighs. "Too much for me, old man. All this talk and all this planning make me want to run from the room. Cili talks and plans too. If it was me, I'd wait to catch Aric alone and then I'd pummel him until he talked or killed me or died, and then I'd go after the next one."

"I understand," I say, getting up and standing beside him. "I'd love to just go on the attack too. If it were only Aric, I would. But there are still seven of them left and God knows how many more in Europe. And they still have Chloe."

Derek shakes his head. "Never could abide playing chess either. Your doing the thinking is fine with me but, whatever your plan is, please let it call for me to smash and rip at someone."

I smile at my brother-in-law. "I promise you, my plan will be for you to get as much smashing and ripping as you want."

We both go silent and stare out the window. I wonder if my brother-in-law's thoughts are on his wife back in Australia. I can't stop thinking about Chloe, worrying about her.

"Something going on out there?" Claudia says as she comes back into the office.

Derek and I both turn. "No," I say. "Just staring at the water."

Claudia nods. "I'd like to be out there right now." She sits down in one of the chairs facing the desk. "Your boy," she says, and looks at Derek, "and your girl are under way."

Derek scowls. "That ponce is nothing of mine."

"What about Ouder Raad's Mercedes?" I ask.

"Our team's in place outside Gables Estates. They'll call

as soon as the car comes through the security gates," Claudia says.

I frown. "If it comes."

"Well, if Thad is the one, they'll be notified already." The woman reaches into her purse, takes out her cell phone and places it on my desk. "Do you really think that Ouder Raad would pass up the opportunity to take her?"

"Oh," Derek says, a smile growing across his face. "I get it. We're going to run down there now and wait for them to show up."

"Not quite," I say.

Derek's smile vanishes as quickly as it came.

Arturo comes through the door. "Got it," he says. He sits next to his daughter. "Talked to Hal Watson himself. He knows the property, said it was bought recently. According to him, the lodge is pretty run-down. He said the new owners haven't done anything to fix it up yet but—get this—they did already dredge out their channel."

"Deep enough for the *Anochi Yagdo*?" I sit down and look at him.

"Watson didn't know."

I sigh.

Claudia's cell phone rings. She picks it up, listens for moment and looks at me. "Well now we can be sure that Thad's a little shit. The Mercedes just came out of Gables Estates."

My heartbeat speeds up and I grin. "How many in it?"

"How many?" Claudia says into the cell phone. She listens and hold up two fingers.

A groan escapes my lips. Aric's decision to send only two of his men surprises me. He is either overconfident of their success or—in the face of his losses—has decided to act with more caution. Either way, my plans for a more substantial blow will come to nothing.

"Two more isn't bad, Boss," Claudia says.

"Is the German one of them?"

She speaks into the cell phone, listens, looks at me and shakes her head.

I sigh and stand back up. "Okay, tell them to wait until the car turns off of Krome and then do it." I look at Derek and say, "We should get on our way ourselves."

My brother-in-law shrugs. "Whatever you say."

"And—" I turn toward Arturo. "I need you to find out . . ."

The man holds up a hand to stop me and says, "Already covered. Before Claudia's call, I was about to tell you. Hal said Everglades City's only a half-an-hour drive from his office. He's on the way to check out Weir for us right now." Arturo glances at his watch. "We should know soon."

"Call me when you do." I motion for Derek to follow me.

"What do you want us to do?" Claudia says.

I stop and look at her and her father. If asked, I'm sure they'd join us and fight as long as they could. But it's not their fight to win or lose. "I want you to make sure we take over Wallenstein, Bearce. I need you to pursue it even if I'm not around for a while. We need to neutralize Ouder Raad."

Claudia frowns. "You say that like you're not sure when you're going to return."

"If all goes well," I say, "it should be soon. But it's possible I may not be back until much later."

"But you will be back?"

"That's the plan," I say, my voice far more confident than I feel.

31

Derek pauses by the passenger side of my Cayenne, his door open, just after I take my seat behind the car's wheel. I frown at him and motion for him to get in. It will take us at least an hour's drive to reach Matherby Farm and I'm anxious to get under way. "Come on, you're letting all the smoky air in," I say.

He shakes his head. "I thought you were supposed to be the planner," he says. "What about the tridents, old man? Shouldn't we be bringing them along with us?"

I groan. As much as I want to be under way, I understand how useful the weapons could be, both for their deadliness and the element of surprise. "I'll pull the car out while you go to Claudia's boat to get them," I say.

By the time I back close to Monty's marina and pop open the car's hatchback door, Derek's back with both tridents. He throws them into the car, slams the hatchback door closed and jumps into the car. "Now let's go," he says. "I can't wait to dig my trident into one of those buggers."

Driving down US 1 and then west on Kendall, through the constant thick traffic that plagues most Miami roads, makes me wonder all over why I wasted so much money on a high-performance car. Even on 874 I barely reach the speed limit for more than a few seconds before traffic blocks and slows me.

The smoky air, which grows thicker the farther west we go, only serves to slow traffic further. By the time we reach the Florida Turnpike on the west side of the county, the sky has darkened so much that cars have their lights on. "Looks like bloody dusk," Derek says.

I nod, throw my lights on and accelerate south, the traffic finally thinning enough after we pass the exit to Metrozoo to allow me to speed past the posted limit.

My cell phone rings and I answer. "Where are you?" Claudia says.

"Just south of 152nd," I say.

"Can you see the smoke?"

I stare out the windshield at the gray, soupy air. "That's all I see. There can't be more than a quarter mile visibility out here."

"No. I meant from the Mercedes. Our guys blew it sky-high. They say there's no chance anyone inside it survived. The explosives they rigged underneath it at the Biltmore could have blown an Abrams tank to pieces."

"Great, but we're still too far north and east of it," I say. "I didn't even hear the explosion."

"Too bad," Claudia says. "They tell me it was spectacu-lar."

"What about Weir?"

"No answer yet."

After I disconnect, I glance over to Derek. "The odds are evening up."

"How so?" he says.

"We just blew up the Mercedes. Two more down."

"Maybe," Derek says. "You know how difficult our kind is to kill."

"In our natural forms, absolutely." I nod. "But they were in their human forms—with no armored scales to protect them. Even if they survived the blast, they wouldn't have the time to heal before they bled to death."

"Hope you're right, old man."

Me too, I think. But I say, "Aric's down to five now. It's going to be time for us to take the fight to him very soon."

"Are you sure of that?" Derek says.

"I have a wife who they may be torturing. I have to be sure of that," I say.

"I don't know, old man." Derek shakes his head. "Five to two doesn't sound all that good to me."

"I doubt their old one can still fight. That leaves us, at worst, at two to one. We can win—if we fight smarter than they."

Derek frowns and goes silent.

My cell phone rings again a few miles later, just as I take the exit to Eureka Drive and stop at the light. "Your blue sailboat's at Weir," Arturo Gomez says.

So close. I slam the steering wheel with my free hand. "All right!" I say.

"Don't be too happy. Watson said the place looked deserted. No cars, no people in sight. He tried knocking at the lodge door. No one answered."

The light changes, and I turn right and go west on Eureka. "The *Anochi Yagdo*'s there for a reason," I say. "Just because no one came to the door doesn't mean no one's there."

Arturo sighs. "I'm on your side, Peter. All I'm saying is that we have no proof she's there."

"That's okay. We'll know soon enough," I say. I disconnect and turn to Derek.

"The boat's at Weir," I say.

"And that means what?" Derek says.

I tell him, and then mindspeak to Aric, "*Aric, you've lost two more.*"

"*So kind of you to notify me, but they've already reported the bombing on TV. I was in the middle of preparing a proper response when you contacted me.*"

"*When you think of it, you can find me at Buddy Matherby's place.*"

"*Shame on you, DelaSangre. Do you think I'd attack where and when you choose?*"

"*You're five to our two. I'd call that to your advantage.*"

"*You know better than to count our elder. I fear he's too old to offer any more support than his advice. We're far more evenly matched than you suggest. Remember you have Cili, who's already killed enough of us for me to take her most seriously.*"

"*Cili isn't here. She never was.*"

"*And you expect me to believe that? We know where she is.*"

I grin. "*Suit yourself,*" I say. "*We'll be at Matherby's.*"

The black column of smoke from the Mercedes explosion finally becomes visible after we pass Krome Avenue. Police cars and fire trucks block the road and slow traffic to a trickle that detours south and winds back north on one-lane farm roads, turning an hour trip half as much longer.

I nod when I finally see the turnoff to Matherby Farm,

take the turn without slowing and accelerate down the road. "We'll be there soon enough, Peter," Derek says.

"Not soon enough for me," I growl.

Thad Campbell's mud-splattered, green Miata looks hopelessly out of place in front of Buddy Matherby's rustic home. I park alongside it, and Derek and I retrieve our tridents from the car's rear and go to the front door. I try the doorknob and smile when it turns. We both go in.

Seated on an overstuffed ancient sofa, her legs crossed demurely, a large purse in his lap, Jamie looks up and smiles at us. Thad Campbell, standing by a fireplace on the other side of the large wood-beamed room, nods a hello, takes out his cell phone and punches a number into it.

"You can make your call later," I say. "We have things we have to discuss."

Thad holds up a finger and mutters something into the phone.

I frown and step toward him, prepared to rip the phone from the insolent man's hands.

"*DelaSangre,*" Aric mindspeaks. "*You've finally arrived.*"

"*We were delayed by your burning Mercedes. I should have had it blown up at a more convenient place.*"

"*I understand. We all make mistakes. Before you compound yours, I thought you should hear this . . .*"

Nothing happens at first and I turn toward Derek. He shrugs. And then Chloe mindspeaks, her thoughts faint, as if from a distance, "*Peter? Peter, I hate that they're using me like this. I should never have let them take me.*"

{*Chloe,*} I mindspeak. {*Where are you? Are you all right?*}

"Not masked, Peter. They'll hurt me more if they can't hear our thoughts."

"Hurt you more?" I can't listen to this and stand still. I throw my trident across the room—so hard that Thad winces when its prongs plunge deep into the room's hardwood wall, even though it's yards from him. *"How have they hurt you?"* I mindspeak.

"Oh, Peter, they've cut and pierced me so many times," Chloe mindspeaks. *"They won't let me rest and eat enough to change from my human form and heal and they won't let me die . . ."*

"Where do they have you?"

"They had me in a room, I don't know where. My eyes are covered. I think I'm in a van now. They drove me some-where . . . I hurt, Peter. I hurt so much."

Anger, sadness and regret overwhelm me. My whole body trembles at the thought of the misery my actions have brought to my wife. *"Chloe, I'm so sorry. I'll do everything I can to stop this as soon as possible. I won't let this go on . . . I promise."*

"No, Peter. No. Don't be sorry. I wish I was stronger than this—but the pain is so, so terrible for me. You must be the strong one. Don't make me promises. Forget me. Kill them. . . ."

"Enough!" Aric mindspeaks and Chloe goes silent.

{*Chloe?*} I mindspeak. I receive no reply.

"Aric?" I mindspeak.

Thad listens to his cell phone, mutters something and then steps toward me. "Sorry, nothing personal," he says. "I just couldn't stand the thought of working for my cousin for the rest of my life." He shrugs. "When I ran into Aric at the

Versailles, his offer was too good to turn down." He offers the cell phone to me.

I take it and Aric says, "Good. We can talk without Cili hearing. It is time we discussed how you will give her to us. Or do you want your wife to feel more pain?"

Part of me wishes that Derek had really brought Cili here, so I could trade her for my wife—but such a thing would go against everything I was ever taught. "No, I don't want her to feel any pain," I growl into the phone. "I want you to."

"Empty threats mean nothing, DelaSangre. We want Cili."

"She isn't here," I say. I hand the cell phone back to Thad. *"She never was. Ask Thad what he sees,"* I mindspeak.

I turn toward Jamie. "Pull up your dress and show him what you've got," I say.

Jamie stands. "Does this mean I can't pretend to be a Hungarian woman anymore?" she says. She turns her back on all of us and fumbles with the front of her dress.

"Now," I say.

"Give a girl a chance to readjust," she says, fumbling another moment before she turns and pulls up her dress.

"It's a guy!" Thad gasps into the cell phone.

"Where do you have Cili?" Aric mindspeaks.

"Nowhere on this continent."

Aric goes silent. Thad nods, the cell phone still to his ear. He steps forward again and hands it to me. "Remember," Aric snarls into the phone. "Remember what we can do to your wife."

"I remember," I growl.

"Where is Cili?"

"Not here," I say, and wince at the thought of Chloe suffering any further.

"Give the phone back to Thad."

Thad takes it with his left hand. The man looks at each of us, his face pale and devoid of expression as he listens again and wanders a few feet away from us, toward a low coffee table. He murmurs something back, placing his right foot on the coffee table, bending over and reaching with his right hand—as if he's about to retie his right shoelace. But he pulls up his right pants cuff instead, draws a small, chrome semiautomatic pistol from a black ankle holster, points it at me and fires before I can gasp.

The first bullet burns into my chest—the crack of the pistol surprisingly loud. A second bullet tears into my stomach. A third strikes my left knee and I fall to the floor, the smell of my blood already flooding into the air. Derek roars and dashes forward, and Thad whirls toward him and fires two more times, each shot tearing into flesh, blood streaming from my brother-in-law's forehead, obscuring his vision.

Sidestepping Derek's blind charge, Thad turns back toward me and takes aim just as Jamie rushes up from his rear, swinging her large purse with both hands. It slams into the back of his neck. He grunts and almost falls forward, firing again, striking only the floor. Jamie hits him with the purse again and again, battering him, keeping him from aiming again until Derek returns with his trident and buries it in the man's back.

Thad gurgles loudly and falls to the floor, facedown. "Bastard!" Derek says. He yanks his trident free and plunges it back into the man until he grows still.

Jamie looks at Derek and at me lying on the floor. "Oh my God," she says. "You're both wounded!"

Derek wipes the blood from his face. "Not too badly," he says.

I nod. Even in our human forms we have much we can do to limit damage—as long as it's not too severe. I've already managed to will my bleeding to slow. With fresh meat readily available, healing will come soon enough after that. "They were just nine millimeters," I say from the floor, and wince as I force myself to sit up.

"Just?" Jamie says. "That's the same as being shot by a thirty-eight."

"Still not a problem." I look around the room. "Know where his keys are?"

Jamie motions toward the fireplace mantel. I nod. "We appreciate your help, but you need to go now," I say. "Take Thad's car. Do whatever you want with it."

"Sure," Jamie says. She grabs the keys off the mantel, walks toward the door, and then stops and turns. "You sure I can't help you in any way?"

I shake my head. "Just go."

As soon as we hear the Miata's wheels crunch away through the driveway, Derek and I both stare at Thad's still body. "Did you ever think he'd have the nerve to try something like that?" Derek asks.

"Not for a moment," I say, shaking my head, tearing off my clothes. Derek strips too, and we both will our bodies to change. Even before we return fully to our natural forms we fall on Thad's body and tear chunks of fresh meat from it.

"*Aric,*" I mindspeak as I feed. "*I'm not finished with you.*"

"*Nor am I with you, my friend.*"

"*I'm glad to hear that. It's time for us to end this—one way or another. After dark, if you don't come for me, I will come for you.*"

"As you wish," Aric mindspeaks. *"After dark. I will be glad to be rid of you."*

"Don't underestimate us," I mindspeak.

"But I could never hold you in as high regard as you do yourself."

I pause from eating and grin. *"You're the one who made the human attack us. You couldn't think he would do us much harm, could you?"*

"He was no longer of use to us anyway," Aric mindspeaks. *"I hope at least he proved inconvenient."*

"He did, a bit," I mindspeak. I take another bite of Thad's still-warm flesh and sigh at its sweetness. *"But it ended up being more of a favor."*

32

As soon as the sky goes black, Derek and I take our tridents and go outside. With the Everglades and its fires so close, smoke has permeated the air so much that after only a few seconds my eyes burn and my nostrils turn numb to any other smell.

Derek blinks his eyes and snorts to clear his nostrils. He shakes his head. {*None of it helps,*} he mindspeaks. {*And you want me to fly through this evil muck?*}

I sigh. Derek has come up with one objection after another since I told him my plan earlier in the day. {*You may be able to fly above it. But even if you can't, it should dissipate as you get closer to Everglades City. The worst of the fires are down here.*}

{*I still think you're wrong to have us split up. I should stay here and fight by your side.*}

{*No.*} I shake my head. {*One of us has to be the decoy to keep Aric and the rest occupied while the other goes for Chloe.*}

{*What good will her rescue do for you, if you die fighting here?*}

{*At least she'll be out of pain,*} I mindspeak.

{*Damned stupid if you ask me.*} Derek snaps his wings open and fans them as he speaks. {*You could be over-*}

whelmed and killed here and I could be overwhelmed and killed there and then where would that leave Chloe?}

{*With no reason to be tortured anymore.*} I look up at the smoke-filled evening sky, the moon only a blur of dim light hidden behind the gloom. {*Aric is no fool. He'll attack here with as many warriors as he can. I doubt he'll leave more than one with Chloe. You'll probably be safer going to rescue your sister than you would staying here to fight by my side.*}

Derek snorts. {*If I can find her.*}

I sigh. {*You saw where it is on the map.*} I point in the direction of the west coast. {*Just fly that way and go north when you reach the coast. When you see the blue sailboat you'll know you're there.*}

Derek and I both leap skyward at the same time, our wings scooping air, our tridents held at the ready, our tails thrashing behind us as we gain enough altitude to shoot north—away from Matherby's and over the Everglades. Even knowing about the fires and smelling their smoke for weeks and weeks hasn't prepared me for the extent of the conflagration. I gasp when the first hot updraft hits me, hundreds of yards from any open flames, and tosses me upward as if I were as light as the ash and burnt leaves it carries away from the earth.

Derek rockets up too and we take advantage of the lift, barely flapping our wings as we ascend in tight spirals, the Everglades below us a landscape of bright, dancing flames and huge fields of burning embers interspersed by calm, dark bodies of water and even darker, teardrop-shaped islands of high land protected by their own watery moats. Hot winds buffet, toss, drop and lift us. Smoke swirls all around, blocking our view one moment, then dissipating the next, and we continue to spiral until we break free into cool, thin air.

{*Bloody relief, this,*} Derek mindspeaks, drawing in a deep breath of smoke-free air. {*Hardly an easy flight.*}

{*I don't know. I sort of liked the ride.*} I look down at the smoke and flames beneath us. {*I'd do it again—at another time, if no one was at risk.*}

{*I'd rather be home, in my bed with my Cili.*} Derek banks and turns toward the west coast. {*Which I want to do as soon as we get this mess finished. If your foolishness doesn't get me killed first.*}

I bank, turn toward the east and readjust my grip on the trident. Soaring in wide circles that take me back almost to Matherby's and then far out over the fire-roiled surface of the Everglades, I gain more altitude and then mindspeak, "*Aric, have you forgotten our appointment? Or have you changed your mind and decided to go back to Europe?*"

"*I am told your father was a wise and able warrior. Didn't he teach you to embrace patience?*" Aric mindspeaks.

"*My father taught me to pursue victory in any manner I wish,*" I reply.

The German's harsh laugh fills my mind. "*Did he teach you how to accept defeat too?*"

I look at the empty sky around me, the bright stars and moon overhead and the gloom and smoke and fire below, and see no sign of Aric or any of his host. "*Defeat?*" I mindspeak. "*The only thing I've been fighting so far this evening has been boredom.*"

"*You must learn how to wait, DelaSangre. Anxiety can*

weaken one's spirits. We will find you when we want. I prom-
ise you, it will be this night."

Except for the slow drift of clouds and smoke and the
constant ebb and flow of the fires, nothing changes. I maintain altitude and circle, readjusting my grip on the trident,
using as little effort as possible, searching the sky for the
first sign of a warrior hurtling through the air at me or the V-
shaped shadow of a flight of warriors climbing into position.
But nothing shows and I continue circling, my mind on my
surroundings, my mind on Chloe, my mind on Derek, wondering how close he is, whether he will be able to free her.

Something ruffles the air above me. I fold my wings and
plummet but an instant too late. Claws dig into the meaty
part of my tail and rip through it as I fall away. Pain shoots
through me. I yowl and twist in midair and see two attackers hurtling after me.

I snap my wings open and shoot off to the side, banking
and turning toward them as they do the same. We rocket toward each other, the warriors' claws poised to strike, my trident tucked close to my body, out of their view but ready to
be thrust into action. Two other warriors emerge from the
smoke far below us and I groan. They circle slowly upward,
too far away to join the attack but close enough to threaten
another should this one fail.

The approaching warriors bellow out roars as we near. I
close my mind to their noise, to the pending arrival of the
warriors below us, and concentrate only on the attack at
hand, the positioning of their claws, the trajectories of their
flights. They intend to hit me head-on and overwhelm me
with their combined strength.

At the very last moment, just before we collide, I fold my

wings again and dive. Neither warrior can adjust in time. Both shoot far past me before they can turn and dive after me. The warriors below continue their ascent, obviously content to let the others strike the first blow.

The wind screams by me as I plummet, too far from my pursuers and too fast to be caught by them. Rather than maneuver to attack them again, I extend my wings just enough to shift course toward one of the warriors making his way skyward and streak toward him. I reach him before he realizes I've changed course and rake his body with all three of my trident's prongs, cutting him wide open, from throat to tail, as I fall past him.

He yowls once, his blood blossoming in the air above me, and then his left wing folds and his right goes slack. I snap my wings open and shoot away from all of them, racing toward the cover of smoke as the dead warrior corkscrews through the air toward the fires on the ground below.

"*DelaSangre,*" Aric mindspeaks. "*Why are you running? I thought you wanted to fight.*"

"*I think your dead friend would acknowledge he was just in a fight. I'd hoped it was you.*"

"*So sorry. I was one of the ones above you. You ran from me.*"

"*Had I known, I might not have,*" I mindspeak.

"*Ah, of course, you have no idea what I'm looking like in my natural form. So you know for the next time we meet, I am the one of us with the longest tail. Unless, of course, you want to come back into view now.*"

"*No. I think it's best if you come after me,*" I mindspeak, flying deeper into the smoke, ignoring the heat, letting the updrafts buffet and toss me. "*You and I will meet soon enough.*"

*   *   *

The smoke blinds me and makes my lungs ache, but I make no attempt to climb out of it. My tail still throbs with pain from my last encounter with Aric and his warriors. I hadn't expected to be attacked by more than three. I wonder what other surprises he might have planned.

I break free from the column of smoke and find myself over a patch of water and a small island of high land, and then glide back into smoke again. *"Don't hide too well, De-laSangre. If you do, we'll never get to end this,"* Aric mind-speaks.

The creature has a point. I have miles and miles of smoke-filled skies to hide in. As long as I'm willing to be tormented by the fumes, I can probably avoid detection. Which would accomplish what? I spiral upward slowly and look skyward as the smoke thins. If Aric or one of his warriors flies too near I can always dive back into a smoke cloud's cover.

None are in sight. I spiral higher, blink my eyes clear of ash, take breath after breath of fresh air and wonder where Aric and his warriors are. If they're busy searching else-where, this is the perfect time for me to fly higher and gain the advantage of altitude.

Something smashes into the left side of my back, as hard as if a sack of concrete had been dropped on me. My left wing collapses and I begin to fall sideways. I bellow into the air. No matter how hard I try to extend my left wing, I can't make it move. Sharp claws sink into my back. I roar and twist and shake my body, trying to dislodge my attacker and rid myself of his weight before it carries us both into the ground.

Another warrior slams into my right side, pins that wing and digs his claws into me too. I yowl and twist and buck, but both maintain their hold as we plummet downward. Their claws dig in deeper. I ignore the pain their claws bring and force myself to think.

No matter how they tear at my back, they lack the time to cause a mortal wound. For that, they need access to my throat and underbelly. Any such attempt would expose them to my trident and my teeth and claws. They only remain safe as long as they stay on my back.

They have to know, as well as I do, that from this altitude, unless we strike water, our fall will kill all of us. So I can only assume they intend to break free of me at the last moment, just before I crash to my death. I cease to struggle and concentrate on the rush of the smoke and air around us and the growing heat below us.

Even with my body shielding them from the worst of the fire's heat, my attackers have to be aware that we're falling into the middle of a large, angry fire. It begins to scorch my underbelly far above the flames. I ignore that pain too, and twist my body so the heat will sear into at least a portion of my attackers' bodies.

To their credit, they maintain their holds and we plummet ever closer to the fire. But when the tips of the fire's flames begin to lick up close enough to almost touch us, I feel the sickening sensation of claws pulling back partly out of my wounds. I readjust my grip on my trident and flex my wing muscles—to ready them to react as soon as I'm free to move.

Still, their release, the sudden freedom from their weight, makes me gasp in surprise. I snap my wings open but my momentum carries me into the flames. Intense heat burns into the underside of my wings and my underbelly, hot air sears the inside of my nostrils and dries the surface of my eyes, and I soar upward as fast as I can, the hot updraft of the fire rocketing me skyward into the blessedly cooler air above.

I break free, into fresh air, only a few hundred yards from one of my attackers. The other glides above him another hundred yards away. Both have their eyes focused on the smoky air below them. I shoot toward the closer one, my trident ready to slash into him, my body in agony from the burns that cover my entire underbelly.

As I close, the second warrior notices me and banks and dives to come to the aid of his comrade. The closer warrior turns to take my attack head-on. But he's unprepared for my trident. I slash completely through his throat, severing arteries, and plunge all three prongs deep into his chest before he can reach me with his claws. He tries to roar but can only gurgle, blood spraying from his throat and flowing from his chest.

I yank my trident free and let him fall into the fire below as I glide into position to meet my second attacker. He zooms toward me but drops away before he comes within striking distance of my trident. *"DelaSangre,"* Aric mindspeaks. *"You've done well so far."*

The other warrior circles me, making sure to stay just far enough away, dodging when I come closer, nearing when I pull back. *"I had to. I've been waiting for you."*

"With a new weapon, too. You are a constant surprise."

Another warrior flies into view, a little larger than the other, his tail longer. *"Aric, I assume?"* I mindspeak.

"It is time to finish this." He flies toward me, the other warrior circling, blocking any move I make that might take me away.

I snort into the air. He needn't bother. I want to confront

Aric. I want to dig my trident into him and see his blood spray into the air. He nears and I readjust my grip and brace myself for his attack.

But a dozen yards from me, Aric flares his wings, slows and points his right front claw at me. I gasp at the large, silver revolver held in his claw just as he fires.

Before I can react, the first bullet digs a furrow through the scales on the bony ridge above my right eye and glances by without any further damage. The second tears through the left side of my neck, missing my arteries and my larynx by centimeters. The third blasts through the scales on my underbody, tears through my left lung and nicks my heart as it exits through my back.

Pain and confusion overwhelm me. My limbs go weak. The trident falls from my claws and my wings go slack and I begin to fall again.

"See, DelaSangre," Aric mindspeaks. "*I can bring a surprise too.*"

I don't bother to answer. The wounds on my back and the burns all over my underbody torment me. Blood from the wound over my eye blinds me on my right side and the left side of my neck feels as if its been torn away. But the pain from my lung and heart make all that seem as insignificant as a scratched knee.

Breathing becomes even more of an agony when I fall back into the smoke. I put my mind away from the pain and gasp in air as quickly as possible, trying to help my one working lung speed badly needed oxygen into my blood, concentrating with all my might on the rip in my heart, closing the open wound, at least, before my energy runs out.

My wings resist but I force them to open and I soar toward the west, too low, too close to the flames to avoid further injury. With rest and food I can survive my wounds, but I can't be sure that either will be available before I succumb.

Derek is somewhere to my northwest; Chloe too.

"DelaSangre. I know you're not dead yet. Don't think we won't find you. You can't stay in the smoke forever."

I don't care about the smoke. I ignore the new pain the fire's flames bring me. I fly on, one beat of my wings at a time. All I want is to know that my Chloe is safe. All I want to hear is that she forgives me.

33

The flames lessen and I fly over acre after acre of blackened, smoldering, scorched ground, parts glowing red like barbecue charcoal, heat and smoke everywhere. Aric continues to pester me with his constant taunts but I pay him little heed. Distance is my only goal. Enough distance to be close enough to mindspeak with my Chloe.

I pass over open water again. It and the cool air over it shock me to awareness. I scan the skies around me, look for the next column of smoke and hurry toward it. *"DelaSangre, I see you,"* Aric mindspeaks.

"If you were close enough to attack, you wouldn't tell me that." I reach the smoke and sigh when it envelops me.

"I just want you to know it's hopeless. You'll be dead before morning."

"Did you notice that it's your warriors that have been dying so far?" I mindspeak.

"I notice that you're so hurt that you can hardly fly. And I notice you're flying west. There's no fire to hide you over there. Do you really think we'll let you reach that far?"

I don't even think I'll be able to travel that far. Every movement of my body becomes more difficult than the last. Every pain seems to magnify with each passing minute. I miss a beat of my wings and dip in the air for a moment before I recover and beat higher.

To keep going, I promise myself rest as soon as I get close enough to mindspeak to either Derek or Chloe. Neither of them answers and I pass from fire and smoke over water and islands and back into smoke again and again, Aric and his comrade never too far away, his taunts ringing in my mind.

Derek finally answers. {*Damn it, man, where have you been?*} he mindspeaks.

{*I've been a little preoccupied with entertaining Aric and his friends. Have you found Chloe?*}

{*I found the ship and the lodge but there isn't a bloody soul here.*}

I groan into the air and circle in the air. Without Chloe, I have no reason to fly any farther west.

{*I did find fresh blood all over one room,*} Derek mindspeaks. {*It could have been Chloe's.*}

{*That hardly makes me feel better,*} I mindspeak.

{*Right you are. Just trying to show you we are close.*}

{*Not close enough.*} I stop my circling and head west again but I doubt my ability to continue much farther.

{*What do you want me to do now?*}

{*For the time being, wait and see if anyone comes back,*} I mindspeak. I break out of the smoke again and look down and see an island with a crescent-shaped lagoon almost directly below me. {*There's an island nearby that I recognize. It has a crescent-shaped lagoon and plenty of high ground. I'm pretty banged up. I'm going to try to take a quick rest there.*}

{*You sure you don't want me to come help you?*}

{*Forget me. It's Chloe I want you to help.*} I bank toward the island and descend.

Aric's warrior hits me from above. Adrenaline surges through me and, this time, I spin in midair before he can sink his claws into me and I rake his underbelly with my claws.

{*Anything else?*} Derek mindspeaks. When he receives no reply, he mindspeaks masked again. {*Peter? . . . Peter?*}

With both of us hurtling toward the ground, I have no time to answer. I grab for the warrior's back, sink my claws into him and mount him, pinning his wings and sinking my teeth into the back of his neck. Though my wings lack the strength to support our combined weight, I spread them just enough to guide us toward the lagoon. This way, with luck, the impact may kill him and spare me.

As planned, he hits the shallow lagoon first, water and mud shooting into air as we strike, the lagoon's water stunning us but cushioning our fall more than I thought it would. I regain consciousness first and listen to the warrior's slow, deep breaths before I roll off of him and try to stand.

My feet sink into the wet sand and I gasp when I try to pull them out and they sink further. I'd forgotten the quicksand that had slowed my prey here before. I spread my wings and fall on my back. To me, quicksand never kills anyone, only panic does.

I've already sculled a good fifteen feet from the warrior when he regains consciousness and groans. He tries to stand and both his rear and front claws sink into the lagoon's bottom as he pushes against it. Rather than follow my lead, he pushes against the sand and tries to yanks his limbs free—and sinks even further.

He growls and yanks and pushes, sinking ever deeper, struggling ever more until only his snout and eyes remain above the water. *"You just need to try a little harder,"* I mind-speak to him.

He throws a growl in my direction and breaks into a paroxysm of movements. Water and sand churn all around him as he struggles and sinks from sight until the water above him slowly grows still again. I stare in his direction and shake my head. Not a single part of the warrior remains to be seen.

"Sehr gut," Aric mindspeaks. *"Wounded and tired and still you somehow manage to win. I have underestimated you too many times."* He flies by overhead, close enough for me to feel the wind from his passage. *"It is a shame your efforts can't be rewarded."*

The German circles back and fires the last two rounds from his gun. One tears through my upper shoulder. The other blasts through my skull and tears into my brain. *"But I didn't get to speak to Chloe,"* I mindspeak, and all goes black.

34

"Dead? He can't be."

"Ah, but he is, leibchen. Your suffering is no more."

"I don't believe you."

"You will soon enough."

The mindthoughts penetrate the darkness that has overtaken my brain and reawaken a small part of my awareness. Pain floods over me and I think to groan but can't. Water laps around me. Wind blows over me. I can hear and feel those things but I can't command my tail to twitch or my eyelids to open.

"See?" Aric mindspeaks.

I hear the rustle of their wings over me. Chloe bellows out a moan. *"No!"* she mindspeaks. *"He can't be."*

"Don't land there, it is quicksand."

A snarl fills the air. *"Don't stop me."*

"I'm afraid I must. We have plans for you."

"Peter, please answer me. Please."

I think to answer. I think to form a thought—but the words slip away from me.

Chloe mindspeaks, {*Peter, please tell me you're okay. Peter, please.*}

The words come. I think to tell her—I love you and I'm so sorry for being such a fool, so sorry for not finding a way

to apologize for the pain that my time with Lorrel caused—
but I can't make the words go out to her.

Something flies close over me and moans. {*Oh, Peter,*}
Chloe mindspeaks. {*If only you could hear me and know
how much I love you. Even as crazy as things have been for
us these past few years, I never felt for a moment that I
didn't love you. I loved you then and I love you now. I will
always love you. I will always miss you.*}

"*Is time to go, liebchen.*"

"*Can't we stay a little longer?*"

"*No. You are still weak from all of what we had to do to
you. We have to feed you more and let you heal . . .*"

"*For what? That's my mate lying dead beneath us. Do
you think I care whether I heal or not?*"

"*Your mate's life is over. You still have one. Remember
you have a child.*"

"*I have children.*"

"*Yes, you do—if you wish to embrace the boy. And you
will have more.*"

"*I hardly think so.*"

"*I understand, for now. Biology will take care of the
rest.*"

"*Do we have to leave him like that?*"

"*He's lying in quicksand. The earth will take him in soon
enough.*"

"*I loved him so much.*"

"*He was lucky to have had you.*"

{*Good-bye, Peter. I'll always love you.*}

I struggle to do something, say something. No words
come. No thoughts go out. I finally manage to flutter one
eyelid and then blackness overwhelms me and takes me
away.

35

{*Bloody, bloody pain in the ass.*} Sharp prongs dig into my scales and pull on my body. It floats ever so slowly in the direction of the pull, and the prongs dig in and pull again. {*It's almost dawn. Can't have you lying in open view. Not that a soul could see you through this soupy air anyway.*}

The prongs pull me along again, and one more time, and then a claw grabs my tail and pulls on it. {*You better be alive, you bastard. You are going to owe me for this. I've been calculating how much and I'd say we need to rethink my ranch in Bidwilli Valley. There's no reason it shouldn't be much more grand.*} Claws grab my lower body and drag me from the water, through the brush onto the island.

Derek huffs and puffs as he pulls me along. {*You're far too heavy for this,*} he mindspeaks. {*If we don't find a clearing soon it will cost you an entire other estate on the other side of the continent. I fancy it being near Perth. Wouldn't you agree? Or should it be a sheep farm in New Zealand? I've seen some of those Maoris. They look like meaty blokes.*}

We come out of the brush and sand crunches underneath me as Derek drags me into position and lets go. {*Good. Now give me a word here.*}

I try. I really try—but nothing comes. I do manage, however, to flutter my eyelid again.

{*Not much, but at least you're not dead,*} Derek mindspeaks, and blackness wells up around me again.

Hot, fresh blood, sweet yet odd and slightly gamey, trickles down my throat. The aroma penetrates my seared nostrils. I try to swallow but nothing happens. Rage builds inside me and I force a swallow. This time a small part of the blood pooling in my throat slides down to my stomach.

{*Good go, that,*} Derek mindspeaks. {*We wouldn't want to let all this good deer blood go to waste.*}

My next swallow goes easier and takes more. Derek drips a little more into my mouth as soon as I can take it. {*No rush.*} He pats me on my snout. {*You've a lot more healing to do.*}

I wake later and manage to open an eye. Sunlight glares through the smoky haze. I try to form the words to call to Derek but still can't. A yellow butterfly hovers over me and settles on my snout. I concentrate on blowing out a huff of air and do it, and the butterfly flies away. I grin and fade back to sleep again.

More blood wakes me. This time I open one eye and gulp it down. The sky has gone dark again and Derek moves his head into view. He stares at my one open eye and mindspeaks. {*Jolly good. You're coming along fine.*}

I try to nod but can't, but at least a word comes. I think it, {*Fine,*} and drop back into the blackness.

*   *   *

The morning sun's warmth wakes me. I open both eyes and squint at its brightness. Derek's snore alerts me to his presence and I manage to turn my head in his direction, pain shooting through my neck as I do so. I have never hurt so much in my life. Never felt so weak. Still, I form the thought in my mind and mindspeak, {*Derek?*}

My brother-in-law sleeps on.

I let out a sigh and mindspeak, {*Derek?*}

But he continues to sleep. I stare at him and force a growl, the sound of it too faint for even me to hear. I try to take in more air with my injured lungs and I growl again, this time loud enough to interrupt his snore. {*Derek?*} I mindspeak.

He snorts a breath, stretches and turns in my direction. {*About time.*} He grins. {*I've been growing damned tired of waiting on you hand and foot. Soon as we get some solid food in you, you can start caring for yourself.*} He gets up and drags a deer carcass toward me. {*Killed the bugger last night. It'll be fresh enough.*}

He puts a piece of meat by my mouth. I take it and chew it carefully, relishing the taste and the slight boost of energy that courses through me. I gulp the next bite down and devour the rest as quickly as I can, concentrating on first healing my skull and brain and then my heart and lungs.

Derek feeds too, and between us we consume every edible part of the beast within a few minutes. Derek mindspeaks, {*Sorry, old man. That's the last of it.*}

I try to sit up and an electric jolt of pain lances through every part of me, from my head to the tip of my tail. I groan and lie still. {*I'm afraid I need much more than that.*}

{*Of course you do, you fool. You've been badly hurt. Let yourself rest for now. I'll bring back more fresh prey later.*}

Rest sounds good. I nod, and wince at the pain the movement brings. I have never felt so tired. I close my eyes and wait for the blackness to take me away again.

Thrashing in the underbrush, the shush of something being dragged over sand and a wet swampy smell intermixed with the aroma of fresh blood near me, wake me from a dreamless sleep. I open my eyes and turn my head toward the smell, and find myself staring into the dead eyes of a huge alligator. {*Couldn't find the slightest hint of any more deer,*} Derek mindspeaks. {*Saw this big bugger though. Should be enough meat on him to shut you up for a while.*}

Saliva floods my mouth and I watch Derek slice the beast's tail open and carve out a large chunk of white meat. It's gamier than the deer's, its blood less thick and satisfying; still, I find it delicious. I gobble down chunk after chunk, as quickly as Derek can feed them to me, my stomach filling, then swelling, as my brother-in-law strips the alligator's carcass bare.

This time I consume more than enough. I close my eyes, not to sleep but to focus on my body, expelling the bullets' lead slugs from my body with tiny contractions of the cells surrounding them, rushing protein to my damaged areas, closing wounds, rebuilding bone and flesh and scales. All of it consumes the energy I've ingested at an alarming rate, and I grow hungry again and in need of more sustenance within less than two hours.

Even though it sends jolts of agony through me, I sit up and look at Derek. He grins and nods at me. {*I'm afraid I'm going to need more,*} I mindspeak.

He shrugs. {*No shame in that. You were as near death as*}

any creature I've ever seen. I'll go out again after dark and get enough for us both.}

I nod. Sleep no longer threatens to overwhelm me and I look around the clearing, noting the gray air and the aroma of smoke that pervades it. {*The fires are still burning?*} I mindspeak.

{*As bad as ever.*} Derek nods. {*The smoke's good for cover though. It lets me get close to prey, when I can find it.*}

{*Tell me about Chloe.*} I stare at my brother-in-law. {*Why didn't you try to rescue her?*}

He pulls his head back and glares at me. {*I bloody well did try. I told you that. I flew there just like you asked me to. I went to the boat first, and risked shrinking my body so I could squeeze through its ridiculously narrow doorways and I searched every damned room. There wasn't a soul on board. The house was empty too. I searched all around there until you mindspoke to me. I don't know what else I could have done.*

{*After we spoke, I waited a while—like you said. When no one came, I decided to go find you. I don't know if I ever would have found that crescent-shaped lagoon you spoke of if I hadn't heard that bloke Aric's mindthoughts—and Chloe's. I flew as near as I dared and ducked into a smoke cloud for cover.*}

I shake my head. {*Why didn't you go after Aric then? Chloe was right there.*}

Derek growls. {*Do you think I wouldn't have, if he was alone? He had two others with him. None of them seemed to be harming my sister and you were lying there mostly dead in the mud below them. You were the one that looked like he needed more help and, frankly, I didn't much relish the thought of dying in a futile attack on three opponents. I took enough risk coming after you and dragging you out of that muck. Had they come back, we both would have been dead.*

{*Instead of accusing me of failing you, you could say, 'Thank you for saving my ass, Derek. Thank you for taking care of me.'*}

I nod. I could hardly expect my brother-in-law to throw his life away. And without him, I doubt I'd still be alive. {*Thank you for saving my ass, Derek,*} I mindspeak. {*Thank you for taking care of me.*}

He harumphs and waves a claw as if to minimize the help he provided. {*You would have done the same for me. The point now is to get you well enough to fly. I can't wait to get out of this swamp.*}

{*Maybe,*} I mindspeak. I try to flex my wings. Pain shoots through my back and brings tears to my eyes, but they move. {*If I can feed again in the early evening, I might be able to heal enough to go a few hours before sunrise.*}

{*It wouldn't do to go back to your island. Aric and the rest could be there and you won't be in any shape to fight them.*}

{*I don't know if I could fly that far anyway.*} The image of Aric and Chloe sitting in the great room of my house comes into my mind and I sigh. {*I hate that she's with him.*}

{*You could try to mindspeak to her, you know. It might be helpful if she learns you're alive.*}

I shake my head. {*I won't do anything that might put her at risk of being hurt again. If she acts in any way to make Aric suspect that I'm not dead, he may use her pain to threaten me again.*}

{*You may risk more by not telling her. You know how our females work. As soon as their mates are dead, their bodies change and they go into heat.*}

I nod. As much as our kind can control their bodies, we have little ability to ignore our instincts.

{*She'll be as randy as she was when she first reached maturity. You know how that goes. She'll fill the air with her scent and the first male who reaches her will have her for life. It may already be too late.*}

{*If it is, it is.*} I shrug. {*At least she won't be in pain.*}

Derek scowls. {*I know my sister. She's a strong girl. She can handle any pain she has to.*}

{*No. I won't do it. I can't handle knowing that she's suffering.*}

We sit in silence for a few minutes. Then Derek mindspeaks, {*I went by Matherby's last night. I don't think anyone's been there. At least no one was there last night. Everything is as we left it, even our clothes and your car. We could go there.*}

I nod, look at my brother-in-law and grin. {*Why, Derek, you suggested a plan.*}

36

We arrive at Matherby's just as the first glimmer of sunlight breaks through the smoke-filled night. Derek and I shift into our human forms as soon as we land and rush into the house. We find nothing disturbed, and scoop up our clothes and dress.

In my human form, my body aches even more than it did in my natural form. I grimace with each new movement and walk slowly, my legs stiff and resistant to bending. "You move like an old man," Derek says.

"I feel like an old man." I take out my cell phone, plop down into an easy chair and dial Claudia's number.

No one answers on my first two tries. On the fourth ring of my third call, someone picks up the phone, and a male voice snarls a sleepy, "What?" into the phone.

I hesitate for a moment. I can only hope that the voice belongs to one of Claudia's boyfriends and not one of Aric's warriors. "Claudia, please," I say. "Tell her it's Peter."

A hand muffles the phone and prevents me from hearing anything more than the murmurs of few words, and then Claudia takes the phone and says, her voice loud with excitement, "Peter? Where the hell are you? What the hell's been going on?"

"A lot's been going on. Who answered the phone?"

Her voice softens. "That was Benny. You know him. He's the veterinarian who's taking care of Max, remember? We've sort of become friends."

I nod as if she can see me. From her tone it's clear she likes him. But right now I really don't care who she's dating. "What's happening there?" I say.

"Chloe called Pops yesterday. She didn't even ask for me. That's not like her. She told him you were dead."

"He asked her if she was sure and she said yes, she saw it herself. And then she asked if we were set up to handle the estate. Pops assured her we were. She wanted to have a meeting to go over it today but, thank God, he put it off until tomorrow morning. It just didn't feel right to him. He wanted to take some time to see if you'd show up or something else would happen to have it all make more sense to him."

I hold back a groan. Chloe would never move so quickly on my estate unless she were under Aric's control. "Where is she?" I say.

"I'm not sure. She didn't say. But remember, she doesn't have a boat anymore. I doubt she'd think to use your new Grady White. It was still at Monty's last night, with its keys on my desk."

Not that either Chloe or Aric needs a boat to cross the bay after dark. "What about Ouder Raad? Do they have any new boats?"

"A big, gray inflatable. Toba reported it yesterday. It's tied up on their seawall, near where their dock used to be."

"Doesn't surprise me," I say.

"As long as you're asking about Ouder Raad, there's something else you should know."

"Like?"

"Chloe said she was bringing some friends with her tomorrow and another attorney, Sam Teasdale."

"With Bennett, Teasdale, Holden Grey's firm?" I say.

"You got it. What's that about?"

I sigh. "It's a long story. How are we doing on Wallenstein, Bearce?"

"Almost all wrapped up. Ian's in Minnesota right now getting the last signature. You're going to be the proud owner of the majority share of a New York investment house and a huge debt."

"Will we have a way to show it all on paper by tomorrow?"

"If we work late tonight."

"Good. Then do it."

Benny's voice murmurs in the background for a moment, and then Claudia says, "Benny wants you to know that Max is pretty much healed up. He'd really like to know when you can take him back home. Seems some of the staff is pretty scared of him."

I grin. I can picture Max baring his teeth at people used to nothing more threatening than bored and usually docile lions and bears. "Tell your new friend he'll have to make do for a little longer. Derek and I will be at the office later this morning to discuss how we'll handle everything. Reserve some rooms for us at the Grand Bay for tonight."

"You're not going to tell me what's going on, are you, Boss?"

I grin. "Just a good old-fashioned takeover. That's all."

"That's all, my foot."

37

The wind turns during the night, blowing cool air from the north, and the morning weather reporters babble excitedly about a storm front making its way down the coast. Derek and I go downstairs to the hotel's dining room and pay little attention to the gray skies outside the windows as we both order steak and eggs for breakfast—with no intention of touching the eggs.

"Are you sure of this, old man?" Derek says while we wait.

I shrug. "We'll see. It all boils down to pride and money. We'll see which they pick."

Derek guffaws. "I know which one I would."

Afterward, we walk the block to the office, my Cayenne left in the hotel's parking lot, the wind blowing in our faces. With its arrival, the air already smells a little less of smoke and a little more of moisture. A sudden gust of cool air slams at us and pulls at our clothes, and I grin. "I wouldn't be surprised if it rains before the afternoon," I say.

"Couldn't be soon enough for me," Derek grumbles.

Marcia Voss smiles when we come out of the elevator and points down the hall. "Mr. Gomez and his daughter and

Mr. Tindall are all in the conference room. They asked if you would join them as soon as you came in."

Ian nods, and Arturo and Claudia smile when Derek and I come through the door, though Claudia's grin slips a little when she sees how stiff my gait is. "Are you okay, Boss?" she says.

I nod and take my seat at the far end of the table. A brown leather briefcase has been placed there and a matching one placed in front of the seat to my left. Derek sits there. We both snap our briefcases open, examine their contents and snap them closed. "Good," I say. "Can I see the paperwork?"

Ian stands up and leafs through the papers he has piled in front of his seat. "Sorry if I'm not as organized as usual," he says. "My assistant hasn't shown up for work in a few days." He grins. "Not that I'm too surprised." He takes a packet of paperwork and passes it to me, following with another packet for Arturo and one for Claudia.

"There's a lot more legal work to be done," Ian says. "But everything you have in front of you is signed and binding. Reversing any of it is almost impossible."

"And this is obvious from the paperwork?" I say, leafing through my packet, looking at the signatures on each section.

The thin man nods. "To anyone who's done business or attended at least a year of law school."

"Good," I say. I glance at Arturo. "When are they due?"

He looks at his watch. "In a few minutes."

Arturo and Claudia murmur something quietly to each other as we wait. Ian leafs through his papers. Derek opens and closes his briefcase, as if making sure the contents haven't disappeared since his last look. I stare out the window, oblivious to the gloomy sky, the whitecaps on the bay, the scudding clouds and the trees leaning with each gust of wind.

My heart races each time I picture Chloe coming through the conference room door. I know she'll be shocked, but I wonder whether her shock will give way to relief or to anger.

The phone buzzes. Claudia picks it up, listens and nods. She hangs up and says, "They're here."

A tall, thick man with a florid face and combed-over salt-and-pepper hair enters the room first. "Sam Teasdale," he booms out in a deep voice. "Bennett, Teasdale, Grey and Levine."

Ian gets up, shakes his hand and motions toward the seats at the other end of the table. Teasdale nods and walks down to take the seat facing me. A tall, broad-shouldered, white-haired, elderly man enters next, his face wrinkled but his movements fluid, followed by a red-haired man and then by Aric.

He freezes in the doorway, stares at me, shakes his head and blurts out, "*Scheisse!*"

Chloe pushes past him and freezes too. Her eyes go moist and she mindspeaks, {*Why, Peter? Why?*}

I look at her and long to rush to her, to take her in my arms. But such a thing will only force a confrontation with Aric. {*It was the only way I could think of to spare you any more harm.*}

{*I would have been willing to suffer for months rather than let this happen.*}

{*Let what happen?*}

{*You know how our females change when their mates die. You know we have no control over it.*}

I nod, afraid to hear what she has to say next.

Sorrow overtakes her face. {*Aric has taken me for his mate. His son already grows inside me.*}

38

I look at Chloe, my mouth open. She stares back, her eyes so sad that I'm tempted to moan in sympathy. But I simply stare, my thoughts too confused to make any sound or even mindthink a word. I hate that she's been with another male, but know she had no choice. I want to tear Aric into small shreds of flesh and I want to cry. Chloe stares back, silent too; no one in the room is talking, everyone but Aric shifting their eyes from me to Chloe and back.

Aric focuses his gaze solely on me, a scowl growing on his face the longer we remain silent. Finally he takes Chloe by the elbow and says, "That's enough private conversation, *liebchen*. I'm sure DelaSangre understands." He forces a grin. "He's played chess before. He knows one does not always get his queen back after she's taken."

He tugs her elbow to turn her away from me. Chloe shakes her head and yanks back on her arm. Aric tightens his grip and holds on. He snarls, "Calm yourself."

She tries to yank free again, but Aric's grip tightens even more and she grimaces. "Let go!" I growl, shoving my chair back, shooting to my feet.

Before I can rush across the room, Derek grabs me by my wrist. "Easy, old man," he says. "Plenty of time for that later."

"Exactly," the elderly man who came in before Aric says. He takes the seat to the right of Sam Teasdale and motions for the redheaded man to sit to the right of him. "We are here for to make business. Please come sit, Aric."

I study the old man's wrinkled face, his eyes as emerald green as mine. From his advanced age and his Russian accent, he has to be the elder, Anatoly Krovyanoy, whom Cili warned about. He motions to the seats to the left of the attorney. "Bring your bride with you. Please to be nice."

His words may be framed as a request but his tone indicates he expects complete cooperation. The German nods and looks away from me. He releases Chloe's arm, guides her on her way toward the end of the table with gentle, open-handed pressure on the side of her arm and follows behind her after she passes.

Once they're seated, Sam Teasdale clears his throat and says, "I won't even pretend that I have the slightest idea of what that's about." He looks at our end of the table, his expression somber. "But I do know we're all here because this young lady"—the attorney nods his head toward Chloe—"experienced an enormous loss very recently. . . ."

Ian smiles. "Sam, do I take it that you're not familiar with Mr. DelaSangre?"

"No." The attorney shakes his head. "Can't say I am. Heard about him. Never met him."

"And obviously you never saw him." Ian's grin widens. He points toward me. "Permit me to introduce Peter DelaSangre."

A red flush rises on Teasdale's already florid face. He turns to Chloe and says, "Is this true?"

She nods.

"Then I don't know what the hell I'm doing here." He

stands. "Mr. Krovyanoy asked me to come here today to help Mrs. DelaSangre review her husband's estate. I'm afraid he's wasted my time and yours."

The elderly Russian frowns at him and shakes his head. "You are billing us for your time, yes?"

"Of course."

"Then at five hundred dollars an hour plus expenses, is maybe a waste for us—but is hardly a waste for you." Krovyanoy points to the attorney's chair. "Please to sit. Mrs. DelaSangre may not be widow, but she has left her husband. We may have need of you yet."

Teasdale glares at him. "Our firm doesn't do divorces. I'm here because we represent Ouder Raad Investering . . ."

"Which is why we're glad to have you here today," Ian says. "Please sit down, Sam. As Ouder Raad's counsel, you'll want to review the papers we have to show to your clients."

Krovyanoy, his redheaded companion and Aric all stare at Ian, puzzlement evident on their faces. Teasdale sighs and sits back down. "Okay," he says. "Since you seem to know what the hell we're all doing here, please educate me."

Ian grins and nods. He takes a packet of information and slides it down the table toward the other attorney. "I'd appreciate if you'd read through that," he says. He looks at the elderly Russian. "We have similar packets for you gentlemen, if you'd care to read along."

With a slight nod of his head, Krovyanoy sends the redheaded man to collect the other packets from Ian. As he does so, Sam Teasdale turns the first few pages of his packet and mutters, "I'll be damned." He turns another page, shakes his head and says, "I'll be damned," again.

Krovyanoy takes his packet, reads the first page and

frowns. "Let me make this simple for you," Ian says. "We've just secured majority control of Wallenstein, Bearce." The Russian looks at his attorney.

Teasdale nods. "I'm afraid so," he says. "It will take a month or two for them to do all the proper filings, but it's theirs."

"Which means you, and Ouder Raad Wereldwidj in Holland, have lost all control of Wallenstein, Bearce, Ouder Raad Investering and VastenZeiling." Ian pauses and studies the Russian's face. Krovyanoy's jaw tightens but otherwise he shows no emotion at all. "I don't think your associates back in Europe will be very happy with how you've handled things here at all. Do you?"

Anatoly Krovyanoy glares at the thin man. "*If I listen much longer to this useless human's insolence, I will have to tear him apart,*" he mindspeaks. "*Please to send them all away. Is time for us to talk.*"

"*But . . .*" Aric says.

The Russian turns his glare on him. "*Have I asked for your thoughts?*"

Aric shakes his head and looks down at the table.

"Mr. Teasdale, please to leave us for a few minutes," Krovyanoy says. "We have things to discuss that lawyers need not hear."

Ian looks toward me and I nod. "Why don't you and Arturo and Claudia take Mr. Teasdale to your office? I'll call you all back when we need you."

Arturo and Ian stand. Claudia remains in her seat and stares at the Russian and his associates. "You sure about this, Boss?" she says.

"Don't worry. Derek and I can handle this from here," I say.

*   *   *

Neither Derek nor I say a thing. Krovyanoy stays silent too, and watches as his attorney and my people exit the room. When only we remain, he turns his gaze on me, his eyes emerald green and cold as ice, and mindspeaks, *"Is best we don't speak aloud. What we have to discuss should stay to ourselves."*

I nod.

"Please not to think you've won," the Russian mindspeaks. *"At best you've embarrassed me and cost me my seat on the Elder Council. But the council will never accept such a large loss. They will have to send more hosts against you . . . enough to ensure your defeat."*

"You are a cheeky bugger, threatening us like this," Derek mindspeaks. *"It's you who should take caution. We've bloody well killed almost everybody you've sent against us . . ."*

"Please, Derek," I mindspeak. I turn my attention back to the Russian. *"Are you planning on just threatening us or do you have a proposal?"*

Krovyanoy grins. *"Is good you know the bad side before you learn the good side. Your father and I once had a conversation like this. He understood that peace always comes with a price. Is my hope, his son will be as intelligent."*

I frown at the creature. *"It depends what the price is,"* I mindspeak. *"And who's paying it."*

"Well said." The Russian stares at the packet of papers in front of him. *"You have control. Is no dispute over that. But our people have been running these companies for many years. It would be very, very hard for you to replace all of them . . ."*

"Wait." I hold up my hands palm out and motion for him

to slow down. "*Before you go into anything like that, what are you offering?*" I ask.

"*Peace of mind. As long as you stay out of Europe, no more of us will come after you. Not ever.*"

"*What about Cili and Derek?*"

The Russian glares at Derek. "*He killed my son.*"

"*I know. What about them?*"

He sighs and mindspeaks. "*We'll leave them be also.*"

"*And Chloe?*"

"*Is bigger problem.*" Krovyanoy looks at Aric and Chloe. "*They have mated. That means they are joined for life. I have no power to change that. Neither do you.*"

Aric frowns and stares at the old creature. Krovyanoy glares back, shaking his head, the two obviously mindspeaking. Chloe joins in, her eyes flashing anger. Finally he turns back to me. "*Excuse our impoliteness. My colleague wanted to know why we were bothering with all this. Is four of us to your two. He said if we attacked you and ended this now, his mate would inherit everything and we would have no problem.*"

"*And?*" I unclick the latches on my briefcase. Derek does the same with his.

The Russian smiles, he tilts his head toward Chloe. "*His mate, your wife, interrupted and said we were three. She said she never would join in any attack on you. She also swore she would pass on any inheritance that came about from your death. She insisted it go to your two children. But Aric still pressed me to attack. I said we've already lost enough good warriors.*"

Aric shakes his head and stands. "*This is wrong,*" he mindspeaks. Chloe doesn't get up from her seat as quickly as he does, and he whirls toward her, grabs her and jerks her up.

"Damn it, let go of her!" I snarl, shooting to my feet again, rushing around the table past Derek, who fumbles in his briefcase for a moment and chases after me.

I block Aric's path just before he reaches the doorway. He hisses and holds out his free hand at the ready, the skin rippling, turning into scales as he shifts it into a claw. *"Move, DelaSangre, or do you want me to rip you open right here?"*

Derek extends his right forearm over my shoulder, a Smith and Wesson 500 Magnum revolver in his hand. *"Shift your claw back to its human form, or do you want me to blow five large holes in your head?"* he mindspeaks.

Aric scowls but puts down his arm, his claw shifting back to a hand. He ignores Derek and keeps his eyes on me. *"It is time for us to leave. We are no longer part of this conversation,"* he mindspeaks. He points at the Russian. *"If this old fool tries to commit anything for me, don't believe it. There is only one way for you and I to end this and, I promise, it will go badly for one of us."*

He forces a confident grin. *"I will come for you tonight, DelaSangre, after dark. Now, please step aside."*

I glare at him, not at all sure I don't want to attack him right now. {*Please, Peter, back up,*} Chloe mindspeaks. {*This will only make things harder for me.*} I sigh and step back a few paces. Aric storms out of the room, holding Chloe by the wrist, pulling her behind him.

Krovyanoy shakes his head. *"Is too much emotion in this room,"* he mindspeaks. *"Is important things for us to decide here."*

He looks at my briefcase. *"Please, before we go on. Is gun in your case too?"*

I grin and open the briefcase, and show him one of the

four loaded Smith & Wesson 500 Magnum revolvers Claudia had placed inside.

The Russian nods. *"Your father did not raise a stupid son,"* he mindspeaks. *"But we will talk now. I will not attack you and you will not attack me. Please to close it and take it off the table."*

We negotiate for more than an hour. In the end, I agree to let the Elder Council's management stay in place, with our managers serving as their chief executives and our people controlling the boards. I also agree to an equal split of all profits—after the costs of our acquisition and financing.

Krovyanoy swears that we will have no further problems from Europe. *"And we will not involve ourselves in your fight with Aric,"* he says, turning his eyes toward Derek. *"As long as he doesn't either—and as long as you fight without any of the weapons you seem to be so fond of."*

"And if I'm killed?"

"Don't think is not very possible. Aric is our best warrior. In truth, I'm tempted to wait to see what happens . . ."

I glare at the irritating old creature. *"You know, I won't give you the same deal tomorrow,"* I mindspeak.

"I know." The Russian sighs. *"So, we agree—if you're killed, your children will inherit everything. Not your wife. And this one"*—he inclines his head toward Derek again and grimaces—*"will be guardian."*

Krovyanoy holds up a finger, as if to punctuate his point. *"But I still hope Aric kills you tonight."*

39

By the time Ian draws up the paperwork and we all sign it, the day has grown dark, the wind has gone still and a light rain has begun to drift down from the sky. Derek accompanies me downstairs and stops with me outside the building's doors. "Sure you don't want me to come with you, old man?" he says.

I shake my head. "It's my fight. I don't want you tempted to join in."

"As if I would." Derek grins. "You're welcome to that one, old man. Aric's a cruel bugger. I was just offering my company for the ride home."

"Sure." I look at my brother-in-law and think how much help he's been. "You're just in it for yourself."

Derek shrugs. "Can't help it. That's the way I am."

"Still glad you came," I say, and hold out my hand. Derek takes it and lets out a surprised, "Oof!" when I pull him to me and hug him. Still, he doesn't pull away.

Under Monty's dock lights, except for the shine on its hull and the lack of any nicks and marks, the new Grady White looks almost identical to my old one. I insert the key and turn it, and the twin Yamahas growl to life. I grin at the sound. It takes all my self-control to let them idle and warm up. Too many days have passed since I was last on the water. I yearn to be away from the marina, out on the open bay.

Water droplets patter on the deck and splatter on my clothes and body as rain replaces the wet mist and the wind begins to blow again. If Claudia has done her job properly, there will be foul-weather gear stowed below, in the cabin. I make no attempt to look for it. I breathe in the wet air and grin at its fresh aroma, almost devoid now of the bitter smell of smoke.

A hard burst of rain batters the marina for a moment, then moves on, leaving my hair and clothes soaked and stuck to my skin. A cold wind follows, and more rain, and I cast off my lines, throw the Yamahas in gear and motor out of the marina.

Even with the rain streaming from the sky and the dark clouds blocking all view of the stars and moon, the night sky seems brighter than all the dry, smoke-filled nights that preceded it. I push the throttles forward and ignore the magnification of the rain's force the speed brings—the raindrops stinging now as they strike me, the cold wind chilling me.

I sneeze and a quick jolt of pain shoots up my back. I wince and stretch my back, my neck and legs, small pains erupting everywhere, reminding me of injuries not quite healed. I shrug. I will be home soon enough. With a few steaks and a little more rest, I should be as prepared for my coming fight as I can be.

A swell rises in front of me, and I turn the wheel and guide the Grady White diagonally across it, the boat barely slowing as it shoots up and down its sides, the water hissing by. I look toward where I know my island to be and frown. With no one home to turn on the light in the great room and few other boaters dumb enough to venture out in the storm, all is black on the horizon.

{*Peter?*} Chloe mindspeaks, masked. {*Where are you?*}

I wonder whether to answer. Whether to tell her. She no longer is my mate. Aric may have prompted her to ask.

{*Peter, please answer.*}

{*I hear you,*} I mindspeak.

{*And you're being careful not to tell me where you are. You're not sure whether you can trust me or not. That sucks, Peter.*} Chloe goes silent for a few moments. {*I guess I understand. You don't have to tell me anything . . .*}

{*I can tell you that I still love you.*}

{*I still loved you after what happened between you and Lorrel. That doesn't mean that I didn't treat you badly.*}

{*I'm not angry at you like that,*} I mindspeak. {*I'm just sad that it happened.*}

{*Do you mean that?*}

I think about it before I answer. Aric hurt and misused my wife. He deserves my anger. But Chloe did nothing wrong. {*I mean that.*}

{*What about my child? I will love him as much as I love Henri and Lizzie.*}

{*The child's innocent. If I survive this night, I will love him too.*}

{*Peter, I am so sorry.*}

{*I'm sorry too.*}

We both go silent. The swells come closer and higher and I slow the engine just a touch and guide the Grady White over one after another. {*Be careful. He's out there already,*} Chloe mindspeaks.

{*Where?*} I take my eyes off the water and scan the dark, gloomy sky.

{*I don't know. Even if I did, I don't know if I could tell you. This is hard. I love you, but my body tells me he's my mate. I should be defending him, not betraying him.*}

I sigh. {*One way or another, this will be over tonight.*}

{*Be careful,*} Chloe mindspeaks. {*He intends to surprise you.*}

She goes silent again, and after a few moments I mind-speak, {*Chloe?*}

{*Please. I can't do any more of this. I am at war with myself. I won't help Aric and I can't help you. Whichever of you wins will have me, and I hate that I have no choice. Please leave me alone for now. It's too hurtful.*}

The rain turns to a mist again and the wind subsides. It feels to me as if I'm motoring through Chloe's tears, and I slow the boat until the mist just settles on me. Even through the mist and the dark, I can see the black shadow of Caya DelaSangre looming less than a mile in front of me. It looks so sad to me with no yellow light to beacon me home.

I sigh and tap the throttles forward just a little more. The entrance to my channel can't be more than a half mile or so in front of me.

A rush of wind suddenly grows behind me. I swivel around to my right—to see what might be there—and gasp as an extended claw brushes by within centimeters of my right shoulder. But another claw digs into my left and yanks me from the Grady White, my full weight suddenly suspended from the single claw's sharp talons. I yowl into the dark, Aric's wings flapping above me, forcing huge gusts of wind downward as he gains altitude and leaves the water and my boat far beneath us.

Aric reaches for me with his other claw and I twist away from it, ignoring the pain the movement brings, willing my body to shift shape. As discomfiting as my position is, I have little fear of facing defeat so soon. It's a simple thing for one of my kind to take and kill a human this way, but a far different matter to contend with an equal in his natural form.

For that, Aric will have to find a way to rip and bite at me or to crash me into the hard, unyielding ground. Neither is possible as long as I dangle beneath him, as free to strike back as he is to slash down at me.

We continue to gain altitude, the dark expanse of the bay below us, a solitary dim boat light far to the south. Aric's free claw slashes toward me again and a jolt of pain runs down my left side as I jerk out of its way again.

Through it all my body expands, my back splits open to allow my wings to grow, my skin turns to scales, my teeth to fangs and my hands and feet to claws. Aric's ascent slows, impeded by my increased bulk. He growls and slashes his claw toward me again. This time, rather than jerk and twist away, I slash forward with my right claw and rake his forearm with my sharp talons.

He growls and jerks his claw back. Rather than wait for his next attempt or to see what he plans, I slash upward with my right claw. Suspended as I am beneath him, I have to strain to reach his underbelly, and even then only the tips of my talons dig into his scales. Still, it's enough to rip into him and the rich aroma of Aric's blood rewards me for my effort.

The creature roars and releases me, and I allow my body to fall away from him. I need distance between us. I need time to prepare for our next clash, time to find an advantage that will allow me to defeat him.

But Aric folds his wings and dives after me. "*It seems to me you're far too fond of running away, DelaSangre,*" he mindspeaks.

"I'm sure you'd rather I turn and wait to meet your attack," I mindspeak. *"Which would grant you the advantages of speed and impact."*

"You think too much. In the end fighting is about will, not strategy."

"But you're so fond of chess," I mindspeak. The black surface of the water looms close beneath me and I snap my wings out, my descent slowing as I catch the air, my momentum shooting me forward, only feet above the water.

Aric roars above me, snaps his wings open and races after me. *"Why don't you turn and face me. Let's end this here and now."*

I flap my wings as hard as I can, my left side stiff and aflame with pain, my breath already ragged, my heart pumping jolts of blood into my veins but hardly energizing muscles still exhausted and aching from my last round of battle. Even worse, my empty stomach, made emptier by my sudden change and efforts, convulses and grumbles to remind me of its need.

With Aric so close behind me, I have no chance to catch a moment's rest and see no way to find any nourishment. *"Be careful what you wish for,"* I mindspeak, and tilt my head down and my tail up. The move turns me head-down, my extended wings blocking any further forward movement and I continue to keep my head tucked so that I tumble in midair for a moment before I begin to fall.

The maneuver leaves me upside-down but facing Aric, and I corkscrew into upright position and shoot toward him. The creature roars as we rocket toward each other and swoops upward just as we close, so he can strike out with all four claws as we pass.

I have no intention of passing him. I adjust my course just

enough to meet each of his claws with one of mine, our
talons interlocking as we collide, my mouth open, my jaws
ready to clamp down. Aric tries to disengage, to pull back
enough to strike again, but I lunge forward and take the side
of his neck in my jaws. My fangs sink through his protective
scales and he bellows, breaking free of my claws and ripping
into my underbelly.

The damp air turns even more damp with our blood, a
thick stream of crimson gore streaming from Aric's throat as
I try to chew through to his arteries, and my fresh red blood
flowing from each successive gouge Aric digs into me. Neither of us makes a sound or utters a mindthought, our wings
no longer supporting us, each of us too intent on inflicting
damage on the other to pay attention to our descent.

We crash into the water. The impact knocks my head
back and dislodges my teeth from Aric's throat, and I push
away from him and his flailing claws as we sink under the
surface. I would like to shift into a dolphin's form and race
away to find rest and nourishment, but I lack the energy to
accomplish such a difficult transformation.

Instead, I flare the end of my tail and use it to scull away
underwater, my wings folded against my sides, my arms and
legs tucked close to my body, Pelk-style. Aric can't hope to
swim as quickly and has no way to catch me as long as I remain underwater. Not that I have the capacity to do so for
too long.

"*DelaSangre!*" Aric mindspeaks. "*DelaSangre!*"

Rather than answer, I concentrate on swimming north,
gaining distance.

Behind me, the water ruffles as Aric breaks free and takes
to the dark sky. "*DelaSangre, stop hiding. You know you're*

going to have to face me. Why do you want to shame your-self?"

I remain underwater and continue to put distance between us. I would like to meet him head-on and see the look of amazement on his face as his life was ripped from him. Had I not been injured before, I think I would win such a contest, but now my body is too racked by pain, too stiff with exhaustion and too in need of sustenance to risk such a thing.

When I think I've gained enough distance from Aric, I swim to the surface and break free of the water, splashing as noisily as I can, as if I've taken to the air. But rather than do so, I sink silently back into the water and float until I hear the rush of Aric's wings.

I dive again and head south, sculling with my tail, shooting away, hidden from Aric's eyes by the dark water above me. My lungs ache sooner than I expect and I push on until they begin to burn. I surface slowly then, and take care not to disturb the water or make noise as I breathe in fresh air.

Two small, dark shadows on the horizon confirm that I've surfaced miles south, close to the Ragged Islands. As much as I study the sky above me, I see no sign of Aric. I sink below the surface again and shoot upward, my wings spread, my tail thrashing behind me, and I break through from the water's surface and take to the air again.

Rather than fly north to take on Aric again, I head south, soaring just above the water so that any eyes peering down from above will confuse my dark form with the black water beneath me. I scan the water stretching out before me and let out a low growl of pleasure when I see that the boat light still bobs on the water only a few miles to my south.

Ordinarily I would forgo such an attack or at least study

the prey before I go after it but my need leaves me with little choice. Fortunately, it's a small boat occupied by only one fisherman, huddled on his seat, a pole in his hands, his body and head covered by a long, dark green raincoat with a hood.

I strike him at full speed, my front claws digging into his flesh, lifting him from the boat and throwing him forward, my rear claws slicing through him and seizing his dead body before it falls out of reach. The aroma of his fresh blood maddens me, but I hold off feeding and fly toward Sands Key and the hidden beach at its center where I hope to feed in peace.

"DelaSangre, I'm tiring of this. Perhaps if I start to hurt Chloe again; would that bring you out of hiding?" Aric mindspeaks.

"She's your mate now. Mates don't do such things to each other," I mindspeak.

"You are naive. We all do what we must to win."

"Maybe you do. I would never knowingly do anything to harm someone I love."

Aric's laugh rings cold in my mind. *"Love is for humans, DelaSangre,"* he mindspeaks. *"Our kind is too strong for such things."*

40

I land on the wet sand of Sand Key's hidden beach, lay the fisherman's body down and slice through his raincoat, cutting his body open, allowing the scent of his blood to blossom around me. I thrust my head down, tear a chunk of meat from his carcass and gulp it down. My stomach convulses as it slides down my throat, and I consume chunk after chunk, the energy of the meat flowing into my blood, spreading to my muscles. I sigh and concentrate on healing the worst of my wounds and something wooshes through the air behind me.

A firestorm of pain erupts across my back as Aric lands on top of me and sinks his teeth into the back of my neck. *"You make this too easy, DelaSangre,"* he mindspeaks, his jaws tightening, his teeth driving slowly through my armored scales. *"I've hardly had a chance to enjoy this."*

I thrash my tail and buck, try to push up with my forearms and forelegs, try to twist my neck away from him, but his weight pins me and his teeth continue to work their way into me. *"Only a few more moments,"* Aric mindspeaks. *"And then this will be all over for you."*

A loud, anguished howl fills the air, and a dark form hurtles through the night sky toward us. It slams into Aric's right side and knocks him off of me. He roars at whoever attacked him and slashes out at the creature, his claws ripping across its side as he bats it away and turns back to me.

By then I've scrambled to my feet. Aric rushes at me and I meet his jaws with my jaws, his claws with my claws, both of us locked in battle, our blood running, staining the wet sand at our feet. But even with the meat I've ingested, Aric still has more strength, more energy. He pushes against me and drives me back an inch and then an inch more, my grip on him slipping slightly, his teeth and claws coming closer to penetrating my guard.

"Please, Peter," Chloe mindspeaks. *"Can't you finish him? He is my mate. I don't know if I can help you any more than I have."*

Aric growls and mindspeaks, *"Quiet, woman. I'll deal with you after this one's dead. You'll learn to be a proper mate yet."*

"I don't know about that," Chloe mindspeaks, twirling around on the beach, her tail digging an edge into it and spraying a line of wet sand directly into Aric's eyes.

He flinches back, and I thrust my jaw under his and drive my fangs into the underside of his throat. Aric bellows and slashes at my body with his claws but I ignore the damage he does—the pain, the spray of my blood—and drive my fangs deeper and deeper into him.

Finally I bite through both of his neck's arteries and his hot blood gushes from him. I ignore that too, and bite ever deeper into him, tearing at his spinal cord until his body goes still and his heart ceases to beat. Even then, I only relax my grip, still reluctant to believe that Aric offers no more threat.

Chloe nudges me. *"It's over, Peter,"* she mindspeaks. *"You can let go."*

I roll away from Aric's body and lie on my back, my heart still racing, my chest still heaving as I suck in breath after breath of damp air, the rainy mist drifting down and settling on my outstretched limbs. *"DelaSangre—is over?"* Anatoly Krovyanoy mindspeaks.

"Is over," I reply.

"I am sorry for that. He was a great warrior. Am I right to assume the female helped you, or did I hear wrong?"

"Chloe was here but Aric died by my claws and fangs."

"She should not have been there."

I pause and think back to our conversation at LaMar Associate's office. *"Perhaps not, but remember, when we made our agreement, you never asked that she be made to stay away."*

Anatoly goes silent for a few moments, then mindspeaks, *"No, I didn't. Is still wrong, DelaSangre."*

"But our agreement still stands?"

"I will be glad to be done with this place and be done with you."

"And our agreement?" I ask.

"It still stands," Anatoly mindspeaks. *"Though I wish it didn't."*

The old creature goes silent and Chloe mindspeaks, {*He can't leave soon enough for me.*} She nuzzles her snout against the side of my neck and lies beside me. {*Can we go home now?*}

I nod. {*In a bit.*}

{*You need to heal.*}

{*So do you.*} I incline my head toward the fisherman's remains. {*We can feed right here, and rest and heal before we leave.*}

Chloe helps me shamble over to the remains and feeds

beside me, pausing occasionally to select a choice morsel for me. Afterward we lie on the wet sand and stare up at the night sky together.

{*I want to bring the kids home as soon as possible,*} she mindspeaks.

{*Me too.*} I shift my body to press it closer to her. {*I can go for them tomorrow.*}

{*I'd like to come with you. It's time I met your other son and his mother.*}

I grin. {*Okay, we can leave for Andros tomorrow—as soon as we find my boat.*}

{*Find?*} she mindspeaks. {*What about mine?*}

{*I have better things to do than tell long, boring stories right now.*} I nudge against her.

She presses back. {*You've already healed that much?*}

{*Enough,*} I mindspeak, nuzzling her with my snout, running the underside of my tail over the underside of hers.

{*No claws or teeth tonight,*} Chloe mindspeaks as I slide into her. {*I need for us to be gentle.*}

I nod and concentrate on her warmth and the uncanny ability she has to move just so, just as I want. Our orgasms come gently too, like the slow, powerful surge of a large swell against the beach. Sleep comes after that and we doze as the mist stops falling and the sky begins to clear.

We wake to moonlight and starshine and Chloe rolls away from me and stares upward. {*The sky's finally clear,*} she mindspeaks. {*It's beautiful.*}

I turn over and gaze at the dark sky, now bright with the lights of millions of stars. {*It is beautiful,*} I mindspeak. {*But I have to ask you something.*}

{*Oh, Peter, you're not going to start asking me jealous questions about Aric, are you?*}

{*No, but you might deserve it if I did, a little bit.*}

{*Maybe, but you said you wouldn't.*}

I mindspeak, masked, {*Aric's dead. I don't care about him. But I wonder about his people and their damned council. Did your parents ever teach you anything about them?*}

{*No,*} Chloe mindspeaks. {*They barely ever talked about Europe.*}

{*Neither did my parents. It worries me to know there are so many of them.*}

{*You have a deal with them.*}

I shrug. {*Sometimes deals are broken.*}

{*If it happens then we'll cope with it—just like we did with this.*}

{*I know,*} I mindspeak. {*Still, I worry what else there is out there that our parents didn't tell us about.*}

Chloe laughs. {*Don't worry, Peter. The way our lives have been going, I'm sure we'll find out sooner rather than later.*}

We lie still for a few more moments, each of us lost in our thoughts. I remember something Aric said and I mindspeak, {*Oh. Talking about things we didn't know, did you know that old chest in the great room has a secret compartment?*}

{*How did you find that out?*}

{*Aric told me. He said both my parents stored their diaries in it.*}

{*Really. I'd love to read them.*}

{*Me too.*}

A sudden shower passes overhead, and Chloe shivers and mindspeaks, {*Let's go home where it's warm and dry.*}

{*In a minute,*} I mindspeak. {*Just answer one more question.*}

Chloe makes a mock groan and then replies, {*Go ahead. Just, please make it quick.*}

{*Why did you come to help me? You told me you couldn't take sides—that there was a war inside you.*}

{*That's true. My love for you was at war with my duty as Aric's mate.*}

{*What happened?*}

Chloe nestles close to me and mindspeaks, {*Love won.*}

About the Author

Alan F. Troop's poems, essays, short stories, and articles have appeared in Miami's *Tropic* magazine, Fort Lauderdale's *Sunshine* magazine, and a number of national magazines. A lifelong resident of South Florida, he lives near Fort Lauderdale with his wife, Susan, and manages a hardware/wholesale business in Miami. Familiar with the waters and the islands off the coast of South Miami, he now often spends his leisure time on dry land, enjoying the sun, the activities and the crowds on the broadwalk at Florida's Hollywood Beach. You can visit him on the web at www.DragonNovels.com.